Who Are You?

A Fiction Novel Based on a True-Life Story

Diana K Robinson

Copyright © 2020 by Diana K Robinson

All rights reserved. No part of this publication may be reproduced, stored in any form of retrieval system or transmitted in any form or by any means without prior permission in writing from the publishers except for the use of brief quotations in a book review.

This fiction tale is based upon the true story of an extraordinary woman's life.

"Lead us not into temptation."

My grateful thanks go to my children, who stood beside me through it all. I could not have done it without you. Also, the author, who knows me better than I thought.

The Main Characters in This Book

- Elizabeth Du Toit, nee Pieterse
- Dion Du Toit – Elizabeth's husband
- Pieter Du Toit – their only son
- Storm Pienaar nee Du Toit – their first daughter
- Robert Pienaar – Storm's Husband
- Rika Pienaar – Storm and Robert's firstborn
- Rick Pienaar – Storm and Riaan's second-born
- Vivienne Venter nee Du Toit – their second daughter
- Andre Venter – Vivienne's husband
- Samantha Venter – Vivienne's first child
- Amelia Van Tonder – Elizabeth's close friend
- Doctor Gouws – a leading Psychologist
- William Pieterse – Elizabeth's elder brother and mentor
- Bessie Pieterse – William's wife
- Lynette Pieterse – Elizabeth's mother
- Miriam – Elizabeth's delightful and loyal housemaid
- Phillip Du Toit – Dion's eldest brother
- Zandri Du Toit – Phillip's wife
- Dr Daan Fourie – the family Doctor in Bloemfontein and close associate of Elizabeth
- Ester – Lynette's adored family housekeeper
- Derek Pienaar – Elizabeth's Boss whom she adored and worked with for years
- Mariah – Elizabeth's head seamstress and confidant

CONTENTS

Prologue: 2010 vii
Chapter One 1
Chapter Two 10
Chapter Three 25
Chapter Four 40
Chapter Five 47
Chapter Six 57
Chapter Seven 79
Chapter Eight 83
Chapter Nine 87
Chapter Ten 93
Chapter Eleven 98
Chapter Twelve 100
Chapter Thirteen 104
Chapter Fourteen 115
Chapter Fifteen 119
Chapter Sixteen 123
Chapter Seventeen 126
Chapter Eighteen 150
Chapter Nineteen 163
Chapter Twenty 173
Chapter Twenty-One 190
Chapter Twenty-Two 196
Chapter Twenty-Three 200
Chapter Twenty-Four 209
Chapter Twenty-Five 212

Chapter Twenty-Six 219

Chapter Twenty-Seven 223

Chapter Twenty-Eight 229

Chapter Twenty-Nine 238

Chapter Thirty: Europe 247

Chapter Thirty-One 262

Chapter Thirty-Two 271

Chapter Thirty-Three 275

Chapter Thirty-Four 283

Chapter Thirty-Five 291

Chapter Thirty-Six 303

Chapter Thirty-Seven: Tochigi Prison 309

Chapter Thirty-Eight: The First Year in Prison 314

Chapter Thirty-Nine 324

Chapter Forty 332

Chapter Forty-One 339

Chapter Forty-Two 341

Chapter Forty-Three 351

Chapter Forty-Four 358

Chapter Forty-Five 365

Epilogue 368

PROLOGUE:

2010

Oh, that burdening feeling of apprehension. I was certainly feeling it today as Adelle's voice rang out in cheerful greeting and she swept across the reception floor toward me. Her vibrant energy was lost on me this Monday morning - I wasn't sure why. Under normal circumstances, her mood was infectious. I wished I could pick up the happy vibrations; this was one of those blue Mondays for some unknown reason.

Adelle looked striking this morning. Her tall frame carried off her outfit to perfection. She'd taken special care in power dressing today; she'd left nothing out. It was an important meeting, and we all hoped she would be awarded the contract she was going after. The company needed a boost in both a monetary and creative way. The 2008 depression had walloped South Africa and now, two years later, more lucrative, attractive contracts were dribbling in; if she secured the deal today, it would be the best one in years. Before leaving, she quickly asked me how the curtaining job for a challenging, elderly customer was coming along.

"Elizabeth, Mrs Van der Byl's curtains, will they be hung tomorrow?" Her radiant energy and self-assuredness irritated me suddenly; she *knew* I'd have them ready. I smiled graciously and answered, not wanting to change her mood.

"We dare not be ready!" I smiled, then added, "we are on schedule; the girls are finishing the last two today. We'll hang them tomorrow at exactly 9.30 am just as the old bag insisted. She made it very clear she didn't want to see us anywhere near her house a minute earlier; apparently, she despises having her breakfast interrupted."

"Oh, really? She's a funny ol' bat, isn't she? Quite a haughty old tannie." Adelle sniffed, raising her nose as if imitating Mrs Van der Byl, then she turned and smiled playfully.

"Thank you, Elizabeth and good luck, I probably won't see you before you head out to her farm in the morning."

"Thanks! We need that luck. Are you out the rest of the day?"

"Yes, I think so. I'm quoting on the naughty Doctor's revamp, as you know, and that will take some time, then I have two other smaller jobs to see. Call me on my cell if you need anything." She turned and left, trailing a whiff of expensive perfume through the air after her.

I'd secretly hoped to go with Adelle to help with the quote - a complete interior revamp of the infamous Doctor's house - but the way I was feeling today I was glad I was covering the office. The good Doctor's divorce had been the talk of the town for several months, and now he'd brought home his new lady, a businesswoman from Johannesburg whom he was more than eager to impress. A big fat budget was on offer and Adelle was determined to ensure the company was awarded the contract.

I sat for a moment, mesmerised by the scent she'd left behind and wished I could shake off the uncomfortable, almost eerie sensation that was churning in the pit of my stomach. It wasn't the typical 'Monday morning blues' I'd woken with; I'd been feeling mysteriously down from the moment I'd opened my eyes. My weekend had been blissfully peaceful without Dion. I should have been feeling on top of the world.

It had rained heavily most of Sunday, falling in sheets from the sky, pelting down on the tin roof; one of my favourite sounds that prompted terrific memories of the farm and my childhood, igniting a warmth in my soul, temporarily elevating my mood, then it was gone as I continued to sit rather mindlessly, doodling on the paper in front of me and reflecting on how much I'd enjoyed the weekend alone when my thoughts were briskly interrupted as Mariah burst into the office looking perplexed and flustered.

"Morning, Missus Elizabeth. We have problem for Mrs Van der Byl's curtains," she said in broken English as her words tumbled out her mouth and sent a shudder down my spine.

"That's not good news, Mariah. What's the problem?" This was one client I didn't want to disappoint.

"Eish, shortage of special curtain tape for last curtain." She stammered apologetically. Mariah loathed making mistakes, and she shuffled uncomfortably, being fully aware of the wishes of the fierce Mrs Van der Byl. It was unusual for Mariah to make an error like this and I could see she was mortified.

"Don't worry, Mariah, I'll get some. How much do you need?"

"Three metres, Missus Elizabeth. Short for last drop. Don't tell Missus Adelle."

I smiled at her reassuringly.

"I won't tell anyone; this is our secret. I've got about that much at home; I'll go and get it for you." A beaming toothy grin spreading across her wonderful warm round face, she held onto the edges of her threadbare apron and her body visibly drooped with relief.

Collecting some spare tape from home meant Mariah wouldn't be in trouble and I wouldn't have to claim from petty cash which, if I had, would have exposed her mistake and Adelle would have been furious. She would never need to know. Mariah was my favourite seamstress; we had worked together for many years. I'd taught her everything she knew about sewing. She was as honest and reliable as the sunrise and just as warm. There was little I wouldn't do for her.

We would be at Mrs Van der Byl's at 9.30 am; I'd make sure of that.

Finishing off a few small errands in the office, I downed my tea, gathered up my bag, front door keys, car keys and cell phone and left Veronica in charge of the reception.

"I'll be back in twenty minutes; I forgot something at home," I said as I left.

"No problem," Veronica replied without interest.

I pulled up to the automatic gates in front of the housing estate where we lived and pressed the button. While waiting for them to open, I glimpsed the back of Dion's car parked in the driveway, and I wondered what had brought him home early. I'd been expecting him back on Tuesday. A surge of annoyance coursed through me, adding to my frazzled mood. It had been so peaceful without him. I'd enjoyed my own space more than I cared to admit and had selfishly primed myself for another evening alone. I allowed the instant testiness to wane as the gate slid open. Our friendship was reasonably comfortable now, I supposed. I knew he'd never change, and I was finally at peace with it. He paid his way, I paid mine. We shared one roof, three grown children, grandchildren and many memories, though the memories were more horrid than good. If I was truly honest with myself, sometimes I felt closer to him now than I had in years; he'd mellowed with age, so it was just when he went on his booze binges that I kicked myself for letting him back into my life. I had a feeling this was one of those weekends that had ended in excessive indulgence.

As I drove down the long, paved entrance toward our parking area, my mind was absorbed with thoughts of trying to remember which box I'd put the curtain tape in; I couldn't be away from work for long but as I pulled up beneath the shade of the massive rubber tree (Hevea tree) that grew near the entrance to our house, I noticed our front door ajar and instantly felt uneasy; neither of us ever left the front door ajar, even though we were in a secure housing estate. It was one of our mutual rules. My first thought was perhaps we'd been broken into, and the cops had called Dion, hence his early return. There hadn't been any break-ins in the past two years but living in South Africa, it was always a possibility.

I pushed the thought aside but still couldn't shake the uncomfortable feeling in the pit of my stomach that I'd been arguing with since waking.

Pulling the keys out of the ignition, I quickly headed toward our open front door. As I stepped into the house, I noticed Dion's keys and cell phone lying on the kitchen counter and fully expected to see him in the kitchen, but the house was silent. I called out, but there was no reply. Suddenly, an eerie sensation trickled down the back of my neck and ran down my spine, raising the hair on its way down, and I shivered involuntarily. Something felt very wrong. Feeling fearful and unusually vulnerable, I put my bag and car keys down on the counter next to Dion's and went through to my room. He wasn't there, nor was he using my bathroom. Strange. I checked his room. He wasn't there either. My mind was racing; it didn't appear that anything was missing or that there'd been a break-in. Could he be outside with the police, perhaps? I hadn't noticed any police vans around, though. I checked in the other bathroom quickly, then checked the spare room, calling out his name as I went. Where the hell could he be? And why was the front door left ajar?

As I entered the spare room, a spine-chilling, throaty rasping sound was coming from outside, instinctively warning me of something ominous. Rushing forward to see what was making the weird noise, I peered out the window; then I saw him.

I knew in an instant why I'd been battling the uncomfortable instinctual sensation in the pit of my stomach all morning. I ran outside and moaned, a deep painful sound, so chilling it didn't sound like it belonged to me. A sense of heart-wrenching loss filled me, followed closely by other feelings I couldn't interpret in that moment, but they took a stranglehold on my chest and made my breathing difficult.

I desperately wanted to go to him, but I couldn't. I didn't dare touch him. He was still alive, but only just. I'd felt this ghastly, familiar feeling of utter helplessness before.

I ran back inside, grabbed my phone, dialled 911 and waited outside. I couldn't go back and look at what Dion had done to himself. He sat slumped in one of our deck chairs, fresh blood was still dripping from his temple, and the .22 calibre rifle had fallen across his knees in a sinister reminder of a life weighed down by a fearsome, deeply embedded guilt.

"Why, Dion? Why end it this way?" I whispered quietly, and though I wanted to cry, not a tear left my eyes while I waited for the ambulance and the Police to arrive.

The nurse in me needed to go to him, and the urge grew stronger as I waited, but I knew there was nothing that would save him now. I stood in silence, willing him to hold on to his life for a few minutes longer. I wanted to say good-bye before he took his last breath, even though I feared he may have already done it. My body began to shake involuntarily as the shock of what he'd done penetrated. I reached out for the sturdy trunk of the rubber tree to support me, trying desperately to take in what I'd just seen. I leaned against it, trying to absorb some of its lifeforce until help arrived.

'If I'd been here fifteen minutes earlier, I could have stopped him,' I thought miserably.

While I waited, only the cherished moments of our life together flashed through my mind. I never imagined Dion possessed the courage to end his own life, and certainly not in this way.

So, he did have a conscience after all. It must have finally got the better of him.

I felt instantly sickened by that thought. I always knew it was there, hidden deep within the recesses of his twisted mind. Everyone else, even his own children, swore he never had a conscience, but years of suppressed regrets, vile, uncontrolled actions and dishonesty must have finally struck at his subconscious, wounding it 'till it manifested into a tragically dark depression. I guessed that being in a depressed, inebriated state all weekend must have finally burst the abscess of a lifetime of accumulated guilt. I'd not noticed a change in his mood on Friday, but I felt sure he must have made the decision not to go on living before he left for the weekend.

He was a master of disguise, right to the end.

I'd not seen this blow coming, especially as his mood had been cheery when he left. He'd not said where he was going, and I never asked nowadays.

"What a macabre end to a life," I whispered, looking up to the heavens through the large green leaves of the tree canopy above me, searching for some mystical comfort and divine reassurance as I stood trying to understand. I prayed then that when he took his last breath, whether I was beside him or not, he'd go to a beautiful, peaceful place surrounded by love and light.

Somewhere in the distance, I heard the ambulance siren bellowing out its torturous reminder that Dion would soon be taken away in it - dead.

I clicked the gate opener and the grinding of it moving along its tracks, scattering sand as it went, reminded me of the rasping sounds coming from deep within Dion when I found him. I covered my ears as the ambulance raced in and parked. Two medics jumped from the vehicle, and we ran in together to where Dion's slumped body waited for resuscitation or escape from his suffering.

So many unanswered questions would be buried with him.

I watched as the medics carefully lay him down on the floor as the police walked in. I glanced up at them briefly; they all knew Dion, and they knew my history too. I looked back to the medics, our eyes connected; they seemed to understand my silent question.

It was now safe for me to say goodbye in their presence.

I knelt beside Dion's lifeless body and finally surrendered to my grief. Would there ever be a day when I'd think of Dion and feel nothing? His breathing was very shallow as I leant in close to him and whispered in his ear.

"Gogga, I will always love you."

The faintest quiver moved across his lips, acknowledging my words, then his chest shuddered, and he let out his final breath. I prayed his soul would be cleansed, then I gently closed his haunted brown eyes for the last time.

CHAPTER ONE

Standing in the foyer of the nurse's residence in Bloemfontein, seventeen years old, painfully shy, rurally raised and frighteningly naïve, an uncomfortable mixture of excitement and anxiety was whirling around in my tummy, tugging and teasing at every part of it. Concern was turning to fear as I lugged my bags down a long passage; I'd lost my way.

An irrational panic threatened to consume me as I searched for signs indicating where in this building this mysterious Room 26 – Left Wing was supposed to be as it was to be my room for the year ahead.

A maze of passages branched off the long corridor I stood in. I felt bewildered. The mouse trails in the cornfields at home instantly flashed in my mind and made me smile; they never confused me as I skipped along them. Somehow, those thoughts comforted me, and the nervous energy I was grappling with, that had my brain racing, stopping it from functioning, seemed to instantly clear.

'Which one should I take?'

Taking a deep breath, I wondered how the mice knew where to go in the fields at home to find the entrance to their little burrow after running across vast expanses of land, hiding from predators up above. I envied them their skills. They didn't have signs; why couldn't I use my instinct? Desperate to find the mysterious clue that would lead me to my room, almost in tears as I blindly dragged my heavy luggage further down the corridor while telling myself to grow up, calm down and think, I stopped near the entrance to another left passageway. Glancing down at my watch, I noticed it was mid-day. While everyone was having their scrumptious Sunday lunch on this lazy afternoon in January 1971, I stood alone on the brink of my nursing career, feeling insecure and overwhelmingly homesick and suddenly I wanted to be a mouse.

Pulling the introduction letter out of my bag to check I'd not misread the directions, the sound of a friendly voice behind was a welcome interruption.

"Hi, are you lost?" I swung around and was instantly drawn to a pair of warm, smiling green eyes looking up at me.

"Yes, I think so," I answered, trying to turn my quivering bottom lip into some semblance of a rather coy smile.

"I'm looking for Room 26 in the left-wing," I stammered and was about to show her my introduction letter when she squealed with excitement.

"Hey, what a coincidence, I'm also in room 26. Howzit? I am Amelia Van Tonder," she beamed and thrust her hand out for me to shake while I felt envious of her confidence.

"Elizabeth Pieterse, it's nice to meet you," I said with relief, taking her warm hand in mine. At last, I wasn't alone in this maze of unmarked passages and had to look away from her mesmerising green eyes and as I did I noticed the room numbers high up on the wall ahead of me; small white signs with black numbers stencilled onto them facing away from the direction in which both Amelia and I had accessed the building.

"That's dumb," I said, pointing out the room number signs. "Why don't they make them visible from both directions?" Shaking my head, I added, "I thought it was just me being stupid. So, judging by the sequence of numbers on that sign, our room must be down the next passage."

"Aagh, No!" Amelia groaned. "These cases are so darned heavy," she rounded her shoulders and screwed up her face while looking down at her luggage, not at all happy she had to haul them along again. I'd been struggling with the weight of mine too, and I was at least five inches taller than Amelia, plus she had more luggage to haul along than I did. Though I wanted to help her, all I could do was smile in sympathy when she looked up at me. Off we went, dragging our suitcases and bags down to the next passage, turned into the entrance and finally located our room.

"Do you have any preference on which side you want to sleep?" Amelia asked, hauling her luggage through the door.

I'd always liked to sleep next to a window and wake to the call of birdsong in the morning, but as both our beds faced the only windows, a French door with windows on either side of it, I guessed it was irrelevant.

"No, I don't mind at all." We were both being very polite to one another, yet it felt to me like I'd known her for years.

"Perfect," She said and relieved herself of her load, threw her handbag onto the bed, taking a deep breath while inspecting our room.

"Not bad, is it?"

"Much better than I expected. Nice surprise."

A vanity table was installed between the two cupboards and served as a dressing table. The bathrooms were further down the passage, but we had a wash-hand basin in our room, which was a luxury. We could fill up our kettle, wash our hands and face and clean our teeth without standing in a queue. This would be the first time in my life I would share a bathroom with anyone other than my family. I wasn't comfortable with that thought.

Pretty floral curtains hung on either side of the French doors that opened onto a beautiful, peaceful communal garden filled with wise old trees, standing tall above manicured lawns — a perfect place to study while listening to the chirping of masses of different birds. Bird calls always made me happy.

"I think we can manage living here." Amelia beamed and unzipped one of her suitcases then suddenly burst out laughing.

"Gee, how tall are you?" she blurted out. I was very self-conscious about my height, but for the first time, I found myself laughing too, responding with unusually good humour on such a sensitive subject.

"Well, the long and the short of it is...." and we both roared with laughter, "seriously, I'm half an inch off six foot. Much too tall for a girl. I hate being so tall."

Amelia chuckled. "Let me tell you it's far worse as a real shorty like me."

"We're never happy with what we have, are we? I'm tall and want to be shorter. You're short and want to be taller. You have gorgeous auburn curls, my favourite hair colour; don't tell me, you wish you were blonde!"

"Yes, of course, I do. Blondes have way more fun. It's a known fact."

"I don't know about that," I responded, blushing furiously. I knew what Amelia was referring to, but I was way too shy to comment. Amelia seemed fun, and I hoped this was the start of a long friendship.

"Jokes aside," she paused, looked a little sad, "I was teased endlessly at school. Short arse, shorty, copper nut, rooi kop, were just some of the horrid names they called me. Kids can be so cruel to each other, can't they?" She was looking at the floor for a moment. I could see how deeply the teasing had affected her.

"I was also bullied at school, mocked constantly for being shy until I finally learned to stand up for myself." I looked at her lovely doll-like face and found it hard to believe she was ragged; she was so sweet and angelically beautiful. I couldn't imagine how anyone would want to tease or insult her.

"We are like Laurel and Hardy. Completely different. I like that, don't you?" I chuckled to lighten the mood again.

"Ja, me too." Amelia agreed and hauled the next heavy bag close to the wardrobe and unpacked it. Banter between us was so easy. I felt so fortunate to have

Amelia as my roommate for the year. It had concerned me that I would have to share a room with someone I didn't like.

"I feel like we've known each other for years, don't you?" She stood up with an armful of clothes ready to hang, shining honesty reflecting in her eyes.

"I've just been thinking the same." We went on nattering, learning what a lot we had in common as we unpacked.

Framed photographs of family members, best friends and special pets were the final decorative bits we added to make our room feel like home. Amelia plonked her childhood teddy proudly on her pillow and looked at me.

"Don't laugh, he goes everywhere with me," she said, as she stroked its face affectionately. "I've had Harold since I was three and we're inseparable; plus, he always brings me luck."

I felt a little tug of sadness as I thought back to my beautiful teddy whose arms and legs moved and whom I'd adored. I'd wrap teddy's arms around my neck when I couldn't sleep after Papa died. It was the comfort I craved as a six-year-old and still did sometimes. Mom had never been one to show much affection and had found it hard to comfort me as she too, was grieving. Several months after Papa passed, she bought me a puppy, a fluffy crossbreed whom I fell in love with until he ripped teddy apart. I never did get another, Mom couldn't afford it, but I eventually forgave my ever-faithful canine companion.

"What made you want to do nursing?" Amelia asked curiously, then her eyebrows raised, and a line creased between them as she sensitively noticed my mood had become a little pensive and she was too polite to ask what was wrong, but I told her anyway.

"My father passed away when I was little. Mom bravely took over the farm, and too many of the years since, she has struggled. She couldn't afford to keep me in school this year. You know we've had drought conditions for a long time. Well, when Papa passed, blistering hot sun and even more severe drought persisted, lasting four long years, burning the lifeblood out of my beloved Papa. Mom once mentioned that the stress of losing my eldest brother during the ongoing drought all became too much for Papa to bear and a heart attack sent him to an early grave. Tough years continued for us after Papa died, but she managed to keep the farm running and provide for us, but now, once more, another bloody drought, which has almost bankrupted Mom."

There was an awkward sombre silence between us for a moment, then I continued with my story.

"I've always wanted to be a nurse, but I did want to finish my schooling first. I know Mom feels very guilty, but there is nothing she can do. Some tough Voortrekker roots embedded in her DNA keep her pressing on year after year; she's amazing and has my brother helping her too. It's difficult to break through that tough exterior, and for years I've craved her affection."

"Oh, I'm so sorry." Amelia reached out and hugged me. "Shame Elizabeth, that's such a sad story. Thanks for sharing something so difficult. So where is your farm?"

"Near Brandfort."

"I know Brandfort; hey, remember how we all learned that crazy town's history at school?"

"Yeah, and anyone born in Brandfort is always labelled a racist." I laughed.

"So, are you one?" Amelia prompted playfully.

"No. I don't think so, nor is my mother, but we understand and respect our differences. None of my family were partial to the ways of that asshole Verwoed, and I do remember wishing he'd never been born in Brandfort."

"Gee, you have had a tough time. I'm sorry about your Dad and your brother. I know how hard it is farming; my Dad has only survived the droughts because we've got irrigation and the dams are good, but he still has to be careful; otherwise, I'm sure we'd have been in the same position." Her voice filled with genuine empathy, and for the first time in my life, I felt comfortable chatting about my childhood.

Bloemfontein was, and still is, the University town of the Free State province in South Africa. For student nurses in the 70's, it was a great city to be in as young teenagers. We fluffed out our youthful feathers and there was no shortage of lively teenagers, many of whom were from the surrounding farming districts like Amelia and I; mostly wide-eyed innocents ready to take on the world enthusiastically.

It was an era of fabulous music and the fashion was colourful and outrageous. Life was fabulous fun, and we revelled in it, especially those of us raised in very conservative households like I was. Our parents were horrified by the way the world was going; young *men* with long hair and lots of facial hair growing in outrageous abandon down the side of their cheeks. The old folk couldn't tolerate the rebellion, but for me, coming to live in a city was an exciting and welcome change.

Living in residence was an education on its own. There was an assortment of interesting characters, but the behaviour from some girls in our wing shocked us both rigid. The city teenagers were far more advanced in the ways of the world than us from the farms. Amelia and I heard that a few of the girls had snuck a man or two into their rooms during the second week in res; we were shocked but secretly enjoyed the gossip when we got sick of studying but I found it hard to grasp that sort of behaviour.

One afternoon I got back to our room earlier than Amelia and was lying on my bed reading through my new notes when she burst through the door excitedly.

"Hey, ready for a party?" She beamed. "We've been invited to join the rest of our wing at a party tonight," she said breathlessly. We'd been in res together just over a month.

"Oh, okay, great. Where?"

"I don't know, some dude's house in town. Probably one of them who has been snuck in here on a few occasions. We are all to meet in the foyer at 7 pm." She winked at me. "So, shall we go?" Her head cocked to one side with one hand resting on her hip, the other she flicked out to the front with a theatrical questioning gesture, and I couldn't help but laugh at her.

"For sure." I was game for a party. "Maybe we can prove we are not the 'prudes' everyone in res thinks we are." Amelia screwed up her face. She knew neither of us was the type of girl who wanted to be known as slutty or cheap; prudish was fine by comparison.

So, off we went. We weren't disappointed by Mr Rich Kid's selection of '60's and '70's music either. Popular songs of the day thumped out through the sound system in the garden, and we did rock around the clock, drinking, laughing and eating off the braai until after eleven, when the music livened up again around the swimming pool. It was a perfect summer's evening; the air was still and warm and, by midnight, the party got interestingly raunchy. Daring couples (or drunk couples) stripped off, dived into the pool and shagged each other openly. Most of the girls participating were from our wing of the res and apart from being thoroughly stunned, I was acutely embarrassed too. I'd never seen such urgent grappling or heard such wicked laughter in an open display of raw sexual lust. Amelia and I didn't know where to look, both feeling awkward, but like insects drawn to bright light, we couldn't help staring, trying not to be too obvious, but then it got too raunchy to go on gawping; it was time to head back to res.

We'd had a taste of the wilder side of life, and couldn't resist hooking up with the city-born teenagers who behaved like racing pigeons released from the coop and, with them, we flew from one party to the next. After that first rather raw introduction, Amelia and I joined in, not for the sexual whirl but the social rush.

Studying, working, and partying became an exciting but essential juggling act and somehow, we got through the first year with excellent results. Then Mom dropped the bombshell and announced she couldn't afford to pay the residence fee for the following year; Government subsidies were only available to student nurses who'd completed their high school examinations and passed.

My world and dreams were shattered. I was devastated. With a heavy heart, I searched for employment during the December vacation and finally found a job in a pharmacy as a shop assistant, and a tiny bed-sit flat quite a long walk from the nurse's residence – I wanted to be close to the res for Amelia and I had a wonderful close friendship and I didn't have a car. I began a seemingly directionless life and felt the loneliness of it like an abandoned child.

CHAPTER TWO

The Corner Pharmacy; on a corner and situated on the other side of the city from where I'd found my little flat meant, for the first time in my short life, I'd have to learn to commute to work on the 6.30 am early bus. I imagined that for a white farm girl to do this would be an unusual occurrence and the thought terrified me; naivety and lack of self-confidence was painful but real.

Though living a sheltered rural life has some incredible advantages, it also has some prickly disadvantages too. I understood the way nature ticked but had not the vaguest idea how life outside of the farm, college and the nurse's res operated, despite a year in the city. I'd never travelled on a bus to work, or even needed to go on a bus. In those days, I assumed it was mostly black people who travelled on buses. Standing alone at the bus stop, shivering as a gentle breeze passed over me seducing my heightened tension, I tried to make a joke of my stupid fears and reassure myself that catching a bus was not a frightening experience; lots of people travelled by bus and while I was trying to convince myself, it arrived. I stepped into the interior and handed my money to a kind old man and was surprised to see a white driver. I felt less nervous then and noticed I was the first passenger.

"Ah, a pretty new face to greet me in the mornings," the bus driver chirped as he took my fare and introduced himself. I could not have wished for a more cheerful face to greet me and settle my nerves.

"Oom, Paul," he said and popped the fare I'd given him into a blue leather pouch strapped around his rotund belly. (Oom - Afrikaans for Uncle)

"Elizabeth," I said and returned his smile shyly, then sat down close to the door. The journey across town, with endless stops along the way, lasted just under forty minutes. I didn't give my nerves a thought as I realised how absorbed I'd become by watching more white people get on and off the bus than black, coloured or Indian and decided this mode of travel was going to be quite fun after all.

The following morning Oom Paul kindly informed me that regular commuters buy a monthly ticket and by doing this, I'd save a fortune. On my small salary, I was very touched by his thoughtfulness. He was a dear old man, and in a matter of days I'd learned everything there was to know about the city, commuting by bus, all about his three beautiful daughters, his wife, how long he'd been a bus driver, where he'd attended school, learned to drive and what his likes and dislikes were. He even described his favourite meals and judging by the size of his tummy, food was high on his agenda. He loved teasing and joking with his commuters, so it was always a cheerful, welcome start to the day. I couldn't help but like him; he reminded me of a joyful Father Christmas.

As we got to know one another over the months, he assumed the role of my fatherly protector. To begin with, I wasn't sure how to receive his light-hearted banter, paternal affections and concerns but in time I found it all very comforting, though it did evoke a longing to have known my father.

"Going home this weekend?" he asked as I climbed into the bus one Friday morning.

"Not home, but out to Amelia's parents' farm. I'm so excited and looking forward to it. I haven't seen Amelia for ages. We're having lunch together today and heading out after that."

"Have a wonderful time, my girl." Oom Paul knew all about my friendship with Amelia, and our farming backgrounds.

"I will; you have a good weekend too, Oom Paul. See you Monday," and I jumped off the bus, but on Monday I felt anything but cheerful; I was getting sick.

An hour at work was all I could endure. I headed home, catching a different bus.

"How are you feeling today?" Oom Paul asked on Thursday, his usual beaming smile spread across his face always raised a smile on mine.

"Better, thank you. How did you know I was sick?"

"Aah, because you haven't been on the bus since Monday," he smiled, then I noticed a different expression on his face, a hint of mischief, a twinkle in his eye I'd not seen before, as if he was about to ask me something or tell me a joke then he stopped himself. When I stood up to leave, he winked at me, pulled gently at my arm, and said in a naughty whisper, "I have someone special for you to meet."

My body temperature soared; I didn't know what to do with myself.

"I don't do blind dates, Oom Paul," I answered quickly, but he took no notice and chuckled.

"Why are you laughing? Blind dates scare the shit out of me. I'll see you tomorrow." I hopped off the bus before he could press for an answer; he was like a fox terrier and didn't let it go, asking me again in the morning.

"So, what's the verdict?"

"Okay," I said, smiling at him. How could I resist his charms? "When?"

"Well……my girl." He paused, interrupted by another commuter wanting to pay their fare as we talked across them.

"He's, um …he's looking for a partner to take… to the New Year's Eve party at the Methodist Church Hall." He was interrupted again while scratching to find the right change in his navy-blue leather pouch.

"He's a good chap, Elizabeth; I think you'll like him."

Should I trust that wicked grin? He read my mind.

"Go on, be a devil," he teased, raising one bushy eyebrow. The twinkle was back in his eyes with an enquiry glistening within their depths.

"I'll think about it and let you know after the weekend."

I'd heard some gory endings to blind dates in res last year, and I wasn't sure I'd be doing the right thing agreeing to this. Though I trusted Oom Paul, I wanted to bounce the idea off Amelia first. I felt sure Oom Paul wouldn't set me up with a serial killer or drug pedlar, not that they were a dime a dozen in Bloemfontein in those days, but I still wanted to talk it over with Amelia; I wanted to know what she'd do.

"Hey, you look happy," Amelia commented as she picked me up for the weekend, and we headed off to grab lunch before hitting the dusty road to the farm. As soon as we were on our way, I blurted out Oom Paul's suggestion.

"How do you feel about blind dates?" I knew she'd be honest with me. There was a smile rising; that was a good sign.

"It depends, but it looks like you are excited. Tell me more." I explained that Oom Paul knew of a friendly chap who was looking for a date for the New Year's Eve party.

"Oh, come on Elizabeth, now who's being the prude? If the old man knows him, you will be fine," she said, laughing mockingly. "You can't stay a virgin forever."

"This is an invitation to a dance, Amelia, not an invitation to a night of bonking. I don't even know the bloke."

We laughed, clinked our glasses and devoured our lunch.

"Cheers to that," she beamed. It was time to head off to the farm.

"Hey, you'd better call me and let me know what he's like - hope he's hot." Amelia giggled.

On Monday morning, I gave Oom Paul my answer, and he roared with delight.

On my pathetic little salary, buying a ready-made, off the peg boutique dress was out of the question. I was good at sewing; I'd make my dress and that would occupy the evenings I spent alone during the week. Amelia and I went shopping.

"You are going to blow his mind in that," Amelia teased when I moved the Butterick pattern book next to her and pointed to the dress I wanted to make.

"It's gorgeous, isn't it?"

"Oh, that it is, but don't you think a slinky, sexy red one would be more fun? Here, one like this," she pointed out another evening dress pattern by Vogue, with a plunging neckline.

"I don't have the confidence to wear a dress like that." I elbowed her in the side. "I wouldn't be seen dead in that on a first date, anyway, but it is very sexy."

"Oh, come on Elizabeth, stop putting yourself down. Of course, you could pull it off, but how long will it take you to make that gorgeous dress, and what material are you planning on using?"

"An emerald taffeta and I guess it will take me about two weeks." I grinned, then, remembering the film I'd wanted to see, so I suggested we meet up to see it.

"Hey, The Godfather is being released next week. Let's go; I want to see that flick."

"Ja, great idea. Can you spare the time?" I noticed a giggle was about to erupt but didn't.

"I know what you are thinking."

"Do you, what?"

"That I should be making that sexy little black number your thumb is on," Amelia roared with laughter.

Finally, in between discussing movies, styles of evening wear and colours, the green taffeta won, and I couldn't wait to lay the material out on the carpet in my tiny little sitting room and pin the pattern to it. A simple, understated round neckline, low back, which was very daring for me, and the skirt panels fell away from the waist in gentle folds to the floor; it was gorgeous. A real fairy tale ball gown, something I'd always dreamed of wearing and a week later Amelia came to view the first fitting.

"Hmm, I love it!" she shrieked. "Elegantly simple but stunning. Great choice," she whistled as I modelled it carefully, trying to avoid being poked by pins.

"You look stunning, Elizabeth. When I need an evening dress, I know where to come," she joked. "I hope he's worth it. Hey, if he is, you can make the sexy little black number next, then maybe I can persuade you to make the slinky red one too." She chuckled playfully.

Family Christmases were always special times for our family, but this year was a bit different. I left the farm on the morning of the 30th December. I didn't dare tell my mother why I wanted to spend New Year in the city, though I was quite sure she'd guessed; there was nothing I could hide from my mother, and she never asked.

The big day was upon me. I was nervous; I couldn't sit still and aimlessly wandered around my flat, unsure of what to do with myself, wishing Amelia was with me to pass the time. Butterflies played havoc in my tummy, and there was an odd metallic taste in my mouth brought on by nerves. At four that afternoon, I jumped into a hot bath filled with bubbles and lay back playing with the bubbles, popping them with my toes as I tried to relax and fill my mind with visions of what he may look like - as girls do. I decided that all I hoped for was a polite man with decent manners and a good sense of humour. The looks were not a top priority, though a bit of eye candy would be a bonus. By then, the bathwater was getting cold.

Seven o'clock was ticking closer, and when I'd finally finished titivating myself, it was five to seven. Swirling around, viewing myself from every angle for the last time, I knew I looked good. My private flaunting session was suddenly interrupted by loud raps at the front door. I jumped; my heart skipped a beat then thumped wildly up against my rib cage, making it difficult to breathe. I froze, feeling absurdly panicky; Amelia would have laughed her head off if she'd seen me like this. Taking a deep breath to steady myself, I picked up my bag, clung to it as if it were my life support and my mother's words came to mind – 'humour is the lubricant of life, my dear child, make sure you use it.'

Trying desperately to stay poised, I opened the door. In front of me stood a tall, devilishly handsome man who oozed sex-appeal from every pore and my knees turned to jelly in an instant.

Why hadn't Oom Paul told me he was the best-looking young man in the city?

Immaculately attired in a dark navy-blue suit, a white handkerchief peeped out from the breast pocket of his tailored jacket and the whiteness of it caught the glint in his dark-brown eyes, as they twinkled confidently. My lips parted to say hello and not a sound came out; too stunned by the sensory input in front of me, I gulped instead. He was mouth-watering; even the cute little dimple on his chin caught my attention.

"Umm…hello," I finally managed. I was doing a superb job of messing everything up, so I burst out laughing.

"Dion," he introduced himself. Not responding to my laughter, he took my hand and kissed it, but I noticed his brown eyes shone with amusement.

"Good evening, Elizabeth." His voice was deep and cultured.

I shivered; there was just way too much exquisite masculinity standing in front of me and I had no idea how to deal with it or how to conduct my reaction to it.

"I'm sorry." I smiled sheepishly and took another deep breath to get oxygen to my brain.

"Don't apologise," he purred annoyingly, shattering what remained of my withered confidence.

"It's a pleasure to meet such a beautiful, happy lady, and, you look stunning." He was as self-assured as I was introverted, which was very intimidating. I laughed again while trying to pull my shaky hand away from his grip.

"Shall we?" he asked politely, pointing to the waiting car. My whole body was shaking so violently I struggled to lock my flat door. My legs vibrated like a banjo; I had no idea how I was going to get down the stairs. Every ounce of poise I'd practised in front of the mirror had disappeared the instant I'd lain eyes on this irresistibly good-looking man, then I felt him slip his arm through the crook of mine and my pulse quickened as he guided me down the stairs and opened the car door for me, graciously lifting the remaining taffeta skirt into the car. I caught another whiff of his cologne; he smelt wickedly good too.

"Beyond my wildest dreams," he said, as he took his seat behind the wheel. "You are gorgeous." Compliments slid easily off his tongue while my mouth dried out rapidly.

"Thank you," was all I could manage. Wouldn't want him to know my thoughts; I couldn't wait to tell Amelia though.

We made our way to the hall and joined Oom Paul and his family.

"Wow-wee." Oom Paul whistled as Dion led me to the table, pulled my chair out and sat me at the table setting where my name card was placed next to his.

"You look stunning, my girl," he said proudly. He always called me, 'my girl' as if I was one of his daughters. He was good to me.

"Thank you," I said again, and it wasn't long before he was teasing me, enjoying how my cheeks changed colour like a chameleon with each gentle jibe. Admittedly, the teasing helped ease my nerves and gradually I began to relax; it wasn't so bad this blind date thing.

A butt ugly bloke would have been easier, but I wasn't complaining.

"Penny for your thoughts," Oom Paul said, and I blushed furiously. I couldn't possibly share my thoughts and definitely not for a penny. I smiled coyly.

Everything inside me was responding nicely to the occasional sip of brandy and ginger ale, and little by little, the alcohol numbed my nervousness.

Dion and I danced endlessly, wowing the group with our foxtrot, our bodies pressed tantalisingly close as whirls of green taffeta swung around my legs. While we danced the slow numbers, he sang along to the music and had the most stunning singing voice. I could feel his breath against my neck, raising the hair along my spine and arms and soon goose-flesh pimples covered my body.

"You have a truly magnificent voice," I complimented him as we swirled around.

"Thank you. I love music; it's my favourite pastime."

"It should be your profession, not your pastime." He smiled at my suggestion but didn't answer; I guessed he'd heard that often before. Then, the clock struck midnight and he pulled my body closer to his and kissed me passionately for the first time. I'd never kissed a man like that before and was only dreamily aware of other couples gyrating happily to the music and singing along to the traditional singsong of Auld Lang Syne. People were hurling streamers across the room and enjoying the celebration, while I was celebrating a heavenly kiss that took us joyously into the 1st of January 1972.

Blinking out of a semi-dazed state, I heard Oom Paul's booming voice wishing us a Happy New Year from somewhere in the room and bashfully released Dion from my grasp.

"You two seem to have hit it off! Happy New Year." He kissed me warmly and slapped Dion on the back and gave the thumbs-up signal.

Our first week together was a busy whirl of blissfully romantic dinners, a movie at the Drive-In cinema, and lunch on two occasions. I was blissfully happy I'd met the perfect gentleman; he was everything I'd ever wanted all in one package. Tall, dark, handsome, funny, had lovely manners, made me feel like a million dollars, he could sing beautifully; how lucky was I? By the end of the week, I felt ready to explore a little more, perhaps invite him into my flat, but I was like a green horse; I had no idea which way to turn or what to do and I didn't want to ruin what was developing.

At the end of the following week, I had lunch with Amelia and on Friday evening, dinner with Dion. I'd not seen him at all during the second week; he'd been away in the country on business and I was aching to see him; lunch with my best friend would help the afternoon pass quickly.

Curious to know how the last two weeks had been with Dion, she rattled off a string of questions like a runaway train, hardly taking a breath or stopping to sip on her milkshake. We shared everything, and this was no different. While I chatted, her smile kept changing with my varying tales of lust and innocence, and then I told her, my face heating up from a rising blush, thinking on what had happened when he'd dropped me home after the New Year's Eve dance. It was, for me, an excruciatingly embarrassing moment.

"Oooh, tell me, tell me," she urged.

"We got back to my flat around two in the morning, and I have to admit, I was so nervous I stood with my back to the flat door, all ready to say goodnight then disappear inside, when he pulled me to him and unexpectedly squeezed me so tight, I farted. It wasn't a little oops, it was like a whoosh of air escaping boldly," I laughed, thinking back, "and no dog around I could blame."

Amelia couldn't contain herself! She was laughing so hard, her laughter made me laugh too. "Did it stink?" she squealed, while everyone in the restaurant turned to look at us.

"Sorry," she covered her mouth quickly as forty pairs of eyes zoned in on us.

"NO! Thankfully not." We were both giggling and the couple at the table next to us were straining to hear what we were saying.

"You're kidding!" she leaned towards me. "What did you do?"

"I wish I was kidding." My face and body were still hot as I remembered the moment and noticed most of the patrons in the restaurant were still looking at us.

Amelia exploded with loud hysterical laughter again, unable to stop herself as she no doubt visualised the moment, and the couple next to us couldn't resist asking what the joke was all about.

"Don't you dare tell," I warned Amelia; her infectious laugh had got everyone smiling.

"Oh my God, I would have died," she stammered through her laughter. "Not even a dog around to blame - love that," she guffawed and the people closest to our table began to laugh along with Amelia's rapture; it was infectious.

"So, what did you do?"

"I burst out laughing, what else could I do? It was the perfect time to say goodbye, and I hastily retreated into my flat, shouting my goodbyes and thankyou's and closed the door, dealing with my embarrassment where he couldn't see me."

"Well, it didn't put him off."

"Oh, no, in fact, he teases me about it now, and I still blush. I think he mentions it to make me blush. We've had dinner twice, we've been to the Drive-in, watched the Bond movie, 'Diamonds are Forever,' and this week he's been away."

"No sex yet?" Amelia teased.

"No Amelia; to be honest, I wouldn't mind, but you know me, I'm too scared." My cheeks flushed again.

"So, when am I going to meet this sexy dude?"

"Soon. We are going out to the farm this weekend. I want Dion to meet Mom and William."

"Oh, wow! That's quick. Well, if your brother approves you are home and dry." she whistled.

We finished our meal and arranged to meet the following week.

"Good luck with your Mom and brother," were her parting words as we blew kisses to each other.

Thankfully, Mom was suitably impressed, though I couldn't read William's thoughts; he never readily voiced his opinion. William's advice was essential to me; I'd badger him and make sure I got it out of him eventually.

He did approve a week later, letting me know just before I was to meet Amelia for lunch.

"My, my, you sure have a glowing look on your face. There's no doubt you are in love, Elizabeth," Amelia said, complimenting me easily as always at our usual Friday lunch meeting.

"I'm looking forward to meeting this handsome man of yours."

"Well, not long now. I can't wait to see Dion, and I'm also looking forward to watching Cabaret. Should be a good movie, then we'll grab a bite to eat afterwards."

"Fab, I'm looking forward to it too."

"Have you done it yet?"

"Amelia! No!"

"I'm just teasing. Remember those randy girls in the res last year?" she chuckled.

"Yes, they were terrible. Sex ruled."

Dion arrived looking as stunning as ever, and I saw out of the corner of my eye Amelia gave him the once over and approved, giving me the thumbs up behind Dion's back.

The music from the film set the mood; Liza Minnelli and Michael York did it for me. I squirmed in my seat while Dion held my hand and tickled my leg. I couldn't concentrate as I lustfully imagined Dion singing the same songs to me and visualised myself ripping the buttons off his shirt and pushing him onto his back on the couch as soon as we got back to my flat, just like in the movies. That was a fantasy; I couldn't pull that off even if I'd wanted to but I couldn't ignore the delicious desire burning inside me. Tonight, I didn't want him to be too much of a gentleman.

After supper, we couldn't get back to my flat fast enough. I slammed the door shut and, in an instant, we were entwined in each other's arms, edging slowly towards the sofa as we kissed. Not as dramatic as I'd visualised, but this was better. We'd even skipped the coffee bit, but there was something I had to tell Dion first, so I pulled out of his grip.

"Dion," I whispered, afraid to ruin the mood. "I am a virgin, and I'm scared." He pulled back from our bear hug and looked at me tenderly.

"Wow, and I'm deeply honoured," he whispered, kissing me tantalisingly on the side of the neck, soothing away my fears and promising to take care of me as he ran his fingers through my hair, stimulating the skin at the back of my neck sending shock waves rippling through me and covering my body in delightful tingling goosebumps. We moved from the couch to my bed, and slowly Dion removed my clothing. My breasts were tight with ecstasy, and I found it hard to deal with such intense physical yearning. I'd never imagined it to be this heavenly.

Dion began by gently kissing my tummy, tickling my navel with his tongue, then he stopped and looked down at my slim body appreciatively while the dimple on his chin deepened. His chest and arms showed beautifully toned muscle formation; I sucked in my breath, holding on to it as his pants dropped to the floor. My chest was tight with desire as he leant forward and gently gripped my nipple between his teeth and provocatively nibbled at me. My body convulsed upward toward him instinctively and, as slowly as he had promised, he gently nudged at my opening, and my body trembled in delicious, fearful anticipation of becoming a woman.

During the Easter weekend, Dion and I decided to live together. He was still living with his parents on their smallholding a few miles outside of Bloemfontein.

"Isn't that a bit quick?" both Amelia and my mother asked, with surprise at our haste, but I was sure this was the man I wanted to spend my life with no matter what anyone said.

We settled into our cosy little nest; I'd never felt so happy. We loved the small home we'd created together. The weekends passed us by in a musical muddle of singing, guitar strumming and passionate lovemaking; even breakfast was a singsong. Dion was my first love in every conceivable way.

One weekend in September, he surprised me by whisking me away to an expensive game lodge for two nights and, while sitting beneath the setting sun inside a waterhole hide, quietly watching an assortment of game come down to drink, filling their bellies with water for the night ahead and listening to the sounds from the surrounding bush as dusk descended, he whispered, "Will you marry me?"

"Yes, of course I will," I squealed with delight, disrupting the tranquillity of the evening, then I said it quietly again, soaking up my happiness and the splendour of an African night until eventually most of the animals had left. In that blissful silence, beneath a black velvety African sky, we celebrated our commitment and love for each other.

CHAPTER THREE

We had our wedding on the farm and William walked me down the aisle. It was a small garden wedding surrounded by a few special friends and family; the type of wedding I'd always wanted. A blissful eighteen months passed then some unusual changes began to occur in the months that followed. I wasn't sure what was causing the sudden eruptions and changes to Dion's behaviour, but his moods swung like a pendulum and sometimes it felt like I was living with a stranger. Perplexed by these weird changes to his personality, I had to find out what was wrong and chose the moment with care.

"What has changed, Dion?" I asked one Saturday evening when he seemed to be in a good mood. I asked as calmly as possible, keeping any hint of accusation out of my tone, and waited quietly for an answer, but as I watched, his expression began to change. It was like watching a chameleon about to retrieve its prey and I was the prey. His face altered in colour from natural tan, through the orange spectrum, and ended with a deep angry crimson. His cheeks puffed up too, just as a chameleon does, but what frightened me was, in an instant, his face went from crimson to a chilling deathly white. 'How on earth does that happen?' I asked myself silently.

This wasn't the man I'd married. I felt a real fear fill me for the first time in my life. His eyes were dark lifeless pools, and he blurted angrily at me.

"Nothing has changed." And the deep red colouring returned to his face again. I had never seen anything quite like this. I knew that any civil discussion wasn't going to be possible, plus he'd had four brandies by then. I instinctively knew to keep my mouth shut.

He'd shown me, during the last few awkward months, that a woman so deeply in love is not the most brilliant judge of character! My fairy tale wasn't panning out quite the way the books portrayed, and, in that moment, I would have been delighted had I turned into a pumpkin and stayed as one. I was not only acutely frustrated by trying to decipher the most peculiar behaviour emerging from my Prince Charming, I was frightened of him now too. Our fairy tale was morphing into a terrifying thriller, and I didn't know how to handle it or to whom to turn.

It was always the fourth drink that turned Oudemeester (A South African Brandy) into an ugly monster and I didn't dare ask him, 'Who are you?

The following day, when he was sober, he was either defensive or apologetic. Somehow, I had to convince him that his love for alcohol was not only changing him and ruining our marriage, but threatening to end it, which was not what I wanted.

I loved him; the real Dion, the one I had married. I was in a quandary for, in our culture, his behaviour was considered taboo and talking about was even worse. It was the sort of conversation one only had in private with someone who could keep it confidential. Being an alcoholic or displaying any form of mental health issues were considered problems that only afflicted the poor or lower classes. I certainly didn't want to tell my mother and least of all my brother, and though I trusted Amelia, I didn't know how to begin describing what was happening. Besides, still spellbound by his sober charms, I lived hoping it was a passing phase brought on by the stresses of his job, which he'd mentioned repeatedly over the past few months. When he wasn't drinking, he'd sing to me as I prepared supper, then all resistance crumbled and I'd forgive him. He'd knew just what buttons to press and would move in close behind me while I stirred whatever was in the pot on the stove, nuzzle my neck and sing; in seconds, I'd have no idea what I was cooking, and supper would be abandoned until later, much later. Those days were blissful and not for a moment did I suspect that the beautiful serenading and confessions of undying love were becoming a cunning disguise. One evening, another opportunity opened itself up for me to discuss the drinking issues and, while we sat curled up together on the couch, I carefully lead the conversation to the issues.

"Please stop drinking, Liefie. I'm worried about you," I pleaded with him. I knew I risked ruining the mood, but I had to express my concerns.

"Don't you dare bitch about my fucking drinking, do you hear me?" he seethed, spittle flying from his mouth like an angry viper. Though I'd prepared myself for retaliation, this venomous reaction shocked me; he'd never hissed at me with such poison in his voice before, and then I noticed his jaw was quivering and his hands balled into fists as he sat upright next to me.

"Dion, that's not necessary," I said, looking at his fists. "Only cowards hit their women and if you hit me, consider our marriage well and truly over." I was struggling to maintain composure. The word, 'coward,' seemed to trigger an angry, uncontrolled rage, and he growled at me. I was devastated and scared at the same time; I didn't dare respond or move. I loathed this sort of confrontation and tears pricked at my eyes and, reaching for the brandy bottle on the coffee table in front of us, I smashed it on the floor shattering the atmosphere then stormed off to bed.

As the months progressed, Dion's personality changes became even more dramatic. My sixth sense was ringing alarm bells in my head, cautioning me that Dion was dangerous, but I kept finding myself excusing his vile behaviour, and though I still loved the old Dion, this new monster was destroying everything we'd built together.

On occasions, we'd have wonderful conversations when he was sensitive and apologetic. For a few days, sometimes even weeks, all was as it had been when we first were married. Often, he'd even admit to behaving like an animal after the fourth drink, but it didn't stop him. Our social life together had dwindled too. Our friends had become bored, often annoyed listening to Dion carry on with ugly criticism of them and others at social braai's, (barbecues) at home or at friends' homes. Consequently, invitations to social outings became rare, and I was living a continuous apology.

After an ugly, hostile confrontation between Amelia and Dion during our last braai together, she vowed she would never come to another, and she didn't, which broke my heart; neither did anyone else. I felt so isolated and from that day on, Amelia and I met in town when we wanted to see each other. She never told me what prompted the outburst, but I guessed he must have been strongly suggestive, which was probably the case, or darn right rude and insulting, neither of which she would have tolerated. Amelia was volatile with admirably strict principles; whatever Dion may have done, she would have struck out at him like an angry cat. He, on the other hand, didn't give a damn that our friends no longer visited, and we never went anywhere. The feelings of others were not his concern; providing he was happy, nothing else mattered much.

Dion was a suave operator when it came to business, and he knew it. His business lunches became his social whirl and were a pre-requisite for the orders he secured, or so he said.

"All part of the window dressing," he said to me and, of course, having their sexy little secretaries attend the luncheons armed with the company credit cards was also part of that so-called window dressing. When Dion's silky-smooth tongue began operating, and the ladies became more mesmerised by his charms, they didn't mind how much he spent to secure the orders he was after. His explanation of how he lured his clients gave him a frightening sense of power and perverse satisfaction, and he loved telling me about how he clinched those deals. His pride and self-belief shone in his face.

"I can see how much you love it, but it's not very ethical," I suggested, then added, "why is all the drinking such a necessary component to seal the deal?"

"My Liefie, (love) closing the deal is much easier when the buyer has had a few 'doppe' (Afrikaans slang for, drinks)." He smiled ruefully and added, "They spend easily then, it's an ego thing, and sometimes they may spend up to half their annual budget in one order, depending on the discounts I dangle under their noses. My monthly sales figures soar, which does wonders for my commission earnings," he said boastfully, then he shifted and realised he had walked straight into something he wasn't sure of how to wriggle out of.

"I'm sure it does. You've never shared that before, or any of your commission earnings," I said matter-of-factly, twiddling my fingers through my hair; something I did when I was feeling insecure and out of my comfort zone, but he was feeling the same insecurity in that moment.

What made perfect, logical sense to him was utterly immoral to me, but he couldn't see that, and there was no point in me causing another heated exchange of words, but I found his sales techniques deplorable. He quickly covered up his financial contribution blunder by saying, "There have been some good commissions, but none big enough to change our financial future." The lie was just too casual.

"But more than enough to change our marriage by putting it into savings instead of spending it on Oudemeester, coke and beer." He shifted around, suggesting he felt like playing the piano for a while, which he did and then came back and we continued chatting.

"Why have you never shared with me what commission you get?" I asked gently, for he was in an unusually approachable mood, despite being a bit uneasy.

He got up and put some gentle music on and came back to the kitchen while I prepared supper.

"You're right babe, I'm sorry. The next commission cheque I will give to you to put into our house savings." I wasn't expecting that answer. It was a refreshing and most welcome change; he was wearing his best apology face, so I was going to keep the mood, hoping he'd not change his mind.

"Thank you, Liefie, it will help you too by cutting back on the drinking. Excessive alcohol makes a person depressed. Plus, we can start to increase our savings faster toward a deposit on a house."

"Aagh, ja, Babes, it'll be good to buy our own home. Ja, I guess you are right, I'll cut back on the drinking for you." He finished up by saying, "It's all about targets, and I always go beyond mine, Liefie."

The atmosphere was a happy one. How I wished it could go back to being constant. I took advantage of the moment and suggested we rekindle our love and celebrate our third wedding anniversary by taking a few days' leave and spending a little of his commission on the celebration. To my surprise, he agreed.

During our getaway, I learned just how hefty Dion's commissions were. I was horrified; over the past year, he'd drunk more than a deposit on a modest home. Perhaps what concerned me more was this indicated the problem was more serious than I'd thought.

I wondered how he could have been so thoughtless and irresponsible, but this unusually idyllic time together was rare, so there was no point in rocking the boat now. Once we got back from our short, romantic getaway, it wasn't long before the mood swings and character changes shot up a gear. I had to turn to someone - I turned to Dion's father for help. I got on well with my father-in-law, and he knew Dion's weakness for alcohol. I prayed he could offer me some guidance for I was desperate by this stage. I badly wanted to talk to my mother but didn't know how to broach the subject with her.

"What's up, my girl?" he asked, hearing the quiver in my voice. I explained tearfully while he listened, allowing me to finish without saying a word. Though I felt better getting everything off my chest, he offered little advice other than promising to speak to Dion; if he ever confronted his eldest son, it didn't make the slightest bit of difference.

I needed professional advice from someone who understood the workings of an alcoholic's mind and whatever else was going on inside Dion's head. I hadn't spoken to Oom Paul for a long time, so I called him to ask if he knew of anyone I could go to, to seek professional help for Dion. I could hear he found what I had to say challenging to comprehend or believe, but he was sympathetic, suggesting I call the AA and ask them for advice, or go to our minister.

"I've tried that. I suggested we go to our minister together and he was furious. He doesn't believe he has a problem," I moaned, feeling helplessness shroud me once more. Maybe the AA could help? I would follow that up and get their advice; but I didn't. I was too embarrassed to call them. Then I thought my boss might be able to offer some sound advice; it took me days to pluck up the courage to speak to him. He was a pharmacist, after all.

"Elizabeth, get your Doctor to give him a prescription for an anti-depressant, and I will dispense them for him." His dismissive attitude rankled me. He didn't give a rat's arse about my problem and spoke down to me as if I was a nothing. Though I was young and naïve, he hadn't learned there was a fire within me; I protect those I love.

"Mark," I snapped more rudely than I'd intended, "those are also addictive. He already has an addiction." Luckily, there were no customers anywhere near us who could overhear how rude I'd been.

"It's up to you, Elizabeth; depression often leads to alcoholism." I could see he was stunned by my bold, rather impolite response to his careless suggestion.

"Why don't you ask him to try it out for a month and see if things improve? If it doesn't help, then he needs to get professional guidance."

"He's a borderline alcoholic who doesn't believe he has a problem. He's so full of his own self-importance I don't see depression. The drinking and mood swings are getting worse and the more he drinks, the nastier he gets. If I get anti-depressants for him, he will hit the roof, or me."

"Elizabeth," he said sternly, "once the depression is under control, he won't have the same desire to drink excessively. You might not think he suffers from depression, but I guarantee he does. Find the right moment to tell him." He was walking away from me as he spoke, but I was so desperate I followed a few respectful paces behind him.

"But...um… it's not just the alcohol," I almost whispered, desperately needing someone to listen and support me through a situation I could not decipher. "He has frightening personality changes, even when he is sober." I suddenly felt agonisingly alone and excruciatingly insecure. The pathetic desperation in my voice must have irritated Mark for he stopped, turned around, stared straight at me and said, "You are a typical woman, always wanting the man to change. It's time to grow up, Elizabeth." Seething, hurt, but not yet defeated, the fire had just been lit.

"I beg your pardon?" I spat, and the argument continued, then ten minutes later I walked out the pharmacy doors and out of a job. Dion was beside himself with rage when I told him - all I was trying to do was help the bastard.

"I don't need fucking anti-depressants, Elizabeth. There is nothing wrong with me," was his snarky, sharp response; exactly what I'd thought his reaction would be and I began to wonder if the fight was worth it, but a chance to get my old husband back was my goal, so I pressed on.

"You have to address your drinking problem, Dion. Maybe if you do take anti-depressants as suggested for a month or two, you may not feel like drinking; surely it's worth a try?"

Dion shook his head and carried on drinking. Our lives together swung like a pendulum, sometimes it swung backwards, life was grim and hard to bear and I was ready to give up on him, then it would turn the other way and times were lovely again, but the swinging eerily forecast an unpredictable future no matter which way it swung.

When our lives weren't on the backward swing, Dion was mostly his old self, but the problems had gone far beyond just alcohol consumption, and in my innocence, I believed it was entirely up to me to help him. I'd made a vow and took it seriously - 'In sickness and health......' I adored his sweet side, and I'd do anything to get it back - permanently.

Alcohol-induced schizophrenia may be a label used nowadays, along with bipolar and all sorts of new terminology that put people in labelled boxes, but in the '70s, his symptoms were more obscure and not openly discussed. Help was very hard to find, especially as alcoholism was not the only problem; there was something more sinister hiding in the depths.

I put on my happy face and found another job in a pharmacy; this one was closer to our flat, so walking to work was quite a luxury with no more bus fares. Determined not to be beaten by Dion's maladies, I went in search of diagnosis within the library during my lunch hour. There, I could spend time researching discretely, reading privately in a quiet space, finding out more on what psychological multiple personality disorders were about and trying to pinpoint which category Dion fell into. I dug up some alarming material, but there was precious little I could do with it, other than store it, clogging my mind with his frightening afflictions. His symptoms were not considered a 'disease' but a social or personality flaw – well, um, that I'd established without the aid of the library. The scary truth was, everything about Dion and his mood swings matched the description of multiple personality disorder, schizophrenia, sociopath and psychopath. I could tag on alcoholism if I wished; all of which would leave him vulnerable to addictions. Who could I get to help me understand the complexities of what faced me? I turned to Amelia and thought I knew she would respect my need to help Dion, but after we had some laughs about it, she said, "Honey, he's fucking mad, loves himself more than anyone else, chuck the arsehole out. You can do better." There was some truth in that, but I wasn't ready to tackle life alone. I wanted my old Dion back; I didn't want anyone else. I prayed, but God wasn't handing any miracles my way. Dion went on drinking and

I went on researching until I finally understood the dire need to seek professional help. My life was going to be a dangerous living hell if I didn't and finding the solutions was going to be up to me. Now my prayers became urgent, grief-soaked and more needy than I cared to admit.

I was still deeply in love with my husband and my primary focus was to help him now that I realised his personality complexities were way beyond my comprehension. I could go on and on, reading and researching, but it was pointless. Beneath his charming, irresistible exterior lurked a calculating monster that only a professional could manage. Dion had two distinct personalities. One turned me wild with passion and giddy with love; the other was a nasty, violent, dark beast that frightened and frustrated me, and this personality was visiting more often. In the blink of an eye, he could switch from one to the other; when his mischievous brown eyes turned to eerie dark pools something far more significant than terror filled me.

I believed my dilemma was providing an eloquent explanation of this strange behaviour to someone else and I had no idea how to handle it. Who would believe me? Would the person I tried to explain Dion's behaviour to understand? Without seeing the metamorphosis, it was difficult to tell the power and sheer terror of it. It was summoning the courage to do it. Picking the right moment seemed out of reach, but a week later, I gathered the mettle to approach Dion on the subject.

"Liefie, I need to get you some help. I can't live this roller coaster anymore. I don't understand some of your personalities, and I want the old Dion back," I said, keeping my tone as loving and as warm as a kitten wanting its food without being a pest but he exploded.

"Fuckin' ell, what's eating you?" Idiotically, the loving, warm kitten in me reacted defensively, damn him, but, the tiger in me hung around.

"You know what's eating me, Dion; we have discussed it endlessly, Dion."

"That's your opinion." He responded with nasty sarcasm that hit me like a blow to the solar plexus.

"Christ, you're not going to go on about my drinking again, are you? *My* so-called problem is all in *your* head, not mine." There was a nasty sneer on his face, but this time the tiger came to my aid and sprang into action.

"Fuck you, Dion Du Toit," I swore, something I rarely did in those early days, but this time it felt incredibly useful, increasing my resolve to fight back. "I'm doing this for you, plus I can't go on like this, it's not just your drinking, and you know it." It was time to release all my pent-up frustration. "One minute you are eating me alive with desire and the next you are spitting fire at me, damming me for being alive and in your life. Alcohol exacerbates the problem, which I am sure you know, but why, in the name of everything holy, can't you remain as just one person, the one I fell in love with." As I said that last sentence, a sadness touched me deep inside and doused my fire. I began openly sobbing as I struggled to explain my feelings, while rivers of tears poured down my face. I couldn't let him know about the research I'd been doing in the library; he would have killed me.

"Don't be ridiculous, Elizabeth. I've never heard such bullshit in my life." I could see he was struggling not to lose his temper. "I'm fucking sick of your accusations. I am neither an alcoholic nor a psychopath. I am one person, Elizabeth, only one person," which he emphasised by violently and deliberately digging his index finger deep into his pectoral muscle to indicate this and finished up by saying, "You don't see two of me do you, or have you been fucking drinking?"

I was flabbergasted by such an idiotic, noxious retort. He ranted on, hardly giving me time to breathe and think. So many of our evenings we spent this way - arguing, or me silently reading and Dion getting drunk.

"Don't be childish. You know I am referring to all those crazy characters inside that complicated head of yours, not you physically," I stated, calmly, but then I saw the monster crawling out of its cocoon and darken his eyes. I quietly backed away and disappeared to bed, filled with misery and desperation. Where was God when I needed him?

Later that night, the *pussy cat* climbed into bed and cuddled up close to me, pushing himself into the small of my back, waking me with his arousal, whispering shallow apologies into my ear while kissing the back of my neck, anticipating a positive response which wasn't forthcoming. He'd reminded me repeatedly; he could fix my irrational female complaints – the stubborn side of me needed to show him sex didn't always work. I lay rod-still, pretending to be asleep; his impatience transmitted to me by his body language and the aggravation I felt in the change to his breathing, but this time I wasn't giving in. He was going away in the morning for a few days, so he'd have ample time to give our conversation some thought if he had any sense at all.

The week without him home was blissfully uneventful, and we'd even had two, almost loving telephone conversations when he admitted, in the quiet time with his own company, he'd given some thought to what I'd said. My heart did little flick-flacks in my chest and I suddenly realised I was looking forward to seeing him.

Later that Friday evening, when I got home from work, I greeted him at the front door.

"Hello, my Liefie, stressful week? You look exhausted," I said, stepping toward him. I kissed him hello then dumped the shopping I was carrying on the kitchen floor and turned back to face him, thinking a hug was in order, but the wild look was in his eyes.

'Oh, God, help me,' I said silently and stepped away.

I hadn't expected this; I'd been so looking forward to having him home - the weekend was probably going to become dangerously volatile if he had anything to drink.

"No. I'm just fucking tired," he swore. "Where were you?" His irrational question prompted an unfortunate snarky response from me. Surely it was obvious where I'd been.

"Where do you think, Dion?" I answered, pointing at the bags of shopping lying on the kitchen floor, all of which I'd just lugged into the house without help.

"I'm fucking hungry, and there's no dinner ready," he snapped. I could scarcely believe what I was hearing.

"It's only 5.30 pm, Dion, and I've just walked in. I work too, you know."

He took no notice and went on swearing like a mad man, pacing around the kitchen gulping down one beer after another. I didn't dare respond. I finished unpacking the shopping then quietly got on with making supper. It was safer not to engage in confrontational conversation or make any further sarcastic statements, then I had a sudden thought and changed my tone.

"Liefie, perhaps you shouldn't have changed jobs; this one seems to stress you terribly," I said, hoping my new sympathetic tone would diffuse the mood, but there was an unmistakable, nauseating threat about him tonight that nothing was going to change.

"Don't be fucking ridiculous. You know how much I love my job." He paused and shook his head. "I don't understand you; it was your suggestion I take the job. Just to let you know, I want dinner ready waiting for me when I get home on a Friday evening." He stood in front of me, defiant as ever.

"You can't be serious; that's impossible, and you know it. If you are that hungry, why don't you have lunch later or make yourself something to eat if you get home before me?" Irritation was rising as fast as disappointment. Our relationship was becoming like my to-do list; housekeeping, cooking, finances, doctors, research, tolerance.

"Cooking is a woman's job," he snapped, popping the cap off another beer and throwing the bottle opener on the counter; then I came apart.

"What? I'm not your slave, Dion. With each passing month, you treat me more and more like I am one. I didn't marry you to be your slave." Now I was seriously pissed off with him; he was goading me; I knew I shouldn't take the bait, but I couldn't help it.

"Some of the best chef's in the world are men, you know. We are living in the seventies, Dion, not the 1940's. Things have changed and will continue to change. Get off your fucking high horse!" I retorted with simmering vehemence and a brooding silence remained between us as neither wanted to speak first.

"Make a plan," he said.

Chauvinist.

The following morning, Dion woke with the anticipated violent headache from excess boozing after I'd gone to bed. I heard him scratching around in the bathroom as I lay in bed, grinning wickedly. Not every binge brought on a headache, but last nights' one had.

"Where are the headache tabs?" he called out. I detected a slight quiver of desperation in his voice; he urgently needed to reduce the throbbing above his eyeballs.

"In the wall cabinet," I called back, but I'd hidden them, hoping a nasty hangover with no pain medication might provoke some thought on giving up drinking.

"There's bugger all in the cabinet, where else have you got some?"

"All the meds we keep are in there; if there aren't any, they are finished," I shouted back and heard him groan. Unfortunately, he had a remarkably short memory of painful hangovers, but he had a back-up plan, like most addicts do; a box of paracetamol in the cubbyhole in his car was tucked away for emergencies. For the rest of Sunday, we tiptoed around each other, scarcely uttering a word to one another.

On Monday morning, we went our separate ways, saying goodbye – another week apart. When I got in to work, I asked my boss if it was possible to reduce my working hours on a Friday. He frowned and for a moment I thought he was going to ask me why. Fortunately, he agreed without lengthy explanation.

I turned Dion's demands to my advantage, for it meant I had the time to meet with Amelia for lunch every Friday, appease my chauvinist husband and do the weekend shopping.

Ironically, from that Friday onward he was never home by 5.30 for supper.

CHAPTER FOUR

Was this how a real grown-up marriage happens? I found myself asking this question more frequently. I didn't feel much like a 'proper' grown-up; I was only twenty-four. I had crept out of the happiness coma I'd been in for eighteen months with a nasty awakening. I didn't want to be all grown up and began to question who I was. Had I turned Dion into this monster? Was I to blame? I was sure it had nothing to do with me, but he made me feel it could be as he continued to manipulate me and make me feel like I was the problem in our marriage.

Amelia kept me believing in myself, and when I got to our favourite restaurant on Friday, she was already sitting there with her back to the window.

"Hey, how is my oldest and dearest friend?" I asked Amelia cheerfully, wrapping my arms around her shoulders.

"I've been fine, well…." I hesitated, "actually, that's not true, I was going to call you, but you beat me to it." I smiled at her and looked around our favourite Italian restaurant, imaginatively named The Italian.

"I'm ravenous! God, it smells good and garlicky in here today," I said quickly.

"It does, doesn't it? Shall we have the normal house wine?" Amelia queried.

"Ja, for sure. Must be home by three-thirty, though." I raised my eyebrows and grimaced.

"Why?" Amelia asked; a questioning frown covered her wide brow, but I sensed she wasn't in a great mood.

"Dion insists I have his supper ready when he gets in at five-thirty." I shrugged my shoulders, knowing I'd surrendered to his demands *again* and felt a bit sheepish admitting my weakness to Amelia.

"Fucking dog. The way he treats you, I'd tell him to go screw himself." Amelia scowled. "He is the reason I was going to call you today, but, as you said, you beat me to it."

"Oh, what's he done to you now?" I sensed I was in for some bad news.

"Not to me," Amelia shuffled uncomfortably holding her wine glass close to her mouth, looking at me over the rim as if it gave her protection from what she was about to say.

"I don't know how to tell you what I *have* to tell you. You are the dearest, kindest, most considerate person I've ever met, and telling you this is not going to be easy, but know I've got your back. Just hear me out."

I nodded and took a swig of wine.

"He's sleeping with Zandri." Amelia spat it out quickly like there was poison in her mouth. Her words hit me like a bolt of lightning. My world turned upside down in an instant, and I nearly choked on my wine. Amelia put her hand over mine as I spluttered. Was this possible?

"Whaaaat?" I eventually breathed out. "Are you sure?" I didn't want to believe it. I'd accepted Dion was a flirt but screwing his brother's wife was far beyond my comprehension and inexcusable.

"Oh, Elizabeth, I wish it wasn't me delivering this shitty news to you. I'm so sorry; your heart must be breaking right now; you've gone ashen white."

I swallowed hard; I didn't want to erupt in the restaurant. I noticed there were tears in Amelia's eyes, too, and both of us were holding onto them.

"It's okay." I tried to smile. "I'm glad you've told me; coming from you I know it's true. The son-of-a-bitch. How did you find out?" The questions tumbled out now.

"I've had the alcohol abuse to deal with, his changing personalities, now infidelity with a sick twist. I can't take it anymore. It's been so hard because I still love him," adding quickly, "that old Dion."

"I know how you must be hurting right now. I hate seeing you in this miserable marriage, my friend. Dion doesn't deserve a person like you."

"He says I'm to blame for everything, Amelia, and the harder I try, the worse it gets."

"Don't go on trying then. He's going to bring you down with him, Elizabeth, and I'd hate to see that happen," Amelia said firmly and deep down inside I knew she was right.

"I won't let that happen," I whispered. "The bitch," I swore, as it all began to hit me, and I wondered if anything could ever be the same again. At the start of the meal I'd been ravenous, but now my appetite for anything had disappeared.

"What are you going to do?" Amelia asked, as she watched me slowly push a little food onto my fork. I looked at it, decided I couldn't eat, laid the fork down on the plate and took a swig of wine instead. Anger was now diluting the pain.

"I don't know, but I'll come up with something. You know, thinking back, I always thought Zandri was after Dion. Phillip is such a sweetheart; he doesn't deserve this either. He's the kinder of the two brothers."

"Oh, my word, Elizabeth, that is so typical of you, always thinking of other's feelings before you consider your own. How about looking after you for a change? Forget about Phillip for now!" Amelia said, then added, "I know what you should do, kick the fucker out." Her red-headed temper was showing as she swore, but perhaps she was right, maybe it was time to face reality.

I smiled feebly – a smile of mixed emotions all trying to express themselves at once; sadness, amusement at Amelia's thoughts, anger and pain that changed the expression into a grimace. I always loved Amelia's forthright manner. 'Kick the fucker out,' she'd said. I needed time to digest all this agony. In one minute, the energy and enthusiasm to help Dion had been sucked out of me, but I wasn't going to allow them to destroy me.

It was time to head home.

"If you need help, a place to sleep or a shoulder to cry on, just shout," Amelia offered. I nodded my thanks, thinking I would probably take her up on her offer in a couple of hours. We gave each other a tight hug and said goodbye.

In the safety and privacy of my car, I sat and cried rivers of bitter tears, which gradually dried and were replaced by anger, then every other emotion born of the pain of infidelity came hurtling in; it all began to fall into place – being away more than usual and now no longer home on Friday evening early. She was probably cooking his dinner now.

Revenge was not the answer, of that I was sure, though the thought was tempting.

I parked under the huge jacaranda tree on the edge of our driveway; it was my favourite tree except when all the purple flowers dropped, covering the driveway and my car with a purple carpet that came alive with bees searching for nectar.

He wasn't home yet, and after what I'd learned, I didn't expect him, but he drove in thirty minutes later. I was so unprepared and wished he hadn't come home at all. Standing in the kitchen, watching him gather up his jacket and briefcase off the back seat, I took a long deep breath filling my lungs with oxygen – not that it guaranteed to help my disposition or clear my head, it was still foggy with conflicting emotions, and no amount of oxygen helped heal my broken heart.

"Hi," he leant down and pecked my cheek, then took a step back and said, "You look like you are ready to kill something."

"Not something, someone," I seethed and watched the frown deepen the lines between his brows.

"How long have you been screwing your sister-in-law?" I growled at him. I couldn't bring myself to say her name. I also hoped, by using her relationship to him instead, it would make his infidelity sound more disgraceful.

Damn, now the tears were back.

His eyes bored into mine while his hands visibly gripped harder on the handle of his briefcase, an action that hadn't gone unnoticed by me. I stood still, my jaw set and ready to retaliate while carefully scrutinising his body language with lasers in my eyes. He stood like a statue in front of me; that spelt guilt. Finally, he spoke.

"I have no idea what you are talking about, Elizabeth."

Of course not! He'd deny it, what else did I expect?

"I think you do. You are sleeping with your sister-in-law, aren't you? Your silence hasn't fooled me." I could feel the pain deepening as I looked at him; as hard as I tried to hold back the tears, they kept on coming. Knowing my husband was having an affair was painful enough, but with his sister-in-law made it a hundred times worse.

"There's not an ounce of truth in what you've heard, Elizabeth. Surely, you know, I wouldn't do that to my Boet."

'Oh, but you'd do it to me!' I thought silently and stared at him while he put his briefcase down and headed straight to the fridge, grabbed a beer, the 'Dutch courage' he was going to need after I'd finished with him. He stood looking at me expectantly then took a swig. I so wanted to behave like a wild woman, scorned and belittled by a ruthless, heartless rogue. Though I felt like physically attacking him, I maintained control and didn't move an inch then I said, very slowly, "that's what I'd hoped, Dion, but it's not that way, is it?" I kept my focus on his eyes. It was shamefully apparent he was lying, holding his cheeks and lips tight, forcing a faint grin and the dimple on his chin deepened, revealing tension there. Before he could answer with more infuriating lies, I spun around and left the house.

Walking around the garden, trying to sift through myriad thoughts, some clear, some confused, I breathed in the fresh air of the early evening. I had to connect my heart and my head again, they'd come detached, but anger merely suffocated my thoughts. Once I had calmed down, I walked back into the house - he was still sitting on the barstool at the kitchen counter, trying to work a more prepared web of lies. I passed him, saying nothing, and put on the kettle.

"Does……does, Phillip know?" I asked with my back turned, focussing intently on the kettle.

"Does Phillip know what, Elizabeth?"

"Oh, come on, Dion. Didn't I give you enough time to think up a new bunch of lies?" I asked sarcastically. A few tears ran down my cheeks. I wiped them away quickly, determined to remain steadfast in front of him despite the agony of this despicable betrayal.

"We need to talk, Dion."

"There's nothing to talk about, Liefie."

"Don't 'Liefie' me, Dion." He was using that term of endearment to cover up, reverberating through me as a painful and insincere stab of hypocrisy.

"There is plenty to talk about, Dion. You can go on denying your disgusting, immoral actions but let me warn you, if you don't end it tonight with a phone call to that slut, I will confront her at the top of my voice on Sunday morning outside Church so the whole congregation knows the scandalous things the two of you have been up to. There won't be any forgiveness, trust me."

The monster within leapt to his defence; there was just enough alcohol in his system to support a nasty reaction. Dion jumped up, grabbed both my arms firmly and stood rigidly stiff in front of me, holding on to my arms forcefully.

"Ouch, you are hurting me, Dion, let go of me!" I yelled at him, looking directly into two dark eyes as they glared into mine and we held each other's scowl. Dion knew, without any doubt, I would do what I'd promised. I felt his confidence withering as he slowly let go of my arms, then I handed him something else to ponder.

"I'm going out now; fix your own dinner while you think about Church on Sunday."

"You can't just walk out, I haven't eaten," he said, shock evident in his voice that I would consider such an action.

I headed down the passage to our room, packed an overnight bag, and as I passed him on my way out, I thought he might try to stop me. Thankfully he didn't; he remained on the bar stool starring into the space in front of him.

"Ignore me, and you will see hell play out in front of you on Sunday and God won't be there to rescue either of you. Decision's yours."

CHAPTER FIVE

A few weeks after the Zandri affair ended, Dion found a job in Kimberly, the famous diamond mining town in the Northern Cape, far away from the tramp in Bloemfontein; so, I agreed to give our marriage another chance.

Settling into Kimberly was surprisingly easy. The whole affair and my response to it had given him a more significant fright than I'd thought. Once we were settled and the pain of the affair lessened, we spent hours chatting, our conversations going deeper than we ever had. He'd done the honourable thing moving away and wanting to try again. We were in a place where we could concentrate on each other.

It was tough for me not having Amelia close to share thoughts; perhaps that was for the best – she'd tried very hard to talk me out of going back to Dion. For now, Dion was all I needed. I loved him, I wanted to help him, and I needed to learn to forgive him. While I was dealing with all that, I also prayed the monster had stayed in Bloemfontein.

While idly looking through the local newspaper, I found a position advertised for a pharmacy assistant and though I wasn't particularly excited about working in a pharmacy again, I thought it would be a good place to meet ladies in the community, so I applied for the job and got it. The pay was better than in Bloemfontein and I didn't have to work on Saturdays.

The company whom Dion worked for rented us a comfortable house with a swimming pool set in a lush garden surround with lovely old indigenous trees and semi-tropical shrub herbaceous borders. It was a beautiful place - the perfect environment in which to heal my broken heart. I spent my Saturday mornings lounging around like a lizard basking in the sun, getting an excellent tan while reading my favourite novels. Life was rosy once more and our relationship was progressing to a comfortable place. Dion was back to his best self. Velvety words rolled off his tongue with ease, making our conversations as intimate and meaningful as they had been in the early days of our marriage.

I lay on the sun-lounger next to the pool, my skin already turning a pinkie-brown after only half an hour sunbathing and it was too hot to go on reading. I closed my eyes and listened to the musical serenade of the birds in the trees; Dion would be back from work in an hour. While I lay there, I hoped the sales manager position for Music & Instruments would afford him the opportunity to showcase his remarkable musical talents too. My hopes were realised just a few short months later - he was a hit in Kimberly, smashing all the company's previous sales records. With the commission earnings, he invested in a second-hand white baby grand piano which took pride of place in our living room. Even a 'baby' grand is a mighty piece of furniture to move, weighing in at around five hundred pounds. We knew it would have to be re-tuned once we'd set it in place, which cost more than the removals company bill but it was the most exciting investment we'd made together - not that we'd made any others before; Dion had drunk all the spare money. Most evenings after dinner, we'd share memories of special times while he caressed the keyboard passionately, singing along and sometimes creating his own stunning music. I still kept thinking such self-taught talent was being wasted in a sales job and was sure if Dion were able to find financial backing, he would have soared up through the ranks to join the famous singing sensations of the day, but for now, he wasn't interested and thinking back, it was just as well. Becoming a small-town sensation was enough for the moment and a perfect place to show off his musicality. His deep beautiful masculine singing voice was soon becoming well-known and our much-needed home therapy was bringing the joy back into our relationship.

One memorable evening, he'd finished playing, 'Gentle on my Mind,' by Glen Campbell, an old 60's favourite of ours, when he turned to me, gently cupping my face in his hands while looking into my eyes, and whispered, "I'm so sorry for putting you through such hell, my Liefie." It was said with such tenderness and sincerity, how could I not forgive him? The critical 'sorry' word was so rare from his lips; I believed him this time. Had the Dion I loved and adored returned home? The passion from our musical interlude took us from the piano to the bedroom and brought with it another celebration - a few weeks later, I discovered I was pregnant. I couldn't wait to tell Dion and raced home from work at the end of the day.

"Babe, I am pregnant," I shouted as I danced across the lawn to greet him, barely giving him a chance to get out the car.

"That's wonderful news, sweet pea." A smile of unbridled joy spread across his face as he picked me up and whirled me around, kissing me, and carried me into the house where Splodge, my precious, newly acquired kitten was meowing as if caught up in our excitement too.

"How far gone are you, my skat?" he asked, as he put me down.

"Nine weeks, I think. I'll make an appointment to see the Doc next week."

"This is so exciting. What a way to start the weekend." He winked at me, turning my legs to jelly and my tummy tingled delightfully. Oooh, he was so sexy.

Perhaps that was part of the difficulty getting over the affair? I didn't want to share the sexiest man in town.

For the most part of me, I was incredibly proud of how well he was doing in Kimberly, even though a tiny part of me was still a little nervous, but I kept reminding myself to cast the niggles to one side; we were starting a family now.

The tiny seed of our lovemaking began to grow, emotions and hormones bounced all over the place joining in excitedly as our relationship grew, until a near disaster struck five weeks later when I had the threat of a miscarriage. Dion was in the country visiting clients, but as soon as he got the message, he drove through the night to get home to be by my side – this was another unusual Dion response.

The Doctor booked me off work for a week and insisted I was to remain bedridden for at least four of those days. Without hesitation, Dion took three days off and did absolutely everything for me; I couldn't remember the last time I'd been so spoilt, with little Splodge often curled up with me until he got restless and entertained us with comical high jinks, throwing around the feather toy I'd bought him and had us in hysterics. I got up on the fourth day and Dion went back to work. On Friday evening, he came home armed with Dr Benjamin Spock's book, The Common Book of Baby and Child Care.

"There are no Afrikaans versions in print, my Liefie," he said as he handed it over. Over the following months, I read it from cover to cover, wondering if I, or anyone else for that matter, would ever fit the role of 'perfect mother.'

"You learn as you go, keep common sense alive and know the first baby is the guinea pig," Mom had said, and her words seemed to resonate more easily than those of the famous Doctor.

The rest had done me good and I went back to work refreshed but without much enthusiasm. I was thinking of giving up my job, but I was hesitant to discuss the idea with Dion. It turned out I didn't have to worry.

"Just five months to go! Why don't you stop work, sweet pea?" he suggested. I was surprised but ecstatic.

"Can we do this without my salary?" I asked, pointing at my growing bump.

"Of course, we can. I got paid out my commission; it's way more than I expected. That alone will see us through the next six months without using your maternity pay."

"You're brilliant. Thanks, I'll resign tomorrow. Yippee," I shouted ecstatically and hugged Dion. "I can spend time doing up the nursery."

This was another first; the first time Dion had willingly shared his earnings. We were making progress, conversation was comfortable and relaxed and though I often didn't see Dion for a couple of days during the week as he visited customers out of town, I wasn't suspicious of him now. A few weeks later he asked, "Babe, how would you feel about going to the company Christmas party?"

"I'd love to, but let me check with Doctor first." I smiled and went on, "The last time I saw him, he'd commented that the rest and swimming was the best thing for me." He had warned that my historic thrombosis issues could worsen during pregnancy but all the elevated leg positions I'd be able to lie in at home, as unladylike as some were, were highly recommended.

"Of course, Liefie. There's plenty of time; I must let them know in a few weeks for catering purposes. No rush."

"If the Doctor says it's fine, I'd love to go, but then we can't stay out too late, which I know is a shame, but baba is more important, hey?"

"Of course! We come home whenever you want to." He rubbed his hand gently over my tummy, grinning proudly.

After supper, Splodge burst into life again with a masterful performance of high jinks and had us both in fits of laughter; then as quickly as he'd started, he lost interest and flopped down next to us, exhausted. It surprised me how much Dion enjoyed our adorable fluffy ginger and white tom who'd got his name from his colouring - stunning white splodges all over his body like white paint had been thrown at him, for he'd never been an animal lover before.

We toppled into bed, our tummy muscles stretched from laughing at Splodge's antics and settled contentedly into each other's arms, holding each other for a long time, then I rolled onto my back while Dion rested his ear against my bulging tummy, listening for a faint heartbeat and beamed when he felt the flicker of a tiny kick. Dion was off into the country the following day.

I hated being alone, but I had Splodge to keep me company and I felt entirely safe in Kimberly. Decorating the nursery kept me occupied. I swam every day, said 'yes' to the Christmas party after my check-up, and at seven months' pregnant, a week before the Christmas party date, I had a scan. I was carrying a little girl. We agreed to keep it secret as none of the family were visiting until after her birth, so I completed the nursery.

Leon Van Der Merwe, Dion's boss, popped in to see me during the week Dion was away. After all this time, I'd not met him before. Leon was a small man with a tremendous attitude and an overloaded ego; I took an instant dislike to him as he sat across from me drinking tea, discussing Dion's incredible musical and sales talents. A roadmap of purple veins crisscrossed his cheeks and bulbous nose which alerted me to a lifestyle of heavy drinking. I sat wishing he'd never come around – his whole demeanour spelt dis-ease for me.

I politely thanked him for coming when I noticed his teacup was empty but before he left, he asked about the staff Christmas party.

"Will you be accompanying Dion to the Christmas do?" He tried to pretend it was an after-thought, but I knew it was the sole purpose for his visit.

"I am not sure if we will be there." I lied.

"Oh. That would be a pity. It would be nice to have you both there. We want Dion to perform a few numbers for us."

I knew there was an ulterior motive for his visit.

"Yes," I tried in vain to smile politely. "If I'm not there, Dion won't be either. Goodbye, Leon." I didn't want to be rude but couldn't help myself.

I bought a pretty powder blue maternity evening dress and off we went. Dion had refused the invitation to sing at the party, which I was happy about; it meant we could leave when we were ready, or if I found sitting on hard chairs too uncomfortable.

A delicious traditional Christmas dinner was served – all the usual fare, roast turkey, glazed gammon, legs of lamb with all the trimmings and more. The table decorations sparkled as candles flickered in their holders down the centre of the tables and the hall was filled with jovial Christmas noises of crackers being pulled and laughter as people read out the joke strips from inside them. I felt terrific. Dion and I had some lovely slow dances together before dinner, but after dinner, the music became lively and energetic, everyone keen to work off their indulgence, so Dion got up to dance with work colleagues. As I sat watching, the minutes ticked by and I began to feel a rising anxiety replace the happiness I'd felt earlier as I caught snatches of where Dion was on the dance floor. An hour later, I tried to catch his attention, but to no avail. Just as I was about to head onto the dance floor and haul him off so we could head home, Leon came past.

"How about a dance? You can't sit there all alone."

"That would be lovely, thank you," I said, having no idea what prompted me to agree but I took his hand, and he led me through the dancers and on passing Dion, he patted him playfully on the shoulder, saying, "Hey, look who's dancing with me."

In an instant, the monster sprung into violent action. Bellowing loudly, he grabbed the back of my dress and possessively wrenched me to him with such force I nearly lost my balance. Driven by an inexplicable jealous rage, the ogre was back with a vengeance.

The dancing stopped; everything stopped. Somewhere in the distance, I heard a woman yelling; then I realised she was racing toward me, coming to my rescue. The chaos happened so quickly.

"Stop that, leave her alone!" the woman screamed as she scrambled toward me, pushing others out of the way. I didn't know the woman, but she pulled me from the grip of my husband and guided me quickly to the ladies' room, leaving the men to calm the fire burning inside Dion.

He'd reached that tipping point; I should have known. I was terrified life would spiral downhill once more; I couldn't deal with that in my last trimester. What had been a glorious evening for everyone, ended abruptly. The journey home was frighteningly stressful as Dion bounced the car from one pavement kerb to another, weaving into oncoming traffic, trying to negotiate the way home with one eye open, alternating with the other.

We got home alive.

I was seething. During the silent journey home, I warned myself not to say anything, but as I wearily dumped my bag down beside my side of the bed, I heard myself ask, with a note of sarcasm, if he was sleeping with the woman he'd been dancing with for so long and before I knew it, I was flying across to the other side of our bed. Slipping off the edge, I hit the floor hard. My nose started bleeding from the force of the punch and the metallic taste of blood was running down the back of my throat. I pushed myself upright. Dazed and disorientated, cupping my hands over my nose to catch the blood, I noticed blood dripping from my forehead too. There was blood everywhere; I had to get to the bathroom. Standing up slowly, my eyes filled with tears and stars, blood and defeat, I staggered to the bathroom. Holding onto each side of the basin to steady myself, I watched, mesmerised by the blood dripping onto the white porcelain while my sobs beat in time with each dark red drop and I felt our baby kicking objectionably. I prayed our baby girl would stay where she was 'till her due date. Then I felt my precious Splodge rub his warm body up and down my calves, entwining himself between my legs as he purred and meowed to comfort me, which only made me cry more. Then I looked in the mirror and noticed the gash ran from my left eyebrow, across my forehead and ended in the hairline.

My nose was swelling and changing colour as fast as my eye socket was bulging outwards. My face had quickly become an ugly canvas of blues, blacks, yellows and deep red.

Dion was passed out when I'd eventually got my face clean, stopped the bleeding, downed two painkillers and tearfully but carefully slid into bed, making sure I didn't disturb the bastard and mercifully fell into a deep, emotionally exhausted sleep. When I woke it was mid-morning, he'd left for work much earlier.

Looking in the mirror was a painful reminder of what happened, my mind filled with all the old questions, bringing with them familiar fears from the recent past. The things I'd hoped we had left in Bloemfontein.

My dear, loyal maid was horrified when she saw me in the morning.

"Eish, Missus," she said, raising her hands to cover her mouth. I told her I'd fallen. She had no reason not to believe me, for only the day before our marriage seemed perfect.

I spent the morning digging deep into my thoughts, contemplating whether or not to contact my mother. Two things prevented me from calling her. Firstly, she would insist I come home immediately and secondly, walking out of my marriage just shy of two months off giving birth to our first child was not what I wanted to do. Mom's intolerance and vehement disrespect for any man that hits a woman, especially in my condition, would be difficult to explain and I didn't have the strength to argue with her. Besides, I certainly didn't want her to see my face all cut and bruised. Thank God it didn't need stitching, but the possibility of a premature arrival of our little girl as a result of the fall concerned me.

I endured a stressful few days while treating my face with ice packs, waiting in the vain hope that Dion would call from wherever he was staying. I had plastered the cut and massaged the area with healing ointments, but by Thursday, there had been no call from Dion and my face was much the same size and the colour as deep. My active baby (I didn't think of her as ours anymore) was growing as rapidly as my anxiety; I seemed to have swelled quickly in the last four days but no threatening labour, which was a relief, and I was sure I'd go full term now. By five that evening, I knew I couldn't delay the inevitable much longer, and just as I was about to pick up the phone and dial Mom, she called me.

The brewed and stored emotion of the beating and the week alone erupted like a tsunami. I couldn't hold it back; it was time to let the matriarch take control. As I predicted, she was outraged and ordered me home. This time I listened, leaving a short note on the coffee table for Dion upon his possible return on Friday evening.

CHAPTER SIX

Mom and William were so outraged when they saw me, they could have happily put an end to Dion. William insisted I lay charges of assault when he saw my bruised, cut face.

"Divorce the swine," William growled, "he doesn't deserve you."

"I will have to go back, Boetie. I must sort this out myself and have my baby there."

"Why? What on earth for?" William responded logically, but when he saw I was close to tears again, he put his arms around me, assuring me he was there for me and always would be, no matter what my decision.

Dion called me after he'd found my note lying on the coffee table and insisted I return home the following day. I refused, pointing out that he'd started the drama.

"I'll come home when I am ready, not when you demand it, Dion."

"I want you home tomorrow so we can discuss this," he snapped. I put the phone down and cut him off and went home the following Friday with Mom and William as chaperones. Dion was waiting, standing on the front veranda, chest puffed out with anger. I could see the annoyed expression on his face as I drove in, then he saw who was in the car that followed closely behind me, and his bravado disappeared. Under normal circumstances, William was an absolute gentleman in every sense of the word until a member of his family was hurt.

Dion was acutely aware of this.

William had suppressed his anger all week and I knew my return was not going to be a happy one. Dion didn't move but stood like a marble statue as he watched William stride across the driveway toward him. He knew he could not turn and go inside; he had to face my brother who he was shit scared of and no sensations of sympathy for Dion filled me; on the contrary, I was quite happy as I watched William launch at him, grabbing a handful of his shirt front as he shoved his nose against Dion's. I was standing too far away to hear what William said to him, but I didn't need to as he dispatched Dion like a rag doll. William came striding back to help carry our suitcases into the house. Mom and I didn't dare look at each other, but I glimpsed at Dion as he got himself back on his feet.

"I won't come in," William said fiercely. "If I get near that arsehole again, I'll fucking kill the bastard, but I've warned him now." It was rare that William swore in front of either me or our mother, but under these circumstances, she graciously pretended she hadn't heard.

"Call me if you need anything, Sis." William wrapped me in a big bear-hug. I felt so safe, I didn't want him to leave.

"If he touches you again, Sis, he's a dead man, even if he is your husband," he called out the car window loud enough for it to be another warning to Dion, though I don't think he heard and I hadn't told him Mom was staying.

The big 'birth' day was fast approaching. True to his word, William called every other day to check Mom and I were safe. I'd been monitored carefully by my mother and thankfully all was well so far. Having Mom with me for the last few weeks in waiting was comforting, though not for Dion, for we had rarely spoken to each other when he was home. Though Mom never asked, I was sure she knew from the nursery furnishing, she would soon be holding her first grand-daughter. During my final check-up and scan, the Doctor asked, with apparent difficulty, whether I'd be staying in my marriage after the birth, openly admitting his concern for our safety, but I didn't answer. I didn't know how to then. I wasn't sure of anything anymore.

My due date was the 14th of April.

"The first baby's due date is always a surprise. They either decide to make an appearance a week early or arrive a week late. Have your bag packed; it's all going well, so relax and enjoy the last of it." The Doctor smiled reassuringly.

"The apple will fall when it is ripe, my kind," Mom added and smiled knowingly at the Doctor.

"No truer words spoken, and Moms are normally more accurate than us Doctors." He smiled back at her while I sat wondering who'd be right, gazing at a picture of perfect serenity – a herd of Zebra mothers and their young around a waterhole. The next time I'd see him would be in the delivery room; that thought made me nervous.

On Tuesday evening, during the last possible week of my pregnancy, Dion called sounding a little more like the old one now baby was due so soon.

"Have you taken the rest of the week off, Dion?" I asked hopefully.

"Leon's not budging on leave, Liefie."

"Why aren't you pushing him, Dion? This is not just casual leave and you are due at least two weeks," I argued, but Dion didn't seem particularly concerned and casually gave me the emergency number of the hotel where he was staying. I was furious and deeply hurt, but I knew it was pointless going on about it; my words would just fall on deaf ears. At least I had Mom with me, and she wasn't unhappy Dion wasn't around.

Late into Thursday evening, the contractions began. This child wasn't going to keep me waiting! Though I was excited, I was frightened and sad to experience this without my husband. The stirrings of labour were gentle, to begin with, and continued that way for quite some time, leaving me to believe it was a false alarm, but by one o'clock in the morning, I knew it was time to call the hotel. It would probably be more than a few hours before I needed to get to the hospital, giving Dion time to get home.

Mom had calculated 3 to 4 hours before I needed to get to the hospital, and I hoped she was right; I had no idea what to expect and hoped her calculations were accurate.

The hospital was only a fifteen-minute drive from the house. If Dion left promptly from the hotel he was staying in, there was more than enough time for him to get home; he was just over a two-hour drive away - I hoped Mom's calculations on my labour were right for she couldn't drive me to hospital.

She'd been born with a slightly deformed foot, and over the years, it had gradually deteriorated to the extent where she was no longer able to drive. I didn't particularly want to drive while gripped by violent contractions either, so I was dependant on Dion getting home in time.

I dialled the number of the hotel, and it rang for a long time before being answered.

"Windy Acres Hotel emergency. Can I help?" said the sleepy voice on the other end.

"I am sorry to disturb you at this hour, but I urgently need to speak to my husband, Mr Dion Du Toit. I'm in labour," I said.

There was a pause; I could hear the man paging through the register.

"There's no one booked in here by that name, Madam."

"What? Are you sure?" I asked horror-struck. "Your number is the number he gave me." I began to feel the prickly sensation of fear and panic grip me.

"Yes, Madam, very sure."

I slammed the receiver down, too angry to speak. Glancing at Mom's enquiring expression, I turned away from her and called the Police Station in Lime Acres explaining my urgent situation to an uninterested, sleepy duty constable.

Like the Hotel receptionist, the duty policeman was equally disinterested that I was in labour.

"Please look for him. I need him home urgently." He sleepily assured me he would do what he could and call me back when he'd found Dion.

Lime Acres, a tiny dusty little hovel of a town in the middle of nowhere, was only popular for one-night stopovers used by salesmen and game hunters. There were a few shops that serviced the farming community, a post office and a bank and that was about it apart from two small country inns, one at either end of the town, which provided the village with its only entertainment. Dion's van had the company logo blazoned across it, so I was sure he'd be easy to find but by 5 am, it was time to get to the hospital; I'd have to drive myself. The contractions were stronger, but nothing I couldn't bear.

I gathered up my toiletries and shoved them into my pre-packed bag while Mom busied herself with filling a flask of hot coffee. She knew me so well. I was a coffee addict; she also knew, being the nurse that I was, I wouldn't rush into the hospital until I *really* had to.

I'd not driven more than twice in the last two weeks. My tummy was huge; the skin stretched, tight and uncomfortable; there was scarcely millimetres between it and the steering wheel. Driving was awkward; I felt alarmingly trapped. Luckily, the journey was not far and the likelihood of any other traffic on the road in the early hours of the morning was slim.

I parked close to the hospital admission's entrance, switched the engine off and looked at my mother. She smiled knowingly and dug out the flask, asking, "have you had another contraction?"

"No, nothing for about twenty minutes. Oh God, I loathe hospitals when I'm the patient," I moaned, pushing the seat back as far as it would go and settled my head against the headrest, taking in a good deep breath.

"We'll go in just now," I sighed. Mom's maternal pride and love was in full bloom.

"That is why I filled the flask. I knew you'd have to have a cup before going in."

I closed my eyes and waited for the next contraction, sipping my coffee slowly, savouring its delicious fragrance.

"I'm scared, Ma," I said, as the minutes ticked on.

"The first baby is always frightening, but you will manage, we all do. Once you have that little bundle in your arms, the memory of the pain soon disappears. What do you want?" I opened my eyes and looked at Mom; confused.

"Ma! Haven't you noticed how I've done the nursery?"

"Yes, I have, but you've never confirmed whether you know or not. I didn't ask for I hoped you'd volunteer the information, but you haven't."

"Oh, Mom, you are so sweet. Thoughtless of me, I'm sorry, yes, it is a girl; it was confirmed shortly before all the shit with Dion happened."

"I'm delighted you are having a girl," Mom smiled, "easier to bring a girl up on your own if you decide to leave Dion."

"Oh, Ma, I wish I had a normal marriage and sitting here like this really brings it home hard, especially not knowing where he is at a time like this is; it shouldn't be like this. Do you think this baby will change Dion?"

"Well," her face said it all. "I certainly hope so, Elizabeth. He doesn't deserve someone like you. If he doesn't change, promise me you'll leave him." It was so unlike her to encourage a separation or divorce, but she despised Dion's vile actions.

"Ma, I can't promise that, but if he doesn't change over the next few months, I will make the decision then."

We sat quietly for a while, absorbed by our thoughts. Then it occurred to me that I hadn't had a contraction for ages. We'd not been timekeeping so I didn't utter a word; it could wait a little longer.

"More?" Mom lifted the flask and broke the silence.

"Do I ever refuse coffee?" I laughed and watched the hot coffee tumble into my cup, filling it up – perhaps not the best thing to be drinking just before an impending birth.

"Ma, it must be at least forty-five minutes since my last contraction. Is that normal?"

"My goodness, has that much time passed? And, you shouldn't be drinking all this coffee," she chuckled, verbalising my thoughts.

"Let's wait another fifteen minutes – let the coffee settle, and if nothing has happened, we may as well head home. Do you think it's a false alarm?"

"No, my kind, not a false alarm; stress and anxiety can halt it though. They will be back, that's guaranteed."

I was so close to my due date; I didn't think it could be a false alarm. We were about to drive off when Leon drove past and noticed my car; he slowed, then turned his car around and came into the parking lot.

He was the last person I wanted to see as he pulled up alongside us, asking if I was okay.

Instead of offering a response to his enquiry, I snapped, "Where the hell's Dion? He's not at the hotel he said he was staying in."

A glazed look covered his face. I knew that look; he knew where Dion was.

"Even the police couldn't find him in your emblazoned company van. Very strange, in a tiny town like Lime Acres. Can you find him and send him home urgently?"

"I will try and get hold of him as soon as I get to the office and tell him to get here urgently," he nodded.

"Thank you. We are going home now as nothing is happening, but it would be nice to have the bastard home today. You could have at least given Dion this time off."

"He didn't ask for time off, Elizabeth, but I will do what I can."

I was confused, he looked confused, and Mom had raised her eyebrows. I looked at Mom and silently thought, should I make that promise now? With disbelief, I asked again.

"He didn't ask for time off, are you sure?" I asked, incredulously. Leon was about to say something else, but I spun the wheels and sped off; I didn't want to hear more and burst into tears.

"Did you notice the way he looked at me, Mom? I hate that man. He knows where Dion is, but why Dion didn't ask for leave is what I'd like to know. Even Leon looked shocked at that. Oh Mom," I sobbed, trying to focus on the road. "Why are they lying to me?"

"Why do you dislike Leon?" Mom asked, not committing herself to anything else.

"He drinks like a fish, and I am sure all the nonsense with Dion again is because of him. He encourages Dion to drink and sends Dion all over the place, playing pianos in hotel bars to get orders; he's such a bad influence."

"Dion doesn't need anyone to influence him, my kind," Mom's chin was set and had gone white. Mom had had enough. "You heard what the man said; Dion didn't even ask for leave. I think you should have your baby and come home, my kind. (my child)

"I'll see, Ma. Let me have the child first. I'm so confused and so torn."

"I'm very proud of you, my girl, you are handling a dreadful situation with such maturity; he's nothing but heartache and trouble, I'm sorry to say. I raised you with good morals and ethics; he wasn't."

"Ma!"

"I'm sorry, but it's true. He's never going to change, my girl. I don't know of any other woman who would give their husband so many chances and now this, it's inexcusable."

I knew Mom was right. We had not talked much about Dion since she'd been with me but voicing her opinion now left my mind in a spin. I loved him; a puzzle I couldn't piece together. If he was having another affair, *I'd* have to catch him, but I threw the thought out.

I wanted to keep sobbing, release the pain and disappointment; at the same time, I wanted to scream, shout and yell to free the resentment I felt that was fighting for space in the pit of my stomach. So many questions raced through my mind as Mom and I waited for a contraction again.

We waited all morning expectantly. Nothing happened. 'Probably because of all the coffee I'd drunk,' I thought, but just after a light lunch, they hit me like a tidal wave from nowhere; fierce, agonising and close together. Moaning loudly as the force of the pain washed over me, I knew without hesitation; this was it. I couldn't drive, I could scarcely move.

It was 2.45 pm. Where was Dion?

"I'll try driving, Mom; we have to go now," I groaned, holding the base of my enormous stomach. Sweat had begun to drip off my forehead and was running down the side of my temples. When the next wave of contractions came, I gripped the car keys so savagely I thought I might bend them. I hobbled towards the front door, gritting my teeth, taking one painful step at a time, and as I stood on the veranda waiting for the contraction to subside, Dion raced into the driveway.

"Oh, thank the Lord," Mom breathed a sigh of relief. "Just in time."

I couldn't remember a time when I'd felt such overwhelming respite. I yelled, "Open the door and drive," as I took the last steps and got in the car.

My waters broke as I was wheeled into the delivery room with a nervous, agitated Dion beside me. He watched his first child being born on the eve of the 16th of April, 1975. Storm was born fifteen minutes after I arrived in the delivery room. A good healthy set of lungs was music to my ears; the life-changing sound triggered a rush of absolute joy while tears rolled down my cheeks. Just as Mom had said, the pain was almost instantly forgotten in those precious moments of ecstasy as my eyes gazed upon a pair of perfect little feet. A human so tiny, so perfectly flawless that I'd carried inside me for nine difficult months was utterly overwhelming. I glanced up at Dion and noticed tears were trickling down his face too.

The midwife handed our little bundle to me. As I held her for the first time, gazing at her in wonder and awe, I could scarcely believe I'd carried this little miracle for nine months! I opened her tiny little hand and examined her perfect long fingers and smiled as the instinctive reflex to grip happened in an instant; her perfect little index finger curled over mine with surprising strength and only then did I look up at Dion and allow our eyes to meet for the first time since we arrived in hospital. There was a softness about them now, but before I gave in, influenced by this exquisite emotional mood, he had questions to answer but for the next few minutes all I wanted was to focus on my beautiful baby girl whose perfect rosebud lips, wisps of curly black hair, long dark lashes and pink cheeks filled my heart with a joy I'd never known possible and this incredible moment was exquisitely mine to savour forever. My baby girl had been through a rough carriage since conception, so, without consulting Dion, I named her Storm. Two days later we were on our way home.

"She looks like you, Liefie," I said to Dion as I settled into the back seat of the car, looking at her sleeping in her carrycot.

"She's as beautiful as you, sweet pea." He lent in and kissed my forehead before jumping into the driver's seat, but forgiveness wasn't within easy grasp for me. The last months clouded the most beautiful moment of my life.

I lay my head back against the headrest. If nothing else, she was at least conceived with love, but for the rest, we'd wait and see.

"I'm so proud of you, Liefie," he said, looking at me in the rear-view mirror. "May I hold her when we get home?" I didn't answer but silently prayed she was the gift that would finally change this man. Then I noticed he was glancing from me to the road, waiting for an answer and when our eyes met again, I nodded.

Mom was waiting for us on the veranda. She'd been so touched by her first beautiful granddaughter and must have struggled being home alone with Dion. I wondered what she may have said to Dion about his behaviour, for her body language in the ward screamed her disapproval. She wasn't going to forgive him or even try and like him again but for now, she graciously enjoyed the excitement of the birth of another grandchild.

Dion helped me out the car and proudly carried the sleeping Storm in her cot into the house then went back to the car to bring in my suitcase and the flowers and gifts I'd been given. Mom had already put the kettle on but I avoided coffee now I was breastfeeding and peeped in at a sleeping Storm and sat down carefully next to her.

"Why didn't you choose an Afrikaans name?" Mom asked. I knew she would at some point, and I noted the disappointment in her voice.

"I couldn't find one I liked and, after the tumultuous journey we had together during the pregnancy, the name fit the turbulence." I smiled. "Dion wasn't impressed either, Mom, but he didn't dare argue; he caused the storm in more ways than one," I said and excused the pun.

"I hope the name isn't an indication of what the child might live through in her future," Mom said, her disapproval obvious.

"Her second name reflects her Afrikaans heritage, Mom, and she will never be told why she was called Storm, but hopefully it will be a constant reminder to her father to behave better."

"Well, my kind, that remains to be seen."

Storm stirred in her cot and I lifted her out. It was time for a feed and Mom and I went on chatting while we had the opportunity, for Dion would be back from the hospital shortly.

"How long before my nipples harden, Mom? I'm so tender."

"A couple of days and you will be fine. As you know, be careful what you eat."

"Yeah, the nurse gave me some tips on what to avoid."

While she suckled contentedly, the sensation, though tender, triggered an amazing maternal bonding and my body tingled while my heart swelled with motherly love and it wasn't long before Dion arrived home carrying in the bouquets and bowls of beautiful flowers from family and friends. Amelia had sent a pure white orchid and on the card, she'd scribed - 'To my most treasured friend, I'm thinking of you cuddling your beautiful daughter and wish I could share the moment with you. Miss you terribly. I chose the white orchid - a delicate, exotic and graceful plant which typifies your wonderful personality and represents love, luxury, beauty and strength. Love you lots. We must get together soon.'

Her message had deeply touched me. I missed my best friend and remembered the tears that had filled my eyes just as the paediatrician had walked into the ward after checking Storm.

"What brings on the tears?" he'd asked, cheerfully. "She's a beautiful, healthy baby girl."

"I know she is; they are tears of joy that come along with a touching message from my best friend," I'd answered. "Thank you, Doctor," I had quickly added.

Soon, the house was filled with all the flowers and Dion settled down in the lounge with Mom and I and gazed at Storm as she suckled on me.

"I've got today and tomorrow off," Dion said and I almost felt disappointed.

"Oh, that's nice. Why didn't you take them before Storm was born?" I snapped more than asked.

"Leon wouldn't give me time off."

"Bullshit!" I barked and upset Storm and her eyes opened wide; then went on suckling from me and Mom left the room. "He passed Mom and I sitting in the car when I first went into labour. I asked him why he hadn't given you time off, and he said you hadn't asked for any."

"I did ask, Liefie, he said I had to meet my targets." The lies fell off his lips without conscience and the ease of his spoken untruths sickened me. I went on with my planned interrogation.

"Where were you on Thursday night, then?"

"Ja, I'm sorry, Liefie. I haven't had a chance to tell you what happened. The owner of Fontein Hotel, south of Lime Acres, ordered a piano and offered me a room for the night because I'd played until late. With that order, I broke last year's record." Dion beamed as if I should be delighted to hear how well he'd done. He was more excited about that than the birth of his first child, or was it just my interpretation?

"Is that all you care about? Why didn't you call and give me the Fontein Hotel telephone number, knowing the importance of me being able to contact you at such a critical time?" I could feel my bottom lip begin to quiver with indignation and hurt caused by the dismissive and careless attitude he was showing. I was glad Mom had left the room.

"No, of course it's not all I care about, but it gives us more money to spend on Storm, which I do care about." He knew how to say the right things at the right time, but his expression didn't quite mould together with his words. I wasn't going to argue with the sentiment though, but time would tell.

"So, why didn't you think to give me that number?" Dion shifted and looked away without offering an answer to the question. Instead, he evaded it like a practised politician with some other bullshit; then silence prevailed as I laid Storm down in her cot and buttoned my blouse. Visions of Dion dressed in black tails, white shirt and royal blue velvet bow tie, the outfit he wore for evening entertainment sessions, suddenly filled my mind. Seated at the piano, perfectly manicured, nimble fingers dancing across the keys, ladies gathered from the sleepy farming dorpe, (village) deprived of good entertainment for months, going crazy, swooning over my husband was a vision I couldn't shake and I had to forcibly drag my thoughts back to the present. Nothing added up.

"Is there anything you want me to get you from the shops?" he asked, tentatively, desperate to get away from my questions.

"Mom and I made a list; I'll get it from her." I disappeared, whispered to Mom he was going out and gesticulated my relief and Mom smiled. Handing Dion the list, he disappeared more hastily than was necessary, providing me with confirmation something was suspicious. Having Mom with us kept Dion on his toes and he surprisingly immersed himself in doing all the right things for his daughter and me. The nappy bit left him terrified in case he was gifted with something he couldn't deal with. It broke the tension while I teased and watched him try, but if the aromas of a full nappy found their way up his nose, he visibly gagged and ran out of the room.

"I'll do anything with her, but not that," he'd said apologetically. He came home every night after work even though Leon complained and gradually the tension eased, and we could spend more comfortable time together, so Mom went home. Then, without consulting Dion, Leon booked gigs at inns and hotels for Dion to do, booking them far from home again. Callous and inconsiderate, all the bastard cared about was reaching the company targets, dragging Dion into the fold selfishly. I was furious.

Of course, once the owners of the hotels and pubs heard Dion play and tallied up their takings for the night, another piano or organ was sold; Leon traded on that and Dion loved the attention. Baby Storm and I were of no consequence to Leon. Dion Du Toit was a lucrative attraction. For nine long weeks, we rarely saw him. I'd had enough. I was exhausted, lonely and depressed, so I called Leon; I was sick of arguing with Dion and never sure he was telling me the truth.

"He's our top rep, Elizabeth. He's brilliant. His reputation has spread across the province. I'm sure you are very proud of him. Pianos and organs are selling faster than we can get them in." It didn't seem to matter what I said, he was focused on one thing and one thing only - sales; but I needed to hear myself say what was on my mind, even if he couldn't care less.

"Let me remind you, Leon, he's married to me, not your bloody company. I want him home, not gallivanting around the country. My daughter doesn't even know she has a father because of you."

"He's too popular to stop booking him out, Elizabeth," Leon stated thoughtlessly. This response wasn't worth me answering politely, as he didn't understand that dialogue.

"You inconsiderate fucking creep. You don't get it, do you?" I swore uncharacteristically, but I didn't care now either. "I want him home this weekend," and I promptly slammed the telephone down with force. It had barely settled on its cradle when it rang again, but I never answered it; I fell into my armchair and sobbed. An hour later, the phone disturbed the peace with its shrill ring and I thoughtlessly answered it.

"I'm not interested in speaking to you, Leon. It's like pissing into the wind; the consequences are not quite as unpleasant but equally as pointless." This was a retort that flew out of my mouth unexpectedly and just as I was about to put the phone down, he said quickly.

"I'm sorry, Elizabeth. We will sort his hours out."

"When?" I screeched. "And where's he been staying?"

"I'm not sure, but I will get him home for you, don't worry."

"You're his boss, you must know where he is staying? I'm not an idiot Leon, refrain from treating me like one."

"I'll find out, and call you back."

"Don't bother, just get him home," I slammed the phone down in rage. Oh, how I loathed the patronising arsehole.

Dion came home that evening.

I wasn't in an attractive mood; every angry, painful emotion had scratched at my innards for three long and lonely months, brewed with a chaotic mix of hormones and post-natal depression; the potion felt dangerous but there was nothing I could say that I would regret. Still, it was an evening of stilted conversation. I had been prepared for battle but somehow Dion managed to steer the conversation cunningly away from what was pertinent and I was too angry and hurt to find the words to steer him back to a place of vulnerability.

When Storm woke for her feed in the early hours of the morning, Dion didn't stir, snoring throughout her feed. He was still in a deep sleep when I finished, affording me the opportunity to dig through his briefcase to satisfy my suspicions. I hesitated a moment; it wasn't something I'd normally do. I opened it up as if it was contaminated with guilt and the sharp sword of infidelity lodged deep in my heart again as I tucked the note into my gown pocket and spent the rest of the night considering my next move.

He and Julie Malan were going to pay. Her telephone number and address were written in what I guessed to be her handwriting, with a few little hugs and kisses across the bottom of it. The address where I was sure to find her was a farm just outside Lime Acres. The dotted line was now forming a picture.

I said nothing to Dion when he woke, and said goodbye as casually as I could, while he was trying to tell me he'd be in the country tonight, but it was to be his last night away. The information lodged somewhere in the recesses of my mind as he pecked me on the cheek and walked toward the door.

"Where will you be staying tonight? I called after him.

"I'll check where Leon's booked me and call you later with the details, Liefie." He stopped, turned and came back and hugged me. I stood, cold as a statue. I didn't want him close to me. He'd just unwittingly confirmed that Leon made his accommodation bookings.

"What's wrong?" he asked, aware he'd just hugged a motionless form as cold as ice.

"Nothing, I'm just tired." He shrugged off my answer.

"I'm probably staying at Fontein Hotel again, but I'll let you know. It is the most convenient place for me to operate from."

"Oh, yes, I'm sure it is," I answered sarcastically.

Once he'd left the house, I arranged with Miriam to sleep in our house that night, telling her I had to leave very early in the morning. She'd take care of Storm while I was away and I'd be back about mid-afternoon.

I expressed enough milk for Storm's three feeds with a little over just in case I got back late and she could mix it in with a few teaspoons of baby porridge and give that to Storm; she was taking a little porridge now. Miriam nodded, obviously troubled by my mood but she said nothing.

I was laser-focussed when I left the house at three o'clock in the morning, the bitter-sweet taste of revenge in my mouth, 9mm pistol loaded, safety catch in the 'on' position, ready waiting in the cubbyhole and off I went. My knuckles glowed white in the darkness of the cab's interior as I gripped the steering wheel as tightly as my jaw was clenched. An aching throb in my head kept time with the whining motor, which was now at full throttle. My thoughts were only on what lay ahead as I drove on recklessly, pushing harder on the accelerator.

The skies were starting to lighten; dawn was twenty minutes away when I arrived at the farm; I'd got there earlier than I'd calculated. It was cold in the car, and I shivered involuntarily, sniffed in the fresh, moist winter air and focussed on the red brick farmhouse draped in bougainvillea that had finished flowering a few weeks back. A few dry purple flowers still had to fall, just like the woman who'd taken my husband was about to do.

I parked, quietly got myself out of the car leaving the door ajar, and with the pistol cocked and ready, I ran across the lawn to the back door and knocked loudly. The sound echoed around me in the silence of the breaking dawn. It wasn't long before two ladies greeted me cheerfully as one of them pulled the door open, obviously expecting to see someone else at the back door at this time of the morning.

Their cheer vanished as rapidly as my murderous intent, and I stared, dumbfounded, at the two ladies who'd quickly slammed the door screaming hysterically. Rage and revenge suddenly drained out of me as the horror of what I'd intended doing came hurtling in. No longer numbed by hatred, everything became flawlessly clear for the first time.

Blurred by hurt, hatred and revenge, the pain and loneliness of the last few months, I realised I had no contingency plan and felt my body give way to uncontrollable quivering while my right arm shook as I tried in vain to unload the pistol, then I knocked again.

"Fuuuuuck offfffff," came a loud retort.

"Get away, you lunatic," said the other. "What do you want here, anyway?" I wondered if that was Julie speaking.

"My husband, Dion du Toit." A guilty silence filled the air, then I heard other footsteps approaching the door and stop.

"Put that fucking gun away, Elizabeth," boomed Dion's voice from behind the closed door, "or I will call the police."

"Call them, Dion. Please, call them. Tell them to get here quickly; a murder is about to take place."

Hushed silence surrounded us for a moment. My mind went blank while inside the house there was panic. My body shook violently from cold and the shock of what I'd been about to do but all the strength had suddenly deserted me. Fuelled by adrenaline, driven by vengeance for too long, I stood at the back door emotionally exhausted, weakened and confused. I turned and staggered across the lawn, fell into my car, slammed the door, threw the pistol into the cubby-hole and switched on the ignition and only then did I take a long deep breath to re-group. I slowly turned the car around and headed home - guided by instinct. I remember none of that journey home; what I do remember is the exaggerated relief of arriving home safely without leaving a murder investigation behind me and stumbled through the door into the welcoming arms of my loving, caring maid, Miriam.

Though she knew none of what I'd attempted to do, she could see I was about to collapse. With quiet wisdom, she knew then it had something to do with my lying, adulterous husband – adultery she knew all about. She led me to the couch, sat me down and with the promise of a hot cup of tea, reduced me to a sobbing heap of broken bits.

Storm was mercifully asleep.

"Oh, my missus," she whispered, understanding the pain of infidelity - it was part of her culture. I always wondered whether she felt the same way I did, or was it just accepted?

"You must sleep, my Missus. I will take care of Storm for the next few hours," she insisted kindly. I was asleep before Mariam had even made the tea.

It was Dion who woke me. I looked up at him through swollen eyes and instantly panicked. I hadn't fed Storm. Why hadn't Miriam woken me? I jumped out of bed, almost knocking Dion over as I rushed through to the kitchen, to find Miriam had taken care of everything. Storm was giggly and cheerful and as happy to see me as I was her while I wiped the sleep out of my eyes. What had Storm been fed?

"What did you feed Storm?" I asked Miriam. "I put water in milk and little bit porridge after milk. Happy Storm." She beamed. She'd sacrificed the care of her own family while keeping a vigilant eye on Storm and me. The depth of my gratitude was all-encompassing.

I didn't want Dion anywhere near me. I hated him. I hated what he'd done to me. I vaguely heard him saying he was sorry; then I heard myself growling at him like the wounded lioness protecting her young.

"Your apologies mean fuck all, Dion Du Toit."

"I know how hurt you are but let me explain," he offered.

"Explain what? There's nothing to explain, and one's not enough for you, I see, you need two at a time." I wrapped my hands around a scalding hot cup of coffee then remembered the note in my dressing gown pocket. Quickly putting the coffee cup down before I dropped it, I pulled out the folded piece of paper, threw it at Dion and walked away.

"Let me talk, damn it. Before you barge out of here, you owe me an apology."

"I owe you what?" I swung round to face him, the audacity of his comment stopped me in my tracks.

"You heard me," he said.

I didn't trust myself to respond. I needed the security of the kitchen where I'd find Miriam with Storm. He followed, trying to explain how kind the twin sisters had been to him, mumbling on about how they'd prevented him from driving drunk and insisted on feeding him a hearty bowl of stew when they got home.

"Do you honestly expect me to believe all that crap?" I flicked the kettle switch to top up my coffee with boiling water, more to keep myself occupied than the need for more coffee. Miriam took up her position next to me with Storm on her hip. The baby had a worried expression on her face and her lips quivered slightly as if she was about to cry, but Miriam soothed and reassured her.

"You are making it sound like everything is my fault. I am the one who has put up with your womanising, drinking and lies and bullying, how dare you ask for an apology. An apology for what?"

"I haven't intentionally wanted to murder two innocent people before," came his sanctimonious response which sickened and enraged me more.

"Because I haven't gone off and had repeated affairs, that's why. You were ready to murder Leon when he led me across the dance floor, if you remember. Don't you dare provoke me, Dion! Innocent ladies? That's a joke, which one ordered the piano, with hearts and kisses on the bottom of the note?" My voice had reached a pitch leaving my throat dry and husky. "Let me repeat, you deserve no apology. The only thing you deserve is to be castrated."

I'd been tempted to put a bullet through my head on a few occasions, stimulated by post-natal depression. The only thing that stopped me was my beautiful baby girl.

Dion tried to reach out to me again on Sunday, but I was unreachable. I refused to talk to him. After he left for work on Monday morning, I packed all I could fit into my car, strapped Storm into her seat while Splodge hopped into the car and curled up on the front seat without an obvious care in the world and we headed off to live with my mother on the family farm 160km from Kimberly.

Who Are You? by D.K. Robinson

I had done a lot of driving in the last few days!

CHAPTER SEVEN

I was in a good mood for the first time in months. The farm was my favourite place, a place where I felt internally at peace with myself and entirely in tune with everything around me; a place where I knew I was truly loved. I'd filled the car with fuel, had the windscreen cleaned and the oil checked before we left the city. Storm was strapped into her car seat and Splodge was still asleep on the seat next to me, purring softly, while his ears twitched every so often. This journey was going to be a happy one, back to where I belonged, back to a place where I felt secure, where I could cleanse away the recent heartbreak and sadness. What had been my happy place as a child was to become my healing retreat, only this time I wouldn't be sitting beneath the wild cosmos growing in our fallow fields; it was the wrong time of the year. My mind drifted back to when I sat watching, with delight, the butterflies and bees busy doing their work. It was there, hidden in that wonderland of pink and white, where everything lives side by side in perfect harmony, that the pain of Papa's death became less troublesome.

The kilometres rolled on smoothly toward the farm and I felt the tension slowly unravel as I soaked in the beauty around me. This was something Dion never appreciated. He wasn't a nature lover. The Dion who'd once made my dreams come true had now shattered them. There was more to life than this pain. I'd left behind a man I'd learned to despise as equally as I loved. I struggled not to lose my grasp on hope and purpose; now, I had to admit, I was too young and too unwise in the ways of psychological complexities to help Dion, but the desire to assist stuck with me.

Would I find the answers to my future in the fields? Would the butterflies and bees bring them to me, show me the signs I was looking for?

A few weeks of precious, quiet time at home would be perfect to let me sift through the confusion and find the path to the next chapter of my life's journey. It was the ideal place to think while pushing Storm down the sand roads in her pushchair, introducing her to the magnificent wonders of nature at the tender age of five months old. The air was clean and unpolluted, the natural swaying of grasses and flowers in gentle breezes and insects all claiming their share of the bounty would not only soothe me but would hopefully fascinate Storm. These were the things that mattered; they were what grounded me.

I'd not wanted to think of single parenthood; it held no appeal but nor did going back to this altered man, a man who was so unlike the man I'd married and was still in love with. How could I throw that away? '*He*,' was still there; it was finding a way to make him stay that had me flummoxed. If I did decide to try once more, would it be worth it? Nothing made sense right now; I would untangle my thoughts and emotions one day at a time, harmonising with the music of the winds, the songs of insects and birds, the dust storms and the setting African sun.

Out on the open road, traffic racket and city noise far behind me, I wound down the window and fresh air blasted its way past my face, and with it, the lovely pungent smell of damp long grass and wild herbs growing in the soil on either side of the road. LM radio was playing some good music and soon I was singing along, the humiliation of another affair to deal with behind me - thank God I'd not pulled the trigger. Those thoughts still brought beads of sweat to my brow.

Recent rains had washed the dust off the countryside. It was refreshingly clean and crisp, reflecting a selection of perfectly soft African greens. The mid-morning temperatures had climbed to 30°C and were rising off the wet earth, making the air close. The dams were full, and the sky was a bright, vibrant blue; it was a perfect day. The kilometres toward home were reducing; soon I would be reunited with my family. We were a close family, unified by tragedy and hardship. I'd grown up with only some of my siblings, a strong mother and guided by the warmth and happiness of our staff. We'd all missed Father's presence, especially my brother, who'd shouldered more responsibility than any teenage boy should. The unavoidable circumstances had forced us to grow up faster than our friends, but we had the gift of the great outdoors. William had taught me such a lot; in fact, he'd turned me into quite a tomboy, preferring to wield hammers and screwdrivers than playing with dolls and learning to cook. William possessed a wisdom far beyond his years, a knowledge I was going to call on now.

Storm began to stir, interrupting my thoughts. We were on the quiet gravel road, so I pulled up beneath the shade of a large acacia tree and switched off the engine. The silence of the African bush always sharpens the senses - I'd forgotten just how blissfully silent it was. Unbuckling Storm from her car seat, I lifted her up and settled her onto my lap. She was hungry and fidgeted as I unbuttoned my blouse, loosened the front of my bra, and released a painfully engorged breast. Her feed time was way overdue, but she'd slept well, and I hadn't wanted to disturb her - must have been the peace, quiet and fresh air, I decided.

A euphoria accompanies breastfeeding. I'd have a glorious high brought on by the release of hormones that accompanied Storm's suckling, and my mind was sharper as I sat listening to the birds in the tree above us while Storm greedily fed on me.

In little over half an hour, we were on our way again. Splodge had settled after yelling for water and mewing frantically, which Storm found particularly funny and she chuckled with the delightful liquidity of a baby, making me go all gooey inside.

During the last leg of the journey, my mind drifted back to Kimberly. Life in the famous old diamond mining town suited Dion. Though we hadn't been in Kimberly long, it was long enough for Dion's reputation as a musician to spread fast. With his natural talent and lots of help from Leon, he was invited to play the piano and sing in many of the quaint historical pubs and hotels in town where young hopeful miners with dreams of wealth had drunk before him a hundred years back, which had boosted his sales and his ego. Kimberly came alive at night and had I not been pregnant and threatened with miscarriage, perhaps I would have enjoyed more nights out with him. Many of the old pubs replicated the energy and vibe of yesteryear when diamonds were discovered in 1871. The area had erupted with the mad scramble for claims, and anything went down - hard-working diggings during the day and hard drinking at night, and just as it was today, there were plenty of loose women to satisfy the primal desires of man. The purpose for our move had been to get away from one woman, and now our marriage had become a symbol of the town's history; blood, sweat and tears, hard drinking and endless womanising - there was no doubt Dion considered himself the Barnie Barnato of the seventies. There was no doubt he possessed the debonair good looks of the diamond tycoon; however, there was a significant difference; they didn't share the same wealth, and there was a sad absence of diamonds, but both men thrived on the attention lavished upon them by adoring women, status and booze.

Bumping over the dirt road close to home, Splodge had moved to my lap and was kneading my leg painfully and purring as if enjoying the pain he was inflicting on me. My thoughts hurriedly left Dion and Kimberly. I was almost home.

CHAPTER EIGHT

Rural African women know precisely how to unleash torrents of unashamedly good cheer and excitement at seeing someone they love after a time apart. This was just what I needed; simplistic, authentic, and heart-warming, in stark contrast to my marriage, ululating while ushering me in to stop beside them.

Word had got around that 'Missus Elizabeth' was bringing her new baby for them to meet, and as I parked beneath the shade of a large white stinkwood tree in the centre of the driveway, they bombarded the car, giggling and laughing, swaying merrily, serenading with high pitched African yodelling excitement, dressed in bright ethnic print uniforms, waving their aprons around. Their happiness was infectious, but Storm wasn't sure how to interpret the merriment, and her bottom lip quivered with uncertainty. Five, happy, apron-clad black women, with an abundance of love in their souls and the warmth of the earth in their hearts, peered into the car at Storm. I loved looking into their shiny black faces, smeared with Vaseline, beaming toothless smiles that shone like the moon against a dark sky, but Storm looked on with an anxious infant stare, on the verge of tears.

Ester, the head lady, reached in and shamelessly grabbed Storm, passing her around like a trophy. Overwhelmed by the enthusiasm and boisterous laughter, she balled her head off, while the ladies cajoled and mocked the infant joyfully. It wasn't long before the tears were gone, and Storm began to enjoy the well-intended love and laughter and pressed out a smile.

A call from Dion inevitably destroyed our quiet Friday evening. I knew it had to come - I couldn't hide from him forever. He'd read my note on getting home and was spitting mad. The fact he'd only found my note on Friday was proof he hadn't bothered to call home during the week for Miriam would have told him I wasn't there.

"What the fuck are you doing on the farm?" he yelled down the phone.

"If you'd called home once during the week, you'd have known. Good-bye, Dion." I put the receiver down, and it rang again seconds later.

"I am here because I can't sit around waiting for you to come home while you screw around with every willing slut in and out of town." This time I slammed the phone down before he had time to answer, but he persisted and rang again. The shrill sound of the telephone ringing again spiked my blood pressure and my mood. Taking in a deep breath, I left it ringing for a bit longer before picking it up.

"Elizabeth, listen to me. You are jumping to conclusions. I'm not sleeping with Julie; that's the truth."

"You don't know the meaning of truth, Dion! I can't trust you. You promised you'd never be unfaithful again after Zandri, but you can't resist, can you? Another promise you made was that you'd stop drinking. My understanding of a promise and commitment are worlds apart from yours. Your promises are said because they sound like the right thing to say at the time, not because you mean any of them." There was silence on the other end, then he asked, "When are you coming home?" The question confirmed he'd listened to nothing I'd just said or was purposefully ignoring it.

"I don't know if I am coming back." Hearing myself say that hit me harder than I'd anticipated. Tears of futility and sadness smeared my cheeks.

"I was not sleeping with Julie; how many times do I have to tell you?"

"Get it into your head, Dion; I don't believe a word you say. You had her details in your briefcase, written in her hand with hugs and kisses along the bottom of the piece of the paper I threw back at you. You and I both know she wasn't looking for a fucking piano."

This time, I gently placed the phone back in its cradle, and when it rang for the fourth time, I left it ringing.

Though Mom was busying herself with Storm while I was struggling with Dion on the phone, she'd heard snippets of the argument and I when I turned to her, falling back into the couch, I noticed a mixed expression on her face; one of pride mingled with empathy for the pain she could see I was struggling to deal with.

They say cats have a sixth sense and Splodge certainly displayed his as he suddenly appeared, jumped on the couch and spread himself across my lap as if to say, 'well done,' and purred like a steam train. He possessed me, as cats do, quietly ruling my life without asking, but I adored him. Though he had the intuition of a cat, he behaved more like a loyal dog. He went everywhere with me, quite happy wherever he was, as long he was with me or protectively loving Storm.

I remained on the farm for ten days and revelled in the gentle quiet of the country, refusing to speak to Dion when he called and binning the letter he'd written to me the evening I had left.

"My kind, (my child) you can't go on like this. You need to speak to your husband and sort things out one way or another. If he calls tonight, have a civil conversation with him," Mom suggested, worried by my refusal to deal with Dion.

"I know Ma, but I don't know what the solution is. Only a small part of me wants to go back."

"Ignoring him isn't going to solve it or help answer your questions. He's not going away; unfortunately, he's your husband." Mom was not often annoyed with me, but this whole episode was wearing her down as she watched me go into a place where no-one could access. She didn't want me to go back to Dion, but it was up to me. My deliberate procrastinating irritated her now, probably because she'd never seen me this indecisive. I knew I could not solve this by a telephone conversation; I had to work this out in our home.

I got up from the chair, lowered Storm into her pushchair and disappeared down the road that led to the farm dam where I sat and contemplated, trying to gather a practical perspective on my situation while moorhens, herons and Egyptian geese watched over me. I envied them, monogamous or not; their lives were simple and without complication. 'How wonderfully simple life would be if I were a bird,' I thought aimlessly for a moment.

That night, I spoke to Dion after re-setting my thoughts at the dam.

"I will be home tomorrow night," was all I said.

CHAPTER NINE

An eerie sense of foreboding raised the hair on the back of my neck as I stepped through the front door into familiar surroundings. It felt like there was someone behind me, right behind me, so close I could feel the mysterious breath blowing down the back of my neck. It was a weird sensation and I suddenly wondered whether I had made the wrong decision. Then, when Splodge reinforced my thoughts by digging his claws into my forearm, leaving a deep red scratch across it that bubbled with globules of blood as he ran off, I screeched and a shiver went down my spine. He'd crossed the floor in a flash with his hackles bristling as cats do to indicate danger or a dangerous threat. He was eerily put out. He'd been okay before we left, I mused. Small droplets of blood were dripping down the side of my arm, but I noticed Splodge's hackles were down and he didn't appear quite so tense. I wasn't a believer in ghosts or the supernatural, but the sensations Splodge and I had just experienced upset us both. Thankfully Miriam changed the mood with her cheer, scooping Storm up in her arms, kissing her chubby cheeks while Storm, instantly recognising Miriam, giggled and gurgled, and the ghostly sensation disappeared.

Miriam and I unpacked and tidied up, but my intuition kept nagging at me - it wanted me to listen, but listen to what? When Dion got home, I was curled up on the couch. Splodge was sleeping next to Storm, who was propped up against me while I read and listened to Abba.

"I'm so happy you're back," he said as he walked into the lounge, leaning down with his arms spread as if to embrace us all. Splodge was having none of that and shot off the couch and disappeared into the kitchen, waking Storm, who started to cry. He was mildly taken aback by his daughter's reaction; Splodge disappearing that quickly had gone unnoticed by him.

"I love you, Liefie. My life is nothing without you in it," he said mournfully. "I know you don't trust me or believe what I tell you, but I can't live without you. These last three weeks have been living hell."

"I love you too, Dion; that old Dion, not the one you have become. I hate that one," I said simply. "You've hurt me badly, and though I might find it in me to forgive you, I can't promise anything. I can't and won't live with your drinking, lies and continuous infidelity. You have a lot to prove its worth it for me to consider. Right now, I'd far prefer to be on the farm surrounded by salt of the earth, sincere people who *genuinely* care about me. I've only come back to see if we can sort out the issues amicably."

There was an honest, anguished expression on his face I'd not seen before. Though I wasn't ready to believe him immediately, yet I also wasn't prepared to divorce him immediately either. What he did need to know was that I wasn't just going to melt into his arms so easily. He'd created this disaster and it was up to him to fix it, but Dion Du Toit loathed being threatened.

"It looks like you'd be more comfortable with just that bloody cat and your daughter as company," he said, with stinging bitterness.

"They've earned the right to my affection, Dion. If you want me back, you have to earn it too." He didn't respond.

Once I'd fed Storm, Miriam bather her for me and put her to bed, singing an African lullaby to her as she'd drifted off to sleep happily, whereas I had a difficult evening ahead with a welcome distraction from Splodge. I could hear him mewing for his favourite meal - sardines. After scooping out the smelly fish into his dish, I rustled up a farmhouse omelette for Dion and I. Splodge gobbled up his sardines and meowed for his bowl of milk, purring like a steam train with gratification.

'Now, why aren't husbands that grateful when we feed them?' I thought quietly.

Our conversation was stilted and uncomfortable during supper and I felt awkward – I wasn't going to start a conversation but he relieved me of that, by saying, "My life spiralled out of control," he began, "the orders poured in, I revelled in the limelight which went to my head and all I could think about was money and more money. You're right, Liefie, I scarcely know my daughter, and I nearly lost you." He reached forward and kissed my forehead which I pulled away from. The old tenderness still didn't provoke a need for forgiveness, but it did relax the tension between us a little.

"I'm not yours, Dion. I never will be. We are two individuals sharing a life; you do not own me. I can't return to our marriage like it has been these past years. I'm not sure how to even begin with the forgiveness process. The only way I can see our marriage working is if you give up drinking, commit to us as a family and come home every single night. Start sharing your thoughts and your income and put quality time into us. I can't switch off the pain you have inflicted like a light. I'm still hurting. I'm still angry - I don't think you understand the extent of what you have done to me." I looked up, unable to hold his gaze and was unprepared for the sadness I saw etched on his face. Maybe my walking out had made him think?

Dion's pure brown eyes were made inexplicably fascinating by the reckless sparkle lurking just behind the concern and sadness. That didn't go unnoticed, though, and I quickly looked down again. I knew the danger in their depths, and just then, felt that same mysterious trickle of breath down my spine and the hair on my arms stood up. Although there were fine lines of fatigue etched at their corners, there was still something sinister lurking there. I needed living proof that the stress showing on his face was because he genuinely loved us. Loving him was indeed painful and complicated. Mom had warned me love was not effortless, but I was sure she wasn't referring to this situation and my husband was no ordinary human being.

"While you were away," Dion continued, as I got up and put our plates in the kitchen sink, "I answered an advert for a General Manager's position for a privately-owned music store in Bethlehem. It's well paid, and I won't have to travel much." He smiled as I plonked myself down on the sofa again.

"That's just running away again, Dion. You are the problem. Until you change your habits, the problem will go with us, so what's the point of moving?"

"Well," he paused, "I went for the interview and got the job. Do you want me to take it?" He took my face in his hands then and kissed the tip of my nose.

"We only move if it's what you want," he whispered - the master manipulator at work once more.

"It's not up to me, Dion. You can't keep running from you. Didn't you hear what I just said?" I responded more irritably than I intended.

"You are just moving the problem to a different location!" I snapped and wondered if I was being unreasonable; he was trying.

"It's a good offer, a better salary, a house and virtually no travel. Will you give me a chance to repair what I've broken, even if it is a different location? I promise to work on me and our marriage together."

I looked down, fiddled with my fingers and didn't respond for a few minutes while Dion, uncharacteristically, remained quiet. Was this a breakthrough?

The thought of starting again in another rural town was daunting, but without Leon's influences, maybe we had a better chance? Dion would have to learn to resist temptation from others, for he'd meet them along the road throughout our lives and Bethlehem wouldn't be any different. I didn't know how to cope with what he'd thrust at me. All he wanted was for me to say yes and agree with him on everything. He'd carefully planned it all while I was on the farm, even down to taking the position before discussing it with me, hoping I'd have no option but agree to go with him. I closed my eyes and rested my head on the back of the sofa. Then he started humming softly, 'Somewhere, over the rainbow, way up high, in a land that I'd heard of once in a lullaby......'

It was almost impossible not to be pulled in by his charms, especially as a part of me still loved him. Personality number one, the Dion I adored, was in 'flawless performance mode' tonight. He went on humming; then I felt him take my hand, and he began to sing for my heart again. 'Someday I will wish upon a star and wake up where the clouds are far behind me, where trouble melts like lemon drops....' I opened my eyes and surrendered to my tears, letting them stream down my face.

"I love you," he whispered.

"Oh, Dion, I love you too," I sobbed.

"It will never happen again, I promise."

"Don't say promise, Dion, I'd rather you show me you mean what you say."

Everything inside me was so tender, so torn, so damaged; then I heard myself begin to answer in a quiet murmur.

"I want to believe you, but I'm scared. It's not just about other women; it's your drinking and all the other personalities that emerge when you've had a few too many drinks or are in a vile mood." His gaze had turned to one of love, tenderness and depth and it burned gently into me. There were tears in his eyes, too, while he gently wiped mine away. It was the most poignant moment we'd had in a very long time. I was watching the lovely side of my husband, but I also saw a dependency on me that scared me.

We went on discussing our future a while longer before he moved away, sat at the piano and sang for me. Splodge and I remained on the couch, comforting each other. Every note, every word lodged deep within me, and when he finished, we moved to our bedroom where he hummed another of my favourite tunes into the back of my neck, and I fell into a deep contented sleep.

CHAPTER TEN

The House of Music, for the era, was a very grand shop - absurdly out of place, I thought. Situated on a principal street corner in a sleepy little 'dorp' like Bethlehem that primarily served farmers, I wondered who their target market could be. There was little relationship to the biblical 'Bethlehem' other than the area was commonly referred to as the 'breadbasket' of South Africa. The town nestled in a broad basin in the heart of a wonderfully fertile farming area; could it sustain such a fancy music shop and do well? It fascinated me, for although it served the surrounding smaller towns too, there were only so many people who would buy guitars, pianos, organs and drums; it all seemed crazy to me. But here we were in one of the coldest places in the country. Founded as far back as 1864, it had grown fast, for its fertile lands were quickly sought after by early settlers. With an above-average rainfall and temperate climate, it was perfect for a wide variety of different crops and cold enough in the winter months for a variety of fruits to be grown successfully, especially apples and cherries. Its natural beauty, sandstone cliffs and steep mountains made the area a charming place to live, but I still couldn't work out the need for such a lavish music shop and hoped it would prove me wrong. And so, it was agreed, swayed by musical melody, that we'd move to Bethlehem and begin a whole new, and hopefully happy chapter of our lives. When I walked into the store for the first time, I could scarcely believe what I was seeing. In front of me lay a spacious, elegantly designed showroom, which provided the perfect platform for displaying the vast selection of beautifully polished instruments. For farmers? I still found it particularly odd. Several pianos and organs stood proudly on display and dominated the shop. Dion couldn't resist taking a seat at the organ and he began playing my favourite hymn, 'Jerusalem'. Of course, passers-by were drawn like flies into the shop when they heard the hymn being sung, accompanied by the pristine sound of a brand-new organ.

Gleaming in a splendid display behind Dion and the organ were guitars, flutes, clarinets, cellos, violins and the sax, the sexy sax, and more, all twinkling like polished gems as if they too were mesmerised by the hymn. Soon, the shop was full of people pressing into each other as they squashed in from the street. It was quite a show. When he finished, the crowd clapped loudly and started singing out – 'nog, nog'. (More, more in Afrikaans)

It was a unique and memorable introduction to Bethlehem, and soon Dion became the talk of the town, much the same way as he had in Kimberly, the difference though was the customer went to the shop and there was no nasty Leon.

Proudly displayed in the main shop window were the newly introduced colour televisions. These were instruments of much controversy in South Africa at the time. We quickly learned many of the folk in Bethlehem frowned upon the introduction of television, feeling it tainted the community, and especially vocal was the congregation of the large NGK fraternity.

I had to admit and only to myself, this job suited Dion. Perhaps he'd made the right decision; all he had to do now was stick to it and take responsibility for his life and ours.

Splodge approved of the new house and roamed around the perimeter marking his territory, satisfied that intruders would know this was his spot, then he returned to the couch and watched us unpack, as cats do. The company had rented us a modest three-bedroom home with a lovely garden that attracted bird species I'd not seen before. Fortunately, Splodge was far too lazy and well-fed to worry about catching birds, but he did catch the odd rat or two when he prowled the area. We had a spectacular view from the lounge and veranda across the hills to eternity; it was where we sat at the end of the day.

Storm adjusted quickly, thanks to the input of Miriam, who'd moved with us and was delighted with her new spacious little flatlet built onto the back of the house. We'd only been in Bethlehem a week when Dion brought home the first surprise, a colour television. I was like a child at Christmas and couldn't wait to switch it on and discover what it was all about. 'Television' was the buzz word across the country at the time. There was great excitement about this new form of entertainment. Bethlehem residents were deeply divided and there was considerable radio and newspaper outrage about its launch, especially amongst the Dutch Reformed Church-dominated communities as Bethlehem was. In some small rural towns, the sale of television was not permitted - I couldn't think of anything more exciting than curling up on the couch on a cold winter's evening, dancing flames spreading warmth throughout the room from the fireplace, a monster bowl of popcorn on my lap, watching colour television until the test patterns came up at midnight. It was also not something I could imagine getting sick of and it didn't interfere with my faith, but the ladies at Bible study were horrified by my attitude, so I left the group. The older folk thought televised media was, in their opinion, undesirable and unacceptable, and, in fact, they were deeply concerned that the type of imported media from the USA would show 'race-mixing' and it became known as, 'the devil's own box.'

"What?" I said to Dion as I read that bit out from the local newspaper. "You better be careful some of the locals don't attack you in the shop, Liefie."

"Ridiculous, I agree. I'm sure that won't happen; we've already sold six this week, seven if you include ours."

"Really?" That was good news to me, and I thought of the ladies at Bible study who told me it was immoral to own one. Soon there were hundreds of immoral families living in Bethlehem, loving their in-home entertainment. The hypocrisy was ridiculous and went on for months but, as the shock wore off the rigidly 'moral' communities, everyone wanted one, even the local ministers who had been outraged.

We loved our television, and I was absolutely certain the good Lord wouldn't mind. One of our favourite programs, launched in 1976, was called, 'The Villagers', a hilarious 'sitcom' that cleverly depicted ordinary life in a Reef gold mine village of the era in South Africa. It was great entertainment; we never missed an episode, but then my days of being graciously unemployed had to come to an end - I was bored. I also needed to top up my empty savings account. The new energy felt great; I was healing, I was rejuvenated and ready to face the world once more. I found a job more quickly than I'd anticipated, working in a clothing store. It wasn't a job that offered much satisfaction; the boss was a complete pig, and I wondered how long I could stick it out after enduring a month there. In the morning, I'd generally begin in the accounts department, then in the afternoon I served customers and tidied the store, or, when the boss felt like it, he ordered me to chase up customers who'd neglected to pay their monthly bills. It was most unsatisfying, but there were lots of cuddles and kisses with Storm when I got home in the evening, which soothed away the frustrations of those difficult weeks back at work. I was working for a man with an ego that even superseded Dion's.

I'd felt guilty putting Storm into day-care so young, but I needed the income; it made feel decidedly insecure when my savings were depleted, and though I was happier within myself and our marriage was good, something niggling deep within always warned me to be vigilant – my husband changed faster than night and day. Dion's promises seemed to be intact, though he hadn't entirely convinced me - then he joined a local band.

CHAPTER ELEVEN

Practice sessions began once a week. The strumming of guitar strings and tapping of piano keys mixed well with the alarm bells ringing in my head. I was struggling with riotous contradictory feelings; I was happy for Dion to show off his singing talents and do what I'd encouraged and hoped for him, but unhappy with my own burdening fears which I couldn't shake off.

It was complicated, he was complicated, my thoughts were complicated too, and my lousy job gave me time during the day to brood. Dion had been so perfect since we'd moved and I wanted to keep the delicate balance undisturbed.

Wrapping Storm in fleecy blankets, we set off in my old car - another thing I had to save for. My 'skedonk' Datsun was due for retirement, but it always got me everywhere, and we headed off to watch Dion during a practice session. As I pulled into the driveway of the dentist's luxury home in my 'skedonk', it suddenly seemed even older as I parked next to gleaming new expensive cars, but she was a car with character and I loved her.

As I lifted Storm and her bag of baby necessities out of the car, I heard Dion singing, 'Morning has broken', a favourite Cat Stevens' song of ours and my heart swelled with pride; God, he had a beautiful voice; I knew he was doing the right thing. Apart from being beautiful, smooth and deep, his voice was an intoxicating aphrodisiac that lit a fire deep within the pit of my stomach; sometimes I cursed it though.

'The Rogues' was the name of the band - it was very apt, but I liked it. It wasn't long before they were in popular demand and miraculously, Dion was still behaving like a perfect gentleman months later. Mom checked on me regularly, Boetie always called once a week, Storm loved the music, and stood, holding onto my knees and bobbed to the music - life was good. The demand for the band grew, so the group needed to practice at least three to four times a week, making it impossible for Storm and I to attend each session, but watching Dion sing once, sometimes twice a week became my drug.

"Hey Dion, you are fuckin' brilliant, bru," Gert shouted out when they finished singing one of Elton John's magical songs in preparation for a gig in Johannesburg. He was so excited; everyone was excited, and the mood in the room was contagious. A few Afrikaans love songs followed, and the end of the practice evening was testament to another brilliant session. They were good and complimented each other well. Back home, I cuddled up to Dion, our naked bodies pressed into each other, and we kissed deeply. When I finally pulled away from him, I whispered, "I am so proud of you; I love you so much." He covered my mouth with his and kissed me hungrily again.

"You're irresistible; you keep me going. Thank you for standing by and encouraging me." His gaze laden with desire, he hummed softly, 'You make me feel brand new.' It was impossible to resist the soft, sexy tones and now my desire for him had reached even greater heights. We lay in each other's arms, exhausted, and it wasn't long before Dion was softly snoring, while I lay sated, relaxed and marvelled that he'd finally thanked me for something.

The opening song the band sang to usher in the new bride and groom was a Rita Coolidge one, 'Your love has lifted me higher and higher.' This was the first Johannesburg wedding they'd played at and they were a huge success. From that, the bookings rolled in, and a month later, I discovered I was carrying our second child.

CHAPTER TWELVE

It was a pregnancy we'd not planned, but we were both thrilled. I kept the occasional feelings of hesitation to myself – brought on by memories of the turbulent pregnancy with Storm. "A new life, a new miracle, how divine," Dion blurted out happily while we sat together in a quiet little restaurant after one practice session and toasted the pregnancy; it was the first alcoholic drink Dion had had in months; the first I'd had in years!

The following day I called Mom; she wasn't overjoyed but wished me well, nonetheless, then I called my closest sister, and all she could say was, "Oh God, Elizabeth, that's just another devious way to force you to stay with him. Why you live with that bastard, none of us can understand. Good luck, Sis."

That was that. My family could not celebrate this news with us and though it stung me a little, I understood their sentiment, even though it was going well.

Five months into my pregnancy, hardly showing, I decided it was time to notify my nasty boss. He was a big man, all too aware of his masculinity, who aroused a deep primal fear in me; I'd never trusted him and was nervous advising me of my pregnancy. He treated a woman with unreserved disrespect which made the situation for me more uncomfortable. I'd arranged a meeting time with him and stood in front of him and after informing him I was five months pregnant, he stretched back in his large leather executive chair and silently gazed at me, running his eyes slowly over my body, his eyes stopping purposefully at my crotch, then my breasts, as he visually undressed me. I knew precisely what was going through his twisted mind and my skin crawled.

"I'm afraid," he began, a disdainful smile creased the edge of his lips, "you are not entitled to maternity benefits and the company is under no obligation to offer them."

"Why not? That's disgusting sexism, Mr Freeman. I work hard here, and you know that." The business world was dominated by men like him in the late '70s and considered ultimately rebellious mentioning anything to do with sexism. He considered women subservient and expected us to grovel.

"It has nothing to do with sexism, Mrs Du Toit," he spat angrily. "It is not compulsory by law, and I don't offer it to any of my female staff."

"Excuse me, Mr Freeman, though you may not have noticed, you only have three female staff, two of which are too old to have children. I have been a loyal member of staff, doing two people's work for months without recognition or thanks or extra remuneration." He gave me a look of disinterest. I felt so acutely uncomfortable I stormed out of his office, sat at my desk, wrote out my resignation and marched back to the schmuck's office and dumped it on his desk.

"What's this?" he asked, looking at the folded letter I'd dropped in front of him.

"My resignation; and the employment agency is going to know about this. I won't work for a chauvinist like you for another minute." I swung around and left, striding across the showroom floor for the last time. I'd been unconsciously holding my breath, and my chest was about to explode. Once I was outside, I stood for a few moments to gather my wits before heading to Dion's work.

I'd never liked the asshole from day one; my first impressions of Mr Freeman could not have been more accurate. Standing on the pavement outside the shop, I felt an overwhelming sense of freedom; happiness pumped through me at a rapid rate now that I'd gotten over the humiliation. Now I had to tell Dion. I went to the employment agent first. Once again, my loyalty and feminism were thrown in my face by another ungrateful, sanctimonious dickhead, who was shit-scared of Mr Freeman and wouldn't take on my case.

I was paid my salary and leave pay, but not a cent was added as a bonus for the extra hours I'd put in during stocktake, or anything else I'd gone the extra mile on.

'Every dog has his day,' I thought as I walked through town to the showroom to explain my resignation to Dion. I wasn't sure how he'd take the news of what I'd just done, for though the band was doing well, the shop wasn't. He was disappointed in me for just walking out, but at least he wasn't angry.

A month after walking out of my job, Dion got a verbal warning for arriving at the shop reeking of alcohol after an extended lunch break. I was spitting mad; if he lost his job, we'd lose the house too. By then, I was just into the last trimester and I didn't know he was drinking during the day again for he seldom drank at home nowadays.

Panic was surging inside me, replacing baby nausea with a more pressing one as I sat in his office after my doctor's appointment.

"You promised no more lies and no more drinking," I said with fiery, frustrated cries when he told me of the warning. "You've been lying to me, haven't you? When did you hit the bottle again?"

He remained silent, looking uncharacteristically embarrassed, then I realised it wasn't his conscience troubling him, it was the fact that his office had a glass front and his staff were watching us argue. In my anger, I'd forgotten that we were visible to all who were in the shop.

"You do realise you are giving me full permission to fuck off out of your life forever this time! I warned you. Do you want that?"

"You bitch; don't threaten me in here," he swore, and my sister's words flashed through my mind as he said it.

"I don't deserve this, Dion. I have never deserved any of the crap you have dished out, but especially now we are expecting our second child. Are you going to make this pregnancy as bad as the last one?" Resentment was rising in my throat like a bitter poison; I could feel it burn. The monster was back.

"Just fuck off out of here; we'll talk tonight at home." He stood up to usher me out and I stood next to him, my nose almost pressed up against his as I glared at him. I said quietly, "Adjust your attitude before you get home." I turned and slammed his office door to make a point, and the glass partition rattled precariously.

When Dion got in, he was still seething from being humiliated in front of his floor staff and customers.

"Don't you ever embarrass me like that again!" he yelled, slamming down his briefcase and turned to me.

"That's a joke, Dion. You don't need me to embarrass you in front of your staff. Being pissed on the job does it for you."

Suddenly, those soft brown eyes I'd seen for months were dark, eerie pools that always unnerved me. He was angry but fully aware he'd stepped over the mark.

"We can work this out, Elizabeth," he said back-pedalling rather suddenly.

"No, we can't, it's too late Dion. I warned you last time."

"What do you mean, it's too late?" A slight tremble of panic sounded in his voice.

"I've warned you so many times, Dion; it is impossible to live this roller coaster life of uncertainty. I'm moving back to William and Bessie's until after the baby is born, then I will decide what to do and where I will live. You have this house to live in if you manage to hold onto your job," I said conclusively.

CHAPTER THIRTEEN

Vivienne arrived on her due date, born in the Bloemfontein Hospital in the Maternity wing, without her father present, on the shortest day of the year, midwinter solstice in the southern hemisphere, the 21st June, 1978 and it was a freezing cold day.

Giving birth to Vivienne was difficult. Though I left the hospital on day three, I wasn't feeling well. Four days later, William rushed me back to hospital after a desperate plea from Miriam, "Boss William, come quick, missus is dying, please hurry."

I was admitted to the Intensive Care Unit, close to losing my life from septicaemia; I'd retained some afterbirth. The sepsis took hold quickly, leaving me seriously ill. I remember looking at the Doctor; absurdly, he wasn't next to my bed, he was walking down the passage, he was leaving me, they couldn't save me. I could hear him talking to a nurse in the passage, but I couldn't string together exactly what he was saying. I felt weightless and acutely aware of everything that was going on around my bed, even what the nurses were doing. One moment I sensed the most beautiful awareness of absolute freedom. I felt no pain and no fear, just wholesome, pure, accepting, all-encompassing love which felt marvellous, then I was pulled away from that magical universal space and it was dark again, then suddenly something mystic was enticing me back to that carefree realm, and I remember thinking how nice it would be to stay there, floating in amongst a rainbow of colours and light, peaceful and divine. During those hours between delirium and clarity, I couldn't make sense of it. All I knew was I wanted to go back to that fairy tale place. Those moments didn't last, then suddenly I was fretting about my two children, smothered with haunting thoughts of them being raised by a drunken, lying, psychopathic father and I was right back in the present. It was those thoughts that pulled me back and kept me firmly rooted to this earth. Doctor Daan had also been fretting, worried he might not save my life and suggested that William call Dion; he was to get to Bloemfontein as soon as possible to say his goodbyes and meet his new daughter.

I'd been hooked up to the oxygen ventilator, pumped full of antibiotics, and had a fever and infection that threatened my life. Though I never felt that exquisite freedom again, the hallucinations coming out of it were terrifying. Apparently, I'd woken screaming hysterically. The one that tormented me the worst was a vision of the two girls lying together on filthy beds, skin and bone, dying of starvation and covered in flies, while their father sat watching them, drunk and disabled from excessive alcohol consumption. The nurses had said they had to hold me down while they injected the tranquiliser. It was those grizzly images that made me hang on to my life. For two more days, nursing staff watched over me until finally, the fever broke, and the nightmares disappeared with the illness. Vivienne was brought to me on day five and William and Bessie brought Storm to visit once I'd moved from the ICU. Seeing them both stopped the fitful nights. I recovered, but the nightmares often haunted me for years after.

On the morning before I was discharged, I lay thinking what a committed nurse I would have been if I'd finished my training, and how valuable that certification would have been for me now. It was one of the few times I'd felt regret about not completing my training, but this was not the time for regrets. As soon as I was well enough, I would be job-hunting again and would begin a new life on my own.

"Good morning, Elizabeth, how are you feeling today?" Doctor Daan breezed into the ward and stood at the end of my bed.

"Feeling better thank you, Daan, just terribly weak."

"I'm not surprised. We thought we'd lost you that first night – kept wondering how I was going to explain that to your family."

"Yes, the nurse just told me." Daan moved round to the side of the bed and looked down at us both. "Beautiful little girl," he said, smiling at Vivienne. "How would you feel about seeing a psychologist to help you deal with the trauma of your marriage and the nightmares?" I looked up at Daan, a man I'd known and trusted for many years. I didn't know how to answer and felt confused.

"Why?" I asked.

"Your nightmares revealed some troubling issues. The nurses called me in when you had the first one. It took three of us to hold you down. I think you were trying to kill Dion," Daan laughed. " I had to sedate you for twelve hours using a hefty dose. I suppose you are not aware of that?"

"I remember one nightmare very clearly, that is bad enough. I don't want to remember more. I'm going to carve out a new future now, Daan. I'm not going back to Dion." I looked at him briefly, then added, "those nightmares gave me the strength to stay alive."

"Do you know you asked, um… well, should I say you violently demanded that we stop Dion from seeing you or your children. You are holding onto a lot of pain, aren't you?" He rubbed my forearm with the palm of his hand. "I recommend you have a chat with a psychologist who will help you deal with your fears and your pain."

I couldn't stop the tears; as soon as anyone offered sympathy, I crumbled. Daan continued to hold my forearm comfortingly and waited for me to calm down before going on.

"I'll make the appointment if you agree." I nodded and wiped the tears away with the back of my hand.

"You're free to go home. William is collecting you and the nurse will give you the remaining antibiotics that you *must* finish." He raised an eyebrow at me like a threatening father.

"Thank-you, Daan."

It was early afternoon when William arrived, bringing Storm with him.

"Mama," she shrieked happily, putting her arms out toward me, as William lowered her onto the bed.

"I'm so happy to see you, my little princess." I kissed her cute rose-bud lips as she smiled and hugged me again, her big, liquid brown eyes sparkling with happiness while her dark auburn curls bobbed in time with her excitement. The purity of love expressed by a child is so wonderfully unique; she melted away all the anxiety and tension I'd been feeling, and my eyes welled up, again.

"Why are you crying, Mama?" she asked, looking concerned.

"They are tears of happiness, my angel."

"Oh," she said. "Why do you cry when you are happy?"

"Not all tears are sad ones, my darling," I said, as she shook her head with confusion.

"How's Bessie coping with being on the farm alone?" I asked William. My sister-in-law had always been nervous about living on the farm and loathed being left alone, even for just a day, so William was keen to get home before it got dark.

"She's coping fine, Sis; she's looking forward to your homecoming."

"I can't wait; let's get out of here." I couldn't remember ever feeling so physically weakened; I was even too nervous to carry Vivienne, so the nurse carried her to the car.

"Daan wants me to see a psychologist," I told William on the way home. "I'm not sure I want to. You know my feelings on psychologists."

"It might help you get over all the trauma," William said.

I relented and went a few days later, but after that first session, I swore I'd never go back to another; it wasn't about going forward, but a traumatic digging up of the past.

I got through it myself, and six weeks later I was sitting in front of a radiantly healthy-looking woman having a job interview I wasn't even qualified for.

Her exuberant good health illuminated my weakened state, making me feel even weaker. Oddly enough, her abundant good health made me determined to get stronger as quickly as I could. Based upon my CV and the initial interview, I'd made it onto the shortlist and waited nervously to be interviewed by the Chief Accounting Officer - Derek Pienaar.

I needed this job badly. I couldn't go on being supported by my brother; he had his own family and I wanted to be independent again.

I was ushered through to Mr Pienaar's austere office and suddenly felt very frail, vulnerable and insignificant as I sat down in front of him - the Chief Accountant of one of the largest grocery chains in the country. I couldn't believe my luck, but I was scared my ill health would put him off.

Derek Pienaar was a short man with a round friendly face, rather spoilt by a thin strip of moustache which underlined his nose and the urge to chuckle was hard to suppress; it could not have been a more appropriate moustache for an accountant. Pale grey-blue eyes reflected his kindness; he had a warmth about him that made me feel comfortable and relaxed, unlike Mr Freeman. I liked him immediately and felt very at ease while I answered his questions. Then he stretched his arms above his head, still holding onto his Parker pen, and his expression changed. My tummy tightened with anxiety; I needed this position so badly.

"I believe you've been very ill," he said.

"Yes, Sir. I nearly died shortly after giving birth to my second daughter. Though it may not look like it, I am well on the road to recovery." I didn't know how convincing I sounded, and I knew I looked anything but well, but I was ready to get back to work. He smiled; I could see he didn't look convinced.

"You have an excellent work record, my dear, with glowing references." He looked up, "Are you a quick learner?"

"Yes, I believe I am. I will certainly give you my best."

"I have no doubt. How much experience have you had with accounting? Can you go to trial balance?"

"Not much, Sir, and to answer your question about a trial balance, no I haven't prepared books to finish off there. I've just done debt-collecting and, as I said, a bit of basic book-keeping in my last job."

"Yes, Mr Freeman told me you were the best worker he'd ever employed." I was stunned. I couldn't believe what I was hearing; he'd been such a bastard.

"What? Did he really say that?" I asked, amazed. "I'm ashamed to say I was rude to him, but he did deserve it. I didn't think he'd ever give me a reference," I said honestly. "Well, if his reference gets me this job, it will be in place of the bonus he refused to pay me," I added.

Mr Pienaar chuckled loudly. "Yes, he did say you are a gutsy lady!"

"Did he call me gutsy? Stroppy feminist, I would have thought. After he cheated me out of maternity leave, stock-take bonus and overtime when he knew I desperately needed the money, I had nothing to lose by giving him a thoroughly well-deserved piece of my mind." I surprised myself by telling this total stranger all about that experience. He made me feel so secure that I didn't see any reason why not. His gentle, quiet, self-assured manner was enormously reassuring. Maybe I'd given away more than I needed to, but 'Que sera, sera,' I thought. Even though I had everything to lose if I didn't get the job, it was a bit late now.

"Well, Elizabeth," he said, looking down at his watch, "I've kept you here quite long enough." He rolled the Parker between his fingers and took a deep breath. I feared the worst.

"When will you be able to start?"

I was ecstatic and speechless. I could have reached over and kissed him.

"Oh, thank you. Thank you so much," I said, excitedly. "When would you like me to start, Mr Pienaar?" I asked.

"Spring day, 1st of September, if that suits you?"

"It certainly does, and thank you very much." I beamed.

"Welcome to the team," he said, pushing back his chair and coming around his desk to quickly pull my chair back. Having not been treated like a lady for a long time, I was rather clumsy in my weakened state.

"In the meantime, get some rest."

"Thank you, I certainly will."

An old-fashioned gentleman he certainly was, restoring my belief that there were still gentlemen in this world. Despite being old enough to be my father, treating me with respect for being a woman was most refreshing.

I had time to sort myself out, gain some physical strength and, hopefully, some weight.

There was bounce in my step for the first time in ages; I wanted to sing out aloud. The relief of being able to support myself and my two children was hugely satisfying. I just had to depend on my darling brother one more time; I had to ask him to pay the deposit on a cottage I rented and the money for the electricity supply.

The girls and I moved from the farm to Bloemfontein during the last week of August 1978.

The cottage was a delightful little space for the three of us, separated from the main house by a beautiful tall hedge, and the garden was perfectly adequate for the kids to play in and for me to maintain. Surrounded by a couple of well-tended acres that was all fenced, it was almost like living on a farm and was cheap enough for me to afford, plus we were safe. I rented Miriam a room down the road that was walking distance from the cottage. Splodge approved of the move, too, and explored the garden, marking his territory as usual, then settled back in his favourite position, spread out on the couch.

I was earning the best salary I'd ever had. My old Datsun was going to *have* to last another six months before I could trade her in; although William had offered to buy me another car, I refused the offer because he'd done so much. Aside from that, I loved my old skedonk; it was a part of me. It still ran on the smell of an oily rag, wasn't expensive to maintain and never let me down. Besides, there would be no financial assistance from Dion for anything, so I couldn't commit to any more monthly payments.

"I'll retire you soon," I said, patting her bonnet as we unloaded the final loose bits - those bits that accumulate and one never knows what to do with, but they still go everywhere with you.

The owners of the property offered to help if I needed anything doing, or help with collecting children and childminding; they were dear retired folk and so typical of warm rural types; people who understand what tough times are about.

The move left me exhausted, so I had a few nights uninterrupted by an assortment of unpleasant dreams I could have done it without. Miriam was a godsend; the perfect surrogate mother who relieved me of so many worries and the children adored her. We settled into our new way of life easily, as if it had been this way forever. Storm rarely asked about Dion now and Vivienne didn't know she had a father.

The cottage felt like home, though it was sparsely furnished, for Dion still had most of my possessions. We were happy and it was cosy. Once I had the energy to sort out the divorce, claim my half and get my treasured personal possessions back, what he had would suffice.

A buzzing in my ear woke me from a deep sleep. Disorientated and startled, I sat bolt upright, then realised it was the alarm clock, a sound I wasn't accustomed to and I flew out of bed; time to get up and go to work again. Hoorah! However, I wasn't so happy when I put on one of the two-piece suits I had. I was horrified by my reflection; I looked awful. No wonder Mr Pienaar had asked if I was able to start work so soon. The deep navy linen suit, which had cost me a fortune a few years back, now hung off me like a family hand-me-down. The only way to hold the skirt up was to put a thin belt around the top of it and fold it over the belt - I'd shrunk from a healthy, curvy 34" to a skinny, grey-looking size 28" and being six foot I looked bulimic. I turned away from the mirror, as I couldn't bear looking at me. I did my face and hair and was soon on my way to work and, despite how I looked, I felt an exciting spark of energy pop back. I got in early, made some coffee and sat at my new desk, thinking back to the interview and how lucky I was to have got this position, when Mr Pienaar interrupted my thoughts.

"Ah, there you are! Welcome, welcome. How are you doing?" he said warmly, glancing over me briefly.

"Better on the inside than the outside." I smiled at him. "All my clothes are miles too big for me."

"Well, I must say you look better than you did a few weeks ago. I want you to know that if you feel too tired, do let me know. No point in exhausting yourself in the beginning - there's an awful lot to learn. You can always slip off an hour early to begin with. When you've finished your coffee, dear, pop over to my office and we can start."

I gulped back my coffee, gathered up my pens and notebook and joined Derek in his very plush office.

"Come in, come in," he said, happily showing me to a chair. A long table ran the length of one side of his office and on it were piles of files and papers all stacked up the length of it. Just the sight of the mountains of paperwork was intimidating.

"Thank you, Mr Pienaar."

"My dear, please call me Derek. Mr Pienaar makes me feel far too old!" He laughed heartily.

To me, he was old; he was thirty years my senior. I considered fifty-eight ancient then.

Moving another chair next to mine, we started to plough through the stacks of files. Before I knew it, it was time to go home; I had to recheck my watch; the day had flown by.

Derek was an excellent tutor, and by the end of the week, I felt alive for the first time in months, and was starving by the time I got home. I was eating like a horse again.

Derek popped his head around my office door one morning when I'd been there a month and asked me to join him in his office. I was terrified he'd decided I wasn't up to scratch.

"Have a seat," he said warmly. I sat bolt upright on the edge of the chair in preparation for the bad news, my legs crossed beneath me nervously.

"Now why are you looking so tense?" I fidgeted then smiled; I couldn't speak.

"Relax, you are doing extremely well. I am delighted to have you work alongside me," he said. "It's time to start believing in yourself again, Elizabeth."

I nodded shyly – he was right, what a relief, I could still afford to support my children.

"Throw out all nasty thoughts of the past, my dear. You have a great mind, you're a strong woman, and you will go far here." They were the most important words I'd heard in a long time after having my self-esteem pulverised by Mr Freeman and my husband.

"You have grasped the job well; you have an excellent accounting aptitude - I'm very impressed." The warmth of his tone and what he'd just said were the best anti-depressants ever. The stars were shining down on me for once – I'd forgotten what it felt like to be valued.

"Thank you."

"It is you I have to thank. The burden of those piles of files is no longer a headache for me. My last assistant died in a tragic motor car accident and I just haven't been able to get through the backlog since. Just look what we have managed to get through," he pointed to the table which was almost clear. "Elizabeth, I have raised your salary now you've completed your probation. I hope it helps." Shaken by the generosity, I wanted to weep. I held onto it, letting go on the way home as waves of relief and gratitude joined hands and I sobbed all the way home.

CHAPTER FOURTEEN

Daily cash checks and balances, general book-keeping, tallying columns of numbers, learning shorthand and all sorts of other accounting tasks kept me mentally stimulated and I began to feel like a functioning human again. I looked more like one too, rather than something that had crawled out of Belsen. I had meat covering my elbows and knees again and my ribs were now covered.

A new part of my job was keeping a vigilant eye out for theft or any peculiar inconsistencies, generally reflected in the daily cash takings. I oversaw new accounts and liaised with security on what went on in despatch. The variety was interesting and kept me on my toes. I'd been alerted that cleverly planned theft happened on a large scale in these big superstores. At first, it shocked me just how cunning some of the plans were, but Derek had taught me well, and I learned to recognise even the remotest inconsistencies and instantly investigated or handed them over to Derek for further action. I became a vigilant accounting policeman and was thoroughly enjoying the investigative work.

I'd been working and living in Bloemfontein for four months before Amelia and I met up again for a lunch date in our favourite Italian restaurant. She was horrified by what I'd been through but delighted I'd finally moved away from Dion.

"Hey, how are you doing?" she hugged me.

"Loving life, at last."

We chatted for hours. I didn't want her to go. She was only in Bloemfontein temporarily, nursing and living in Durban, in a relationship and blissfully happy. None of my friends liked Dion, so, throughout our married life, I hadn't been able to make any other genuine friendships.

"So, when are you getting married?" I asked.

"We haven't set a date yet, but we will. There's no rush; we thought about sometime next year, and you will make sure you are there," she laughed happily.

"I will have to bring the children too, but I'd love to visit before you get married."

"We'd love to have you; you know that. I haven't met Vivienne yet."

"I'm not sure my old 'skedonk' will get me to Durbs, but I'm willing to give it a go!" I laughed. "For now, I'll have to be satisfied with regular chats on the phone, won't I?"

"Yup, guess you will. Shame, Elizabeth, what a lot you have been through. I hope this new start gets you back on your feet. You don't need that swine back in your life; you know that, don't you?" I nodded. I had accepted I would never have the old Dion back. It was time to say a sad farewell.

My life continued much the same. I'd gained five kilograms; I was ecstatic with that, happy with my job, adored my children and the new life - six months had disappeared somewhere. It was hard to believe how the time had flown.

One morning, with my nose buried deep into the worksheets on my desk, I came across a mystery; an accounting discrepancy I'd been flummoxed by for the last two days and couldn't solve; the deeper I dug, the more complicated it became. It was time to pull Derek's sharp brain in on the problem. I'd been suspicious of despatch for a few weeks but I couldn't pinpoint the ringleader and hadn't wanted to pounce prematurely.

"Is it possible for the Arabella four-piece lounge suite to disappear out the store, along with two coffee tables and a stereo system?" I asked Derek and he looked up at me and said, "Oh yes, anything's possible, dear, these people are masters at grand theft, you should know that," he smiled. "If they want something, they always find a way. Why? What have you found?"

"You know I've been suspicious that something is going on at despatch? Well, I think it is a bigger problem than I anticipated. It is looking more and more like a syndicate of thieves are at work there; look here." I spread all the papers out on Derek's desk and showed him what I suspected, how I'd come to tie it all together and with the proof I was holding now, we could catch them at it. I'd been tipped off that a yellowwood dining room suite was ready to go.

"I think you've cracked it," he beamed. "Well done."

"Yes, but there are some issues I need you to check through with me to make certain." He grinned and soon we were both utterly absorbed by the process of piecing the puzzle together of an enormous furniture theft operation costing the company thousands. We were so engrossed in tracing the leads, neither of us noticed Dion standing at the door of the office, watching us. He made his presence felt by coughing, and I looked up, straight into the monster's angry eyes. What stunned me was how frightened I was at seeing him again and in seconds, my inner peace was blasted to smithereens.

How had he'd known where to find me?

Derek was about to ask if he could help, when Dion spun around and stormed out of the office.

"Who on earth is that?" Derek asked, then noticed I'd gone as white as a sheet; he understood in an instant.

"Was that your husband? You look petrified, my dear," Derek said with an honest look of shock.

"I am. I have no idea how he found me." My hands were shaking so violently I couldn't hold my pen.

"That is not a normal reaction, my dear. You've been through more than you've let on, haven't you?" Derek asked gently, genuinely concerned. "Let us take a break, have some lunch, and we will get back to this later."

"NO!" I said too sharply and with too much emphasis. "I'll go on here; I'm not hungry."

Derek looked worriedly at me.

"Do you want to go home? Collect the kids and bring them here? What do you want to do?"

"I'm not sure but seeing him has shaken me more than I ever thought it would."

Derek shook his head, "Shall I make some coffee?"

I didn't want to go home in case he followed me to my little cottage; it was my only sanctuary now he'd found where I was working.

"Good idea, maybe chuck some whiskey in it," I half-joked.

Before I left work, I thought it prudent to call Miriam and find out if she'd noticed any strange cars passing slowly by the cottage or going up and down the road. She'd not noticed anything suspicious at home, which was a huge relief. I scrutinised the car park before I left the office, then drove all over town, making sure Dion wasn't following me before I headed home.

CHAPTER FIFTEEN

Dion was waiting in the car park at the office the following morning. I saw him as I drove in.

"We have to talk!" he bellowed, as I jumped out of the car and rushed toward the entrance of the office block. I knew I couldn't avoid the confrontation much longer and he appeared calmer than he had been in the office the day before. He was catching up to me as I looked back and with relief, I noticed Derek pulling into the car park.

"When can we talk, Elizabeth?" he asked, as I ran through the foyer and jumped into the lift and the doors closed before Dion could get in with me. However, as the lift doors opened on the third floor, he was standing in front of me.

"I'm not ready to talk to you, Dion. Please leave. I must start work," I said as Derek stepped out the lift.

"Leave her alone please," Derek asked Dion politely, but Dion's response was far from polite.

"Fuck you, old man! This is my wife; she ran away from me, and we need to talk."

"I believe she ran away for a good reason. Can't you can see she's terrified of you? Come on, Elizabeth, let's get to work," Derek said and waved me toward the entrance of the office.

"Who the hell are you to protect her? Her new lover?"

"Oh, grow up, young man," Derek said, pushing past him, closing Dion out the offices. Later that morning, Dion phoned asking if we could meet at Wimpy for an early supper, insisting that he needed to see the girls, *his girls*, he'd emphasised. It wasn't something I could go on denying him even though he paid nothing toward their keep.

"Yes, yeah, um...." I stuttered. "Okay, we will meet you at 5.30." I put the phone down to guarantee no more conversation would be forthcoming until our meeting – a meeting I wasn't looking forward to at all.

I left work early, picked up the girls and told Storm we were meeting Papa at the Wimpy. Although Storm was a bit hesitant at first, she was happy to see her father. Vivienne was indifferent, after all, she didn't know who Dion was and she was too young to show any reaction to him. After we'd ordered, Dion explained some of what had gone down in Bethlehem; how much truth was in his story, I wasn't sure, apart from being fired and always drunk - that I knew to be the truth. A little later, he asked why I had ordered his removal from the hospital, despite my condition. It was an awkward evening; I purposefully ended it as quickly as I could. I didn't want to regurgitate the terrifying visions I'd had while almost dying; he didn't need to know.

"Thanks for supper. We'll get going after this," I pointed to my coffee, "and, please don't follow me home. I'd prefer you didn't know where we live for now. If you want to see the children, we can meet once a month in a neutral place like this."

"Once a month? That's a bit unfair, Elizabeth."

"No, it's not Dion. If you were not so attached to alcohol and bullshitting people, your children would be living with you, and so would I. You have not made any effort to contribute to their living expenses either. It's been seven months, Dion." He raised his eyebrows and managed to contain himself as the waitress put the bill down in front of him; I left him to pay, said our goodbyes and left.

Not trusting that he wouldn't follow, I drove around the streets again before heading home, being advised by Storm that I was going the wrong way.

Dion's arrival back in Bloemfontein rattled me more than I wanted to admit. Sitting beside Derek at work the following day, my concentration span kept fading in and out as I thought about our security being compromised by Dion once again.

"How did your Wimpy meeting go?"

"Without a hitch, amazingly. It got a bit uncomfortable when he asked about the hospital, but I never answered. Storm was happy to see her father, and we left soon after we'd eaten." I paused, knowing I could share my thoughts. "His return to Bloem has rattled me; I'm more afraid of him than I realised."

"I can see that, Elizabeth!" He'd been watching me try to focus on the work at hand, but I couldn't.

"Yes, I'm sorry, it is all so confusing - I can't make any sense of my feelings. I know I'm scared, but there's more. I didn't ask for a divorce last night because I know I'll have to pay, and, quite simply, I don't have the money for that and a new car. And, of course, discussing divorce in front of Storm wouldn't have been fair; even though she's little, her ears miss nothing."

"Give yourself time, my dear. You have your own life now, don't forget that."

I couldn't afford to make any changes quickly and shoved Dion out of my mind and got back to focussing on finding another sort of criminal. Later that day, we stumbled upon the weak link in the chain; we found it in receiving. We'd broken the syndicate that had been going on for months; what a terrific feeling - perhaps I should have been in forensics.

Derek called in the police to make the arrests of seven staff, and later in the week, the proof we had pulled together was presented at a disciplinary hearing. The company wanted to make a spectacle of these thieves, hoping to prevent it from happening again. The careful attention I'd paid to bringing an end to the syndicate earned me a bonus big enough to put a 50% deposit down on a new car and trade my little old Datsun' skedonk' in, which reduced the monthly payments. I never, for a moment, thought I'd be so sad to say goodbye to a motor car.

CHAPTER SIXTEEN

I never did ascertain how Dion discovered where I worked, mainly because I never bothered to ask - there wasn't much point. Besides, he knew Bloemfontein better than most people. I was an idiot thinking he wouldn't eventually locate the cottage either; we were still married, and he had a biological right to get to know his second daughter. He didn't realize I'd invested in a new car, so I hoped that would throw him off my trail for a while.

Dion called the office a few times asking me out for dinner, but I refused the invitations, then he called and asked if he could take Storm to a movie.

"She's too young to sit through a whole movie, Dion."

"It's the new Walt Disney one, The Aristocats; she'd love it, come on, let up, Elizabeth."

I finally agreed to let Storm go. She approved enthusiastically, but I insisted on chaperoning her and arranged with Miriam to care for Vivienne. Storm loved the movie and I did too, who wouldn't, but towards the end, I could see Storm was ready for bed and suggested to Dion that the next time he went to the movies with Storm, the afternoon shows would be more suitable for her.

"Would you like to come to my place tomorrow? I'd like to see Vivienne, and perhaps we can have a chat over some lunch." I stood looking at him in disbelief longer than was necessary, and before I found an appropriate answer, Storm interrupted.

"Yes, Mama, can we please go to Papa's house?" I looked down at her, not knowing whether to agree or not, fully aware I couldn't deprive the girls from seeing their father now he was back living in Bloemfontein. He *was* trying to extend the olive leaf, and I was a bit bristly; I just couldn't help myself.

"Okay, thank you, but we must get home now so poor Miriam can go off." Storm kissed her Papa goodbye, waving to him as we set off.

Over the following weeks, we spent a few balmy evenings enjoying each other's company again after the Sunday visit to Dion's place. Storm kept talking about the movie and how she wanted to play the piano again.

"When's Papa coming here?" she asked one night while sitting cross-legged on the kitchen counter next to me as I peeled potatoes.

"I don't know my precious; I haven't spoken to Papa for a few days."

"Why, Mama?" she asked, pressing her mouth onto the top of her knee, her legs tucked under her pyjama clad bottom and I couldn't help marvel at the way children possess such a unique way of making *everything* seem so simple.

"Well, Papa has got to be a good Papa and stop getting drunk before I let him come here. We don't want any trouble, now, do we?"

She shook her head but kept her mouth pressed against the top of her knee while she processed what I'd said in her innocent mind.

"Are we having chippies and tomato ketchup for supper?" She suddenly asked as she watched me peel the last potato, thoughts of her father gone in a flash.

"Yes, we are, with fish and veg too." I pinched her cheek affectionately.

"Yay, yummy! I love chippies……. and the rest." She had quickly tagged on, 'and the rest,' to please me. After we'd eaten and I'd put the girls to bed, I found myself wondering what to do about Dion.

We'd been purposefully avoiding the topic of divorce. Friendship was okay for me and as far as I knew, he still wasn't aware of where we lived. I'd collected some of my clothing and personal effects, telling him I'd get the rest sooner or later. Essential, I thought, to make it abundantly clear I had no intention of going back, though he'd mentioned he wanted our marriage to continue.

For months, Dion carefully guided me toward that place where he knew the doubt would end. One thing he hadn't considered - I knew him well enough now to know all his games - I wasn't going to fall for his lies or gentle manipulations. We'd sorted out a few differences; he was paying toward the children's expenses, picking up the tab for Storm's schooling, too, and there was no doubt the fantastic Dion, personality number one, was back; only I knew that could change in an instant.

I was amazed the band was still going. The Rogues were hugely popular in Bloemfontein, but had he done enough genuine work on himself, or was this just Act 1, Scene 3? He'd said the alcohol poisoning, then being fired, losing me by his side and not knowing Vivienne had shattered him, but Dion du Toit had a short memory. I drifted off to sleep on the couch and woke around three in the morning with a stiff neck and a sore back, and though I climbed into bed, I couldn't get back to sleep. I had a shower instead and got on with the usual morning routine and got to the office half an hour early. It was 6.38 am when I sat down at my desk, sipping on my coffee, inhaling the scent of a rich Kenyan roast, which I'd sprinkled with chocolate powder.

I'd just swallowed the first blissful mouthful when I was interrupted by the phone, shattering the blissful silence of the early morning when no-one else was around. There seemed to be an urgency to its ring and given the week I'd just gone through, I wondered whether more accounting forensics was on the cards; then I heard Williams' distraught voice as I put the receiver to my ear.

CHAPTER SEVENTEEN

"Mom was attacked on the farm last night. It's bad, Sis; I'm scared she's not going to make it." Williams words echoed down the line, shattering my world. It didn't seem possible.

"Oh God, who would want to attack Mom? Where is she, Boetie? What happened?" I asked all at once in crushed disbelief.

"She's in theatre right now, Sis. I'm at the Police Station, err…sorry Sis, hang on." I could hear him talking to the cops in the background.

"Aagh, sorry Sis, questions to answer for the police, - um, let me call back in a few minutes. Hang in there." He put the phone down, and my whole body began to shake, while my thoughts whirled in panicky chaos.

Who would want to attack an elderly woman and nearly kill her? Everyone loved her; all the farm staff adored her. None of this made sense.

Trying to gather my thoughts and calm myself, I went on sipping at my coffee and waited for William's call. The waiting didn't last long, thank goodness.

"Hi." I snatched the receiver after one ring. "Tell me she's going to live Boetie?" My voice was quivering with emotion; no amount of deep breathing could waylay the fears that we might lose our beloved mother.

"She's in surgery, Sis. Daan is with her; all we can do now is pray, Sis."

"In surgery?" I repeated, horrified. I was struggling to comprehend this ghastly news. "Oh my God, William, what have they done to her?" Revenge and hatred became genuine parts of my helpless feelings in that moment, surging through me like a runaway veld fire somewhere in my chest, spreading quickly to my gut turning it into red hot grief as William explained.

"She was badly beaten up, Sis. Torn to pieces and God knows what else." I could hear the restrained anger in my brother's voice. "Mom wasn't able to talk much on the way to the hospital, but from the little she said, it was one man who attacked her in the orchard after she'd closed the store. Can you get time off work and get to the hospital?"

"Yes, of course, give me an hour. Where shall I meet you?" Panic was still surging through me.

"In the main foyer, Sis. Mom will be in theatre for a while yet."

A while yet! Oh, God, the hour hand had just passed seven o'clock when I put the phone down and raced through to Derek's office, praying he'd got into the office early. 'Oh God, if you are there, keep Mom alive, pleeease,' I begged aloud, quickly putting my hands together and looked up to an invisible source then ran upstairs, half-knocked then pushed Derek's office door open at the same time. He glanced at me with a stunned look on his face as I barged in.

"What's the……," he looked up at my grey-white face, "not that bastard husband of yours?"

"No, it's my Mom. She was brutally attacked on the farm last night; she's in theatre. Please, can I go?"

"Oh, I am so sorry, my dear. Yes, of course; let me know if there is anything I can do."

"Thank you. I'll keep you posted," I said as I turned and disappeared down the stairs to my office and called Dion; he'd have to take care of the girls for the next two days. I had no other option, then I raced home.

A year earlier, William and Mom had swopped houses. William's growing family needed the more significant farmhouse, the one we'd all grown up in; the cottage was getting too small for them.

Her living in a sizeable, four-bedroomed rambling farmhouse, with its wrap-around veranda, where William and I used to play endless games as children and where Mom had rattled around in alone for too long, being haunted by memories of our father in every room, was pointless. Moving her to the cottage had been the most obvious thing to do and she was quite happy to move. The main house was also conveniently situated next to all the farm outbuildings, the office and sheds and made Williams life far easier.

Mom loved the cottage; it was the perfect little retreat for her, but I doubted she would want to live there on her own after this incident. That thought ripped into my heart; the farm was her life. She was connected to it not only because she'd farmed it herself for so many years but my father and brother had been buried in the garden – a special remembrance corner surrounded by banks of white Iceberg roses and agapanthus. So many memories kept flooding into my thoughts as I raced around, trying to arrange my day, so I could get to the hospital quickly.

I remembered how Mom had pestered William about running the farm store. She bothered him for months telling him she was bored; 'I'll grow old fast with nothing to do,' she'd moaned. It was so like her; always needing to be busy. The thought of sitting on the stoep all day watching the birds on the dam, reading, knitting or crocheting would have driven her scatty. Retirement was not a part of her vocabulary, so William gave in, and she started her 'job', serving the staff twice a day, opening the little store at nine for an hour and again at four in the afternoon.

One of her favourite little sayings, when we were young and doing nothing other than irritating her, was; 'the devil makes work for idle hands,' and she'd put us to work. Even at 67, she couldn't sit still for long despite her gammy foot, but now, due to some evil, ill-gotten person, she lay critically injured in the theatre, being stitched together by miracle workers. It seemed hardly possible.

I parked, grabbed my bag and ran across the car park to the front of the hospital, pushed the doors open and saw William, looking grey and suddenly years older, pacing up and down the foyer.

"Oh Boetie," I cried as I hugged him. "Have you heard anything more?"

"It's shocking, Sis," he kept on repeating. William rarely lost control of his emotions, but I could see he was struggling to keep it all together now. "Let's sit down."

We sat on two comfortable armchairs, away from the mainstream of visitors, and he began to explain what he knew of the attack.

"I shall never forget the desperate expression on Mom's face as our eyes met when I opened the bedroom curtains; that look will haunt me forever, Sis." He pulled a handkerchief out of his pocket and wiped his eyes and his brow, the memory, then anger and the helplessness bubbling perspiration on his forehead.

"I ran from our room like I'd never run before, screaming to Bessie to phone Daan and arrange for a team to meet us at the emergency entrance of the hospital. Mom was so weak when I got to her, I thought we'd lost her then, but she hung on. Adrenaline had taken over my body and I picked her up and got her into the car." He paused for a moment as he looked at me. Mom was not much more than a few kilograms overweight, but she was a large-boned woman and quite tall. "She's tough, Sis." He shook his head sadly as he recounted those moments. "She'd lost a lot of blood, she was in shock, dehydrated and exhausted and once I'd got her filthy body into the car, we wrapped her in a blanket and Bessie kept her awake by talking to her, asking what had happened. Her speech had been affected by endless screaming and she kept fading in and out of consciousness. Bessie made her sip on warm water throughout the journey and I drove like a man possessed; it was the worst journey ever; I was literally racing against time." William was shaking as he took another swig of his lukewarm coffee.

"The police have been fantastic. They got hold of the army, and both troops and trackers were deployed soon after Bessie called, but you can imagine how far Mom's attacker could have got with her *bakkie* (truck) from six o'clock in the evening to three in the morning when she got us. A helicopter went out at first light too. We'll catch the bastard, that's for sure." William nodded with grim determination.

"Shit, first light? How long have you been here?"

"It's been a long night, Sis, a very long night. We got to the hospital somewhere around four. Daan was waiting with a team of trauma nurses and they raced Mom to theatre. Once she was there, Bessie and I went to admin, signed what I had to, then I left Bessie to deal with the wheels of bureaucracy, which took ages, you know how it is. Meanwhile, I raced back to the police station to make the full report. That's when I called you. I was there for what seemed like hours. Because the attack took place out of their jurisdiction, everything had to be confirmed with the Brandfort Police first." William glanced down at his watch. "They should have finished with Mom by now, though; let's head up to theatre."

"Where's Bessie?" I asked William as we got into the lift.

"In town; she's gone to get Mom all her favourite lotions and little treats. I think this is all too much for her, to be honest. You know how sensitive she is; she is probably with Martha now. She'll need that comfort and a shoulder to cry on for a while. She's been courageous and handled the situation with remarkable calm. I am so proud of her, but she needs her best friend now. She'll be back shortly."

As we approached the entrance to the theatre, Dr Daan Fouche was pushing through the swing doors, looking exhausted, followed by a team of doctors we didn't know with dire expressions. One glance at Daan's face, I feared the worst.

"A whole team of doctors?" I heaved as I held William's arm as Daan came toward us. He separated himself from the other doctors, waving his thanks as they went on their way and came to stand next to William and I.

"How your mother is still alive is a miracle," he began. "I've seen some pretty awful stuff in theatre before but seeing what only one savage could do to an innocent elderly lady, someone whom I have known all my life, being torn apart so brutally, was beyond belief. Looking at her under the scrutiny of blazing white theatre lights made it even more shocking. The cruelty of her wounds made every one of us in theatre weep."

The only words that penetrated my brain in that fleeting moment were the words that Mom *was still alive;* the rest began to sink in as I looked at Daan's shattered, exhausted face. I knew how bad it was if Daan needed the assistance of a team of specialists to help him save her life.

Daan put his hand on William's shoulder and shook it with affectionate reassurance as men do. They were great friends. I could see the unspoken gratitude William felt for Daan's commitment to saving the life of our Mom, a woman he'd known since he was a small boy. Having Daan look after Mom helped ease my tension and fears as I know it had for William too.

"What are her chances of survival, Daan?" he asked, his chin quivering, just managing to hold on to the last bits of self-control.

"Look, Boet, she's badly injured, you know that. She lost a shit load of blood as you saw yourself, her pulse was racing toward an early grave, and there was serious internal haemorrhaging. However, she's stable now, thanks to the team; if she gets through the next twenty-four hours, she should be fine."

"Was she raped too?" I asked, with abject horror. William hadn't mentioned that part to me; no wonder he'd turned grey with a vengeance.

"I'm afraid so; two or three times, with the most brutal results I've ever seen," he said, looking down at his feet, struggling to make eye contact with me, and I noticed he was about to cry as grief and exhaustion were rapidly setting in, intensifying and heightening the emotion and stress of three and a half hours in theatre piecing Mom together.

"How the hell she managed to walk about three or four kilometres in her condition, only God knows. They bred them tough in her day." Daan paused and took a deep breath. "Nobody deserves this, least of all your special mother. I'll keep a close eye on her. I'm sure she's still fighting in her anesthetised sleep. I must warn you; her wrists will carry the scars for life. I struggled to stitch such thin, fragile skin on the inside of her wrists." Daan paused again; suddenly there seemed nothing left to say. "Listen, I must be off, if you'll excuse me." He cocked his head to one side with a look of sincere sympathy. "See you later."

William and I headed down to the Intensive Care Unit in silence, each dealing with our own torn thoughts.

"I'm perfectly sure Mom won't give a shit about the wrist scars," William said and I knew it was his way of managing the hell that was playing out in his mind that he couldn't express. I let go a little smile, more a feeling of admiration on the inside, than a smile on the outside; an inconsequential statement to help suppress his emotion. My nursing instincts, on the other hand, had taken over my mind, temporarily blotting out the emotional trauma. My immediate worry was septicaemia and pneumonia now my brain had registered she was still alive.

"Our poor, precious mother. A dangerous, life-threatening, tormenting ordeal," was all I could say as a sob of relief broke. William put his arms around my shoulders protectively and said nothing. Then I felt another set of arms surround me. It was Bessie. I turned to her, and we hugged, then sobbed into each other's shoulders; I could see she'd already shed many tears.

"Has Ma just come out of the theatre?" William and I nodded. "Do you know yet how long she will be in ICU?"

"No idea. Probably the next two or three days. I'm going to stay with her, Boetie; Mom needs someone near when she comes around."

"Will you get that amount of time off work?"

"Yes, Derek said I can take off as much time as I need," I reassured him.

"That's great. Jesus Christ Sis, but what about the girls? Who is going to look after them?"

"Dion has agreed to take care of them." Williams eyes hooded suddenly, like an eagle focussed on its prey. The very mention of Dion's name made his hair curl. I left it there. Then William said, "Well, I won't stop 'till we catch that son-of-a-bitch, but Bessie and I need to head home now, Sis. We'll be back tomorrow afternoon. Keep us in the loop if there are any changes, either way." William reached forward and kissed me goodbye, then I stepped into the ICU.

Mom was lying silently in her cot, pipes leading in and out of every orifice connecting her to life-support machines. Her face, what little peeped out from the bandages, was covered in maddening bruises, swollen beyond recognition, her hands and arms were also wrapped in bandages while the buzz of the heart monitor reassured me she was still fighting. I gently touched her ice-cold, motionless fingertips that peeked out from the bandaging.

Mom had always taught us never to hate anyone, but looking at her, lying broken and fragile, I couldn't help hating the person who'd done this to her and for now, I didn't deny myself the sensation. I needed to feel it in order to deal with my grief and anger. Mercifully drugged from the anaesthetic and other medicines, I knew she might not hear my whispers, but I said what I needed to.

"We love you, Mom," my whispers strained with emotion. She was going to be asleep for a long time, so there was no need for me to stay at her bedside now. I shot home to gather up what I needed with me for a twenty-four-hour vigilant stint at the hospital, or until I knew Mom was out of danger.

When I got home and told Miriam, she was shattered and very angry by what had happened.

"Oh, my Missus, oh my Missus, ay, ay, ay," she kept saying, repeatedly apologising as rural Africans do in their natural, humble ways. I shoved my book, toothpaste and brush, hand cream, cosmetics, a flask of coffee and some biscuits into a carry bag and gave Miriam instructions and a quick hug; she still begged me not to allow Dion to take Vivienne and Storm for the night.

"I will sleep here, Missus. I will take care of *my* babies," she said urgently. I couldn't help but marvel at her loyalty and I nodded, wondering how I was going to explain that to Dion. Miriam's suggestion made perfect sense, so I called Dion before going back to the hospital.

"I am so sorry, Liefie," he said as he answered the phone. I quickly informed him that Miriam was staying over and would take care of the children and just as I suspected, it didn't go down well. He insisted on staying with them; in my cottage.

Miriam wasn't happy with the arrangement, but under the circumstances, she accepted graciously, saying she would sleep in the house on the floor in the lounge; she wasn't leaving the girls alone. I hadn't wanted him to know where we lived but there was nothing I could do.

I stayed at Mom's bedside for the rest of the day and throughout the night. Caffeine and anxiety were an excellent combination to keep me awake. Just after seven that evening, Mom stirred for the first time. I took her bandaged hand in mine and whispered to her gently. There was a faint movement on her lips as if she was trying to smile and she moved her fingertips, acknowledging she'd heard me, then disappeared back into the beautiful deep, drug-induced healing sleep she'd been in for hours. I was ecstatic; it was all the confirmation I needed; she was going to fight through this – she would survive.

I slipped out of the room, popped downstairs to the public phone and called Dion.

"How's everything going?"

"Fine, the girls are as delightful as ever. How's your Mom?"

"A few minutes ago, she half-woke, acknowledged my presence by moving her fingers in my hand and slipped back into a deep sleep. It is such a relief."

"That's great news. Are you still staying next to her the whole night?"

"Yes! I want to be here when she wakes fully. It will make all the difference to her."

"I'm sure it will. I'll get the girls off to bed shortly. Call me at the office in the morning if there is anything I can do. Oh, and by the way, was it essential to have the maid stay over too?"

The casualness of words irked me - I never took the bait. I didn't want to tell him that I'd trust Miriam long before I'd trust him alone with our children. I couldn't help the cynic in me, but I kept it silent. I suspected he would use this tragedy to try and lure me back. After speaking to Dion, I called William.

"Hi, good news, I'm sure Mom will be off the critical list by morning; she responded to me by trying to squeeze my hand."

"Thank God, that's wonderful, Sis and thank you for being there with her."

Mom stirred again around one a.m. This time she was far more lucid, but with it came the reality of her pain, and she groaned. I felt every part of her pain shoot through me too. It wasn't much more than a minute or two before she was asleep again; a perfect time for me to put my head down in the family room and catch up on some missed sleep.

When I got back to her, she was awake. In an animated state, the facial swelling and bruising, though severe, hadn't seemed quite as severe as it appeared now she was awake. Moving her lips, with her eyes open reflecting the pain within, everything seemed visually worse and I tried not to show my own shock and pain; instead, I smiled at her affectionately grasping her fingers comfortingly and leant over her, gently kissing her forehead. Then she tried to sit up, but excruciating pain distorted her face and she fell back on her pillow. I grimaced.

"Don't move, Mom," I said, and propped the pillow up to support her head. "Just rest."

Wanting to sit up and get herself more comfortable was a celebratory sign for me – she'd passed the critical stage. For Mom, it was a horrid realisation of the pain she'd have to cope with over the next week but I knew her determination to live was winning the battle, and though she'd not come out unscathed on many levels, she'd handle it all in time in her own private way, just as she did after losing Papa - she'd reject any form of sympathy and get on with life. Being treated like a victim would hurt her more. It was going to take the courage of a lion to come through this trauma and the visible scars savagely engraved on her inner thighs and wrists would be a life-long memory she didn't deserve.

When William and Bessie arrived, I escaped home, exhausted. My everfaithful Miriam stepped in, keeping the girls occupied, fed and bathed so as not to wake me while I slept off my own internal shock and weariness.

Dion was standing over me when I woke the next morning, holding Vivienne on his hip and with Storm standing beside him, ready for school. It took me a moment to process and I couldn't believe I'd been asleep so long. Rubbing my eyes, I sat up and stretched up to kiss Storm good-bye while Dion tucked Vivienne into the other side of the bed so we could cuddle up together after they'd left.

"Can we see Ouma?" Storm asked.

"No, my precious, you can't see her yet. As soon as she is stronger, I will take you to see her, I promise. Have a good day at school. I'll fetch you later."

"Mommy, are you home tonight?" Storm asked quickly.

"Yes, I am darling," I reassured her, and she sighed with apparent relief which left me wondering what was going on in her little mind. I'd find out later.

Mom's injuries were worse than any of us could comprehend. No wonder Daan had looked like he'd been hit by a bull elephant when he emerged from theatre. Only she knew the unspeakable extent of what had been done to her while we struggled to fight off the demons of revenge, especially when we learned from *her* the despicable horrors of what had taken place. Recounting the attack a few weeks later was her form of therapy, her way of letting it all go and she insisted on explaining the whole grizzly experience to me; she held nothing back.

The little farm shop was not far for Mom to limp across to in the morning, supported by her walking stick, then back again in the afternoon. It kept Mom fit and was a place of happy social gathering for the staff, their children and Mom. She'd been generously doing this for the past year. The shops' existence was purely for the convenience of the farm staff, stocking only the fundamental grocery requirements - sweets, cigarettes, tobacco, tea, sugar and bread, a few tinned foods like sardines and tomato relish, bath soap and washing powder. The farm provided the staff with free maize meal, (their staple diet) dried beans and salt. The nearest shops were thirty kilometres away and William's truck shipped them into town once a month for their other needs.

When she started, we'd all worried the walk to and fro might be too difficult, but she'd insisted she loved doing it - it kept her fit and youthful, and she treasured the time there for many of them, whom she'd employed as youngsters, were adults with their own families now and were always proud to introduce her to any new-borns. They all adored Mom; many of them even called her 'Ouma' (Afrikaans for Grandmother); they'd been working and living on the farm that long.

She sat more upright and held my hand.

"I'd locked the shop at 5.30 pm," she began. "I popped the keys and the cash in my apron pocket and set off for home. It was always a slow walk, hampered by my blasted stupid foot." She put her head back on the pillow and closed her eyes; the memories were rushing back at her as I sat silently, apprehensive.

The pathway from the shop led straight to the back door of her cottage, passing the pathway to her beloved vegetable garden on the way to the back door. A few shallow steps lead into the hallway where a key rack hung conveniently above the shoe store cum walking stick stand Mom was so dependent upon. Off to the right was the kitchen, to the left two large comfortable bedrooms down a short passage, hers with a bathroom en suite. Straight ahead was the spacious sitting room fronted by huge sliding doors that lead on to the patio where she sat in the evenings watching the sun go down, listening to and viewing, through her binoculars, the birds on the dam bathing and taking in water for the night – Mom was an avid birder and always noted any new species arriving at the dam. The dining room led off the sitting room and joined the kitchen as one.

Mom's routine was probably her downfall in this instance. William and I agreed her attacker had been monitoring her routine for some days before he made his move. *They* say things always happen for a reason; walking to and from the shop had kept her fit, which was what ultimately saved her life.

"I'd noticed a couple of tiny peaches appearing on the lovely early-ripening hybrid William had planted when the cottage was built and couldn't wait for them to ripen. I wanted to check they weren't getting stung, then pick some carrots for my stew. Thank goodness I hadn't started the stew, or the cottage would have burned down."

The early evening was Mom's favourite time of the day. From her vegetable garden, she'd pick what she needed for supper and soak up the chattering calls of numerous bird species that roosted in the trees close by. The evening breezes and the endless bird song relaxed her tired shoulders. It was difficult walking with a gammy foot and a stick and always caused tension in her neck and shoulders. Once supper was bubbling away, she'd put her feet up and watch the sunset, soaking up the others sounds of approaching nightfall, and she did this every evening without fail.

"I'd put my stick down beside me and had the wicker basket over my arm and had pulled down one of the branches that was laden with baby peaches- there was no insect damage yet but I also wondered how many the birds would leave me," Mom tried to smile, but it was still too painful.

"Suddenly, I was grabbed from behind and wrenched to the ground. Dazed and caught off guard, I wasn't sure what the hell was happening, but it quickly became abundantly clear the danger I was in when I hit the ground, winded and gasping to get my breath back, I caught a whiff of stale wood smoke and dirty, old, masculine sweat and my skin crawled, alerting a primal instinct to come to my aid. The situation was serious, so I reached out for my stick and scooped up a handful of sand which I tossed as hard as I could into his eyes, for he was stooped over me, then I swung my walking stick striking out at his shins, but it made no difference. I don't even think he felt it but he responded like lightning to my unexpected fight for survival. Scrawny, nimbly quick and absurdly strong, he hauled me back onto my feet and grabbed my hands, binding them together with old rusty barbed wire." Mom shook her head and took a breath. The concern on my face was obviously blatant, for she looked long and hard at me before she'd mentally decided I could take what she was going to tell me.

"I let go some almighty screams and went on screaming at the top of my voice while I struggled against him and prayed Ester, or someone would hear my desperate cries." Mom started shaking as she released the pain of the ghastly memory, now etched into her swollen face.

"I didn't realise it then, but luckily, he'd bound my hands in front of me, not behind my back, but either way, the barbs dug painfully into my wrists and tore the skin. I remember wondering why he was tying my hands in front of me. Later I realised what a stroke of luck that was. Standing this close to me, he reeked; his breath was the most revolting smell I'd ever smelt; rotting, putrid, decaying on the inside - I wanted to vomit."

Mom needed a moment; I could see the memory of the smell was up her nose again as she swallowed furiously.

"I glared at him, looking directly into his yellowed, evil eyes, stained from years of living in a smoky hut, drinking disgusting homemade alcohol and smoking dope. I put both my hands out in front of me and tried to push him away, but he blocked my feeble attempt casually, while rubbing some sand out of his eyes. I was no match for him, he knew it and taunted me. Then, without warning, he swung his fist hard into my chest and I fell hard without my hands and arms to slow the impact. My head hit the ground then snapped forward with such force I bit into my tongue and blacked out."

Trying to visualise what she was going through made me feel quite ill. I reached for some water, but Mom went on.

"I'd lost my stick by then; my eyes were full of tears from the fall and biting my tongue, which hurt like hell, and I was swallowing blood while trying to get my breath my back. I screamed again, a shrill, blood-curdling liquid yell but the sounds got lost on the breeze."

The young black scoundrel had every advantage over Mom. Half of me wasn't sure I wanted to hear more, but I had to let Mom go on and purge what plagued her. Talking this way, in private, her and I, was her way of clearing the toxin from her system.

"The evil urchin began tearing my clothing, and I kept ripping my vocal cords 'till I was hoarse and my throat burned, then he was standing over me, dominating my helpless form on the ground. I tried to manoeuvre myself away, hitting out at his legs with my bound hands; the barbs caught on his trouser leg, ripping the filth-engrained, ancient fabric." Mom shuddered. Gravely handicapped, the sudden exertion must have tired her quickly, even though I imagined the massive injection of adrenaline pumping through her veins would have helped.

"He was looking down at me as he stood over me with a triumphant look on his face. He had straddled my body, and started making a weird, mumbling sound like he was in a trance as revolting strings of saliva trailed down his chin and dropped on my chest -it was repulsive, but I couldn't move, I was trapped between his legs and I yelled at him to let me go." Mom stopped, then tears began to roll down her cheeks and she began to sob, deep, ribcage-rattling sobs and I held her quietly.

"Mom, you don't have to go on." I could see the memories were tormenting her. I passed her the box of tissues.

"Oh, my child, I have to go on, I have to tell you, then I can bury it forever."

"Okay Ma, as you wish. Can I get you something nice and warm to drink first?"

"That would be lekker," she said and smiled. I popped out and got us both a cup of hot chocolate.

"Then, panic and horror paralysed me, and I screamed, Nee! Nee! Nee. I was yelling for my life when I realised his intentions. I kept screaming at him to leave me alone, begging him not to hurt me. I was utterly helpless. It made no difference; I was sure I was about to die a terrible death in the orchard." The colour had drained from Mom's face. Tears, which had made a pathway over her still swollen cheeks, kept on rolling down.

"He was grinning at me, that disgusting spittle started pouring out his mouth again; he was relishing the fact that he was in full control of me and I was terrified." Mom sighed and closed her eyes for a moment. She was being so brave.

"He was crazy, rabid with disease, the most disgusting creature I'd ever laid eyes on, and then he began struggling with the zipper on his torn, filthy trousers and I couldn't stop screaming." Mom squeezed her eyes shut again - I knew what was coming next and I grimaced.

"Oh, my kind, (my child) this is so hard." She coughed and cleared her throat.

"My throat was sore from screaming, the metallic taste of blood, fear and helplessness had dried the inside of my mouth and the back of my throat. I wasn't sure how much longer I could endure the torture." I was gripping Mom's hand now and her body began to quiver.

"A weird, wounded sound rose from somewhere deep within me when I saw his huge erect penis protrude through the opening in his trousers. 'Neeeeeeeeeeeeeee,' I bellowed at him then I felt him savagely rip into me, grunting viciously as my screams faded into deep, mournful cries of pain and humiliation. As quickly as the rape happened, it was mercifully over."

My poor mother. Tears were tumbling down my cheeks as I listened in horror as she released her trauma. She was shattered by recalling such violence and I suggested she finish the story another day, but she shook her head vigorously; she needed to go on to get rid of the demons. Watching the raw expression of pain and torture written across her face was one of the hardest things I had ever witnessed from someone so dear to me and I was struggling to deal with my internal rage, living the nightmare with her.

Mom lay back; the shivering began to subside. I couldn't bear thinking about how hard it must have been for her. One of the nurses popped her head around the door and asked if everything was okay. I nodded but asked for a sedative; Mom promptly turned it down, saying she needed to finish the story of her horrific ordeal first, then she might take a sedative.

"Thank God my skirt was still on; it saved my butt from being grazed to pieces. The bastard then dragged me along the ground, up the steps and dumped me in the hall next to the walking stick stand. The edge of each step jarred my back, but I couldn't scream anymore, no sound came out."

The vision of my poor mother lying in a bloodied crumpled heap, dirtied and broken and unable to do a thing to help herself stirred some disturbing desires of what I wanted to do to the rapist if I ever got my hands on him. Now it was my turn to have a moment to process what she'd just told me. I *had* to get up and walk around. Hot chocolate, as comforting as it was, wasn't enough.

"Mom, I'm just going to the loo," I said quickly and ran to the bathroom, slammed the toilet door and hurled into the toilet bowl. Bile and hot chocolate were all that was in me and up they came. I splashed my face with water, swirled my mouth out and dried off my face with some paper towelling and went back to Mom. I wasn't sure how much more I could listen to, but I had to be there for her. She went on almost before I'd sat down next to her, then I took her hand.

"He started shouting at me, demanding to know where I'd hidden the shop money and asked for my gun. He'd already ripped all the keys off the key rack and emptied them into his pockets, then, without warning he took off, running through the house, shouting demands in Zulu.

"Nginike yona noma kufanele ngibulale wena!" (Give it to me, or I will kill you)

"I cannot begin to describe the kind of relief I felt when I heard the bastard speak Zulu. It was then that I knew with certainty the nasty savage wasn't from our farm, not even the district. It was a weird feeling, given my dire circumstances. I could hardly talk by then and my teeth were chattering violently; I couldn't seem to control it. I could hear the smashing of my precious collection of vases and ornaments Papa had given me crash to the floor. I wanted to yell out, but he wouldn't have heard me."

Both of us started crying. Mom treasured every piece as if Papa's loving energy was still attached to each precious ornament.

"I prayed, my kind, hell, I prayed. I prayed for God to remove me from the onslaught, take me quickly to avoid being subjected to more pain and humiliation, then he appeared again making a strange tongue clicking chant and launched a hefty kick into my rib cage and screamed that I was a liar. Then he said in English, 'You whities have all the money. iMali, kuphi, kuphi?" (Money, where, where?)

"I hoarsely replied in English, because of evil thieves like you, us farmers don't keep cash in our houses. It was a foolish thing to say, it only made him angrier, and I paid with a powerful punch to my jaw, and I felt it go along with the need to fight a moment longer. I wanted to die."

Mom's challenge wasn't over, though.

"My mind had gone numb, my body defeated, then, he suddenly pushed me onto my back and dropped onto me, forcing the air from my lungs. Searing pain shot through my jaw and ribs. With a knee on either side of me, I hoped he'd kill me and spare me from the nightmare, but he raped me again, not like the first time, but far worse."

I was expecting that.

"He began by tearing into my womanhood with his fingers, ripping at me with his pinkie fingernail – grown long and razor-sharp, then he tore at the skin of my inner thighs before inserting his enormous penis deep into me; mercifully, I passed out."

This was the internal damage Daan had referred to when he explained how he'd had to do extensive internal stitching. My body was wet with sweat.

"Then he was gone, leaving me in a pool of blood with my arms still bound, my wrists in shreds; I was sure more than one of my ribs were broken and my jaw. I vaguely remembered hearing the back door slam and my Toyota pick-up being crashed through the gears as he drove off at high speed. Part of me hoped I'd die quickly; another part of me knew I desperately needed to get help – this part was won, but if I hadn't got myself free of the rusty wire cuffs, Ester would have found me dead on the floor in the morning. I had no idea how to free myself of the barbed bondage that had already gouged through the flesh on both my wrists. There was no doubt I faced a horrible, slow death if I didn't free myself and get off the floor."

We were interrupted by the arrival of lunch; fish and chips with a side salad which smelled really good; it was time for a break.

Miracles do happen, and though the emotion that filled me then was complicated, now I was intrigued to find out how she'd got herself across to Williams house, and after we'd eaten, she explained.

Luckily, the wire used was ancient. Mom manoeuvred herself over to the walking stick stand and hooked the wire over the decorative knob at the bottom of the stand and worried at it till the wire snapped. Thankfully, William had secured the unit to the wall when she'd moved, so she was able to pull herself upright, but as she did, she felt a stream of hot sticky blood rush down the inside of her legs leaving her gasping from the pain. Grabbing another stick from the stand, she hobbled carefully to the phone but the line was dead; the bastard had cut her off from that too. Very slowly, she hobbled to the bathroom, plugged the basin and filled it with warm water, dropped in some Savlon and attempted to clean herself.

"Oh, that warm water was so soothing. Then I made myself a sanitary pad with a dry facecloth which I folded over a wad of toilet paper, then staggered to the chest of drawers and dug out a fresh pair of panties. By then I was exhausted, but I sat on the edge of my bed and inched them up and placed the home-made sanitary towel inside the panties, hoping this would help absorb some of the blood and help stop the bleeding. Getting to William's house was my priority. Every bloodied inch of my body hurt; it took me ages trying to pull a light jacket on, knowing I'd need to keep warm as the night temperatures dropped. All I could think of was getting out of the house, for I was scared the bastard would come back. Before I left my room, I looked around and wondered if I'd ever see it again," she said, her swollen bottom lip vibrating gently.

"I was so shaky, but when I got to the back door, I convinced myself I could make it across to William's house. I'd had some sugar water, taken two pain killers, protected my private parts, and I needed to get going. Standing unsteadily with two walking sticks supporting me, I looked up at the approaching night skies and knew the cover of darkness would come quickly now. Without the guiding light of the moon, my walk to William's would be slower, but safer."

Attacker and victim shared the same road in and out, creating another challenging dilemma for Mom. No-one else would be using that road; mercifully, she knew every inch of it. She set off, one precarious step at a time, supported by her sticks. She'd only gone about four hundred metres down the road when she heard vehicle sounds far off in the distance; sounds she dreaded but had expected and another surge of adrenaline-filled energy came to her aid. Moving a few metres deeper into the long grass and with agonising difficulty, she crouched down, praying the grassy spot was not going to be the place where she'd take her last breath. Hiding about ten metres off the edge of the road, he passed her. With immense relief, she realised she'd got herself just out of range of the headlights. He wasn't going to find her in the house, but on the return journey, he would be scouring the edges of the road looking for her. Shooting pain stabbed from every part of her battered body, but she forced herself to remain as still as possible. The silence of the night was startlingly loud as she listened.

It seemed to take forever before she heard her 'bakkie' racing back towards where she hid, passing without the headlights exposing her. Driving at breakneck speed, he would never have located her hiding place, and as the sounds of the vehicle slowly died away, she allowed herself to sob, deep pitiful sobs; her pain was temporarily numbed by relief and the painkillers she'd swallowed earlier were working through her system.

Now the sounds of the night became comforting melodies as frogs croaked and insects chattered; it was the perfect musical ensemble to reinforce Mom's determination to live. Even the nightjars called out to her, urging her on her way, as she stumbled down the edge of the road leaving a bloody trail behind her. Blood had seeped through the homemade sanitary pad and was dribbling down the inside of her legs again. The physical struggle was sapping her strength, and her prayers became more pleading.

"Do you remember that precious carved Swazi walking stick Henry gave me?" Mom asked.

"Yes, I do, Mom."

"It was that one I used the most because it's top was wider and gave me support, but it got so stained from all the blood that had oozed from my wrists that William tossed it out. When Henry gave it to me, he wouldn't have thought it would one day save my life."

Dehydration had become a frightening companion and was another genuine hindrance.

"Fine sand from crouching down on the side of the road had stuck to the blood on my inner thighs and dried, creating a skin of living sandpaper which was now rubbing them rawer and a deep burning consumed the inside of my legs."

Eventually, Mom could see the farmstead looming in front of her out of the darkness. The worst part of the ordeal would soon be over. Mom's gammy foot had been rubbed raw and was bleeding, surrendering to the difficulty of the journey like every other part of her; she was nearly there. Standing unsteadily, Mom tapped on William's bedroom window. William was asleep, lying with his head on his deaf side, so he never heard the taps of her stick on the window, but Bessie did. Always a light sleeper being nervous about living on the farm, she responded to the sounds by sitting bolt upright in bed, instantly petrified and alert. She urgently rattled at William's shoulder to wake him.

"Mmmmm, what's wrong, Liefie?" he asked, sleepily.

"Someone is knocking on the window," she whispered.

"Are you sure?" William knew what a light sleeper she was; most noises woke her.

"Yes, very sure, that was not an animal sound, it is definitely someone knocking," and as she said it, Mom tapped again, more urgently this time, knowing she wasn't going to be able to hold herself upright much longer. William jumped up and quickly walked around the end of their bed, stood at the curtained window, and pushing some of the fabric to one side, peered straight into the desperate eyes of his severely injured mother.

Mom gasped; the horrific experience was behind her. She lay her head back on her pillow and incredibly, minutes later, she was snoring in a deep, restful sleep as if revealing her savage attack and her long walk to get help had released her of the emotional trauma. Later that afternoon, Daan popped in on his rounds.

"Mum told me what happened to her; my God, it's gruesome. Like you said, Daan, it is a miracle she's alive, but she seems relieved to have gotten it out of her system. Thank you for saving her life," I whispered.

"Well, when I first saw her, I didn't think I could, nor did the team I'd called in to help me."

The news of Mom's savage attack sent shock waves rippling through the community. Both black and white were angry and wanted the man found. Local farmers joined forces with the police and the Army Tracker Unit to assist in finding the man that had brutally raped Mom and torn her to pieces, very nearly killing her. The search was relentless, paying off the following week when they found Mom's bakkie, parked and abandoned, full of dents and scratches; her brand-new bakkie was a mess.

"Mom is going to be furious," William said in passing to a local farmer standing beside him. "That bakkie was precious to her; it was the first new vehicle she'd ever owned, and though she didn't drive it herself, she'd be as livid as her driver Joe is."

Thankfully, Mom never saw it.

The search for the rapist continued. On the ninth day, they found him cowering in thick bush next to a river only three farms from ours. The police showed no mercy and our friends agreed it was the swine's good luck that William hadn't gotten to him first. Rape, in anyone's eyes, is an inexcusable crime, but done with such savagery to a lady in her late sixties who was the darling of the community enraged everyone.

William and I found the court case intolerable; hateful vengeance was not a part of our upbringing, but neither of us could feel anything else. Forgiveness was not a sensation that fitted with what we were feeling in the courtroom that day. Listening to the verdict gave way to some of those nasty emotions. Life imprisonment - we were satisfied with the sentence, but none of us would ever truly forgive what he'd done to Mom. Seven weeks after the incident, Mom left the hospital, still shaken, but on her way to a full recovery. She never went back to live on the farm she so dearly loved; he'd taken that from her too.

William and Bessie found a suitable house for her in the nearby town of Brandfort and Ester, her loyal housekeeper, moved with her, but Joe, her dear old driver, remained on the farm, collecting Mom once a week to take her shopping.

CHAPTER EIGHTEEN

Only six weeks after Mom's brutal attack, Dion's mother passed away. Mothers were having a massive impact on my life, and the two tragedies united us again. Dion had been there for me after Mom's near-fatal attack and I felt it my duty to be there for him during his time of loss.

Timing wasn't a gift we'd had during the history of our married life. We'd both been living separate lives for a long time, and though it suited me, it never suited Dion. Not long after the death of his mother, Phillip called to say Hennie wasn't coping well on his own.

A month after that phone call, Hennie sheepishly asked Dion if the two of us would move to the plot and take care of him. I was very hesitant but after endless discussion, I agreed. My family, particularly my mother, were mortified.

My positivity and determination to make things work evaporated quickly not long after moving, being faced with one nasty surprise after another. The first was one I could deal with, having been raised on a farm with a generator; there was no mainline electricity to the house. However, this generator was manufactured at the turn of the century and was on its last legs, screaming for an end to its hard life, deafening us when it was on. When we had visited in the past, we'd never stayed overnight and took modern electricity supply for granted, so it hadn't crossed my mind that we'd be going back into the dark ages. The second shock, and this one angered me, none our furniture was permitted in *his* house, being relegated to a rickety old shed that was waterproof but not rodent-proof and thirdly, what I thought was the worst; there was not much clean water — wrong move.

The death of Hennie's beloved wife had turned what I knew as a dear, kind old gentleman, into a grumpy, aggrieved, bitter old bastard, and I struggled to hold my tongue. When I woke sore and crippled from sleeping on a bed with an old coir mattress, I didn't keep my mouth shut and ordered the gardener to swop it for our bed. This obvious violation of his rules enraged the cantankerous old Hennie and I thought his red puffed-up face was going to explode. I was on the warpath and checked the children's beds; fortunately, they had reasonably new beds.

Round number two, which happened a few days later, was indeed about the children. Instead of being overjoyed by the sound of his happy grandchildren bringing cheer and laughter back into his home, they infuriated him. Storm's gregarious character was too lively, Vivienne was messy and far too nosy. He wordlessly tolerated Splodge because he fitted in anywhere without a fuss, putting Oupa's Maltese poodle in its place in the first five minutes we were there. Just as distressing was his housekeeper, Selina, a woman shrouded in a malevolent energy; a woman I was convinced was created in hell with severe Arabic features, sharp, almond-shaped eyes that viewed me with mistrust and venomous, unprovoked hatred. She'd been with the family for years, and though she had been a devoted and loyal housekeeper to Mr and Mrs Du Toit senior, she refused to take one instruction from me and was determined to make my life on the plot an absolute misery, which she achieved.

I called on dear Miriam. Luckily, she'd gone to her family home for a break before looking for another job after leaving me. I was just in time - she didn't hesitate, despite her previously trying to convince me not to go back to 'Mr Dion'. Miriam cleaned the parts of the house we occupied, did our washing and ironing and prepared the vegetables for me for dinner. She did some of the cooking for me on occasions and was nanny to Vivienne. But Hennie always had to have the last say and told me that even though I had brought in Miriam to help me, I still had to pay Selina's salary. I took that up with Dion.

"He's got an absolute cheek, Dion. He's your father, and they are your children too, so you talk to him, but I am not paying a cent toward Selina's salary. She does nothing for any of us, is downright rude to me and won't even greet me."

"Calm down, Liefie."

"Calm down? Like hell will I calm down. I won't tolerate any more abuse from your father, I am sorry to say, and I am certainly not paying toward that bitch's salary."

I realised then I had been crazy to agree to this move.

"Besides," I went on, "*he* asked us to move here, and he's not in the slightest bit appreciative. You don't see or hear what the girls and I have to put up with." Dion nodded, but he didn't seem to get it or had gone into selective hearing mode.

"Did you hear what I said?"

"Yes, I did, my Skat, but I cannot ask Papa to change anything."

"Well, you pay the nasty Selina. Not one cent of my hard-earned cash is going anywhere near her pocket." Dion nodded again; that was the end of the conversation. There was something sinister and dark about the relationship between Hennie and Selina, and I felt sure Dion knew some of those dark family secrets I'd never picked up on before now.

Miriam was the angel at my side with a smile as big and as sunny as her personality. Her lovely characteristics highlighted Selina's mean ones and, admirably, Miriam never allowed Selina's repugnant ways to disrupt her. She just got on with the job as usual.

The water that fed into the house came from a brackish, underground supply and was as utterly vile as the maid that ruled the house. One of Miriam's daily tasks was to boil it for the kids to bathe in at night and a massive pot boiled away on the woodstove all day, cleansing it, so the household had drinking water. Then, before Miriam left in the evening, she popped a new pot on for Dion and I to use for our baths. It was the ultimate in discomfort. I'd lived without often during my life, but bodily cleansing under a jet of clean water was, for me, not a luxury but an essential part of balancing my psyche. Now, this ultimate discomfort and the despicable attitude of Hennie Du Toit and his sidekick made everything around me close to impossible to deal with rationally when I never felt refreshed and properly clean.

When I got home one evening, Hennie suggested I should, "beat some discipline into my naughty children." This was the straw that broke the proverbial camel's back and put an immediate end to my tolerance. I roared back at him about how ungrateful he was and he responded by saying, "You are a hopeless, immature woman who has no idea how to bring up children."

An exchange of colourful, creative vocabulary flew out my mouth. He was furious and muttered continuously about the disruption we'd caused in his home, what awful food he was forced to eat and how he loathed the ghastly noisy children. I stopped cooking for him and left his food requirements to the loathsome Selina.

Daily life became a battle of wills - one in which Dion refused to participate. Hennie's grieving was over, Dion never mentioned his mother again, and I was in the middle of all this – I grieved my decision more than the two men grieved their loss, as if their shallow lives were perfectly calibrated.

Hennie preferred to spend his time with his youngest son, giving us some welcome peace on the plot, but living there was going to end for me and end soon. I hated the house; I hated having to stoke the stove to boil water for a bath over the weekend - in fact, everything about the house was depressing. Not a blade of grass had ever been planted around the house; it stood alone in a desert of red earth, the walls of the house painted a sand colour which emphasized the emptiness and exaggerated the gloom and barrenness. The roof was covered in the same colour of dust, everything reflecting a loveless environment. I couldn't imagine anything worse than growing up here. It was a beacon of despair.

I got home early one evening and found Hennie back at the plot. Greeting him civilly, I continued through to the kitchen, for that morning, of all mornings, I'd asked Selina to peel potatoes for me, leave them in water to soak and I'd cook them that evening - Miriam was on a day off and since Dion was still paying her salary, I felt no hardship in asking her, but she'd prepared nothing for me, so, ensuring I wasn't rude, I enquired why. She sensed I was annoyed at having my instructions purposefully and spitefully ignored and stood staring at me then put both her hands on her hips and smiled victoriously. I'd reached the end of my tether.

"If peeling potatoes for us is too difficult for you, Selina, then I suggest you leave. Mr Dion pays your salary, and, as you will do nothing for any of us, I am letting you know now, we do not need you any longer."

Hennie had been listening and burst into the kitchen shouting angrily, waving his arthritis-gnarled index finger under my nose.

"Selina isn't going anywhere." I glanced her way and noticed a triumphant look had risen across her face.

"Well Hennie, you choose, it's her or me."

"She's going nowhere!" he repeated stubbornly.

His words were like a lance penetrating deep into my heart. I'd tried hard for the ungrateful old bastard. I stood in the dark, dingy kitchen, quite shaken by these events, and quietly admitted the odds were stacked against me and I was never going to win, but a suspicious thought entered my mind then; had Hennie been having a long-term affair with Selina? He was much too affectionate and protective of her, far from an ordinary servant – employer relationship. I left them in the kitchen, headed to my bedroom, dropped down on the edge of the bed and pondered my next move, my body vibrating with rage.

Dion wouldn't be home until Friday evening. I wasn't going to wait for him; it would be futile, for he was on his father's side anyway. It was time to leave.

Jumping up, I yanked all our suitcases off the top of the cupboards and packed everything in the room that belonged to us.

"What are you doing, Mama?" I heard Storm's little voice come from the direction of the door and I swung round to face her. She'd listened to the argument and was standing in the doorway looking stunned and frightened - a picture that tugged at my heart. I knew my two children weren't happy, and neither had any affection for their Grandfather; in fact if anything, they didn't like him at all.

"Come here, my precious," I beckoned putting my arms out for her to walk into, then I wrapped them around her and held her close to me.

"Don't say a word to Oupa. I'm going to find a new place to live when I get to work in the morning. Come on, let's go and make supper. I'll pack the rest later." A happy smile lit up her face.

"Go and get Vivienne and join me in the kitchen."

"Okay Mama," she said, as she skipped off toward their bedroom. We made dinner for ourselves and ate it in the kitchen. After kissing the girl's goodnight, I packed what I could, and we left earlier than usual the following day. After dropping Storm at school, I bought a newspaper, checked for rentals and found a place that sounded suitable. I called the advertiser at 8.30 am, secured the property unseen, begged Derek for a company lorry to move with and, by nightfall, I'd shifted all our stored belongings into our new house with help from the lorry driver and Miriam.

Neither Hennie nor I uttered a word to each other while we loaded and packed. Selina watched from the side-lines with an elated sneer all day whenever she saw me.

Dion got home as we were busy with the last load and went off at me like he'd been detonated, which took me by surprise, for I knew he wasn't happy on the plot. Suddenly, I felt those nerves again, but I stood my ground; there was no turning back.

"Your father gave the ultimatum. The girls and I happily accepted."

Dion looked stunned. "What ultimatum?" I didn't bother to go into all the details but offered him one of two options.

"You can stay with your father, or you can come with us; choice is yours." I handed Dion a piece of paper with our new address scribbled on it, jumped into my car, and followed the lorry off the property. There was no suppressing Miriam's mood as she took her place in the front seat, while the kids on the back seat were standing up looking back at their angry, rather bewildered father, who stood watching us drive away, and with each passing meter of gravel road the car crunched over, a mountain of stress lifted off my shoulders. Splodge was a happy cat; even he had become unusually subdued and had given up teasing Dot, the grumpy Maltese.

Dion didn't follow immediately, but later that evening, while I was unpacking and sorting out the mess, he arrived. The monster look wasn't quite there, but I was pretty sure it wouldn't be hard to trigger. He'd found it tricky dealing with my new independence. He wasn't in control of me, and that was a dangerous situation living under the same roof again.

The more I tried to explain how Hennie had chosen Selina over me, the worse the argument got. I didn't want to start this new chapter on shaky foundations, but I wasn't backing down. The children's happiness came before anything else in my world.

He came towards me, threatening with a warning finger, and suddenly reached out to strike at my face. As he lunged at me, I brought my arm up in an instinctive protective action and my fist accidentally connected the delicate spot on his temple, knocking him off balance and he fell. I was shocked; the sudden reflex action to protect my face had more power than I realised.

It took a few minutes for him to focus and get back on his feet, but he was seething from the humiliation, especially being knocked off his feet in front of his children and Miriam; he wasn't going to swallow that accidental blow - I was in trouble.

Once he was up, he went directly to the bathroom without uttering a word. Then a short while later the screeching of tyres were the last sounds we heard from Dion for a week.

By the end of that week, I was feeling apprehensive for his home-coming. I had no idea what to expect but he was in an unusually good mood when he got back.

Dion had given up on the music industry and was now working for Nestlé. He arrived bearing gifts of atonement; in the back of his car lay tins of instant coffee and hot chocolate, bars of chocolate and an assortment of other sweets, instant puddings and luxury breakfast cereals. The kids forgave Papa instantly.

Damaged packaging rendered goods unfit for sale in the stores, so it was sold off to the staff at cost and Dion took advantage of the opportunity to obtain this cheap, but yummy peace offering.

Storm and Vivienne gobbled a large Bar-One each, putting them on a hyper-active sugar high within minutes. They buzzed around the house and garden playing games with each other as if they were powered by Duracell. After supper, Storm dragged Dion to the piano, urging him to play, but it wasn't long before the sugar high dumped her, and she struggled to keep her eyes open, while Vivienne was already asleep on the sofa.

With the children tucked away in bed, Dion and I chatted, purposefully avoiding the issue of the unexpected punch and his absence the whole week. The chemistry was surprisingly good, so I didn't dare raise the subject. It had been a long time since we'd made passionate, meaningful love - I gave in to the call of nature and the need for passion that night.

After a month away from the plot, I noticed Vivienne had recovered from a strange, undiagnosed illness she'd suffered while living there. We'd had endless blood and urine tests done on her that had revealed nothing. She'd been referred to several doctors, none of whom found a cause or gave a diagnosis to her unexplained and unusual illness that had caused ghastly vomiting attacks, high temperatures and fever that burned her little body up at night. Vivienne had been a desperately ill little girl; medication had cost a fortune without much relief and we had no answers; now it was miraculously gone. Since the day we packed up at the plot, she'd not had another attack, but with everything going on, I'd not paid attention to the fact she'd not had another disturbed night. This was living proof what a devastating effect a toxic environment can have on children and without the vocabulary to express it.

I had a sudden thought; had it been Selina slowly poisoning her? She'd had an aversion to Vivienne. I shook the thought away. I'd also learned that the week Dion was away after we'd moved was spent with his father and two months later, he was dead. A sudden heart attack - I got the blame; *I* was the one who'd abandoned him. I could scarcely believe what I was hearing. Later that week, I received a phone call from Phillip. We'd not spoken since the affair Dion had had with his wife.

"I'm so sorry about your father, Phillip," I said, offering my condolences.

"Do you know where Dion is? None of us can reach him," he said, coldly and I guessed he too believed I'd killed his father.

"No, I don't. Have you tried his offices?" I suggested.

"You killed him, Elizabeth. You know that, don't you? *You* abandoned him and left him to die," Phillip said suddenly and without provocation.

"I did nothing of the sort, Phillip. That is a cruel and unnecessary accusation. *He* told me to leave." I slammed the phone down and sobbed my heart out. I was forbidden to attend the funeral, but I went. I felt it was the right thing to do. The family shunned me; nobody sat on the pew at the back of the church with me, not even family friends, and though it hurt me, I'd anticipated being received with disdain.

Later that week, the family gathered for the reading of the will. Money was left to each surviving brother, and, what shattered the brothers but didn't surprise me at all, ten thousand Rand had been written into the will for Selina, confirming my suspicions. The property was left to the brothers to work out what to do with it.

Somehow, I had to prevent Dion from having his part of the inheritance deposited into his account. He was drinking again, and I knew, without hesitation, he'd drink it away. Protecting the inheritance for him and trying to arrange it was going to be almost impossible.

A plan was sent to me from the heavens as I lay awake early one morning. A visualisation of the plot all renovated with a garden, vegetables growing in abundance, fruit trees everywhere, lawn all around the house, clean water and electricity - it would not only be a good investment but a great place to raise the kids. It was far more than I could offer them if I didn't stay with Dion. In spite of the initial tension over the death of his father, but in fairness to Dion, he was supportive and knew how hurt I was; we'd also chatted about his drinking again.

My suggestion came as quite a shock to Dion. He couldn't believe that I'd even suggest buying out his brothers and moving back to the plot, but after I'd explained my vision in detail, he enthusiastically agreed, even letting me deal with the lawyers handling Hennie's estate. Eventually, Dion's siblings decided they'd rather have the money than a useless share in a property they all hated and had no emotional attachment to.

Signed, sealed and completed, we celebrated our first home ownership. I was ecstatic. Youthful dreams and hopes of *'happily ever after'* were always there in the back of my mind. I knew the *real* Dion; he was being that incredible Dion now and I dreamed of making our relationship work, helping him over his problems, and I considered this move to be the right one.

Dreams and hopes aside, there was not the remotest chance I was going back to the plot before sorting out the water situation. I booked a month off work to sort it out, which raised some questioning eyebrows. Me, plumbing? Thanks to the skills training in all things farming, mechanical, building and home maintenance that I'd learned while growing up with William as my mentor and tutor, fixing up the plumbing was not a daunting task for me - William was only a phone call away if I got stuck.

Miriam and I started dismantling the rusty old pipes, ones that had been laid in the early 1940s and crumbled between the teeth of the shifting spanner as we loosened them from their ancient stronghold. Lots of skin went missing, fingernails got broken too, but we had fun. As the days passed, Miriam learned, with lightning speed, the art of wielding shifting spanners, pipe cutters and threaders and our new home was almost ready for the professionals to come in, check our handy work, make any necessary changes, then connect us to the municipal water mains and sign it off; job done. This was quite acceptable in those days. Once that was behind us, we gave the whole place a coat of paint, inside and out. Four weeks later, we'd both earned a fabulous new level of fitness with weight loss a bonus, and we moved in. Dion was impressed, but I sensed a little vulnerable jealousy, interpreting my work as just one more display that I didn't need a man in my life and at any given time, I could just walk out, but for me, it was about saving money and having a fun challenge.

Miriam and I had loads of laughs, ruining many clothes, but the luxury of clean running water, both hot and cold, was worth it. We'd put a shower into

Miriam's unit too. With my savings just about depleted, it was time to let Dion know he'd have to cover the electrical installation, which caused a few sideways glances. Dion hated paying for anything.

The following Sunday, William and Mom came to view our handy work, bringing with them a surprise housewarming gift of a brand-new gas stove and a few gas lamps. I was thrilled; it was a most unexpected gift, for they were not partial to Dion and I being together again. It was the children and I they were concerned about, though, and they made it very clear. I loved cooking with gas, but I couldn't toss out the old wood stove that the coffee percolator sat on, burping away all day, reminding me of my childhood.

Without electricity on call, candle-lit dinners lost their appeal after a few months, and the only way to get Dion into forward gear was for Miriam and me to start doing something. I drew a plan on paper of where plug points and light switches needed to go and proceeded to pencil it in on the walls. A week later, Miriam and I began to chase into the cement surface where the electrical conduit piping would need to be placed. Poor Miriam was left to fight with a fine dust storm that covered the house. Dion wasn't amused, but three months later we'd done the dirty work and electricians came in to connect us to the mains.

"Eish, missus," Miriam's smile was brighter than our new lights as I switched on the overhead one in the kitchen for the first time. The girls were just as excited when they got home from school and ran through the house, switching on every light, checking they all worked then rushing back to hug me, Storm babbling on about how easy it was going to be to do her homework now.

Eighteen months later we'd transformed the plot from a depressing dusty dump into an oasis, gorging on our home-grown fresh vegetables every day. The garden was gradually taking on the landscaped form I'd designed - roses were flowering, shrubs had taken hold and were growing well and the seeds I'd sewn for cut flowers were budding. The lawn looked like a carefully tended fairway and being blessed with an excellent rainy season that year, my garden of Eden was thriving.

The vegetable garden was one of the girl's favourite place to play. Shrieks of laughter could be heard as they searched through the carrot bed for the fattest ones, hopping about on all fours pretending to be bunnies with carrots between their teeth as they played fantasy games with each other and named it 'The Disney Patch', so we painted a sign for the gate. They were happy days.

CHAPTER NINETEEN

My job as Derek's PA kept me on my toes, and by the time we'd renovated the plot, I was earning an enviable salary. Dion had managed to stay in one job for longer than a year and life had been close to miraculous with him. Although he was still drinking, he'd become more disciplined about it, and the monster hadn't appeared for a long, long time.

I was dreading Derek's retirement, which was looming. He'd not said when he would leave, and he wasn't particularly keen on retiring, but I wasn't looking forward to the day when he'd had enough and would pack it in.

One evening, after the girls had gone to bed, I curled up in my big armchair, its wings closing me into a world of blissful comfort and security while I dreamily switched on the TV to check if there was a movie worth watching. I didn't feel like going to bed, and Dion was out. It was just Splodge and I; the peace was idyllic until suddenly it was shattered as the front door flew open; Splodge scattered as Dion stumbled in, collapsed over the arm of the sofa and toppled off it, hitting the floor with a frightening thud. He fell so quickly and so hard, my instant thoughts were that he'd suffered a heart attack like his father. I flew out of my chair as fast as Splodge had disappeared and looked down at Dion. He looked dreadful and all I could think of in that moment of panic was to call Daan.

"Hi Daan, it's me, Elizabeth. I, um…. I'm sorry to disturb you this late, but I think Dion may have had a stroke or a heart attack. Would you mind coming out?"

Without a moment's hesitation, he said, "I'm on my way."

Those were the days when doctors still did emergency house calls, but Daan was more than just our GP. I put the phone down and quickly rushed back to where Dion lay - what an idiot I felt. I should have checked him over more closely before allowing panic to rule me; the son-of-a-bitch was so drunk he appeared unconscious. I was devastated; he'd been so good. As I bent down to feel his pulse, the putrid stench of alcohol and stale cigarette smoke made me want to vomit, but a more potent smell of defeat filled my nostrils.

"What the fuck," I muttered as I stood up, my eyes still focussed on the pathetic heap of humanity at my feet. How I wished the bliss could have continued. Three incredible years of happy family life on our beautiful plot gave the girls a taste of the best of both worlds. Dion had been sober for most of that time. The girl's friends would come and go; they loved the farm life as much as we did, and now this. All gone in one selfish, thoughtless evening.

Twenty minutes later, Daan arrived and I met him at the front door, feeling embarrassed and ashamed.

"Oh, dear Elizabeth, it must be bad, you look like you've seen a ghost!" Daan said.

"I have; the ghost of the past just smacked me in the face, Daan. I'm sorry to have called you; I should have checked him better before calling; he's pissed out of his mind. I didn't think of checking before calling you; he's been dry for so long."

Daan shook his head sadly.

"I'm sorry to hear that, Elizabeth, but as I'm here, let me check him anyway and make sure he's okay."

Coming back into the house, the stench of stale alcohol fumes assaulted our nostrils.

"A bad case of alcohol poisoning. Let's roll him on his side; he'll move into a more comfortable position later on, but keep an eye on him. I don't envy him; he'll have a hangover from hell tomorrow and will probably be as sick as a dog for a good few days, but maybe that's what he needs. If there are any changes during the night and you are unhappy, call me, but I'm pretty sure he'll survive providing he remains on his side; we don't want him drowning himself if he vomits."

"He has been so good; I never expected this, Daan. I thought the drinking was under control." I was close to tears, knowing what lay ahead.

"Something must have prompted this. Has he appeared depressed or agitated recently?"

"No, he's been a model father and husband."

"See me at my rooms in the morning, Elizabeth. Let's chat through this and your next move."

"Okay, Daan, thank you. I'm so angry and disappointed too, of course."

"I'm quite sure you are. It's time for Dion to get professional help."

I raised my eyebrows; I couldn't see Dion agreeing to professional help. Daan left, and I closed the front door behind him, covered Dion with a blanket and went to bed. Dion was still sound asleep the next morning, precisely as I'd left him and in a feeble attempt to cover for him, I told the girls a fib - the look on Storm's face suggested I hadn't fooled her. There was a deafening silence in the car on the way to school; both girls were unusually subdued; they knew. I popped into the office and left a note for Derek, then headed down to Daan's consulting rooms.

"Good morning, Elizabeth. How's Dion's head this morning?"

"He's still out for the count. Miriam's at home if he needs anything."

"Do you think we can convince him to see a psychologist when he wakes up?"

"That's a bit radical! I thought about that last night. I know he's got more issues than just alcohol, but I can't see how a psychologist is going to help him. Don't you think AA would be more effective?"

"Not at all radical, Elizabeth. Seeing a psychologist may help us discover the root causes of his addiction and personality disorders. I don't want to see you and the girls go through hell all over again. We need to establish why, after all this time, he's suddenly drunk himself into oblivion. We have to establish the triggers then we'll have something to work with."

The logic made sense. I nodded in agreement despite feeling defeated.

"I think *you* will have to call and discuss it with him. He'd never agree if I suggest it, but he's probably feeling sick enough today to agree to anything you suggest. Let him know you did a house call to us last night; that might shake him."

"Yeah, good idea. I'll recommend he see Dr Gouws; he's reported to be one of the country's leading psychologists. He has an excellent reputation for getting to the bottom of difficult psychiatric cases. He's worked with the worst." I smiled, trying to keep the cynicism out of my expression.

A torturous hangover worked in our favour; Dion agreed to the assessment. Daan wasted no time making the appointment before Dion had a chance to change his mind. When Dr Gouws finished the assessment, he sent Dion home to sleep off the alcohol poisoning and booked him off work for a week.

The following day, I was back in Daan's office when Dr Gouws called. I watched Daan's expression change and wondered what the discussion could be about, then Daan answered irritably.

"There is no question, Dr Gouws, I sent you the right patient," he stated; I turned purple with rage and was ready to climb over the desk, grab the phone and yell at the psychologist – how dare he suggest I was the problem? Feeling like a whirlwind in a mealie field on a hot day, I struggled to stop myself going from one emotional extreme to another as I felt the anger give way to burning tears. Humiliated and deeply insulted, I insisted on meeting Dr Gouws myself, but Daan managed to dissuade me.

That was the level of brilliance we were dealing with, with Dion. A master manipulator, and the crème de la crème on Dion's list of talents. He was a genius at it; it even surpassed his musical prowess. When Dion felt he was cornered, particularly with a professional like Dr Gouws, the game was on; instead of fighting his way out, he turned up the charm and performed with more panache and style than any Oscar-winning performance required and had the person gasping, agreeing with everything he had to say and laughing at his marvellous humour. No-one ever believed he was a shallow, selfish devil in disguise with the scruples of a shark. So, Dion Du Toit had managed to manipulate one of South Africa's leading psychologists and cunningly placed the blame on me - a polished act to alleviate his dented ego, the son-of-a-bitch, but it backfired. Dr Gouws was acutely embarrassed and promptly ordered a series of more in-depth tests on Dion, finally exposing just how unpredictable and dangerous he actually was.

A shiver ran down my spine as I read the report. What I was reading, and the enormity of Dion's psychological complications, terrified me. How could he find it so easy to masquerade as the ultimate charmer and enjoy living such a double life? I was far too young to cope with this; I didn't even know where to begin. I always knew he was not an ordinary rogue, but I wasn't aware his condition was quite as complex and dangerous, despite my constant efforts to help him.

'Gifted with intelligence on a MENSA level; a talented, arrogant, egotistical, cunning and sly sociopath, psychopath and schizophrenic;' this was my husband they were describing. I had a sneaking feeling even the professionals were not quite sure how to handle Dion's case. The investigation exposed a rare glimpse of what lay behind the scenes in the Du Toit family's dark secrets. The cracks were getting more profound, the crevices darker, and I wondered what else we'd dig up.

Alcohol was Dion's escape when the gremlins and demons in his head got too much for him, drowning out the noise of the past, dulling the pain, but all the while increasing his anger levels till he passed the point of no return, then he was aggressively in control of everyone; he was invincible in the nastiest of ways and exceedingly dangerous.

"Though we've laughed at Dr Gouws expense, this is no laughing matter," Daan said thoughtfully, then revealed, somewhat tentatively, what Dion had said about me.

'Stubborn and wilful. She is committed only to her children and her own needs. Egotistical, selfish and pig-headed.' This was how Dion had described me to Dr Gouws. There was more nasty stuff, none of it remotely fitting my character or how hard I'd tried for him. I sobbed unashamedly in front of Daan; those words ripped into me like a hurricane, tearing me to shreds. How dare he!

"Don't let it upset you, Elizabeth; he's covering his arse, it's all his stuff; besides, his type would never hear of putting someone else first, you should know that. Unfortunately, the gift of a high IQ exacerbates the problem." A frown wrinkled Daan's brow, carving two deep grooves between his eyes; he was disturbed by what lay ahead for the children and I.

"We'll just have to wait and see what comes of the next procedure before making any decisions."

"How long does that take?"

"He will be admitted tonight and discharged from the psychiatric ward by four o'clock tomorrow afternoon. Dr Gouws will advise us once he has all the results. I'm told he has called in a colleague to assist. As soon as I have the reports, I'll call you, and we can go through it. Dion will be permitted to read the reports." That was not good news; in fact, there was no good news on the horizon for me.

I left Daan's room with a heavy heart, collected the girls from school and had to tell them another white lie which sickened me. Storm was particularly distressed by the news that her Papa was in hospital but watching the Mork and Mindy comedy show meant she'd quickly forgotten.

Pages of medical jargon on Dion's condition were faxed through to Daan; lots of it didn't mean much to me, but it also covered some bothersome childhood issues he'd disclosed that he'd never revealed before. Dion was made explicitly aware of the consequences of continuing his current lifestyle and was advised to stay off alcohol for life. Mood enhancers and brain chemical drugs were prescribed, combined with a few other drugs I'd never heard of; also prescribed for life. I didn't like that. Another assessment was required in four weeks to establish how well he was responding to the medication and whether it needed tweaking or not.

"The patient requires continued treatment. Our investigation will be worthless if he consumes alcohol in the next four weeks of the trials. Should he give in to his addiction within the prescribed four-week period, we will be forced to commit him to six months of confined rehabilitation." Daan read out Dr Gouws's comment.

"He's been off binge-boozing for three years. Those tests haven't revealed the triggers; all they've done is dug up some rather unsavoury bits in his past. That's what I don't like about psychologists. I'm not comfortable with it, Daan. They've also prescribed potentially addictive drugs that have other side effects too. He's already an addict." Daan looked at me thoughtfully but said, "Let's take this first step, Elizabeth. It is important to see how he responds to the medication, and then we can assess how he is after the one-month trial. We need to give it a chance; cases like Dion are not solved overnight."

"Okay, but there's something I don't fully understand. Is it being suggested that none of this behaviour is Dion's fault?"

"No, no, that's not what they are suggesting at all. Dion is in full control of his faculties; alarmingly so. He controls precisely what he wants to be in control of, and that's what makes him calculatingly lethal. Unfortunately, you are his primary victim. Although people like him believe there is nothing wrong with them or their emotional state, they need help on a grand scale, so promise me not to go doing the woman thing and feel guilty about anything." I smiled and nodded although not feeling guilty was difficult for me.

"All you have to do now is to encourage Dion to keep up with his medication and stay off all liquor so we can get the best results."

"I'll do what I can," I said, looking down at the floor – I was convinced.

The month of medication and no alcohol went better than I expected. Dr Gouws still recommended three months in rehabilitation, and to our mutual amazement, Dion agreed - this was what we needed to go through to stay 'dry' forever and on an emotionally stable future; he even packed his suitcase and was admitted to the drug and alcohol Rehabilitation Centre in Welkom without any force or forceful persuasion.

On the drive home, I wondered why on earth they, whoever *'they'* were, had chosen a town like Welkom in which to establish a rehabilitation centre. It had a flat, dreary, dusty, dull landscape and, like most mining towns, was like Liquorice Allsorts, with diverse people gathered from around the world and generally, they were hardened drinkers. The positives and negatives of the city aside, if confining Dion to a rehabilitation centre worked and I got my *real* husband back, it didn't matter to me where it was.

Neither the kids nor I were permitted to visit Dion for the first month. We waited out the isolation period then set off on a two-hour drive for our first visit 30 days later. Dion appeared to be responding, but during the second month he became increasingly depressed, so his stay was extended. The next time we visited, he didn't want to talk to us. He wasn't even interested in seeing his children and I expressed my concern to the Superintendent who said his condition had been reported to Dr Gouws and his medication adjusted. I didn't like what I saw. I feared they were turning him into a prescription drug-addict too.

Dion came home at the end of the fourth month, depressed and unusually subdued. I finally managed to get him to talk to me about what went on in rehabilitation, and the stories were grim (if he was telling the truth.) Over the following weeks, his mood improved a fraction, but for several months after being discharged, it remained unchanged.

Shopping in town one day, I happened to bump into a social worker who'd worked with Dion while he was in rehab and who was often on duty when the children and I visited. We greeted each other, then she casually asked if I was still with him. I nodded the affirmative.

"Leave him," she snapped venomously.

"Why would I want to do that? I'm not into kicking a dog when it's down," I replied. I hadn't liked the girl much when I'd met her at the rehab, and I liked her less now as she rudely continued.

"If I were you, I'd get out now before he kills you. It's just a matter of time, and if it's not you he kills, you can guarantee he will molest one of your daughters. Let me tell you, I've never met such an evil beast in my life; that man is subhuman."

I was so flabbergasted all I could do in response to her words was to glare at her but the element of truth in what she had said had already penetrated my brain and stuck itself to the frontal lobe. When I did finally respond, I surprised myself by loyally defending Dion when he'd not earned it or deserved it and she ranted on as to why I should leave the union as soon as possible.

"I'll be the judge of that," I snapped at her finally. I desperately wanted to get away from her quickly. Her issues with Dion had nothing to do with me; or did they? As I walked away, I heard her say, "stupid woman," leaving me asking myself a string of new questions.

There was no denying her words shook me more deeply than I wanted to admit. I also knew that while Dion had been in rehab, she would have seen the worst of his character. This was my justification, but despite knowing that, I was indeed, deeply rattled.

CHAPTER TWENTY

After living for years with someone who could morph into a terrifying freak in moments, I was close to burnout and had to finally concede Dr Gouws was right.

Perhaps even the vicious carer from rehab had been right - he was evil, or was he? The sensible part of me was telling me it was time to make radical changes again. My intuition was telling me he had a mental illness that was still misunderstood but that afternoon, I made up my mind and announced my intentions to Dion as soon as he walked through the door, and before he had time to head to the fridge. I even neglected to say hello in case my train of thought and intention was interrupted.

"It's all over for me, Dion, your drinking, character shifting and the bullshit that tumbles out of your mouth has finally come to an end. I want a divorce!" I blurted at him, suspending his calculated journey to the fridge.

"You want what?" he asked with an expression of shock, temporarily delaying the well-worn passage to his favourite piece of furniture - the fridge. 'How could he be shocked?' I wondered. The children had had enough of it too. Our few short years of bliss had ended and, as far as I could see, we were not going back to that beautiful place in the foreseeable future, if ever. He cared only about himself and had successfully eroded *my* self-belief, murdered my self-confidence to the point where I was suffering severe bouts of depression and felt myself spiralling down toward a nervous breakdown which Amelia had warned would happen. It was time to listen to the threads of *me* that were left. Someone else could work out his mental health issues, as it was time to end the combat with my inner saboteur; we'd been fighting for years. I had to stop bluffing myself that Dion would change and that I was the catalyst that could help him make those changes.

The girls had listened to more aggressive verbal abuse and angry threats of physical violence than any child should ever hear. They'd seen their father so drunk he had no control over his faculties; it broke my heart. I needed to get them away from him. I didn't want them to hate and despise him. Miraculously, they still loved him, and I wanted to protect the purity of his children's unconditional love; I envied it because I understood it. He could be so easy to love but sadly, the impact he'd already had would carry into adulthood and become part of their baggage and contribute to their emotional imperfections.

Dion seemed impervious to guilt. His love was a dangerous dependency. Love had a different meaning to Dion, even toward his children, and their love for their father was becoming more diluted. So, before it was all but gone, I felt it my duty to remove them from the unhealthy environment they'd been exposed to off and on. (more on than off.)

Dion had never physically hurt the girls; he adored them in his own way; he seldom disciplined them - that was my job; Dion had no idea about boundaries and self-discipline and certainly couldn't teach his children about them. It was his indifference that was perhaps more eroding and hurtful, and they hated the way he treated me, apart from being terrified of him when his mood changed. I knew and accepted that their experiences with him thus far would have an impact on their thoughts and actions in the future, but it was time to limit the possibility of further damage to them and/or me. Vivienne was not the bubbly child she used to be. Storm was a stronger character, but she'd had enough. There was simply no point in living this illusion anymore.

"Don't leave me, Liefie," he pleaded pathetically, having quickly processed what I'd said, understanding what it meant for him (a selfish knee-jerk reaction). Knowing I meant it, he whimpered, "pleeeease."

Bittersweet emotion may have been tugging at him, but I'd long forgotten what it felt like to be overwhelmed by sympathy for him. His pleading just made me feel sick, angry and disappointed.

"Oh, come on, Dion, you've had so many chances. We've been over this path so many times it's now boring. It is **over**, get it into your head now that it is not blurred by your imaginary life support system; alcoholic bliss."

"Please, my skat," he begged again, which only made me feel more contempt. "How many times have you promised to stop all your bullshit? I give you a chance, try and help, and you abuse that too. And, how often have you dumped the blame on the children and me? We don't deserve it." He looked at me with a sad expression I didn't want to acknowledge as genuine. I went on now I had his undivided, sober attention.

"The amount of money you have wasted on booze is staggering; it could have paid off the plot. I can't remember when you last made any meaningful financial contribution to anything other than the bottle store and the pubs." I could feel ugly resentment starting to ooze out of my mouth and I stopped it going further; I wasn't in the mood to regurgitate all that crap, knowing it would just trigger a nasty reactive fire within him; besides, I could see he'd gone into shut down; what I was saying was not penetrating. The curtain of harsh truth was now drawn.

"Give me another chance, please, Liefie?" he begged again, putting on his best quivering voice, yet in the past, he'd not even had the good grace to break a sweat when screwing me over, leaving me to foot the bills, protect our children from their psychological woes as a result of his despicable behaviour and keep on working. There was no denying I felt a huge loss and a pang of genuine sadness, but there was a sense of relief that blended well with my decision.

The following day, I filed for divorce. The papers were served a week later, and despite what I'd told myself, I was devastated. I couldn't ditch the feeling that I'd failed him in some way, which my mother and William found absurd and said so.

No more jokes, no more piano lessons, no more singing, no more of the man who could be a darling; all a distant memory, as I couldn't fight the monsters that consumed him any longer.

My work kept my mind busy, and Derek's kind words of encouragement helped soothe the rocky road; he and my colleagues got me through the painfully tricky weeks that followed.

"The storm will pass, Elizabeth, it always does, then the skies of your life will clear, and you will look up and see only sunshine." The hand-written words in a 'congratulations' card colleagues had got for me; profound words indeed, and reading them over and over, I realised how much they'd all been a part of the tragedy with me. How fortunate I was to have a boss that grounded me. Relief was what I was feeling now. Guilt was no longer annoying me, sitting on my shoulder, shouting at me, 'you should do, you should have.' At last, I felt a surge of renewed hope flood through my soul. The birthing of an overwhelming gratitude for the internal strength born of past difficulties I'd learned and grown from. The road ahead would be tough on my own, but it would be worth it.

It felt amazing to be standing firm in the world by myself.

I couldn't contain the excitement bursting in Storm and Vivienne since telling them we were spending the December holidays with Ouma. We packed our bags a day earlier than the official end of term, piled Splodge and our bags into the car and headed for Brandfort. Mom's house was filled with their laughter; those wonderous, uninhibited sounds neither of us had heard for a long time. A few days with Mom to begin the holidays, then we shipped ourselves across to be with William and the family on the farm for a week.

I hardly saw the girls during that week. They discovered the mysteries of nature under the watchful eyes of tens of loving staff following them everywhere; they were never alone, but I was. I spent that week soaking up the timelessness of nature I missed so much, allowing its incredibly pure energy to earth me, rejuvenating what had become a rather battered soul. As hard as I tried, no amount of persuasion could get Mom to come with us, sadly. The attack had shattered every strand that had made up her life and love of the farm. The trauma was too great. Nothing could fill the void since being forced to leave her beloved land, whose earth she carried in her heart and soul, but there was no way she could summon the courage to go back though we all knew it was what she needed to do. After a refreshing week on the farm, we livened up her life again as the girls got stuck into making Christmas decorations from tree seed pods, grasses and other natural things we'd gathered from the farm and used to decorate Mom's house, just as I'd done as a child.

Dion didn't bother to call the girls on Christmas Day, nor did he send any gifts, and though I appreciated Christmas was not about gifts, the girls didn't. Mom was our Christmas cheer as we were hers until Vivienne shattered the cheery mood while they ripped the paper off their presents Mom had placed beneath the tree.

"Papa playing the piano with us, and….and, singing with us, oh, and…. oh yes and, remember, 'member… how we used to tease Papa with a mouse," she squeaked with mirth, then whispered, "I miss Papa, and he's forgotten us, Mama."

Mom and I looked at each other, our hearts dissolving like soap left in hot water. I struggled not to allow the tears to form that stung the back of my eyes. Storm stepped in, rescuing us from response. As quickly as the sad moment was upon us, it had gone again, and the two of them launched into reciting stories of chasing after Dion while holding a precious, albeit terrified little field mouse that they'd found in the vegetable garden in the palms of their hands. Petrified of rodents of any sort, Dion took off to loud guffaws from the girls and as more stories came tumbling out, their voices got louder and sillier as they imitated their father, collapsing in a heap on the floor, laughing hysterically, the sadness lost in the moment as only children can do.

The holidays passed too quickly, and soon it was back to the routine of daily life. Only this time it was all different; we were living with Mom in Brandfort. Getting to work from Mom's to Bloemfontein was awkward and expensive until I located a lift club. The girls were now at school in Brandfort and between Mom and Miriam, they took care of that responsibility for me.

On the day of the divorce hearing, I took my car and nervously headed to the courts. It was the end of January. Dion had not contacted the children yet. I felt edgy and uncertain about meeting him in the courts, but the verdict was that Dion was to remain living on the plot. The courts awarded fifty percent ownership of it to me, which ignited Dion into a blaze of crimson fury. He was further ordered to pay alimony for the girls, school fees for them both and they were to be added to his medical insurance scheme immediately. I'd won a battle, but not the war. Visitation rights would only be granted once it was proven he was no longer dependent upon alcohol and *not* until then.

I was overjoyed, in fact, so happy I felt like having a few drinks myself and partying all night. It felt so good to see him squirm with the realisation that responsibility was being imposed upon him by the law.

But it wasn't long after the divorce hearing that I learned more of the horrors that lurked below the surface of a psychopath sociopath and had to visit Dr Gouws. After leaving his consulting rooms, armed with his advice, I headed down to the police station and placed a restraining order against Dion. The duty constable handed me over to some other disinterested law enforcement officer who wasn't particularly empathetic or helpful, but I got it done and vented my frustrations with Mom that evening after the kids had gone to bed.

"They have no idea the perils of being closely associated with a psychopath, or is it because most black men here treat their wives with such disdain anyway, they can't understand why us white people demand more respect? I'm gatvol." (had enough, in Afrikaans)

It was at times like these I hated Dion Du Toit.

"Did the police suggest other ways that you could be protected?" Mom asked.

"They don't give a shit, Ma, if the truth be told. They informed me it is not a criminal offence that Dion can drive up and down the street shouting abuse at me. It's so embarrassing that I want to die, but it's not a crime. The worst is, there's no alternate route to take to the office. The cops tell me he must become a public nuisance before they can step in and act. Just proves that we women don't matter in this man's world. I can't see how the restraining order offers me any protection, but it's what Dr Gouws suggested I do, and I don't want him to think I am ignoring his advice because if I do, it may bounce back and hit me. It's a waiting game, we know that. I am to wait for him to hang himself, so to speak, for there is no doubt he will break the law, it's just a matter of time, then the police will step in." I sighed hopelessly, feeling beaten again. "In my mind, he's already broken the law by causing endless traffic jams during morning rush hour. It's chaos, Ma, but I'm going to follow instructions and see what happens."

Mom swallowed her last mouthful of coffee, patted her lips with a tissue and sighed. She wasn't convinced the advice was going to support me and I could see she was concerned for my safety.

"The traffic gets blocked for at least 10 minutes while he yells obscene and belittling abuse at me. It starts from the point I'm dropped off – yes, he discovered that, all the way to the office."

"I'm worried, Elizabeth. Let me see if Jannie Pienaar will get involved. Bloem is out of his jurisdiction, but you never know." Mom suggested.

Jannie Pienaar was the station commander in Brandfort who'd actively tracked down Mom's attacker after the event. He also had a soft spot for my mother. I'd always hoped it might come to something, but it didn't. He'd said she could call on him if she ever needed help.

"Thank you, Mom. I need someone of authority to step in. What's amazing is all the other drivers sit on their horns, hooting at him to move on and he ignores them. I'm sure he gets a perverse sense of satisfaction by pissing everyone off, though embarrassing me is his first goal, especially as he knows I am helpless to change the situation. His wearing-down tactics at play. What is another worry is, his drinking buddies are half the police force!"

"No one will ever work out the thoughts that go through that man's mind, my dear. That's proven." Mom said, graciously voicing her guarded opinion.

The following day was the straw that broke the camel's back for me. No guilt, no love, no sympathy or empathy, only a deep loathing so intense I changed direction and marched to the Central Police Station instead of my office and raised hell. The policeman on duty was enjoying the moment, watching me lose my temper. The urge to slap the patronising look right off his face was teetering on the brink of becoming a reality and my palms tingled with desire, but I managed to control myself, even though he was blatantly goading and offending me. I let rip verbally instead.

"I took out a fucking restraining order against the bastard. You do not know how dangerous this man can be!" I yelled at him.

"Yes, Mrs Du Toit, we understand," came the automated and uninterested response.

"No, you don't," I yelled louder. "If you did, you would have done something to stop him, like being at the scene to witness what happens to the morning traffic during rush hour, let alone what I have to endure."

"Mrs Du Toit, shouting at me is the same as your husband shouting at you, it does not constitute a crime even though it is unpleasant." He'd momentarily disarmed me, but I wasn't backing down.

"Don't try that on me," I spat with anger and resentment, but I knew I was getting nowhere.

"The man is a certified psychopath. If anything happens to me, the blood will be on your hands. I'm going to go to a higher authority." I turned and left him to ponder my words, but I actually had nothing else to say.

As I expected, Dion was waiting for me the next day, and just as before, he drove alongside me at walking speed, baiting me, yelling, to anyone who could hear, the ghastliest accusations and disgusting comments, and it took every ounce of resolve to ignore him and keep walking.

"Missing my dick inside you?" he shouted out the car window as loud as he possibly could. I felt my face turn crimson, which was followed by more revolting questions for all to hear.

"How many penises have you had since mine?" The abuse was relentless and headed down toward the police station again, but a man in the queue of cars felt like I did, jerked up his handbrake, flung open his car door and ran to Dion's car, reached in, grabbed him by the throat and lifted him off his seat while yelling at him, their faces inches apart.

"Listen here, fuck-head! I'm warning you, leave that poor woman alone." He dropped the grip he'd had on Dion's shirt front as if discarding a piece of trash and returned to his car, by which time the queue of cars behind him extended for miles back, causing a serious traffic jam.

"Prick!" he shouted as sirens suddenly interrupted the air around us, and four police cars arrived on the scene at last. The degree of congestion was considerable and irritated commuters now leant out their car windows and were shouting, horns were hooting, and it became a cacophony of vehicle sounds mingled with angry shouts from drivers late for work; now the traffic police had their work cut out.

I smiled as I watched them take in the seriousness of what I'd described the day before. Eventually, they cleared the backlog of traffic and took Dion down to the charge office. I watched the charade; it was more fun than going to work this time and for once, I had the last laugh.

The morning harassment stopped but Dion's stalking me didn't. I had to find a cottage to rent and move us from Mom's house. I couldn't put her through any more of the nonsense.

I found a small, quaint, thatched cottage with two big bedrooms, two bathrooms and an open plan living area in Bloemfontein and moved the girls back to their old schools. It was perfect; Splodge thought so too. A high wall on two sides enclosed a small but pleasant garden with tall hedges on the other two sides; it was secure, private and quite adequate for the three of us. That was, until late one April night, when Dion came flying through my bedroom window, showering the entire room with a hail of glass shards, waking me rapidly. I sat bolt upright, confused and terrified and became fully awake in an instant. There he stood, at the foot of my bed, still dressed in his suit with his tie half undone and frighteningly drunk.

"Where is he?" he screamed, frenzied by a dangerous mix of jealousy and alcohol.

"Where is who, Dion? And what the hell do you think you are doing?"

In the soft light from the streetlamp, I could see he was in one of his dangerous moods, and no amount of reasoning was going to penetrate. 'Was I ever going to get away from this man? How the hell had he found us?'

"Theerr bastard youse sleeping whiff." His words rolled out of his mouth with dribbles of alcohol-infused saliva while he scanned every inch of my bedroom suspiciously. It hadn't registered to him that he'd woken me from a deep sleep, and I was alone in my bed the moment he crashed through the window.

"You've gone mad, Dion!" I bellowed, "Go and look for yourself, look through the house. Let the girls see you searching for the mystery man in your mind that is supposed to be living here, then maybe, just maybe, you will realise what idiotic games your mind plays, and you might see for yourself what an arsehole you are!" I shouted, and pulled the bedclothes up under my chin and flicked the glass shards off my bed.

The crash of breaking glass in the dead of night had woken the girls and they rushed to my room barefoot, stopping dead just inside the door as I yelled at them not to come further in, to go back and get their slippers on. The two of them took one look at their drunken father and slunk away. Storm, in her wisdom, quickly ran to the phone to call the police, but before she dialled, all hell broke loose as the neighbour burst through the front door and into a sobbing, terrified Vivienne whom Storm was now trying to soothe.

"The police are on their way," dear old Mr Venter, my wonderful landlord and neighbour, announced.

"What's going on here? I heard a shout and breaking glass?" he asked an embarrassed Storm who didn't know what to say. Dion was still standing at my bedroom door, but he'd heard Mr Venter saying the police were on their way. I heard Dion laugh, an evil laugh that scratched its way up his throat as it escaped into the room and sent those familiar shivers down my spine.

"They're my drinking buddies," he leered toward Mr Venter with ugly intent.

"Don't you dare," I yelled at Dion when I saw what he intended to do to the old man, when suddenly, the cops swooped in and cuffed Dion. It was one moment I wished I'd captured on camera. It was reassuring to know that not all the police were his friends.

"Fuck you." Two policemen ignored his drunken curses while they handcuffed him, but his two devastated daughters stood by and watched, with grim fascination, their father's removal from our cottage and burst into tears simultaneously. So traumatised were they by the events of the night, I kept them home from school and booked a day off myself, having to arrange for a new pane of glass to be fitted to my bedroom window. Dr Gouws was the next person on my list to call and he made preliminary arrangements to have Dion committed. Then I called the police station, and to my horror, learned Dion was no longer in custody.

"Who the hell authorised that?"

"I don't know Ma'am," came the reply.

So, he did have more 'buddies' in the police than I'd thought.

"You'll live to regret this, trust me," I snapped and slammed the phone down.

Dion never did get committed.

We had a few months of peaceful reprieve but guardedly waited for the harassment to begin again as I knew it would.

This time, it started with telephone calls in the middle of the night and all that came through the receiver was heavy breathing, then the phone went dead. I knew it was him. This went on for weeks, always around one o'clock in the morning, purposefully disturbing my sleep patterns, and often the two girls would wake to the ringing sounds of the phone.

Grouchy and exhausted, the three of us concentrated on getting through the days. I'd advised the headmistress. Their teachers were understanding, but a drop in their work and falling asleep in class was hard on them both and children are positively cruel to each other for the teasing started because they couldn't concentrate. As if the phone calls in the dead of night weren't enough for us to endure, he began depositing dead animals at our front door. Storm found the first one - a dead crow. At first, she innocently asked, "Mom, how would a bird manage to die at our front door?"

"I have no idea my darling; weird, isn't it?" I answered, while the hair on my arms stood up, and a cold shiver ran down my spine. That crow hadn't decided our front door was a good place to end its life. A few days later, a dead tabby cat lay at the front door, one that had been dead for a few days and rigor mortis had set in. Its lips had stiffened, curling up and exposing its teeth in a macabre smile and unfortunately, it was Storm who opened the door; this time she knew who'd left the animal at our front door and she screamed, a scream that expressed all her fears, her anger, the terror and revulsion she was feeling in that moment. I pulled Vivienne away from the door and covered her eyes and ears, resulting in another day out of school for both girls. I called the headmistress and wondered whether I should call the police, then decided not to. Still shaking with anger, I called my brother. To put an end to this, I had to get William involved. None of us could tolerate any more harassment, and I knew the only person in the world that Dion was afraid of was my brother. The hardest part was asking Storm and Vivienne to participate. I didn't want them to feel they had to be dishonest or disrespectful to their father, so I carefully and truthfully explained what my intentions were. They agreed to help, much to my relief, for I was not going to allow Dion to humiliate and terrorise us all again.

William arrived at my cottage an hour before the pre-arranged children's collection time; Dion was supposedly having the girls for the day. It seemed feasible, for they hadn't seen him socially for months; they hadn't wanted to go and still didn't, but Dion didn't know that.

Bang on time, Dion knocked on the door. William was ready for him and flung the door open with such force I thought it would fall off its hinges and he sunk his fist into Dion's chest. That first punch knocked him backwards, the next blow rearranged his nose and dentures as he squirmed on the floor clutching his broken, bleeding face, begging William not to hurt him anymore but William had seen enough of how Dion had hurt us and nothing was going to stop him; he pulverised Dion then hauled him to his feet like a useless puppet, dragged him to his car, opened the door and hurled him headfirst across the front seats where his beaten body lay limp - his hearing was still intact.

"No more calls late in the night. No more dead birds and cats deposited at their front door. No more harassment. Let this be your last warning, Dion Du Toit. Behave yourself, or you will never see Elizabeth or your children again. Do you hear me, you useless fucking drunk?"

Dion didn't answer but shifted his torso, then William walked back into the house.

"Has Papa gone now?" Storm asked her uncle William.

"Not yet, Storm, Oom William has given Papa something to think about; he will probably leave shortly." Storm nodded, innocently confused but accepting of what she'd been told.

"Did he promise not to bother us again?" Storm needed a bit more reassurance.

"Yes, he did, and I hope this time Papa keeps his promise." Storm nodded again; wisdom shone through that innocent look of hesitant acceptance; she wasn't sure her father could ever stay away. Vivienne was sitting on the edge of the sofa in stunned silence, suffering her silent trauma as I squeezed her hand gently and suggested Coco Pops for breakfast and a home-made milkshake. William called me to one side and whispered, "If Dion's car is still there in half an hour, call an ambulance." I nodded, but my eyes were widened by his comment.

William returned to the farm, knowing as I did, the beating served to give me time to act.

Slowly, carefully, Dion pulled himself up, then holding onto the steering wheel, manoeuvring himself into the driving position he slowly disappeared down the road.

Thankfully, the girls didn't witness the beating; they never knew their beloved Oom William had even touched their Papa, they thought he'd just warned him, and we left it at that. When William got home, he called on Jannie Pienaar for some advice on what to do next if the harassment continued. If Dion laid a charge of assault with intent, how were we to respond?

"Shit, William, he could have you for attempted murder."

"Ha, let him try, then I will fucking kill the doos, (idiot) it would be worth it." Jannie roared with laughter, knowing how William felt about Dion.

The next time Dion saw the girls, collecting them from school, was four months after William had pulverised him. There had been no charges laid against William. Dion had asked if he could take them to the movies – now it was hours later, and they still weren't home. This time the police flew into action, and when they found them, both the girls were in a terrible state.

"Mama," Storm cried hysterically, "Papa locked us in the car and drove scarily fast, telling us he'd kill us all if we didn't agree to force you to go back to him." Their little bodies were wracked with sobs, both deeply distressed. I went cold.

"Oh my God, what next?" I wailed. Thankfully, the police got to them before disaster did.

Dion was arrested and jailed.

The following day, Dr Gouws called me after visiting Dion in jail, and what he suggested appalled me.

"I can't possibly do that. You have got to be joking, Doctor. You need to come up with a better suggestion, I am afraid," I said with finality.

"Mrs Du Toit, you must understand the longer you are apart, the more dangerous he is going to get; that's guaranteed. He will feel nothing for taking his life and your daughters with him. He will do anything to prove to you he cannot live without you. You are in grave danger, my dear."

"Well then, have the bastard committed. That's what you promised last time," I snapped back at him.

"Mrs Du Toit, we can do that, but it is a complicated process. What you need to grasp is - he will come out again, then you will be in greater danger than you are now and that I can guarantee. If we commit him, it is unlikely he would be in for more than six months; he understands the system intimately and knows how to work it to his advantage. You, of all people, know that. You are his *possession;* he is obsessed with you; dangerously so. I can guarantee he's not taking his medication, though he swore he was, but as we both know, he is a particularly good liar. He admitted to drinking heavily again, so even if he were taking his medication, the alcohol would obliterate any good the drugs might have done him."

I cringed as the doctor's words sank in. I couldn't answer, I couldn't agree; I didn't know what to do. An uncomfortable silence settled between us, then I remembered.

"In the divorce court, he was warned that he would not see his children until he was dry. That is contempt of court. Surely, we can stop him from seeing them again?" I asked, clinging to whatever I could.

"He knows the law, Mrs Du Toit. It is how these people operate. Eventually, he will commit a serious crime; that's what we want to prevent."

I understood his underlying message, but I couldn't bear the thought of living with Dion again, let alone being anywhere near him.

"I have arranged for him to come in and see me. He will be brought here cuffed and in a police car. They are keeping him in jail for a few days to give him time to think about the consequences of his actions. He might realise that not all the cops here are crooked and support what he does."

Sobs rose out of nowhere suddenly - I couldn't control them, but I managed to stammer, "I can't do this Dr Gouws, I just can't."

"Give yourself time to process it all, Mrs Du Toit; you have a few days. When I meet with him, I will tell him that we have spoken. I'm prescribing different medication and will offer him two choices; get back on his medication and give up drinking to get you back or be committed to an asylum for two years. Are you happy with that?" he asked, but no words could leave my mouth. Then he said, "Just a thought, would you consider meeting with him here after his first appointment?"

"How will that help? In front of you, Doctor, he's charming and sweet. He will promise to do anything for the girls and me, you know that. I've said it before, and I'll repeat it now, it's what you and everyone else doesn't see that scares the shit out of me, to put it bluntly."

"It's worth a try, Mrs Du Toit. I'll leave it with you."

I called him back after twenty-four hours and agreed to meet with him and Dion.

CHAPTER TWENTY-ONE

Twenty-four hours of sleeplessness, tossing and turning, fighting with myself, sweaty breakouts, shivers and sobs filled my night - somehow, I had to prevent Dion from coming back into our lives, no matter the circumstance. I skipped over the nitty-gritty but asked the girls how they felt about having their Papa back with us, living as a family again. Neither gave me an answer; neither needed to, their expressions were enough.

I sat at my desk in a daze, staring blindly out the door, trying to process the events and information I'd been forced to address. I'd run through the suggested details from Dr Gouws with Derek; he was at a loss as to what to advise me too.

"My wonderful mother always said to me, when life is not going your way, you have to see the funny side of it. Well, I'm sure when she said that, she didn't know another human being like Dion existed. I cannot find anything funny about any of this crap."

"You have my sympathy, my dear. No-one could find anything funny about what Dion has done to you. He's a head case," Derek said as the telephone rang and I leapt, realising how edgy and vulnerable I felt.

"Hello," I said with a shaky voice. It was Dr Gouws; he'd spoken to Dion.

"Dion is happy for you to join the conversation. The appointment is tomorrow morning at nine."

I felt queasy.

"I will be there, Doctor." I put the phone down, crushed and defeated. It had become the way of my life, I felt cursed. If only I had answers other than terminating his life or mine. The rest of the day passed in a blur. I couldn't focus; I couldn't concentrate; everything was a jumble; I was numbed and confused.

The following morning, I arrived at the doctor's rooms fifteen minutes early and was sitting reading a magazine in the waiting room, when Dion sauntered in.

"Hello!" he greeted me with a triumphant smile; I nodded; he sat down beside me and smiled again.

An hour of what I can only describe as an 'interrogation' took place in Dr Gouws's office. I expressed my opinion without reserve, my fears and uncertainties, and though I sensed Dion's annoyance by my blatant honesty, outwardly, he was calm.

I was not going back to live with Dion, not now; he had to prove himself first, then I may consider it because the girls had suggested, if Papa went back to how he was at the plot, they'd agree to be a family again and if we all had to go to court for Dion to hear his children saying that, that's what I was happy to do.

"One last try, Mama," Storm had said. Had it been my decision only, I would have never considered it.

Dion agreed to everything, of course, taking his meds, being monitored, no more drinking, not a drop. He'd already been put on new medication - if he consumed even as much as a teaspoon of alcohol, it would make him so ill he would be put in hospital. He'd agreed to six months of close monitoring.

I knew he could do it; he'd done it before for three years, but then what?

That evening, the girls and I curled up on the couch together and I explained, skimming over the main details of what Dr Gouws had suggested, and they both agreed Papa had to prove himself first.

"Is Papa able to change?" Storm asked, thoughtfully, with wisdom beyond her years and as she said it, I wished Dr Gouws could have heard the truth spoken from a child's view of Dion's behaviour. Storm had read her father like a book, and they, too, were suffering the uncertainties of living with their sociopathic father again.

"We can only hope so, my precious. Let's see what happens over the next few months." Vivienne remained silent all evening, refusing to talk, which worried me; she found it difficult expressing what she was feeling; by closing up it was easier for her to manage her insecurities. Mom was disgusted that Dr Gouws had even suggested a reunion of any sort, and William was outraged. However, that didn't diminish the fact they were concerned for my safety, so they remained as my rock, supporting me through the most awkward and trying decision of my life - stay single with the kids and risk our lives, or go back and pray this time, under Dr Gouws's guidance, he'd be cured.

Six months later we were back as a family, living on the plot once more. I was naturally more guarded than the two girls; their little thoughts were more focussed on being let loose with the space they'd once enjoyed than worrying about what their father might do. Shortly after the move back to Dion and living on the plot, Derek retired. I was heartbroken, and though he'd been talking about it for nearly a year, I wasn't ready to release his solidarity in my life; but it was an obvious time to make a change to my career. A few days later, I gave in my notice and decided to take a month off before looking at what to do next.

I'd been home for two weeks, being blissfully lazy and enjoying some vital quality time with the girls, then Dion took some leave too.

Life together was still a bit raw and touchy. We didn't avoid each other but it was going to be a massive effort for me to rebuild a foundation of shattered respect and trust. The crumbly bits of what remained as cement to the relationship were the girls, and I'd promised them I would do whatever it took to make sure they were safe.

It took several more months to gradually become more comfortable in each other's company.

Dion began to open himself up a little more and I became less cranky. Dion found vulnerability difficult but he was working on it and began to share snippets of deep inner secrets which provided me with a tiny glimpse into what had moulded him from the tragedy of his childhood. It was complicated, he was complicated, but it left me with no doubt; in his peculiar way, he loved his two beautiful girls, and he adored me.

He was still following Dr Gouws' guidelines religiously, taking his medication, and the tension and stress eased considerably. I was guarded and a bit sceptical, but under the circumstances, we were making progress. At the onset of this trial period, I had put in a few clearly defined boundaries and gave Dion a new affectionate name - 'Gogga'. This is a word with multiple descriptions in Afrikaans, but in this instance, I used it affectionately to describe Dion's somewhat devious character.

We had all agreed that only kind, loving and positive words were to become a part of our daily conversation, and the transformation seemed to be working. The girls were doing well at school again, and with faith in their father's change, their self-confidence grew to what it had once been.

Storm had a powerful singing voice which, with Dion's careful coaching, was developing beautifully. Coaching his daughter was the highlight of his days. As it always had, music settled him better than any drug, including alcohol. He was proud of Storm, as I was. Her voice showed a lovely, sensitive, gentile side to her character when she got lost in the music as she practised.

None of Dion's past misdemeanours affected him; he'd brushed them off now and found it enormously difficult to understand why I was still guarded and cautious after all this time. I had to remind him I'd only been home for a few months. I was ready to seek out a new job, for I felt isolated on the plot.

Amelia called often to find out how the kids and I were doing, but she refused to visit the plot and, when she was transferred back to Bloemfontein, we'd meet in town and as always had. During the first week of my search for another job, Dion tarnished the status quo by asking me to marry him again. I declined each request, though it didn't deter his resolve in attempting to convince me it was what we should do. He went on patiently begging until finally, nearing the end of our third year back together, with the children older and secure, I felt it was safe to say he'd proved himself and I gave in, convinced our roller coaster life was finally over.

We married again at the Home Affairs offices without a wedding party. Derek agreed to be with us as a witness for William had refused, and Mom stayed at home.

The girls excitedly witnessed the proceedings, happy we were marrying again, although they were disappointed that our 'wedding' didn't have the typical trappings and was over in fifteen minutes, and our dress was smart but nothing fancy. No youthful, romantic swirl this time around. It was a beautiful sunny day; our moods were as bright and happy. With the formalities complete, we walked out of the offices holding hands, feeling optimistic, while the girls bounced their way down the steps ahead of us.

Standing on the last step, Dion turned to me; his sexy, beautiful dimple set deep in his chin, the twinkle in his mysterious brown eyes shining like the sun, and as mesmerising, just as they had been on our first wedding day many years before. Holding both my hands, he captured my gaze; it was a special moment, until he said, very quietly,

"Now you belong to me again!"

I froze; a fearful chill ran down my spine, as it had so many times before. The monster was back as he bent forward and kissed my hand.

The kiss of death?

Happy smiles, which moments before had spread across my face, evaporated in the warm sunshine and withered away like a flower in the desert.

CHAPTER TWENTY-TWO

It was hard to believe the scoundrels were back – the whole lot, with carte blanche to do as they pleased, now I'd signed my life away. I was their legal possession once more. They owned me, each one of those complicated personalities lurking behind that handsome face. I'd never known another human like him - the change happened in an instant. There, on the steps, in front of my eyes, I watched him morph once more from a loving, sober companion of three years, into a venomous ogre. It was this distinctive switch that beggared belief, and that's what I'd tried so hard to explain to Dr Gouws and everyone else who'd dealt with him all these years. No-one could understand it, not even me. I kept up pretences for the sake of the girls and then, to my utter horror, discovered I was pregnant. I didn't let anyone know, including Dion, until one evening when he was particularly smarmy and intolerable.

"Cut the crap, Gogga; I don't need the window dressing. Why did Phillip call you?" I asked. The two brothers were not close. Dion had damaged their relationship years back but I sensed there was something unsavoury being born.

"Well…………" he paused, trying to work out what was the best way to lie to me now he was aware I knew him better than he knew himself. Spread out across the couch in much the same way Splodge typically lay, owning the space as only he could, but without oozing the sincerity that Splodge had, he said, "Phillip suggested we sell up here, move back to Bethlehem and buy the Elna sewing machine franchise."

I stared at him in total disbelief.

"I hope you said no. What do you know about sewing machines anyway?" I asked, while dipping a rusk into my coffee; he purposefully didn't answer.

"Sell up here and buy a sewing machine agency with the money from our home? Are you out of your tiny little mind?" As I asked the question, the girls burst into the lounge before Dion could find an appropriate answer. Soaking wet hair flying everywhere, their bodies wrapped in bath towels, they stopped, noticing a rise in my voice and a change to the tone and their playful look instantly dissolved. They looked at each other, back to me, decided all was good and continued the chase, shrieking with happiness; the sound tugged at me. How long was it going to last now?

Dion went on trying to convince me that his brother's idea was a good one, between interruptions of hysterical laughter from Storm and Vivienne, until Dion couldn't take their merriment a moment longer and reprimanded them. In seconds, the room was quiet, the spell of the 'happy mood' broken, and they disappeared hastily to their bedroom; I followed, reassuring them Papa wasn't angry and then went back to the sitting room.

"Then what, Dion? Back to renting a house? Not a chance……," I sighed, my legs curled up underneath me with the weight of the world on my shoulders once more.

"Who is going to run the business anyway, Dion?"

"We'll run it together, build it up, sell it and buy another house in two years." Dion smiled confidently.

"Besides, you won't be working, and it will give you something to focus on," he offered enthusiastically. I couldn't fault that, but reality was a different story.

"That's not the point, Dion. Why put the girls through this? It means a change of schools, disrupting their lives again, removing them from their friends at a crucial time and I don't want to move from here. It's a healthy environment for the girls to grow up in and we own it."

Dion was becoming agitated with my fierce resistance to his suggestion. He didn't mention the idea again for a few days, but I also knew that when Dion went silent, it was dangerous; he was planning something devious. I was right; when he got home, he announced he was buying the shop – no regard for the way either of the children would feel - I erupted, barely able to articulate my thoughts into words.

"Does the safety, security and welfare of your family ever enter your mind when you make decisions? Let alone having discussions with me? I'll buy you out, the girls and I will stay put, and our next child will have the pleasure of growing up with space around him like every little boy should."

Dion's eyes narrowed. I should have told him earlier. Delaying it those few days may have been the wrong decision. I watched the colour drain from his face, turning his complexion from a healthy brown to a pale, sickly grey. For the first time in a long time, my statement left him without an instant retort.

"What? Are you…, are you pregnant?"

"Yes, five months along and it's a boy, from what they can see."

"Why didn't you tell me before?"

"Perhaps I should have, Dion, but you've been so wrapped up in your own life again you scarcely notice we exist, let alone my changing shape, with or without clothes on; now you want to disrupt our lives again. I can live without you Dion, you know that, with two children, or three. You go on and run your little shop with your brother; I want no part of it."

He sat for a moment, shaking his head, looking at his feet

"Why didn't you tell me you were pregnant?" he asked again, quite perturbed by the news.

"Because you don't give a shit about us, Dion, that is why I never told you. All we are is a make-believe anchor for you and you hold us to it. There is only one person that matters in your life, and that's you. Cast your mind back to the trouble I had with contraceptives and recall the doctor telling us that because I'd been on the last contraceptive for so long, I'd be sterile. Early on in this pregnancy, I didn't think anything of the missed periods."

"You and the family will move with me, Elizabeth." He'd not taken in a word of what I'd just said.

"Not a chance. This was your decision; you go ahead without us."

A very slight flicker of concern showed on his face; my threats weren't idle ones, and he knew that. He also knew it wouldn't bother me if he never met his son – that, I hoped, was my trump card.

"I will run the shop successfully, Elizabeth, I promise," he tried to redeem himself. "You know I can't live without you."

"It was your rash decision, so now you are going to have to learn to live without us, Dion."

"Don't you think I am fucking capable of running the shop successfully?" he asked, angrily.

"Quite frankly, no I don't, and promises – well, I'm sorry, they mean nothing to you, so don't bother making any. Your history is in sales, (and I wanted to say steeped in lies) not retail. Running your own business requires commitment and responsibly, neither of which you own." That struck a sensitive chord. He walked out of the house, slamming the front door defiantly. Though I had no idea where he was going, I had a nasty hunch.

The next day he called to say he'd signed the deal; he'd sold the plot.

The bank loan I'd secretly applied for was approved twenty-four hours too late.

He'd caught me in his net again.

CHAPTER TWENTY-THREE

Storm and Vivienne were devastated by the news and sobbed for days. Not even the announcement of a growing baby brother lightened their mood; mine was as bleak. I wasn't looking forward to the rest of the pregnancy; he'd doused any excitement too. How I had wanted our little boy to grow up with the freedom his sisters had experienced for six years of their lives. It was where little boys should grow up, but he'd snookered me again. The yin and yang of my life couldn't find a harmonious link.

The thought of leaving our wonderful plot, the place I'd turned from a dry, dusty shell to an oasis paradise, broke my heart. The children were secure and happy, and after pouring so much work and love into it, it meant the world to me. The mere thought of having to say goodbye to it when the school term ended was unbearable heartache for the three of us. Much to Dion's disgust, paying out my half of the property and his part of the franchise left him with very little. Phillip was a silent partner and insisted he remain in his secure job and living in his own house in Bloemfontein.

On the 9th of December, we made our way, with shattered hearts, to Bethlehem. Kneeling, with their tummies pressed against the backrest, the girls quietly sobbed as I drove slowly down the road and with every metre we covered, my heart was being slowly ripped out of my chest as we gradually left the property we adored, for good.

The girls waved sadly to Miriam, who stood watching us go, crying into her apron that she'd lifted to her eyes until eventually, she was out of sight. How I wished Dion had been there to witness the heartache he caused us - except it wouldn't have moved him.

"Mama, why can't Miriam come too?" Vivienne sniffled as she turned away from the back window and sat down.

"Why did Papa do this?" Storm asked angrily, at the same time, her bottom lip quivering with the pain of her loss. Both girls had walked every inch of the property in tears, storing memories that morning, and hugging Miriam and begging her to come with us, just as they had pleaded with me to stay on the plot. Their lives were falling apart around them; their beloved home had been sold and they were helpless to change anything, and now as we drove on, emotional exhaustion took its hold on all of us. I turned on the radio, hoping the music would lift the mood.

"Pleeeeeeze go back Mama, please," Vivienne sobbed and tugged at my arm in a desperate attempt to stop this happening. Losing Miriam and their treasured home was agonising.

"We can't, my girl, Papa sold the plot."

Vivienne sat with her arms crossed, pouting. The grief pulling at her as she sobbed, taking deep shuddering breaths while tears poured down her cheeks – all I could do was hope she'd eventually fall asleep.

I'd secretly made a promise to Miriam that I would call her when we settled, but I didn't want to tell the girls in case it never materialised. Just as Vivienne's chest-shuddering sobs were subsiding, Storm said, "I hate Papa."

"So, do I," Vivienne whispered, before fatigue took over and she fell asleep. We arrived in Bethlehem a few hours later, emotionally depleted.

To appease me, or so he thought, Dion had rented a comfortable home in a pleasant suburb on the side of a hill overlooking the town. The town lay sprawled out below us, and the views of the rugged mountains beyond helped lift my dampened spirits a little, but it didn't have the same effect on the girls.

We had our evening meals on the veranda and watched the molten ball of spectacular African sun setting as it melted into the horizon, leaving a delightful palette of vibrant colours in the sky, but not even that put a spark back in the girls, who remained sombre and miserable; all they wanted was to be back in the home they loved.

Compulsory franchise orientation training in Johannesburg for six weeks was something Dion had to attend to ensure that the standards laid out were maintained. With him out the way, I had some quality time with the girls and ran the shop in Dion's absence. To my surprise, it was busier than I'd expected, which was a welcome relief, and I began to feel a little more positive.

Perhaps we could buy another house in two years.

When Dion got back from Johannesburg, he took over again; I was too far into the pregnancy to go on working all day and he needed assistance in the repair division. He employed a man called Bernard, a ruffian alcoholic with a most unpleasant manner whom I didn't approve of, but he had years of experience in sewing machine repairs.

Pieter made his appearance during the evening of the 28th of February, 1984. He was a big boy and I struggled, but the struggles and pain were soon forgotten when I had him in my arms. Dion was ecstatic he finally had a son, and the girls were charmed by their baby brother, smothering him with love and cuddles as often as they could, fighting over who got to him first, who changed him and helped at bath time. Despite the fun with baby brother, the girls were still moody and unhappy; the time was right to contact Miriam; she didn't have another job and shrieked down the phone, promising to be with us in a week.

I didn't tell the girls of Miriam's arrival. It broke my heart seeing them so quiet and depressed, but within a few minutes, Miriam would change that. They scraped their chairs out and plonked themselves down at the table and hardly spoke before lunch.

"Close your eyes; let's say grace," I ordered.

"Aaw, Mom, do we have to?" Vivienne moaned.

"Yes, we do, we have to give thanks for our food."

With their eyes tightly closed, Miriam crept out of hiding and stood beside Storm. I stretched grace out to last fractionally longer and when they opened their eyes, pandemonium broke out as the two girls exploded with delight, bouncing off their chairs, knocking into each other in their haste to wrap their arms around Miriam's ample waist, joy on their little faces once more. Miriam was over the moon to be back and meet our delightful little Pieter; the timing of her return could not have been more perfect - Dion was back on the bottle.

"I do not believe it, Dion, you've just thrown away our home, now you're throwing away any chance of buying another, and running the risk of losing your children and me, again."

"Oh, don't bloody start. Whine, whine, whine. It's all you ever do. I'm also fucking sick of that, you know. I suppose you're going to find me a psychologist in this town too and try and have me committed," he spat with stinging sarcasm.

His reaction was confirmation that, no matter what I did, he was **never** going to change. It was time for me to gather my wits and cut the cord – forever. Dr Gouws and all his advice wasn't worth the monumental effort and sacrifices I'd made.

I found a job and Miriam stepped in as surrogate mother again, a role she played with excellence. She cleaned the shop three times a week, keeping an eye on what Dion was up to, while I filled the position of relief housemother at the Mother Teresa Orphanage. I took the job because I could take Pieter to work with me. The salary wasn't what I was used to, but it was better than nothing, and I still had most of my portion from the plot in savings. I hadn't been at the orphanage long when they offered me the live-in position as House Mother of the group of boys I taught and looked after during the day. The post included a quaint cottage and I was sorely tempted to take it on my own, but I didn't.

Moving to the cottage meant saving the rent, so I accepted. Miriam rented a room close to the orphanage and in the morning, she worked there, and in the afternoon, she worked for us.

Ten wonderful young orphaned teenage boys, their ages ranging from thirteen to seventeen, lived in comfortable, homely surroundings in a large house adjacent to the cottage. Two boys shared a bedroom, there were three bathrooms, a spacious open plan lounge and dining room which led out onto an expansive veranda looking onto manicured gardens. A beautifully equipped kitchen wasn't used by the boys, as meals were prepared in a central kitchen; I decided I'd teach them all to cook too. It was a lovely, homely environment for the boys, who'd had all experienced tragedy in their short lives but despite that, they were polite and respectful to the girls and made settling in next to them worry-free.

They were good lads who soaked up my teachings, proving to be hungry to learn boy stuff like changing light bulbs, attaching plugs to electrical cords, changing car tyres, mending bicycle punctures, using a screwdriver and hammer effectively among the other necessary activities boys of their age like to learn and hadn't been taught. Once they'd perfected some simple boy skills, we moved onto knitting, sewing buttons onto clothing and fixing clothing with tears or where seams had come adrift; these all-important little necessities they grasped quickly and enthusiastically. They enjoyed their knitting so much I managed to persuade the local haberdashery store to donate wool and knitting needles, and we set up an in-house competition to see who could knit the best scarf in the shortest time, with monetary prizes for the best three scarves. Then, I started the cookery classes but in time, all the attention I paid to the boys triggered the nasty, jealous ogre to emerge in Dion and he'd have sudden outbursts of ludicrous resentment toward them. They considered me their adopted mother for no-one else had ever offered them this level of care and guidance but Dion viewed it all with his own brand of twisted thoughts, and the tension began to rub off on us all, especially when he insisted they stop calling me Mama. They became very protective over me, so in an urgent effort to include him, I suggested he get involved too; there were lots of lovely children keen to learn to play our piano and teaching those keen to play would keep him out the pub. The boys responded with enthusiasm, and soon girls and boys from the other houses lined up for lessons and our house became known as the happiest place to be in the orphanage.

A few months later, Miriam called me to one side, telling me I needed to check the shop – "not good," was all she'd said. Curious, I popped down during one lunch hour and was horrified by what greeted me. The shelves were bare of stock and neglected – a business in trouble - and though I was disgusted, I didn't have the energy to care anymore. There was only one solution and that was to get out for good this time.

School holidays started the following week, so I bundled the kids into my car and took off to spend a few days with Mom, who'd recently had a hip replacement. Our stay was cut short when, on the fifth day, I was summoned to return to the orphanage and report to the headmistress's office immediately. I wondered why it was so urgent and prayed nothing had happened to one of my special boys or any of the other orphaned children in the home. I dropped the kids at the cottage and rushed across to the offices.

Standing in the Headmistress's office was reminiscent of my own school days and I smiled at the memory of how terrified we used to be by being summoned to the Head's office, even if no *crime* of naughtiness or disobedience was the reason.

Mrs Venter, the head of the orphanage, was a lovely warm, compassionate woman, but she didn't have a look of warmth about her now. A tense, rather unpleasant atmosphere dominated the room, and I wondered what could have happened that was so bad in just five days.

"Elizabeth...," she began and hesitated, magnifying the uncomfortable atmosphere.

"I am sorry to inform you......" she took a deep breath, "that I have to ask you to resign."

What? I was shocked rigid. Was I hearing her correctly?

"This is very difficult for me, but......um...your husband............" I froze.

"He was caught sexually molesting one of the girls." I stood, feeling the internal tremors begin to shake my entire body.

"Whaaat? Oh God no, no. Who?" I stammered.

"The first night you were away, he was excessively drunk, behaving in a particularly unacceptable manner, which he repeated the following night and he was asked to leave the property if he could not behave while you were away."

'She could have been talking about a child,' I thought.

Shaking my head in shame, I didn't know what to say as I fought a nasty mix of emotions and I couldn't speak.

"I am so sorry, Elizabeth. You are the best housemother we've ever had. We are all devastated."

Nothing could have prepared me for this news. My cheeks were hot with rage and all I wanted to do was castrate the bastard. He didn't deserve to live, in my opinion. Mrs Venter went on, and I almost wished she hadn't, as her words ripped into my heart.

"I am so sorry," she said again, the warmth in her voice returned and touched me deeply. "You have led by example and given the boys more than duty required - we are eternally grateful for that, as I know they are. They will miss you terribly."

I bit down on my bottom lip to prevent myself from sobbing as the grizzly reality rapidly sunk in.

"Oh, my God." I covered my face with my hands, pushing back the tears. "Who was the girl?" I asked in a whisper, at the same time, dreading the answer.

"Moira," Mrs Venter said sympathetically.

"Oh, dear Lord, no, not Moira. Oh, God, I should have known better," I sobbed. "How could he have even considered it? Will there be a court case?" I asked.

Mrs Venter nodded, "She was the girl he was teaching to play the piano, wasn't she?"

"Yes; I feel sick, for it was my suggestion. I hope they lock the son-of-a-bitch up for good and throw away the key. Where is he now?"

"In that shop, I would imagine, my dear, but do not blame yourself."

"I can't help it, Mrs Venter." To think the father of my children had committed this evil deed was beyond redemption. How was I going to explain this to the girls? Do I even dare? Storm was not much younger than Moira. My heart was thumping in my chest.

"How is Moira coping?" I felt an urgent need to go to her, comfort her, hold her. Nausea moved into the pit of my stomach as I thought of her. A young, beautiful, orphaned girl - her innocence being so callously violated in the most insensitive of ways could not be forgiven, I had to make sure of that.

"She was in a terrible state and only found the courage to tell us yesterday. It was rape, though she said, he sweetly coaxed her into exploring her sexuality."

I moaned aloud; I knew just how convincing Dion could be.

"Poor, poor Moira," I whispered, shaking my head, looking into space, my guts in knots. A young girl like Moira would not have known how to cope or say no to his coaxing; agreeing to his persuasions would have been her only way out. I also knew he would have twisted it to make her feel it had been her decision in the end. She'd carry the guilt and the scars; an emotion he carelessly discarded.

"I know how hard this is for you, Elizabeth. Immediate resignation or divorce are your only two options. He is forbidden access to the property. I'm so sorry."

"Yes, of course, I understand," I answered, wanting to run from the world to a place where no feeling existed. Defeated, disgusted, humiliated, angry; I didn't want to feel anymore.

Another divorce was now pending, and this time I would ensure the swine was jailed, but right now, my thoughts were on how to protect my beloved children from the embarrassment and the cruelty their school associates would surely dish out once this humiliating information found its way around the town.

The sordid scandal spread like wildfire, as I knew it would. Everywhere I went, people whispered or avoided eye contact and conversation; that was the natural human part, the sickening struggle was trying to help the girls deal with the cruelty dished out at school.

The disgraceful pig somehow snivelled out of the court case. He paid a handsome mound of cash to some unscrupulous police officer, and the evidence disappeared.

Was there no end to this man's wicked ways?

Just when I thought it couldn't get worse! I never did learn who that someone was in the police force, though I tried. I tried for Moira's sake, I tried for my children's sake but, with evidence destroyed, I was hamstrung.

CHAPTER TWENTY-FOUR

None of us quite knew how to respond to the situation in which we found ourselves. It took the urgent search for a new home and my mother's reassurance that she'd be with us soon to keep going during the dark days when it felt the world was against me. The whirlpool of hardships was trying its best to suck me under. The children were what I had to stay strong for. I longed for the day when I could face the world again without being confronted by the prying, questioning eyes of others, but the beauty of life is that it seemed to give me the strength to draw on somehow, even in the most dire situations and just when I thought there was no hope, change popped in from the most unexpected place; a simple, tatty old piece of furniture changed the course of my life.

I'd found a house to rent, Mom moved to Bethlehem to help me regroup from the recent devastation, being the lifeline who kept me from coming apart at the seams. Mom settled in and we were sitting on the tatty old piece of furniture, commenting on the state of it, while sipping our coffee, discussing the shocking state it was in. I couldn't do anything about it other than chuck a pretty throw over it and then Mom piped up and said, "Why don't you recover it, Elizabeth?"

"Mom!" I exclaimed, laughing. "Don't be absurd; I barely have enough money to feed us and I have never done upholstery before."

"I'll give you the money. We'll take it apart, one chair at a time, and do this last," she said, patting the cushion of the couch she was sitting on. The simplicity and logic of her statement resonated somehow; I could sew and was pretty good at it, so, why not?

"We can cut the pattern from the pieces we undo, sew the new pieces together and see what happens," she chirped. I wasn't sure what to do with the emotion of the moment. The timing of her inspiration could not have been more perfect.

"Ma, you are wonderful. What would I do without you?" The words sounded oddly shallow as they left my lips, but I was deeply inspired.

"It's what mothers do. Look what you have put up with for your children – I think you overlook that, my kind."

She was right. <u>Up to now,</u> I'd navigated my life for everyone else - it was her magic steering me in a new direction. I nodded with a gratitude I couldn't express.

Over the weeks following the Moira rape, I refused Dion access to the kids, wanting nothing more to do with him - ever, then the law turned against me. I was not permitted to deny him access to the children; *he'd committed no crime.* He seemed to get away with the most despicable behaviour at every turn; surely one day he'd have pay for it?

Thankfully, and I say this in this kindest possible way, the girls were so disgusted and ashamed of what their father had done to Moira, *they* refused to see him – the law was forced to consider that.

After Mom's innovative suggestion, I lay in bed, emotionally and physically spent, staring up at the ceiling and trying to summon the freedom to feel charged with excitement, but it wasn't happening - I was too scared to be optimistic - that was my last thought before drifting off to sleep. A flutter of excitement was trying to nudge past the confusion. The challenge of recovering the lounge suite was what I needed - it turned out beautifully.

"Well, my talented daughter," Mom said, looking on, proudly, at what we'd achieved in a few weeks. "Why don't you start your own upholstery business?" I burst out laughing but the tatty old piece of furniture sprouted a brand-new life.

CHAPTER TWENTY-FIVE

No more job hunting for me! *I* was the boss. *I* would write my salary cheque. These and other exciting thoughts were whipping through my mind. I had some savings left and, together with a small loan from Mom, I could launch an upholstery business. I understood the risk, but I was determined to make it work.

I named my business - La Provence Interiors, sounding considerably more upmarket than the humble beginnings that it was. I placed the first small advert in the classified section of our local paper and sent it on its way with a sprinkling of colourful prayers. The response was more than I could ever have dreamed possible and the most liberating, expansive feeling, filled me with hope and a sense of purpose.

Job lot, 001 in my invoice book; re-cover loose cushions for a cane lounge suite. This was my dispatch note to freedom and from that first job, my business grew.

Dion had not been in the town since the Moira incident - the coward had bolted; no one could have been happier than Moira and me. Our visits were frequent and fulfilling, and we developed an incredible bond, fortified by tragedy, and we pieced the bits of our lives back together to a place where we both could rise tall, claiming our feminine power once more.

Toward the end of the second year, La Provence Interiors was doing so well that Mom decided to sell her house in Brandfort, and between us, we bought a rambling property, which had once been a doctor's consulting rooms, and had it converted into the business offices, workspace and our home.

I had to keep pinching myself, reminding myself this was real; this was *my* fantastic thriving little business.

Though Dion may not have been in town, the nasty Bernard was; a thorn in my side who reported to Dion our every move, seen only through his inebriated eyes, of course. I could only assume the twisted lies and ghastly untruths he would have fed back.

I interviewed several ladies who claimed to be seamstresses and finally whittled them down to one delightfully funny, rather shy coloured lady called Mariah. She had considerable experience on domestic sewing machines but was terrified by the power and speed of the industrial machines. I overlooked that, for she had everything else I was looking for in an employee.

"Eish, Missus," she laughed when she first started, "like airplane, too quick," she beamed. She soon got used to its power and after only a few days, skilfully guided metres of fabrics under the footer guide, becoming the asset I knew she would be. Not only did she bring her sewing skills to the business, but along with it, barrel loads of delightful humour so typical of people of colour from the Cape.

Mom opted to spend her time helping Pieter with his schoolwork, being the girls' support system and cooking tantalising meals for us all for lunch and dinner. Into her seventies, her gammy foot was very arthritic and caused her constant pain; her knees were weakening but her hip replacement had been successful. She never complained but I knew how much effort it took to prepare the family meals.

I was starting to tot up a handful of happy years in business on my own.

Storm had grown into a beautiful, self-assured young lady who was in her last year at senior school and happily took many of the household chores away from Mom. Vivienne, on the other hand, was growing into a hormone-dominated handful, with many inherited paternal traits, and she deeply resented the close relationship Storm and I had. If her current attitude was the gauge for the next two years of her schooling, we were headed for a nasty nightmare that would undoubtedly disrupt my life.

She proved me right by ruining a peaceful evening when she let out a blood-curdling scream at the front door. Scrambling hurriedly out of bed, I grabbed my gown and ran to see what was happening. Viv had gone out to the movies with friends. A devastating sight was waiting for her, and the ghosts of the past came rushing in for us both. I had a horrible premonition that Dion was back in town and up to his dirty old tricks again.

Distraught and sobbing, garbled words toppled out her mouth, mixed with sadness and alcohol, making them undecipherable, then I saw him — my most precious companion of so many years. Darling Splodge lay dead at her feet. I dropped to my knees; my heart tightened in my chest as I reached for him. He'd lived so many lives with us, he'd seen me through the darkest days of my life, and I felt a disturbing emptiness as I stroked his cold, stiff body. Picking him up carefully, I carried him through the house to the back veranda, where I found an empty box and laid his body down inside it, covering it with a towel. If Splodge had passed over due to old age, why at the front door?

To be sure Dion didn't have a hand in ending my precious cat's long life, the vet assured me he'd died of old age; then I allowed myself the freedom to release the grief I was holding onto. The house was empty without Splodge. SPCA was where we headed next and came home with two delightfully fluffy kittens. Pieter named his Harry and Vivienne called hers Daisy, and she got more attention from Pieter and I, for boys took precedence for Vivienne. As they grew from kittens into cats, so La Provence grew from fledgling company to the largest interior decorating company in the town. For the first time in years, I was making a comfortable living.

Dion rarely phoned and contributed nothing toward his children's expenses. He hardly knew his son, which broke my heart for Pieter's sake, though he assured me he didn't yearn for any paternal influence to enhance his youth.

Storm was finishing school and joining the Metropolitan Police and, after her initial training, was to join the drug squad, saying she believed she could make a difference to the lives of children ruined by drugs, or those who'd fallen off the wagon as a result of being raised by addicts, for she had first-hand experience of living with an addict. Vivienne, we didn't know, but her belligerent determination to be as difficult as she could be was blatantly clear. Trying to have a civil conversation with her was as rare as water in the desert, and her behaviour became more and more insufferable for us all. Pieter, on the other hand, was a sensible and balanced child and wanted nothing to do with Vivienne, but he adored Storm, and this caused different ructions - where was the manual for parents on raising opposites within a household?

"What's the matter, Sis?" Storm asked with genuine concern, as Viv came to breakfast sobbing. Plonking herself down next to me, she rested her head on my shoulder. We all sat quietly waiting; Storm looked across at me with raised eyebrows, and Pieter looked bored.

"Ma, I'm pregnant," she blurted out.

My brain felt like a battalion of busy ants had suddenly invaded it, causing a tactical muddle of indecision. Storm's mouth opened - nothing came out, and Pieter was watching my reaction.

"I'm going to leave school and get married," she announced and her 'crocodile tears' dried up.

"Don't be ridiculous, Vivienne; we need to sit together and work all this out sensibly."

"You heard me, Ma." Her chin jutted defiantly.

"Vivienne," I snapped, "that is the craziest thing that has come out of your mouth recently. Go and wash your face, and we'll talk this through when you come back."

Pouting, she pulled her pyjama top down to cover herself and sauntered out the room. Storm was still staring at me as Pieter got up and shouted from the kitchen.

"Slut."

Vivienne erupted.

"I'm not a fucking slut," she screamed at her brother.

"That's quite enough swearing from you, young lady," I reprimanded Vivienne, then Pieter fired her up again.

"She's not a lady, Ma."

"That's quite enough from both of you!" I shouted back. "We need to work this out as a family."

"She doesn't want to be a part of this family, Ma, don't waste your time," Storm joined in.

"Whoa, stop, stop, stop - all of you; what is done, is done. There is no turning back now; Vivienne has to accept the responsibility of what she has done."

Storm got up and left, leaving Vivienne and I alone.

"Don't ask me to have an abortion, 'cos I won't," Vivienne snapped before I had said a word.

"You know that's against my principles, Vivienne," I said gently. "We do, however, need to talk. I'd like to know who the father is, what does he do, and does he know?" Vivienne stared at me; her lips had formed into her theatrically rebellious pout again.

"His name is Andre Venter, he's twenty-two years old, and he's training to be a diesel mechanic. He wants to marry me, and he's happy I'm pregnant."

"Well that's a good start, but.... um, I'm very disappointed in you falling pregnant before leaving school. So very young to shoulder such responsibility. You know you will have to give up your drinking and partying, young lady. You have two months left of this school year, which you will finish whether you like it or not," I said with finality.

"Okaaay," Vivienne said, sighing her best irritating sigh, emphasising how unhappy she was about finishing school but fully aware she'd got off lightly. "I'll finish this year for you, Ma, but then we are going to live in Durban," she said. There was no point in trying to stop her.

"Oh, I see! How long have you been planning all this, Vivienne?"

"Not long," she smiled triumphantly – she was so like her father that a shudder ran down my spine.

My mind was spinning - my youngest daughter fleeing the nest, pregnant at seventeen and gone in just three months. Storm would be gone too. I'd heard about the empty nest syndrome; now I was feeling the threat of it closing in but at least I still had Pieter and my Mom.

"Before you go anywhere young lady, I want to meet Andre and his parents."

"You will meet Andre this afternoon. I'm spending the night with him and will be back tomorrow evening. You won't meet his parents; they live in Durban," Vivienne informed me with about as much disrespect as she could dig up – I let it go and said nothing but I thought sadly, 'Insolent and arrogant, just like her father. Not a thought for anyone else's feelings, no remorse, no apology, no shame.'

Andre seemed a pleasant young man and obviously adored Vivienne. Storm was happy her sister was leaving home, though angry at her for hurting me. Pieter spent the night with a friend. He didn't want to see his sister or meet her husband-to-be. He needed space and time to deal with what his sister had done.

At the end of November, Vivienne left us and didn't bother letting her father know any of the details. I waited, wondering how long it would take for the news to filter back to Dion via the sly Bernard. It took longer than I expected. He called, for the first time, after Christmas but offered no words of encouragement and good wishes to his eldest daughter, who was starting her career in January – one of the biggest milestones of a young person's life.

"Vivienne is long gone, settled in Durban and expecting in April. She sounds happy and secure," I said, and he was furious neither she nor I had told him.

"Neither of them want anything to do with you, Dion, and I honestly don't blame them. If you'd bothered to call regularly, you'd have known. Didn't Bernard tell you?" He ignored that dig.

"Can I speak to Pieter?"

"He's not here; he's with a friend playing hockey."

"Playing hockey?" He sounded surprised.

"Yes, Dion and what a disgrace you are as a father. You've broken their hearts, embarrassed them, you've not been there for them when it mattered, so don't push yourself on them now." I put the phone down.

For three years he'd not provided for his children, had rarely spoken to them, and now he expected to weave himself back into their hearts after the careless, cruel scars he'd left behind; but there was no point in saying it to him – there was always someone else to blame and he always protected himself from the corrosive effects of shame.

CHAPTER TWENTY-SIX

"Mom, is it wrong to sit and wish Vivienne wasn't my sister and Dion wasn't my father?" Pieter asked, looking burdened by guilt.

"No, my precious, it isn't wrong; under the circumstances, I think it is natural. Sisters often irritate their brothers but in your father's case, it is all so different. One day, you may find it in you to forgive him, or maybe not. Time will tell, but don't feel guilty if you can't," I assured him.

"No way can I forgive him, Ma. *You* protected and cared for us, and this is what they do to you." I wondered where Pieter was going to take this conversation.

"I wish I could do more for you, Ma, but I don't know how to handle my anger. That's why I escape to my room and bury my thoughts in my computer; it's the only way I can suppress my fury," he said apologetically. I'd bought him a second-hand IBM 286 Hercules, of which he was immensely proud.

"I've just installed CGA Gold from a DOS program. Hey Ma, I love computers." I smiled at his enthusiasm. Was the conversation on his sister and father going to continue, I wondered, or had the joy he was expressing about his computers diverted the conversation?

"Hey, Ma, I have a new golfing game; it's hysterical, it's such a massive program and runs so slowly, when the golfer lifts the club to hit the ball it's all in slow-mo. It cracks me, then the birds and crickets in the background have to pause so the animated man can complete the swing to hit the ball, then the birds start to chirp again." We roared with laughter together and decided it was time to get him involved in my computer that had Lotus 123 on it. He was ecstatic.

"I can write my very own programs now, Ma; it's so cool." He beamed and never broached the subject he'd opened our discussion with, so I left it.

"I'm proud of you, my boy; these self-taught skills will be a huge asset to you one day."

Pieter was playing a new golf game, Mom was on the other couch dozing, and I was watching her. She was struggling, her eyes were closed, though I knew she was listening to the background noises coming from the golf game Pieter was playing, but I could see how fast she was withering into old age now and it scared me. I couldn't bear the thought of her not being around.

"How's Jan doing, Pieter?"

"He's a good friend. Shame Ma, he's had a hard life too, that's probably why we get on so well, he's like a brother to me."

"He certainly is, and you are both so good at hockey and indoor cricket. How's he with computers?" Pieter burst out laughing, "Can hardly switch one on."

"Mom, do you miss Storm as much as I do?" Pieter asked - back to where we started earlier.

"Even more than you do."

"I can see how your face changes when Storm is home, Ma. You love her so much don't you?"

"Yes, I do, but I love you all just as much. I don't always like what Vivienne does, but I still love her like I love you," I said and wrapped my arms around my computer Wizz-kid.

The following morning, the 7th of April, 1998, Andre called to say Vivienne had given birth to a beautiful baby girl, my first grandchild, and despite the circumstances, I was overjoyed.

"Congratulations to you both. Give my precious Vivienne a big hug. We'll chat when she's home. Have you let Dion know?"

"No, and I have no intention of doing so either. I'm sorry," He said firmly.

The next encounter we had with Dion was another unhappy one. We'd not seen him for a long time and in he walked through the back door and into the kitchen one evening, grabbing a knife on his way through. By the time we saw him, he was heading straight my way.

"Don't you dare touch her," Pieter yelled but, being fifteen, I was sure he wasn't going to be able to stop this rampaging, knife-wielding father without getting himself hurt. Time stood still as I watched Dion poised to stab me. Pieter was moving toward us just as I blocked Dion and grabbed his arm, the point of the knife millimetres from my face. Fortunately, Storm was home that weekend, heard the commotion and moved in on her father as swiftly and silently as a leopard and launched, protecting Pieter by pushing him out the way as she pulled Dion off me but it was too late, the knife had sliced through the top of my eyelid, splitting the skin up into my forehead. Blood gushed out of the wound like an open tap and ran down my face in rivers of red that descended to the floor.

Pieter stayed crouched down with me while Storm dealt with her father, pushing him back up against the wall using tactics she'd been taught in the police. I whispered to Pieter, "Phone the police my boy, I need to get to hospital," while the battle between father and daughter continued.

"We've got to get Mama to hospital!" Pieter shouted above the racket; then I heard Storm screaming at her father, "I hate you, I haaaate you, get out."

Sounds and actions all faded into a singular noise as my shirt front became drenched with blood. I eased myself across the kitchen to grab a tea towel to curb the bleeding and heard Mom on the phone to the Police. Dion heard her too and fled like a stray dog caught digging in a dustbin, and by the time the Police got to the house, Dion had gone.

Fingerprints were taken and the knife placed in a plastic bag as evidence and Storm whisked me off to hospital leaving Mom and Pieter to clean up the kitchen that resembled a war zone.

Thankfully there was no damage to my eyeball - eleven stitches held the gaping wound together.

When I got home, Pieter said, "Mom, all I wanted to do was grab that knife and thrust it into Papa, end his life so he'd never hassle us again."

The stabbing had traumatised Mom.

CHAPTER TWENTY-SEVEN

The doctor had done a beautiful job stitching my eyelid but, looking at it in the mirror, the scar would be another constant reminder that evil in human form was never far away.

Pieter suffered deeper emotional turmoil for its roots were embedded deeper in anger and helplessness and youth. I suggested trauma counselling might help him deal with the rage, but, like Storm, he said we could work it out. And between the magical therapy his computers offered and regular conversations with Storm, Mom and I, we did work through it.

"No matter where you are, Dion will never leave you alone for long." Dr Gouws words rattled in my head once more, but Mom was my immediate worry.

William and I discussed the possibility of her returning to live on the farm with them - she would be safe. It took an awful lot of persuasion, but she eventually saw the sense in it.

Packing up her belongings and saying goodbye to my mother was one of the hardest things I'd done. The day Mom left, I organised for the place to be burglar-proofed. I also had external cameras mounted, so if he did return, I'd have evidence of him breaking in or trying to break me.

I sobbed as Mom was driven away but she would be safe with William.

The Police came back and suggested I lay attempted murder charges, but I refused to do that; he'd make a fool of me again with his unscrupulous friends and could boast that he was untouchable.

"Are you quite sure, Mrs Du Toit? It could happen again."

"I know, and it will happen again," I shrugged my shoulders but did not want to tell him I'd had cameras installed. I was never sure who in the Police was friend or foe. With cameras, I'd have evidence that he couldn't escape from.

The cop was nodding his head and writing on his pad. I could see he was thinking I was mad, then he said, "There's still time to change your mind. If you do, call me, I'm not on his side," and handed me a card with his direct line number on it.

"Thank you," I said, feeling relieved that not all the policemen in town were friends of Dion's.

"Mom, why didn't you lay charges? You need to teach Papa a lesson," Pieter urged.

"How many times have I tried before? For now, my boy, he's won again because we've had to send Ouma away, but we will catch him soon enough."

"We have to, Ma." Pieter was frustrated, and I understood, but it was pointless.

"I know we do, and we will. It's just a matter of time." I hugged Pieter, feeling fatigued and old beyond my years. I'd lost every battle, but I wasn't going to lose the war on Dion Du Toit. For some inexplicable reason, Dion always made me feel like I'd failed him somehow.

Some weeks after Mom left, an old-established carpeting company happen to come on the market and I snapped it up, putting me back into debt but adding value to my business, making La Provence Interiors a one-stop interior decorating company.

Andre came to mind to run it for me - he and Vivienne had just been made redundant within weeks of each other, and they were struggling to find employment.

My head told me it could work; my gut was telling me something very different; they were my children - I went with my head.

Andre accepted happily and managed the job well - it was after working hours they exhausted me. He and Vivienne spent most evenings out after dinner drinking with Dion, who'd now moved back to Bethlehem. Apart from being nanny, I found myself paying for everything too. It was time to bring their freeloading to an end and set the boundaries.

"Andre, I can't take on the burden of financially supporting you and your family. Living with us didn't mean I pay your way too; it's time to pay for your boarding," I snapped, rather more aggressively than I'd intended but I was annoyed by their thoughtless behaviour.

"And Viv needs to get off her arse, find a job, pay for a nanny and contribute or you can all find another place to live." I grimly watched Vivienne follow the same cycle of financial abuse she'd inherited from her father, and when she came begging for more financial support I refused to help.

Carrying barrel loads of bitter resentment, they moved out, and on that day, the sun set on my darling mother. My *forever* rock ascended to join my father in a happier place, reunited again after all these years.

I went home. The farm, to me, was always home. Storm and Pieter followed a few days later for Mom's funeral. She was laid to rest in a specially prepared sanctuary at the bottom of the garden, deep within the earth that had given her life's purpose, the land she loved so dearly, and for a few more days, I sat next to her grave, thanking her for all she'd taught me. Alone and quiet, I released the pain of my loss; whispered conversations healed me but I was going to miss her, even if she was always there in spirit.

Woes were ever-present in my life; Andre had disappeared for a week without letting anyone know where he'd gone. When he returned, he bragged about all the cash he'd earned in the week away. I was flabbergasted but his commitment wasn't to me. I suggested he look for another job.

Coincidence - meaning – the fact of two things happening at the same time by chance, in a surprising way.

I didn't believe what happened next was a coincidence. Dion called suggesting he could take over where Andre had left off.

"That's not a good idea, Dion. I can't trust you. It wasn't that long ago you tried to kill me; you can hardly think I would want to employ you."

"I never tried to murder you, Elizabeth; when Storm and Pieter grabbed me, the knife slipped."

Metering out the blame as always.

"Our opinions differ on that. I cannot employ you, goodbye, Dion."

"Listen Liefie, wait, wait, wait. I don't have a job, and I would like to help you out. Genuine. Even if it is only for a few months."

"Firstly, I am *not* your Liefie. Secondly, I have told you, I cannot employ you."

"Please, Elizabeth. I'd also like to see more of Pieter."

"Why now? You've had plenty of opportunity. You abandoned him, and he feels it. I'm not sure he wants to see more of you, Dion. You've hurt him so deeply the odds are not in your favour, now goodbye."

"When will you let me know, Elizabeth?" he said quickly.

"Keep looking elsewhere." I snapped, losing patience.

"Why can't you give me a chance? I'll get you lots of business."

"I don't have to give you any more chances, Dion; I've given you so many, now goodbye." I put the phone down before he could go on antagonising me.

That evening, I mentioned Dion's absurd telephone call to Pieter.

"You owe him nothing, Mom, remember that, and I don't want to see him. All he is trying to do is make you feel guilty again. Don't fall for it this time, Mom. The bastard should work for you for free; he owes you so much, Mama."

Some home truths to mull over.

"Papa sees you are successful now, but on second thoughts, Ma, by *not* employing him, that could trigger his nasty, vindictive streak, then who knows what he will try next?" Pieter looked down and picked at his fingernails while thinking.

I called Dion in the morning.

"Hi, it's me. I gave it some thought last night and chatted to Pieter; we have all agreed my initial decision still stands," I said bluntly.

"That wasn't your decision, was it?" he yelled down the phone.

"There's nothing more to discuss on it. Good-bye."

I'd decided to keep Dion out of my business for multiple reasons and began interviewing. I employed an educated, well-spoken African man who'd worked for the previous owners of the carpet business. He came with a glowing reference and was delightfully humble. Joseph took over what Andre had abandoned.

I decided I needed a holiday and sat at my desk, dreaming about booking myself into a health retreat for a week, imagining myself submerged in a steamy hot jacuzzi, bubbling with spring water, staying in it until my skin crinkled and all my stress had been bubbled away. Sadly, Joseph wasn't suitable, and the interviewing process began again – and with it, a series of events that were to change my life.

The day I said goodbye to Joseph, Vivienne called to say she was pregnant again. Andre had been made redundant for the second time - I was not to worry, he was going overseas on one of his 'trips' but could they move back with me?

Storm was my light, the warmth, the rainfall, the gentle breezes, the sunshine in my life when I needed her. Vivienne was my night, dark with the occasional twinkling star, her moods like the lunar phases. What should I do?

Pieter was different; he kept himself absorbed with his computers, his friends and his sport, but Jan, his dearest friend, was living with us after losing his parents in a tragic car accident. Viv, Andre, Annie and the one on the way moving in would be a disaster and I had no-one to run the carpeting.

This kind of chaos was the story of my life and then Vivienne added another dimension to the already existing chaos – she insisted that her father should be given the chance to run the carpeting division and I stoically fought against it and decided to sell the carpet division. Vivienne blew, fuelled by vengeance; she was brutal. She accused me of cutting off her father, blaming me for his behaviour, spitting out her fury like a viper and her final injection of poison was a vicious reminder that her father couldn't live without me.

"Your success has gone to your head," she spat venomously.

I called Dion the following day and gave him the job. Anything for peace at home.

CHAPTER TWENTY-EIGHT

"Morning, Elizabeth, excuse me barging in on you but I think you should see this," Carol, my bookkeeper said, handing me a bundle of papers before sitting down opposite me. Carol had been with me a year after I started La Provence Interiors and I trusted her implicitly. She was as sharp as a ray of early morning sunshine and always there. When she called my attention to something, I listened.

"What's the problem?" I asked, as I stretched back in my chair and took a deep breath – I was so tired.

"You look exhausted, my friend, and I think this is going to make you feel worse, but there's a problem in the carpeting section."

No sooner had the words left her mouth, than my stomach lurched. Words I'd feared I may hear.

"Explain," I said, noting the empathy etched in her kind face.

"I found a discrepancy that rang alarm bells, especially as it was associated with carpeting and your ex. If I'd had all the facts to hand, I would have brought it to your attention last week. Dion has spent his three-month probationary period cunningly ripping this company off. I can only imagine he came in with this plan."

"What's he been doing?" I grimaced, cursing myself for trying to appease Vivienne and letting her come home.

"He's been syphoning money off - now it's serious. I'm sorry, Elizabeth. I could kick myself for not picking it up earlier, but it wasn't obvious. I also didn't want to ask too many questions in case you'd authorised some of it."

"When it comes to Dion, I authorise nothing to do with money. So, how's he been doing it?"

Carol swallowed deeply.

"He introduced a personal invoicing system. The bigger jobs went through our books, which threw me off. I couldn't match his purchases to a job lot, and as you know, we have had quite a considerable number of teams working in houses all over the place, not just here in Bethlehem. He's been invoicing the small jobs from his invoice book and receipted payments in cash using a false receipt book with the company stamp on it, buying all the materials for numerous cash jobs on your supplier accounts, and of course, no-one questioned him."

"How much has he taken?"

"Fifty-nine thousand Rand," I heard her say.

Anger wasn't what I was feeling; it was far worse. Murderous was more apt, with the same intensity I had all those years ago, and though I'd promised myself never to allow those sensations to overcome my rationale again, they were back.

'So, this was how he was going to crucify me finally, was it?' I asked myself quietly. I had to resign myself to the fact that he'd now won that war too.

"Oh my God, Carol. I never learn with that swine," I admitted. "I gave in to keep the peace at home with Viv, and being so fucking tired, I couldn't fight her anymore."

"I'm so sorry, Elizabeth. Don't be hard on yourself. I should have been more vigilant, knowing his history. I wish I'd picked it up earlier, but I didn't have enough proof, and in honesty, I wasn't looking for it - to begin with."

"It's not your fault, Carol. The most important thing now is to find a way out of this mess." Carol nodded and left my office.

"Do you want a coffee?" she called out as she left.

"Yes, please." I never said no to coffee, but caffeine wasn't the answer I was looking for.

Lumbered with debt, the children draining me, and my business now financially ruined, it was time to have some questions answered, not just from Dion, but Vivienne and Andre too.

I had a message sent that Dion was to get to my office urgently.

"Sit," I scowled, pointing at the open chair opposite my desk when he appeared. Carol closed the door behind him and took her seat.

"What the fuck? What's up?" he asked, then added, "It's like the Spanish inquisition."

"This is no time for stupid wit, Dion, but yes, and I believe you know why. You have an awful lot of explaining to do. Before we go on, you are fired as of right now."

If I'd had my pistol, this time I would have used it.

"What do you mean?" he said, putting on the 'innocent victim' look and glancing from me to Carol and back.

"How many jobs have you pocketed the cash for in the last four months?"

"None. Why?"

"Of course not! How stupid of me," I said sarcastically. "Dion, Carol isn't stupid, but I have been, we have proof. There is absolutely *nothing* innocent about you. Your act of vengeance is actually fraud, Dion.

"You are to leave immediately without remuneration. Get out and never step foot in these offices again and leave me alone."

He got up and, stopping at the door, the devil personified grinned at me triumphantly and left.

"My God, Elizabeth, what did I just witness?" Carol had never seen the other Dion. She was ghostly white. I collapsed onto the sofa and sobbed until there were no more tears left. The following day I needed to action account-holders.

"Carol, can you make appointments for me to see the Directors of each of these companies?" I handed her the list I'd made last night. "We need to keep these sweet; they are vital. The others we can write to and arrange extended terms. for most of them won't be necessary without the carpeting division."

"Yes, sure, Elizabeth."

"How many jobs need to be finished?"

"I'll check and let you know. Teams went out with Johannas today; he's on it."

She turned and left me to wallow in the turmoil Dion's lies had caused.

By 2001, I couldn't go on. Not only was I on the verge of a physical collapse, but emotionally and financially I was sunk. I found myself lying to creditors, something I'd never done nor would have ever considered outside of this mayhem.

My sister was furious with me for employing Dion, Vivienne was livid I'd fired her father, Storm was tearful and desperately worried about me, Pieter was focussed on his computing and William suggested it might be better for us all if he stayed away, though he was emotionally supportive of me.

Night times were the worst times when the last rays of sunshine dropped behind the horizon, and the horrors of darkness swept in bringing thoughts that triggered panicky sweats, leaving me sticky with fear. Creditors were hounding me like flies and I was making empty promises to keep them off my back. I had every intention of paying off my debt; I just had to find a plan to do it quickly.

"Ma, may I come in? I have a suggestion and would like to talk it through with you?" I was a bit taken aback by Andre's request – there was no harm in listening.

"Sure. I hope it's a good one. Where's Viv?"

"With her father. Listen, I have a contact in Johannesburg. I know you won't like what I have to say, just hear me out. They pay tens of thousands of Rand for certain jobs. Those weeks I was away and came home with money, remember?" He smiled looking a little embarrassed – would I forget those weeks?

"Well, I thought I would do one more and give you the money. You've helped us so much, and I know it was a huge strain on you having us live with you. I also know the clashes you and Viv have didn't help and employing Dion at her insistence and what he did, I feel I owe it to you."

Andre was a good man, but the suggestion had an ominous tone to it, and if anything happened to Andre, Vivienne would surely blame me.

"I don't want you doing anything illegal. You have a wife and children to care for before helping me."

"No, Ma, it's cool, I will do another job."

"Don't do anything stupid and get into trouble," I warned him. "The family has been through enough without inviting more."

"It's no trouble, Ma," he lied. "There are a few risks, but its good money," he assured me, but something didn't feel right. I felt uneasy and couldn't sleep that night. I needed more information from Andre on what he planned to do. We got together again the following day, and he explained.

"Nee, Andre, you are not to do that. It is not right," I warned him.

"I knew you wouldn't approve Ma, but it will get you out of die ding! (Slang for being in a tight spot) I will happily do it for you; it is the least I can do. I've contacted the Nigerians -it's a week to Japan, drop off the package, then I will pick up in Paris then fly back. All expenses paid and forty thousand Rand is yours."

"Nothing is that simple Andre. What's in the package?"

"They never tell me, Ma; apparently this consignment is diamonds. I know it is not ethical, but I am prepared to do it one last time."

I didn't like what I was hearing. After Andre left, I sat at my desk calculating the exact amount I needed to pay off my debt and kept asking myself whether it was worth Andre taking such a risk. I wished then I was clairvoyant and could see into the future. I discussed the job again with Andre, and just as we were about to finish up, Storm called.

"Mama, can you look after Rika over the weekend?"

"Yes, of course, my angel," I responded without hesitation, and glanced at Andre and indicated with my thumb that I was satisfied with what he'd told me.

Storm and Robert were moving - a perfect opportunity to think quietly while babysitting. After breakfast on Saturday morning, I popped into our local shop and grabbed something for us all for lunch. I was looking forward to a day of peace and relative quiet. I was feeling a little easier, now there may be a glimmer of hope on the horizon.

I didn't tell Storm what Andre was planning; keeping it from her made me feel devious- I normally shared everything with her.

I'd read that people got hung for smuggling drugs. I wondered if being caught smuggling diamonds was as dangerous. Andre had done it before, and I assumed the last two trips must have been drugs. Had he said he would be moving drugs this time, I would not have agreed to let him go. The stories Storm told me of what she'd already seen working in the Drug Unit raised the hair on the back of my neck and broke my heart. So many children between the ages of ten and fifteen die as a result of drugs. Though she'd grown up with an addict, she'd had a tough time too, but nothing compared to the horror stories she told, catching greedy drug dealers who swooped on children before they turned innocents into liars and thieves, needy of nothing but the poison their minds craved gave Storm real purpose. As I thought of those children, my conscience tugged at me;

at least, if Andre did this run, diamonds wouldn't hurt any children and would give one child a chance for a future he dreamed of; a university education in IT.

I shook my head to clear my thoughts. Little Rika had slept most of the day while I read my book, interrupted at times with all these thoughts. It was well after sundown before Storm and Robert finished carting boxes and breezed in carrying a few hot cheesy pizzas; the smell brought a rush of saliva to my mouth, reminding me I hadn't eaten all day. I devoured my Hawaiian; it was delicious. I left Storm's house somewhere around ten that evening, ready for a restful night's sleep, until I opened the front door of my house and walked into mayhem.

Drunk neighbours looked up at me with pathetic vacant stares that only drunks can deliver. I was livid; how could Andre do this? I threw them all out, those half-sober sheepishly sidled past me and there on the floor, a tangled mess of drunken humanity, was Dion. Where was Pieter? I called out to him, but he didn't answer. I hoped he was asleep, not too sad to talk to anyone, including me. I went back downstairs and ordered Andre to wake Vivienne, who lay slumped inelegantly across the sofa, and get to bed, warning them they had to clean up my house in the morning.

"This is it. I've had a gutful, Andre. How dare you do this in my home!" I looked around my lounge, not sure whether to scream or ball my eyes out, then I heard Dion retching and in moments, he was spewing vomit all over my lounge carpet.

"Get him out of here, Andre," I roared, noticing Dion had wet himself, which repulsed and disgusted me more.

"When you get back from Japan, you will have to look for another place to live. I cannot deal with this shit anymore," I warned him. Disappointed and angry with Andre, at life, with everything - all I wanted to do was run away and hide; disappear to a place where not a solitary human resided. I needed the space of a deserted island more than ever.

I knocked on Pieter's door again; there was still no response. Leaving the disgusting chaos behind me, I closed my bedroom door and sobbed, gut-wrenching sobs that rattled my core. Maybe someday I would be released from the hell I was living. I climbed into bed, closed my eyes and tried to find answers.

"Oh, God, why are you doing this to me? Why do you never hear my prayers? Why do you never answer them either?" I asked, my voice laced with bitterness. "Do you even exist?"

I felt disillusioned and betrayed and couldn't work out where I'd gone wrong; if *I'd* gone wrong at all. I had asked for His wisdom and guidance so often. He'd surely seen how hard I'd tried. He knew my conscience better than I did, and now I couldn't help feeling He was a figment of the imagination. It wasn't long before I found myself begging *Him* again, to listen to me, then a thought popped to mind, 'Maybe I should go to Japan.'

Trouble was, I wanted to be sitting at a place called, 'God's Window,' high up in the mountains above Pilgrims Rest in Mpumalanga, gazing out across the vast expanse of unspoilt Africa, breathing in pure air and relaxing peacefully, cicadas screaming, wild herbal scents permeating my nostrils, and bird calls soothing my frazzled nerves. Maybe, if I were seated on the edge of the mountain named after Him, He'd hear my desperate pleas - I needed guidance now, more than ever before.

I woke on Sunday morning still thinking about God's Window, but more pressing was the thought that maybe I should be going to Japan. Plain old simple conscience was working - *I* should be doing this 'mission' to get *myself* out of trouble. Either way, a week's break in Mpumalanga or a week in Japan, I couldn't hang around much longer, or I'd be driven to do something I'd regret. I needed to get away from Dion before I snapped for this time there would be no holding me back, this time I would pull the trigger. I could see no way of getting the evil out of my life other than getting back to nature for a week to clear my mind.

Andre would be back from Japan, I'd have money to resuscitate my business, I would have had a week's rest and I'd be up and running again. Andre and Vivienne would be living elsewhere, I'd be eighty percent free of debt, Pieter could get through the end of his school career without the stress he'd been exposed to recently and go on to University in early February and life would be tolerable again.

I was in no hurry to leave my room until I knew the others would have thoroughly cleaned my house. Apart from the thoughts of trying to sort my life out, I lay in bed feeling relieved my house girl was not in on Sundays – seeing the state of the house would have embarrassed me terribly.

CHAPTER TWENTY-NINE

I needed to meet with Andre before he left, and I didn't want Viv in on this meeting. Since the Saturday night debacle, he and Viv had moved in with some friends, giving me space while things settled. I'd arranged to meet Andre at the Wimpy and got there before him. I ordered a large coffee for myself, and as it arrived, Andre walked in.

"Before we talk of anything, Ma, I want to apologise again for Saturday night. I'm ashamed of how it went down." He had the decency to look sheepish and embarrassed.

"Yes, I was not impressed and very disappointed in you all. Let's not talk about it, just make sure it never happens under my roof again. I appreciate your apology and for moving out; Pieter and I needed some space."

"That's a promise, Ma. Nothing like that will ever happen again. So, what's on your mind?"

"This mission you are going on shortly - I've been thinking, why don't I do it?" I asked, and a look of utter shock formed on Andre's cleanly shaven face.

"No, Ma, that is not a clever idea."

"Why not? I thought you said it was relatively easy!" I raised my eyebrows, looking enquiringly at him, but he sat in stunned to silence for a moment and then hastily ordered coffee.

"Ma, it is quite a dangerous mission; I don't want you doing it."

"Yes, I am aware of that Andre, but they, (referring to customs officials) would hardly suspect a grandmother, would they? Find out from your contacts what they think. It is not resting well with my conscience – it is my debt, not yours." I thought about that for a moment, then said, "well actually not my debt, that bastard's debt, but he's too useless to do this mission, isn't he? Though he should be the one finding the solutions."

"I agree, Ma, we cannot depend on Pa. I'll call them, but I'm quite sure they won't agree. Rather let me do this alone, Ma."

"Let me know when you've spoken to them. I'm not happy about you doing it and my reasons are - you have a wife and children to consider, and God forbid, I'd rather die than have Vivienne blame me for the rest of my life if anything happened to you." By the expression on Andre's face, he hadn't thought of that consequence. We finished our coffee, and he promised to call me later.

I spent the rest of the day thinking of the pitfalls. The do's outweighed the don'ts; or was my list born of innocence? I knew nothing of this underworld Andre understood. I'd never even flown out the country before. How would I manage flying halfway around the world? When Andre called, I felt quite nervous suddenly.

"Can I pop round to the house, Ma?"

"Yes, of course! Have you heard from your contacts?"

"Yes. See you in ten minutes."

I put the phone down and waited. I certainly had reservations about doing it.

"I'm not at all happy about this, Ma," he said as he walked into the house. Pieter was in his room studying, so we had some time to finish the conversation without him knowing Andre was in the house and there was no chance of him eavesdropping.

"They said you could do it, but *I'm* not sure you should," he rubbed his brow.

"I insist. You must be with your wife and children."

"No, Ma, I can't let you do it. I know how they operate."

"I know you do, Andre, but I've made up my mind; however, there is one thing I need to know first - are you certain it is diamonds and **not** drugs? Once that is confirmed, I'll do it and you can prepare me for the trip, what I should and shouldn't do."

"Ok, Ma, if you insist. I'll keep your business running with Carol the week you are away. Is that a deal?"

"Okay, and you vow to me that neither Storm nor Pieter will know about this. As far as they will be aware, I am going on holiday to God's Window. Does Dion know anything?"

"Guaranteed. Yes. Ma, he does know I'm to go but he hasn't said anything."

"You mean he hasn't considered that it is something he should be doing? It's his debt after all."

"Ma! You know him better than that." We laughed together; I wasn't sure why I'd even asked. "He couldn't do it; he can't take instructions and carry them out, you know; he listens to no-one. You don't want to know what they do to people who let them down."

That was a warning. I trembled inside.

"I know, and that thought doesn't make me feel secure doing it either. Tell me how it all works."

"Ma, don't you want me to find out what will be in the packages first?"

"Yes, I do, but there is no harm in telling me what to expect. I may not do it anyway."

Andre and I spent an hour going over the pros and cons; I felt ashamed and tarnished and I hadn't even left or had my request confirmed, but suddenly, the thought of me doing this seemed the only answer. I didn't really have the money to spend a week on holiday, even though I was dangerously close to a nervous break-down - I did have a little in savings but it was all I had to fall back on.

Then, the appalling thought of lying to Storm and Pieter about where I was going for a week filled me but superseded the wilful need to exterminate my ex-husband. My decisions terrified me. I *had* to get away.

'I've managed fear before,' I said to myself, more boldly than I felt.

Andre called.

"Ma, we need to go to Johannesburg tomorrow to organise a British passport for you."

I swallowed hard.

'A British Passport?'

What was wrong with my South African one? Then I remembered I would need a visa. My stomach filled with butterflies and they were in chaotic flight; like my mind, round and round they went, leaving my legs feeling quite weakened. It was all happening - paving the way to financial recovery with hard truths and unpleasant lies, but off we went.

My new British passport would be ready in a week; a week filled with nervous tension, sickened by a guilt I'd not experienced before.

'Only a week away from the business,' I kept reminding myself, while the whispers fluttering through my head were saying - 'don't do it, Elizabeth.'

It was my only salvation. I had to do it.

Storm was excited for me - "Ma, I'm so envious! You'll have a wonderful time just relaxing, doing nothing other than resting, reading and walking in that divine fresh mountain air. It will do you so much good. I wish I was coming with you."

I felt ill.

Time ticked on; it was getting closer to my departure date — days filled with gnawing fear and a crippling sense of shame.

I would be flying to Paris first, staying over, then getting on the flight to Japan, deliver the package - a box contaminated by lies all wrapped up in desperation, then fly home. Just a week - that's all it would take to sort out my life and pay my debt. Andre had primed me; it was a waiting game. I was to keep calm and follow instructions. He'd done it, so could I.

The thought of seeing Paris and a glimpse of Japan filled me with a detached sense of excitement. On weighing up my options now, this one was better than being tried for murder and me being locked away.

The day was upon us. Everything was organised except me. I was a nervous wreck saying tearful goodbyes to Storm and Pieter who laughed at me for crying.

"Enjoy it, Ma! It's only a week away, and no-one deserves it more." Storm chuckled into my ear as she hugged me. I didn't want to let her go. I held Pieter close to me, kissed him goodbye, then Andre whisked me off under the pretence that I couldn't miss my bus from Johannesburg to Pilgrim's Rest and we were on our way.

"You can do this, Ma, just breathe deeply. Once you are on your way, you'll be fine," Andre said, looking concerned.

"Of course, just drive," I snapped. "What I hate the most about this is lying to Storm and Pieter; it makes me ill."

"They will understand, Ma."

Margaret Barnes; my new name, was on her way to Paris. The week before, in the privacy of my bedroom, I had practised being Margaret. I'd pinned my hair back like she did, I wore glasses like she did. I had to have 'Margaret' firmly entrenched in my mind.

"Remind me, what is Margaret supposed to do once she gets to Paris?" I asked Andre as we got closer to Johannesburg International Airport.

"They will tell you, Ma. Just follow their instructions precisely as I told you and you will be fine."

"Oh Andre, I feel sick, can you stop?" I asked urgently. Saliva was rushing into my mouth as Andre pulled off the road. I flung the car door open as it came to a stop and vomited, hanging my head in shame out the car. Andre passed me a tissue to wipe my mouth and another to blow my nose that burned from the bile.

"Right, let's go," I said and had a few sips of water.

"Ma..."

"Don't talk, just drive."

I needed to deal with the last minutes of this journey in silence. I was to collect my ticket with further instructions from the Nigerians who were meeting us at the airport; at least for this early part of this loathsome decision, Andre was with me. Then suddenly, Andre was pulling into the first-floor parking area, and my stomach lurched again.

"First stop is the loo, Andre." He nodded patiently, remembering how it was the first time he did this journey.

Sitting on the toilet, I felt trapped; I wanted to stop it all.

"Am I mad?" I whispered to myself, covering my face with my hands while I waited till the trickle of urine ended. The airport was noisy; people rushing here, rushing there, some crying, some rejoicing. I felt numb.

I was about to board a plane for the first time in my life, at fifty-two years of age, with a false passport and very little money, fly to a city I had only ever seen in the movies, filled with the knowledge I was embarking on a particularly unsavoury mission, guided by people with no conscience, with guilt written all over my face.

"Have faith," I whispered into my chest. "It's only a week away."

Once again, I joined Andre who was standing with the Nigerian organisers. There were two tall black men, dressed similarly, one wearing black jeans and a red sleeveless 'T' shirt, showing off massive toned biceps and a well-developed body. Not a physique one would voluntarily want to mess with. The other was also well-built and wore blue jeans and a white 'T' shirt, also with cut-off sleeves, his expression more fearful than the other's build. I instinctively knew they were trouble. They were the types that, with just one glance, you intuitively know they're dangerous. The man wearing the red shirt handed me an envelope with some foreign currency in it, the plane ticket and my new British passport. My hair was pinned back like Margaret's photograph, and my glasses were in place, though I wasn't wearing them in the passport photo. He opened the passport to check, looked at me and nodded his approval. I opened the envelope and counted the money and looked at him questioningly.

"How am I going to live on this for six days in a foreign country?" His expression was dismissive; all he said was, "You will be contacted when you land at Charles de Gaulle. Follow instructions, as we have explained, and you will be fine. You won't go hungry."

"What if I no-one meets me in Paris?"

"Margaret, you must just listen. If you are not met, they will call you on the phone and tell you what to do. Do not panic."

"Do not panic? I'm terrified." I muttered.

"You will be fine, Ma," Andre said, as he put his hand on my shoulder to reassure me.

It was time to check in, say goodbye to Andre, then *wait* to board.

Wait – as a verb – stay where one is – I was numbed with fear. To hold back, stop, cease – I'd felt the sensations in the lady's toilet. All and more.

As a noun - a period of waiting - an interlude. I wanted to get on the plane now and get the ordeal over and done with, get back home and go on with my business.

Andre hugged me, wished me luck, shook hands with the two men and disappeared. My mind was reeling, my feet rooted to the spot, too terrified to move, feeling absurdly alone and abandoned. My mouth dried out in an instant and the butterflies in my tummy took off again in frenzied flight around my stomach, leaving me nauseous with fear. I felt faint. Out of my depth. I'd never done anything purposefully illegal before - this was huge, and the enormity of my decision hit me hard.

I moved off slowly, my feet leaden from the burden of apprehension, and I headed toward the check-in desk, smiling nervously at the lady who was beckoning for my passport and telling me to put my suitcase on the conveyor for weighing; then she handed me the boarding pass, saying, "Enjoy your flight."

"Thank you," I answered, and followed the signs to Terminal A, through security and by now I was desperate for something to drink. I sat down at a window table and glanced at my watch. Only an hour and a half to wait before boarding at gate 28. I sipped alternately between hot chocolate and water, then wandered around the duty-free shops, bought a book and headed down to the boarding gate.

Soon, I was standing at the entrance to a massive jet airliner for the first time in my life, wishing the reasons were different. The smiling stewardess indicated where I would find my seat, and I followed the others down the narrow aisle. I had a window seat, which helped take my mind off the reason for this flight and the trepidation I was plagued with. I secured my safety belt and nervously read the safety instructions listed in the in-flight magazine.

30th March 2002. The aircraft doors closed, everyone was seated, and I felt the plane begin to move and held onto the arm of the seat. The gentleman sitting next to me smiled sympathetically.

"Is this your first time flying?" he asked.

"Yes, and I'm terrified." My body was visibly shaking as we taxied onto the runway in preparation for take-off. Then the engines shuddered and whined; I wanted to die. I closed my eyes, gripped the armrests firmly and stopped breathing as the plane gathered speed, the engines whined and I felt myself being pushed back into my seat. The sensation made me gasp for the breath I'd been holding, while oxygen and adrenaline surged through my veins and the magnificent flying machine lifted gracefully into the air. I was on my way to Paris.

CHAPTER THIRTY:

Europe

Eleven hours later, I arrived in Paris and disembarked, following the crowd off the plane, through immigration and joined the hum of people in the 'Hall des Arrivées,' and had a good look around me before finding a seat and doing the proverbial 'waiting', as instructed, keeping a vigilant eye out for a tall black man dressed in a dark suit, as described. Another Nigerian, I assumed.

The hum of people arriving, leaving and greeting loved ones would have been far more exciting to watch if my brain wasn't playing tricks on me; suddenly, all the black men I saw were dressed in dark suits, they were mostly all tall, aloof and unfriendly. My mind was racing, wondering how *they* would identify me, and what if *they* didn't contact me, among a jumble of other terrifying thoughts.

After sitting for half an hour, I got up and wandered around in weary awe of my surroundings. Coming in from Africa, the first time off the continent, I'd never seen so many white people in one place in my life and for the first time in hours, I managed to enjoy a little smile to myself. Fifteen minutes later, I sat down with a bottle of water and checked my phone for messages or missed call alerts - there were neither. The momentary smile vanished, tensions elevated and the flood gates to irrational thoughts opened, then I had to remind myself of the Nigerian's words in Johannesburg; 'They will contact you, just wait.' That blessed 'wait' word again and I remembered what Andre had told me about the army, 'Hurry up and wait.'

As the minutes rolled into hours, waiting became more and more challenging. I couldn't even focus on the women's magazine I'd bought to pass the time. My heart was racing; I desperately wanted to go home.

'Why the hell did I agree to do this?' I murmured under my breath, as another hour ticked by and an icy fear gripped me. I was tired, panic-stricken, alone in a strange land with nowhere to go.

It was light now; a new Paris day was dawning, and Margaret needed to take control and make a decision. I was too tired to think; all I wanted to do was sleep, but the new day was nearly upon us. I dragged myself to the information desk and asked where I would find a cheap hotel and how I would get there. A well-spoken information clerk efficiently booked me into a cheap hotel and kindly drew out instructions on getting to the hotel after I'd explained to her I'd never been in Paris. My travels weren't over; I had to take the underground train to get to the hotel.

Alarmed - the Underground! I'd never been on a train in my life, let alone an underground one. Trains were not the mode of travel many white South Africans used much, and there was no such thing as an underground one. Collecting my thoughts, I followed the signs that lead to the Underground station and managed to find my way to the hotel and checked in. Walking up the steps to the entrance of the hotel, I was surprised at how grubby the façade was, having a preconceived notion that everything in Paris would be glitzy and glamorous. The threadbare carpet in the foyer was as tired as I felt, but it was a cheap place to stay until they called.

Having the key to a room on the second floor, I dumped my suitcase and asked where I could have breakfast before I fainted; I was starving.

I was guided to a pleasant little bistro not far from the hotel, and as I got to the door, the smell of good coffee and hot bread made my mouth water. Sinking my teeth into a freshly buttered croissant was heaven. The scrambled eggs were good, the coffee topped me up with a good dose of caffeine and now I wanted a cigarette. With a full tummy and coffee, a cigarette was essential to complete the meal. I hadn't brought many packets with me, but I couldn't hold out any longer. I paid, walked outside and lit up; it was the second cigarette I'd had since leaving Johannesburg. I pulled every bit of the smoke deep into my lungs to calm me, and as I exhaled the first puff, my phone rang. Grappling for the phone in my pocket, I noticed it was Storm calling; I let it ring and she hung up. I could not have answered that call. The appalling stirrings of deplorable guilt came rushing back, ripping into my gut. I took another long draw on the cigarette.

I had asked the family not to call while I was supposedly relaxing at God's Window, many thousands of miles from where I was now, but I couldn't help wondering why Storm should try calling. I guessed if it were urgent, she'd call back a bit later.

I'd just got back to my room, nestled my head on the pillow when the phone rang again. I jumped up thinking it was Storm, this time I would answer, but I saw on the screen it wasn't her.

"Hello," I said hesitantly.

"Get on a train to Brussels," a deep male voice said. "You will be met in Brussels in the morning." The phone went dead.

'Oh great, how the fuck do I get to Brussels?' I mumbled to myself. 'No time given, nothing. What kind of instructions were these?' Andre had said they could be very blunt and leave you wondering what to do, but somehow it worked.

I didn't have the faintest idea where I was in Paris; now I had to get to Brussels! Why Brussels?

I sat on the edge of the bed, suddenly alert again; it didn't last long. I lay back and fell into a deep sleep, waking after seven the following morning. With all my wits about me after sixteen hours of sleep, I began to question why I was being sent to Brussels and not on to Japan. This diversion had not been mentioned before I left Johannesburg. Something didn't feel right, but for now, I needed to shower, pack up and find out how to get to Brussels.

The receptionist kindly explained what I had to do and how I would get to Brussels. Three-quarters of an hour later, I was seated on a train to Brussels, desperate for a cigarette to calm my nerves but there was no smoking permitted.

During the journey, a different voice shouted down the phone at me.

"You're doing well, lady," he said.

'Yes, I thought so too!' I didn't dare verbalise my thoughts.

"When you get to Brussels, lady, you will be met. Now listen carefully," he said.

"I am listening," I replied sharply. "And I hope there will be someone to meet me, not like at the airport." He ignored me.

"A tall, well-built black man will meet you. He will be wearing a red shirt with black trousers." The phone went dead, as before. I was furious. This was ridiculous. Andre never told me it was a cat and mouse guessing game played around Europe.

"Damn them," I breathed out loudly, and the lady sitting across from me frowned. I smiled back, politely. The most frustrating people to deal with - the lack of adequate instructions annoyed me. Wouldn't have been so bad if I knew where I was going and what I was doing. My shoulders were on fire, my neck as stiff as a rod, my mood sharp and fear was on the prowl again down the avenues of my mind; I needed nicotine.

I arrived in Brussels, starving, shaky and disorientated; my stomach felt disconnected from my mouth. I'd spied a small cafe coming in and went directly to it, grabbed a sandwich and sank another cup of coffee, defiantly thinking; 'If they can't find me, they can phone me.' I'd get the hang of this.

Living off rubbish like sandwiches and snacky type meals since I'd left Johannesburg was making feel ill. With the tight budget I was on, I didn't have much choice. The sandwich I'd just eaten tasted like another; it was the freshest one I'd had so far, chicken mayonnaise on whole-wheat bread, dripping with the best mayonnaise I'd ever tasted. With the second one consumed, I collapsed on a bench and lit a cigarette, inhaling deeply, my eyes closed in the ecstasy of filtered nicotine. I lent my head back before exhaling smoke circles above my head when I felt someone tap my shoulder and my eyes flew open. It was a uniformed man carrying a baton - it wasn't the baton that terrified me but looking straight into the face of a man in uniform. He said something to me, and I looked at him dumbly, indicating with my hands that I had not understood him and in perfect English, he said, "No smoking in public, Ma'am."

I squashed the tip of the cigarette out and dropped it back in the packet; something I would never have done at home, but these weren't normal circumstances.

The next man that tapped me on the shoulder asked if I was Margaret. For a second, I was about to give him a piece of my mind, then remembered, I *was* Margaret.

"Yes," I said, "that's me."

Holding my shoulder so he didn't lose me in the crowds of people racing around the station, he marched me out of the impressive station building, then reached for my hand, which I ripped away disapprovingly.

"I will keep up; you don't need to hold my hand." I snapped.

Soon we were walking down a rabbit warren of quiet back streets and entered the lobby of Hotel van Jeanne, another low-budget, ancient-looking hotel. This one was smaller than the hotel in Paris, and in worse condition. The nameless man in red and black paid the bill for my room, two meals and refunded me what I'd spent on the last hotel and meals, adding another meagre allowance for food.

"Wait here," he said, then quickly disappeared before I could ask him for more precise instructions. One syllable instruction from nameless faces in foreign places was most disconcerting and thoroughly intimidating and I wondered how Andre had coped with it.

'I guess men handle it all differently,' I thought. The whole purpose of me doing it was I looked and behaved like a little innocent, rather reserved grandmother. It was what we needed to present. Andre, on the other hand, was about as big and muscular as the men I had to take instructions from, and had that burly, South African rugby player look.

I was shown to my room by a surly, rotund woman, who motioned I should follow her up a dark, dingy staircase to the first-floor landing. She only just fitted between the wooden bannister rails as she heaved her large frame up each step, catching her apron frills between her bulk and the bannister rails and puffing like a steam train, cursing all the way up until we came out on the landing. I thought she was going to expire from the exertion.

"All.... the....rooms lead off... this landing... Madam," she said breathlessly, gasping for air. "You....... are.... room 13," she said, pointing to the door and handing me the key.

"Oh no, not number 13," I moaned superstitiously. Under these circumstances I didn't need bad luck; I'd had enough of that in my life. Four steps to my right and there I stood in front of room number 13, feeling very apprehensive, and inserted the key. The room was minute; just enough space for a narrow single bed, a tiny wardrobe with two single coat hangers hanging in it and two shelves. A single glass door led onto a small balcony and was the only source of natural light. At least this one had a bathroom en-suite.

As I was stepping out of my jeans, preparing for a much-needed shower, the phone rang.

I answered, waiting for the next one syllable instruction. The voice instructed me to remain at the hotel until they called with further instructions. I felt my shoulders relax a bit; I had some time to myself. I had a shower, washed some clothes in the basin and hung them up to dry, draping them over whatever furniture was available. I was too tired to bother with supper and too depressed to feel hungry.

Later that night, the noise in the room above woke me. It took me a few moments to establish where I was, then try and work out the noise; aah, I got it. I struggled to block the sounds and stop myself from chuckling wickedly, wondering if the couple above knew I could hear all their orgasmic groans, sexy little shrieks and even louder cries of ecstasy. Snickering gently, I pulled the dusty pink duvet over my head, and eventually, the sounds of erotica died away, and I fell asleep again. The following morning, I packed up my things and headed downstairs to the dining room for a leisurely cooked breakfast, my first hot meal in three days. Back in my room, feeling satiated and comfortable, I pulled out the book I'd bought at the airport in Johannesburg and started reading, but the picture of a windmill standing alone on a farm in the barren Karoo on the cover reminded me far too much of home; I began to sob. The burden of this mission was getting to me; the deep sense of guilt, fear and homesickness snatched at my chest and I put the book down, allowing rivers of salty tears to pour from my eyes. How blessed I had been to have grown up on a farm in Africa, surrounded by wide-open spaces, beautiful clean air, solitude, and peace, unlike here. A constant cacophony of busy, over-populated city life, and I wondered how many people here had ever experienced the silence of the African bush. With swollen eyes, I ventured out onto the streets; I couldn't read, it was hopeless even trying. I wandered around close to the hotel, peering into shop windows, fascinated by how different it was to home. A little side street beckoned to me and I found a quaint café tucked in at the end of the street. I snuck into a seat right at the back and ordered a salad, a glass of water and a cup of coffee. My heart ached for home, my children and conversation in my mother tongue.

Back in the room, I mentally ran through the instructions so far. Everything was different; I wondered why but it wasn't for me to question. I was itching to get the job done and get home and beginning to think I should have sent Andre – he knew what to do. I had not heard from anyone all day, and that night I lay awake with the burden of this decision weighing heavily upon me. I was about to drift off to sleep when the phone rang, as it always seemed to do, but this time it was one o'clock in the morning. I answered, feeling quite spikey and annoyed by the disturbance but braced and ready for the next veiled instruction - it was Dion.

"JesusChristElizabethwhereareyou?" His words all ran into one jumbled question from the interference of humming and crackling sounds on the line. I listened, then killed the call and switched off the phone. He was the one person I did *not* want to talk to. It was because of him I was here and in this mess. Sleep came in waves between terrorising thoughts.

In the morning, just after switching the phone back on, the Nigerians called. I was to stay where I was; they would see me later that evening. Another day's delay, which added to my tension and anxiety and gave me more time to think; I didn't want to think; I needed to get the hell out of Europe, on to Japan and home. I had dinner and put it on a tab for the men to pick up later when they collected me.

A loud knock on the door startled me. I opened it hesitantly - two strangers stood at the door, men I'd not seen before, and I was about to slam the door shut when one of them spoke.

"Take the train to Amsterdam tomorrow; leave here at 6 am. There will be someone to meet you there."

"Why do I have to go to Amsterdam? I was told to collect a case in Paris and go on to Japan. Why am I being lied to and kept in suspense like this?" Neither of them answered; instead, I was handed a bundle of money, and they left without providing an answer.

A young man was there at the station to meet me and informed me we were to make the journey to Amsterdam together. Relieved by the news that I'd have company on the next leg to Amsterdam, my tummy began to make noises that it needed filling again - I was starving. Breakfast - another bloody sandwich, but this time, I bought an apple and a banana which I ate on the train to Amsterdam.

Our train arrived early. This escort was a little more talkative - I wouldn't learn his name, but he was friendly and polite; quite different from the others. Chatting openly about how often he'd escorted South Africans, he said he'd show me around the station when we got there. 'Bizarre,' I thought, train stations in South Africa were buildings you didn't want to hang around in too long.

Once we'd got off the train, he started the tour – this was no ordinary train station. Above me were impressive high-arched roofs, healthy manicured gardens, a perfect spectacle, a delightful mingling of nature and chaos. Then we went outside; I was speechless. I'd never seen architecture like this in my life as I gazed upon the iconic Renaissance façade the building boasted; it was stunning. I was awestruck. Railway stations in my mind were dirty, scruffy places that no architect would want to put their name to. I wished I'd had a camera. He was very kind, but I found it awkward trying to strike up a conversation with a person with no name.

"This really is beautiful. Thank you for showing me. Do you mind if I call you Jack?"

"Nope," he answered cheerfully. The conversation seemed to flow more smoothly after that. Jack told me a bit about his life and how difficult it was as a Nigerian living in Holland, how he missed his family and how unhappy he was doing the job, but he made good money and supported his family and his parents. They were poor rural folk who scraped out a living only if the rainy season was kind to them, growing maize and vegetables and selling eggs. His mother made a special bread which she sold too and I couldn't help feel sorry for him, even though he irritated me by insisting on wanting to buy me small gifts which I quickly declined.

Eventually, he got the call he'd been waiting for, and we hurried off to find a taxi which took us to a grubby suburban sprawl in a seedy, dirty part of Amsterdam. Rows upon rows of red-brick terraced houses stood shoulder to shoulder; they were unkempt and here the architecture was ugly. As the taxi wove through the dingy streets of what I'd heard was a stunning city, I wished again that the circumstances were different so I could see the tourist spots, the beautiful parts. I caught a few brief glimpses of the famous canal system as we crisscrossed over old arched bridges built in the same red brick as the terraced houses. As impressive as the bridge was, living in row upon row of houses all attached to each other was utterly alien to me. I was glad I was only going to be here for one day in this run-down part, where the pavements were dirty and decorated with ugly dustbins that stood along both sides of the narrow streets. Even the trees looked tatty and tired; no wonder Jack wanted to get home. Then the sickening realisation of why we'd come to Amsterdam suddenly dawned on me - we were in the drug capital of the world. I wanted to vomit, to get rid of the lies that polluted my innards. For a moment, I naively hoped that what I'd just thought was not going to materialise; it still could be diamonds. I left without Andre confirming it.

"What the hell are we doing here, Jack?" I asked, feeling the quiver in my lower jaw. He was aware of what had just passed through my mind, so he smiled casually, "collecting the suitcase you will be delivering to Japan," he said, with casual obviousness.

"I think this whole trip has just been continuous lies, Jack. I wasn't told any of this in Johannesburg."

"Ask no questions; they tell no lies." He waved his index finger at me.

The taxi dropped us outside one of the grubby-looking terraced houses where we met with another 'no-name' Nigerian. Looking at their living conditions, who they were and the underworld they operated in, I wondered how it was possible they got into these European countries to live, work and manage to send money back to their families, but as Jack had warned, 'ask no questions.'

Waves of shame gripped me like menopausal sweats.

'Had Andre lied to me? Were diamonds a smokescreen to appease me?'

I'd not paid attention to the street name or the number of the house, all I could think of was what lowly, dishonourable and filthy levels I'd stooped to in my desperate state of mind. Sitting inside an empty lounge on a tatty old chair, looking down at a threadbare green carpet, knowing what I was waiting for, mortified me. Would I ever get over this disgraceful act? At the time, I thought I was acting in the best interest of my family and my business. Had I known the truth of how this mule thing really worked, I would *never* have agreed to do this, but I reminded myself it was too late, and it was futile trying to fight with the noise in my head and the hundreds of voices screaming at me; there would be time for recrimination once I got home. Two more days left; I could do this. I had to do this.

"Did you bring the suitcase?" Jack asked the new man.

"No suitcase yet," he answered, shrugged his shoulders and quickly disappeared without a word and there we sat in a cold, heartless place, the stench of unscrupulous dealings crept into the crevices of my soul, dirtying every living part of me.

We sat in silence. Jack lay down, seemingly oblivious to the world around him, and slept. I watched him and envied the way he could switch off and sleep in the most uncomfortable of surroundings and under such circumstance. I wondered then if people like Jack felt the same vulnerability and fear that I was experiencing. Perhaps not. He seemed totally at ease and accepting of the situation, even though he'd expressed how much he missed his cultural norms and his family. We were both in it for similar reasons; to support family. He'd explained that if he didn't do this, his family could die of starvation. If I didn't do this, I'd have murdered my ex-husband and been flung in jail, but, as in Jack's case, family were primary; without a business, I couldn't afford to send Pieter to university.

No matter how small or brief my part, it *was* unforgivable. Self-loathing was often overwhelming. Finally, the other man returned, pulling a small black suitcase up the steps and shoved it towards me.

"For you," he said. Hearing voices, Jack stirred and jumped to his feet as if he'd never been asleep and urged me to hurry.

"Take it, take it, time to leave," he insisted. Uncharacteristically irritable, he grabbed my sleeve and dragged me roughly out the house and off we went at a pace, back-tracking some of the way we'd come in the taxi, then we took a short cut back to the station. My feet were killing me when we got to the station; then in a blur, we were on the train back to Brussels.

"You get off, go back to the hotel and wait."

"This is fucking ridiculous, Jack." I'd had enough of their bullshit. He never answered, looking at me with a strange enquiring expression.

"Why are you looking at me like that, Jack?"

"What are you doing this for? You don't look like the kinda person who should be doing this job."

I'd wondered why too, more than once.

He handed me a tightly wrapped bundle of Euros and nodded; he'd understood.

I got back to the hotel, dragging the dirty black suitcase and my little red one, and hauled them up the narrow stairway, unlocked my room and collapsed onto the bed. I was exhausted, tearful and filled with bitter regret.

I counted the notes Jack had given me, dialled room service and ordered a hot meal. Twenty minutes later, there was a knock at my door and the smell of roast beef and gravy was the best thing I'd smelt since leaving home. The plate was loaded with the vegetables I craved; carrots, broccoli and potato wedges.

As I put my knife and fork together on an empty plate, I noticed the ominous black case with its malevolent aura – it was staring at me, beckoning me to open it and an hour later it got the better of me. Gripping the zipper tag, I peeled back the lid and gagged. A dirty old 'T' shirt and a pair of men's jeans lay at the top and the whiff of stale, dirty male body odour drifted up to my nose and I had to swallow rapidly to prevent my dinner coming up. Bracing my jaw and swallowing hard, I stood for a minute or two with my eyes squeezed tightly shut. Eventually, I turned back and lifted the clothing. Two brown paper packages bound with endless string, shrouded in suspicion, lay on the bottom of the case. Jack's words reverberated through my mind; 'ask no questions, tell no lies.' It wasn't for me to question what was in the packages, all I had to do was get them to Japan, hand the suitcase over, collect my plane ticket and fly home; job done, except.......

Halfway around Europe, just for this? Why didn't someone bring it to Paris for me? None of it made much sense unless I'd been misled from the start.

Later that night, tossing and turning in bed, unable to stop millions of thoughts swirling through it, the primary thought as the night wore on was – how do I get out of this? Now I had the packages the implications were ominous. I had enough money in my savings to book into a cheap hotel somewhere else, lie low for a few days, giving my sister time to get me a ticket home. These thoughts, interspersed with a few logical ones, warning me of the consequences of ducking out at this late stage, and what could happen to both Andre and I wasn't worth contemplating; or was it? These guys were ruthless. In the end, I decided there was no way out; I had to go through with it.

The room stank now I'd opened the case. It was stuffy enough without the overbearing stench that hung in the room, which only served to reinforce the menacing feeling that tormented me when a knock on the door startled me.

"Who is it?" I called out. It was Jack, so I opened the door a fraction and noticed Jack was not alone. The stranger with him spoke quietly.

"Tomorrow we buy plane ticket to Japan," he said. "One man meets you at ticket office; you get money, buy ticket and bring back to this man," he said, pointing to Jack, then he handed me a little more money for the hotel bill and my food.

The following morning, I boarded the train to Charles de Galle once more. Weakened by a fitful night, my intestines knotting up rebelliously, I couldn't concentrate. I was a nervous wreck, ached for home and was desperate to get the hell out of Europe as fast as I could.

Just two days left, but the worst was still ahead of me.

Jack was there to meet me as promised and handed me the money for the plane ticket to Japan which I purchased.

"You will be met at the airport by a tall black man dressed in blue jeans, a denim shirt, and a cap with a football emblem on it." He smiled, then added, "It's the football World Cup on in Japan."

What did I know about the football club emblems? Everyone would be wearing football regalia then.

Timing was everything now. I had to get off the train and run like a woman possessed, get through passport control and onto the plane in minimal time.

"They didn't give me much time, did they?" I said to Jack, who just shook his head and said farewell.

"Good Luck. Eyes wide," he said, indicating with his fingers as he pointed toward his eyes, then he left.

A power failure halfway to Charles de Gaulle brought the train to an abrupt halt, leaving me a jabbering nervous wreck and all the other passengers in an uproar. All I seemed to hear was the rapid beat of my heart in my chest.

I had to be on that flight. Five long minutes later, the power came back on, and we were on our way again, then I learned through incessant jabber in the coach, there were some essential footballers on board the train; the flight to Japan was waiting, but we had to do everything quickly. We were ushered through, our luggage checked in, and we raced to the boarding gate and ran onto the waiting plane in record time.

Once I was seated, I wondered how the ominous black case had got through the airport x-ray machines. Dismissing the thought…, 'ask no questions….'

Flight attendants quickly got everyone into their appropriate seats, the aircraft doors closed, seatbelts fastened, and we were in the air in minutes. The intercom announcement warned of tight security at Narita airport, Japan. Korea-Japan World Cup Soccer - expect delays at the airport, we were advised.

In less than a week, I'd been halfway around the world for two brown paper packages.

We disembarked, and by this time, my bad shoulder was throbbing riotously and hurt like hell. It was almost too painful to move, but I was one step closer to home.

CHAPTER THIRTY-ONE

I stood nervously at Immigration check-in, trying to appear as relaxed as possible. An unsmiling Japanese immigration officer's face with lifeless jet-black eyes was staring at me, beckoning for my passport. I smiled and handed it to him and watched him fingering the pages of my fake British passport till he found the photograph of Margaret and looked up at me, then looked back to the passport photograph with a doubting stare and looked up at me again. The second time he frowned; a primal fear gripped my gut, a sensation so powerful, I struggled to maintain a semblance of normality. He glared at me just long enough for me to understand I could be in trouble.

"Do you have any other form of identification?" he asked politely. This time I flashed a smile at him, shook my head.

"No Sir," I said, politely praying my lips would not quiver. Putting my passport down on the counter in front of him, he picked up a magnifying glass.

I went rigid. The fight or flight instinct was fully activated.

Desperately trying to keep myself from fidgeting, licking my lips, fiddling with my fingers or doing anything else that may give me away, I fixed my focus on watching him run the magnifying glass over my photograph – ironically it was the only part of the passport that was authentic, but then, as I feared, he carefully checked the rest of the document. The photograph had been taken with me wearing my hair pinned back. Today it wasn't tied up, so I quickly smiled at him and nodded and pulled my hair back into a ponytail. All I got in return was a cynical glare.

"Please wait here," he said. I knew in an instant what may happen to me if they suspected I was a fraud. I had to abandon the black case.

'Leave it pressed up against the counter or in the toilet,' I thought, but to leave it up against the counter, the passenger behind me would surely alert me to it; I needed the toilet.

There was no name tag on the suitcase so that they couldn't link me to it.

I was panic-stricken and rapidly running out of options. I had to think quickly, but the official was back before I could do anything.

"Come with me please," he said, very politely and led me to a glass cubicle and motioned for me to take a seat on the wooden bench.

"May I use the toilet, please?" I asked politely. He nodded, pointing to the toilet signs but ordered me to leave my suitcases where they were. There was no fooling this immigration officer; he'd seen it all before; foiled again. With crushing dread, I realised that unless I could somehow talk my way out of this situation and convince them the suitcase wasn't mine, I would be arrested.

I found the toilets, sat down but nothing was working. I couldn't release a drop of urine. I sat for a few moments longer and willed myself to empty my bladder, then everything released.

In my innocence, I'd not given 'being caught' that much thought before now, probably because Andre had done this twice and got through and I believed I would too. The Nigerians and Andre skirted over the possibilities of arrest in our interview. We agreed that it was unlikely that customs would suspect an older woman being a 'mule' but that was idiotic naiveite! As I stood up, I began to shake violently and struggled to do up the zip of my jeans. Primal fear was clicking in; it was so real I could smell it - a sickly sweet, metallic smell.

I returned to the cubicle and sat down on the bench. My bladder and everything else empty, my tummy felt more able to deal with what was to come next. Then three Japanese policemen marched into the glass cubicle. I didn't dare look at them. Starring ahead of me, I remained as outwardly motionless as I could, then one of the officers said something I didn't understand. The one who'd spoken motioned that I should follow him. I could hardly breathe by this point. I was escorted into a small office and ordered to sit down. Survival makes every sense crisp; even the din in the airport intensified as waves of panic and terror swept through me.

The interrogation began.

They asked where I was from and what my name was. I told them I was from Britain and gave them my false name, a name that I'd engraved to memory. I was her; she was me. Then they asked for my passport number, and I recited that too, realising then I may have walked into the trap. How many people bother to remember their passport number so readily, unless…

Then they asked for my residential address in Britain.

I glanced at them, not knowing what to say while attempting to prevent the insufferable fear I was feeling from showing on my face. The three men looked at each other, then looked back at me. Their expressions mirrored my thoughts. Time stood still; the silence was tormenting.

"Sorry Ma'am, but this is not you," one of them said, pointing at my passport photograph while shaking his head. It genuinely was me, but I knew they were not referring to only the image, more to the fake passport.

"That is me, Sir," I said. (amazing how one's tone changes when one is telling the truth) They ignored me.

"What's in your suitcases?" one of the other police officers asked.

"I have only one suitcase, Sir," I responded.

"I see there are two with you." He was taunting me and enjoying it. My insides shifted uncomfortably.

"Only the red suitcase belongs to me, Sir," I responded as politely as I could under the circumstances, then explained how I came to have two suitcases.

"My train was delayed in Paris, Sir. In a rush to get on the waiting plane, one of the men who was on the train with me and booked on the same flight asked me to take his hand luggage through for him."

I noticed one of the officer's shift and appeared to be listening intently. I prayed he was considering that I may be telling the truth for they knew about the delays.

"The airport staff forced us to hurry and get on board because of the delay, Sir. So..." I breathed out to control my voice. "I agreed to carry it through for him and had every intention of giving it back to him, but the immigration official told me to follow him to the glass cubicle before I could hand it back. The owner is probably still waiting for me, Sir." I looked boldly into the eyes of the policeman. He turned and nodded to the other. I didn't dare drop my shoulders or change my position even though the tension was excruciating.

"May we look inside that suitcase, Ma'am?"

"Yes, of course. I don't care what you do with it, but perhaps it would be polite to return it to the gentleman it belongs to," I said, as calmly as I was able and watched the officer open the case and whirl away from it as the putrid smell of stale, male body odour assaulted his nasal passages, just as it had done mine, and prayed that might get me off. I watched him dig through the men's clothing with a grimacing expression from holding his breath as he lifted the layers of filthy clothing, then found what he was looking for. Lifting the two bound paper packages out of the case, he handed them to his co-worker, then looked back at me.

"Are you aware of what is inside those packages, Ma'am?" he asked with an icy cold tone.

"Of course not, Sir. I have already told you that is not my suitcase," I said sharply and shifted my body weight insolently for I genuinely didn't know what was in the packages.

He began opening the packages in front of me. "What is this?" He asked.

"I don't know, I have never seen anything like that in my life." And once again, I genuinely hadn't, but that didn't save me.

"It is about 5kg of marijuana." He lifted the packages up and down as if to assess their weight invisibly.

One of the other police officers took some away for testing.

"What? No wonder that bastard wanted me to take his case," I snarled, trying to ignore the nasty sinking feeling in the pit of my stomach. What I'd thought while sitting in the dingy house in Amsterdam was now confirmed. I felt crushed; betrayed by my son-in-law? I was sure he would have known the package would be drugs. Viv must have known too. How was I ever going to forgive myself for this? Storm would never forgive me, how could she? Switching my thoughts back quickly to the present, remaining steadfast in my determination to convince these two officers I knew nothing of this, I vaguely heard the officers talking, one believed me; the other two didn't.

"I told you Sir; it is not my suitcase. There has been a big mistake. Check my red case to satisfy yourselves, then let me be on my way."

"You are a liar," came the scornful response from the man who didn't believe me. I was losing ground, and I knew it, but I stuck to my story and raised my voice a little.

"Sir, you are making a false accusation, which I consider demeaning." I could sense all I was doing was irritating him further; then he prodded his finger into my shoulder, which, just my luck, bounced off the rolled-up tissue I had tucked under my bra strap which triggered a whole new line of questioning.

"What are you hiding in there?" Incredibly, I remained composed and stared angrily at him for touching me, which I understood was not permitted – I should have caused chaos for him for doing that, but I didn't.

"It's a roll of tissue, Sir," I said. I pulled it out and shook it defiantly in front of him, then the results came back positive for drugs.

"What else is on you?" he demanded

"Excuse me, Sir; you are rude. I have nothing on me. I own my handbag and my red suitcase, nothing else. I'm here to meet my aunt and watch football." I lied then gave him the address of the hotel they'd booked for me. They hadn't pressed again for my residential address in Britain, and I prayed they wouldn't. The only city that came to mind was London, and I couldn't think of a proper street name in English. Fear had terminated my ability to think clearly in English and made me stutter when I spoke; thankfully, a mixture of anger, resentment and adrenaline came to my aid.

The nasty officer was like a fox terrier, determined to break me, shake me and bury me with others caught for drug-smuggling. I was shocked when he asked permission to have me X-rayed. I didn't refuse. I didn't need to, and I was keen to prove the son-of-a-bitch wrong.

"Yes, you may x-ray me," I said, keeping my eyes focussed on his as I answered. Because I'd agreed without hesitation, I heard the officer who believed me begin speaking in Japanese to the other. It was dangerous to assume under such circumstances, but he thought I was telling the truth. My hopes were in vain as I watched angry gesticulating between them and he was ordered out the cubicle. He came back about five minutes later and shook his head, saying something briefly to the mean officer, who smiled. I was bewildered and wondered what was going on; whatever it was, it didn't appear to be in my favour. I was left alone in the office while they collected the X-ray results that seemed to take forever, but there was no point in making a run for it, so I sat and waited.

The two nasty officers finally returned and, pointing to my suitcase, he said something to his companion who unzipped the lid and flipped it open and began making an inventory on an official pad of everything in it, what I was wearing and what was in my handbag; then I knew this was it. I'd been caught. I refused to hand over my phone when they asked for it; it was my lifeline to my children.

"Why are you doing this, Sir? You have no proof that I have committed a crime." He didn't answer, but his face suggested I shouldn't anger him further.

"Let me ask again," he said forcefully, "I want your phone."

"Why, Sir?" A hot sweat began to melt my icy resolve. My pulse racing now. We stared at each other; I tried to keep a steely look of anger but acting and lying were not my strong points.

"You are guilty of drug-smuggling into Japan with a false passport. You are under arrest. Now hand over your telephone." I wanted to die at that moment; his words confirmed my thoughts.

"Who are your contacts?" he asked.

"Who? I don't understand."

"The people that got you to do this act," he said. My lips stuck together, my mouth had dried out, and I couldn't answer. I sat motionless and silent until he prompted again with the same question.

"I am sorry, I do not understand. What act?" I managed to say, smoothing my tongue over my lips; he was getting more annoyed but kept his composure and asked a third time.

"Who are they?"

"I don't know who you are talking about!" I snapped at him, refusing to let go of this tiny thread of hope, but he was relentless, and I finally broke down. It was over, everything was over, and I fainted. When I came to, I was lying on the floor looking up into the face of a petite Japanese lady. There was no emotion in the lady's eyes, but her voice had a gentle timbre to it, and she asked kindly, "Are you all right, Ma'am?" I nodded, disappointed I was still alive, and tears began to pour down my cheeks.

She packed everything I owned back into my suitcase and when she'd finished, marched me out the office in handcuffs down to the holding cells within the airport buildings. Every muscle in my limbs quivered wildly, and my temples threatened to explode. She ushered me into a small room where we were met by another lady officer who searched me physically, violating the very essence of my womanhood. Stripped naked, asked to bend forward, and, with a gloved hand, she inspected deep into my anus and then my vagina. I let out a guttural animal sound which came from deep within; the sound of naked fear and terrifying humiliation, which then gave way to uncontrollable sobs.

Something in that moment died within me.

From somewhere, as if it were far away, I heard a different voice saying an 8-year jail sentence was imminent. Committing suicide was a very appealing fate as I stood, naked and vulnerable, while the two women removed the underwire from my bra. When they gave back the bra, they handed me a pair of old trousers with an elasticated waist and a pull-on shirt with a V-neck and collar. Any clothing with buttons and zippers on is not worn in the holding cells. Shoes weren't allowed either. Socks were permitted, and I was handed a second-hand pair and marched off down to the cells.

I looked and felt like a dirty, worthless tramp, an experience more humiliating than losing my business.

All I had left in life were memories; some I treasured, many haunted me. Everything I owned had been confiscated, including my life. Not even my toothbrush, toothpaste and personal toiletries were permitted to go with me. All I wanted to hear were Storm and Pieter's reassuring voices, just once more, but there was no way of contacting them or anyone else in the family.

CHAPTER THIRTY-TWO

"Look what you've done." I ran toward Papa, screaming hysterically, waving the local newspaper under his nose.

"You've killed my mother."

Revenge was pressing and suddenly, without a moment's thought, my right fist connected with his jaw, and the drink he was holding flew across the carpet.

"It's you who should be dead; you're a nothing, and now you've taken Mama down too." I stepped back, tears of anger and devastation pouring down my cheeks. I was shaken by what I'd just done to my father, but I had no respect for him; that had gone long ago. He was no role model and never had been, merely a biological attachment and even that I wished he wasn't.

I learned of my mother's fate in the worst way possible - as an impressionable, vulnerable teenager. It came through in the jeering chants and nasty whispers from cruel fellow scholars who savoured the gossip and revelled in watching my pain.

Back in my room with the door locked, inconsolable and angry, I couldn't fathom how Mom could have done what she did. It was so unlike her. The more I analysed the situation, the more deep-seated the hatred for my father grew. Even though, I knew Mom would have been doing whatever she did for me so we could get away from him, but that made me feel worse.

Concentrating on studying for a science test in the morning was impossible. There were so many conflicting thoughts swirling around in my head. I had to find somewhere else to live and someone to help me through my last year of school. But who? I couldn't go on living with my father; I didn't trust myself to be near him. Now I understood, with greater clarity, why Mama had a desire to end his life on occasions. It was his fault Mama was in jail, and I'd never forgive him.

Then I heard a light knocking on my door and Storm's tearful voice calling my name. We fell into each other's arms, sobbing bitterly and I closed the door, locking it to keep Papa out.

"Why did Mama lie to us, Sissie?" I sobbed.

"She wouldn't have meant to hurt us; she went to do this for us. Andre told me he was going to do the job, but she insisted on taking his place for she felt he should stay and look after Viv and the children."

"Why didn't that useless drunken father of ours do it then? He got Mama into this mess in the first place."

I couldn't stop crying. The visions of my precious mother in a prison cell, terrified, alone and very far away, while Papa sat in his comfortable armchair, drinking.

Storm tried hard to soothe my brokenness, and eventually, I calmed down. She'd been sobbing too; we both had swollen eyes and puffy faces from endless crying.

"How are we going to get Mama home, Sis?"

"I don't know; we have no contact with her. The consulate contacted me today. They will send her a little money, and apparently, she will be able to write soon."

"Oh, Sissie, why? Why did Andre and Viv let her go?"

"It's too late to think about that, Boetie; we have to be strong now and support each other."

Storm left my room an hour later, and I cried myself to sleep. In the morning, I raced through a bowl of muesli then hurried off to school to write my science test. I hardly remember writing it, and I could barely hold my pen, but somehow, I got through it. Luckily, it was the last test before the final exams in a couple of months.

The days after Mom's arrest passed in a blur and my future suddenly seemed very dark. I only had a few months left of high school, then what? College wasn't something I could look forward to any longer. My hopes, my dreams, everything dashed, taken from me by a self-centred addict. That night, I knelt beside my bed as I had done as a child and prayed someone would take me away; only a few days later, my prayers were answered.

Uncle Ernest and his business partner, Uncle Niels, came to my rescue. I moved in with Uncle Ernest and his family for the remainder of my school year. It was a huge relief to be away from Papa.

I missed Mama terribly.

Leaving home caused another huge row with Papa.

A friend helped me move out one night when Papa was passed out drunk on the couch. We thought he was too drunk to know what we were doing. I'd handed Frikkie my computer and ran back upstairs to grab my suitcases, but Papa was waiting for me when I came down the stairs, blocking my exit. He was no match for me and this time I screamed at him to move out of my way. He took no notice, encouraging me to make a move on him again. Instead of hitting him, I pushed past him, knocking him out of my way, and put the cases in Frikkie's car boot and went back for the last few things in my room. I wasn't going to be intimidated by a drunk who had no conscience, even if he was my father. As I walked into the house, Papa locked the front door behind me and followed me up the stairs. I grabbed the last satchel off my bed and turned to face him. I wanted to do the decent thing and reason with him, but he lurched toward me aggressively and tried to hit me. I ducked to avoid his flying fist, and the next thing I remember, I was stepping over him at the bottom of the stairs. Taking my own set of keys out of my pocket, I unlocked the front door and left home forever.

CHAPTER THIRTY-THREE

Adrenaline was pumping rapidly through my veins; I was sure my temples were about to explode. Ahead of me were the temporary holding cells at Narita. The sight of them made me want to retch again, to spew out the shame, the pain, the lies and humiliation that was poisoning me. I violently pulled back against the two ladies holding me; like a child refusing to go to school, I sat down, my heels firmly pressing against the cement flooring to create the desired friction. I was not going to go into one of those cages.

The vision of what lay ahead was far beyond my grasp. Another guttural sob sounded from the pit of my stomach as I fought the two ladies who took little notice of me. They waited beside me while I put my head between my knees trying to gather my thoughts, then they pulled me up off the floor. I stood still, shivering and weak; my legs trembling, and I was petrified all urethral sphincters would let go leaving me wet and more humiliated, but my legs gave way again instead and I collapsed in a crumpled heap on the cold cement floor once more.

"Just breathe," the lady warders said, kindly, trying to assure me I would be fine. My mind was numbed, and my body paralysed by fear and refusing to co-operate. I couldn't move; nothing moved as my eyes stayed fixed on what was ahead of us. Patiently, they coaxed me into believing I would survive this ordeal. I took a few deep, oxygenating breaths and rose to face my fate.

The wire mesh cages were getting closer with each step we took. I wanted to yell out again that I couldn't go into them; instead, I whispered pathetically about how sorry I was.

There was no response from the two ladies. No-one gives a shit how sorry you are or how badly you needed money. In their eyes, all you are is a criminal.

Before they put me into the cells, I was shown where the lockers and cupboards were. The bedding store cupboard remained locked and was only opened at night for us to collect our bedding. My closet had in it a spare set of second-hand clothing similar to what I was wearing. Finally, they guided me to the cell block.

It was eerily quiet in the hall, everyone quietly mourning their capture. I was expecting it to reek of stale urine, halitosis and dejection, but surprisingly the place was immaculate except for the stench of crime, and I smelt like that filth.

Futons, the Japanese 'beds', were what we slept on. They sounded rather fancy, but when I saw them, they were far from what I'd seen in furniture stores.

At a prescribed time, we collected our futon set, which comprised of a sparsely padded mattress, a quilt and a pillow. The pillow was a strange cushion filled with masses of tiny little plastic pipes to give it some semblance of buoyancy.

On entering the cell, I was handed a cushion to sit on; a crumpled old square made of tired foam that had seen the bums of many prisoners before me and wasn't going to provide much comfort.

The cell block filled the more significant space in the middle of the hall and was grouped into multiple cells, separated by sheets of clear Perspex, which ensured the low life within could be viewed from anywhere in the hall by the roving police. There was nowhere to cower and hide from the shame and guilt I was feeling.

The floor covering was made from interwoven grass matting the Japanese called 'tatami'; it helped to hold back the cold, but nothing could hold back the cold I was feeling inside. A layer of this woven matting was about three inches thick; had it not been so old and tatty, it probably would have worked well.

Clutching my cushion, I slunk into the cell. If I'd had a tail, it would have been firmly between my legs with my spine curved upward in submissive fear. Entering with me was a deep, penetrating self-loathing, along with other fearful feelings that rapidly filled the crevices of my mind and soul. I didn't want to be alive.

I put the cushion on the floor, away from the other prisoners, and sat on it, propping my back against the Perspex wall. I wrapped my arms around my knees, pulling them up to my chest in a protective manner. The sweet musky odour, the initial fear response, had settled and dried on my skin and drifted up to my nose ensuring the memory of the interrogation became firmly etched in my mind.

My new 'home' for God alone knows how many days, was three meters by four meters. There were six of us crammed into that small space for three days. In the corner of the cell was a western-style toilet which my eyes fixed on, registering with horror that its Perspex surrounds were only blacked out to waist height.

"I can't do this," I wailed, and the other inmates looked at me with blank stares. This was not a place where sympathy could be found.

How was I to do my ablutions? I didn't even do that in front of the people closest to me. I surrendered to oblivion, removed from this horror for only a moment, and came around hearing the police officer saying to someone that the holding cells were busier than usual. I was forced to face the truth of my new world once more as I looked about somewhat dazed, then someone else mentioned the Football World Cup was to blame for so many being caught; airport security had been on high alert, as I'd experienced.

A crushing emptiness filled me. I stayed on the floor and curled into the foetal position on the matting, putting my head on the square cushion, and tucked my hands between my thighs, trying to shut out this grim reality.

'Oh, Storm, what have I done?' I whispered very quietly into my chest. I was still trembling from the inside out, feeling raw and vulnerable; then it was time for supper.

Seated cross-legged on my futon, I watched with numbed single-mindedness as 'dinner' got slid into the cell through a small opening at the base of the door. On the plate was some rice and a strange, unappetising pinkish slop which I was supposed to negotiate with a pair of chopsticks. I starred at it and suppressed a groan. I couldn't eat. When the plates were collected, a small styrene cup of hot green water that had an awful pungent smell, and a mug of cold water was pushed through. I drank the water, then took a sip of the hot green water and spat it back into the cup - I'd never tasted anything more disgusting.

I moved my futon back against the Perspex walling and propped myself against it again, closing my eyes, trying to breathe rhythmically and ignore the aches in my body. I went on rocking gently backwards and forwards throughout the night, asking for water every time a police officer passed the cells. The hunger pangs had gone with everything else I was dealing with, but I was severely dehydrated.

The cell was as silent as a desert at midnight, and just as cold. I constantly shivered, both from the cold air that surrounded me and my raw shameful thoughts. In the early hours of the morning, a million little voices were screaming accusations and questions, none of which I could answer. None of them would have been satisfactory had I found an answer. Nothing was going to change my predicament.

The only sounds were the intermittent sounds of police officers checking on us, like black cats scuttering through empty streets in search of rats that may have escaped. I hadn't sought an escape route.

During the night, probably nearer the early morning hours for my watch had been removed, I signalled to one of the officers and pleaded for water in a much bigger cup. My mind was foggy with exhaustion, and my vision was blurred; I desperately needed to rehydrate. I knew I had to put the embarrassment of peeing or defecating in public behind me somehow, but I had to drink, or I would end up seriously ill. Water, in copious amounts, was what I needed to get my kidneys functioning normally again as I watched my feet swell to double their size.

"Two cups, please," I asked, showing a sign with my fingers. The police officer shook her head, indicating just one. I shook my head, urgently gesticulating; I needed two large ones, and she nodded. I thought I saw a glimmer of a smile. She came back with one large cup which I downed while she stood outside the cell, waiting for the empty mug. Then I asked for one more which she obliged, drinking the second one more slowly.

The life-restoring liquid flowed into me and an hour later, my system began to function. Clarity of thought returned, but a burning sensation in my bottom shot hot spikes of pain down my legs and a tingling sensation in my feet. I had to get up and move, but there was so little room. I stood up and rubbed as vigorously as I could manage until the pain eased, then I needed a pee. There was nothing I could do but succumb to a bladder that was now about to burst. I sat on the seat-less cold porcelain, closed my eyes and let go; oh, the relief; I'd done it. Most of the prisoners were still sleeping but peeing with my eyes closed felt less exposing.

Now that my focus of attention had moved from my bladder and the hardships of sitting exposed on the toilet, other thoughts tormented me. They rampaged through my head like a runaway bush fire, burning through the passages of my mind, scattering ashes of disgrace and erasing memories of happiness while horrific scenes I'd seen in movies of ladies' prisons played around in my mind.

Suicide felt like a comfortable, almost exciting option.

This living hell continued all day and into the following night, and I kept wondering when I could make a call to South Africa.

The sequence of events is not particularly clear, but I stopped rocking on my haunches, I had to – they were bleeding and too painful to continue rocking, they were almost too painful to sit on for any length of time. I'd not intentionally hurt myself, but what I'd done by marking my cushion with blood was frowned upon and would not serve me.

Finally, at lunchtime on the third day, they told me I could make one internal call only.

"One internal call? That doesn't help me. I don't know anyone in Japan," I sobbed. "I need to call South Africa." International calls were not permitted.

As the days passed, the other prisoners were transferred or released, and I was the only prisoner left in the holding cells. I was sure there must be something wrong. I was expecting to be in the holding cells for five or six days. The silence was eerie, and I beckoned to the lady police officer whom I sensed was more sympathetic than some of the others and asked her what was going on.

"You can write a letter," she responded quickly.

"I have no paper, no pen, no money; how can I write a letter?" I wailed helplessly in response.

She shrugged her shoulders and walked away.

That afternoon, a young Philippine girl was admitted to the cell. She spoke a little English and Japanese. That night we communicated quietly between officers' rounds, and I felt a glimmer of hope. She explained she'd asked the officer to arrange for a lawyer to see me the following day. Touched by her thoughtfulness, I gave her a quick thumbs-up, blew her a kiss, then lay back on my futon.

The lawyer arrived, but he neither spoke nor understood much English. However, between us, we got a letter drafted to Storm, giving her the address of the holding cells, and the detention centre where I was to be moved to in a few days.

I spoke as often as I could with my new friend. She wouldn't be in the holding cells long; she'd been in before and understood the system. While we were out in the exercise area, she provided me with information on what lay ahead. She also taught me the importance of drinking green tea, and I slowly got used to its taste.

"It will nourish and re-hydrate you," she told me. Sip by delicate sip, I ingested it, and it did hydrate me; I began to embrace its known healing properties.

The following afternoon, my Philippine friend was moved and once again, I was the only prisoner in the holding cells.

Overcome with despair and loneliness, I began rocking on my cushion again. All I could think about was how much I longed to brush my teeth and have a shower. The only reassuring knowledge at that time was the family would soon know where I was, what had happened and my contact address.

In the silence of the empty cells on day five, I wondered how my fellow countryman, Nelson Mandela, had dealt with twenty-seven years of this kind of hell. I couldn't bear the thought of another hour of capture. I speculated on what his initial thoughts must have been when he was caught near the main Johannesburg - Durban railway line in the heart of the Natal Midlands and was arrested. He would have kept his strong demeanour, I was sure of that; he had a political purpose and I assumed his only thoughts would have been on freeing his people from the burden of apartheid; he never lost sight of that, and I knew that was what I had to do - focus on a purpose. I pondered on these thoughts for a long time and remembered that he'd said, documented somewhere, I could not recall where, 'A saint is a sinner who keeps on trying.' I had to keep those words in my mind forever.

Four prisoners came in on day eight, and the lawyer came back to see me the same day. Depression became a part of my daily life, as it became clear an eight-year prison sentence is what I would have to face. Eight years? I couldn't be in jail for eight years. I wept for hours. Dying would be preferable.

CHAPTER THIRTY-FOUR

After waiting ten long days, the Japanese Consulate informed the South African Embassy that they were holding me and someone from the Embassy was to visit me. Two days later, they arrived and provided 1000 Yen for me to buy the articles I needed. I thought it wise to request an Afrikaans translator for the court proceedings, which I did, and then learned later the request would delay my release from the holding cells. Then I learned that before I could be transferred anywhere, the South African authorities had to verify who I was.

There was no other way to describe what I'd got myself into other than a fucking mess.

Boredom becomes the catalyst. Boredom that made me whisper to my limbs and argue with my thoughts every minute of the day, even though I had a few books from the library. Finally, by day twelve, I had passed the stage of asking myself why? It was the time to dig deep and analyse internal factors that were to be crucial in my healing process and the development of what makes me a human being and accept that the universal fear of poverty had destroyed all common sense and I had to forgive myself. There were parts of *me* I began to look at through different eyes and question; who am I? How honest, how sincere, how generous, how vain, and so the list went on. I took the time, in the silence of the confinement, for introspection without harsh criticism and to take advantage of the quietness to find the path to deep spiritual matters and be gentler on myself, as tough as it was.

On day thirteen, a list of what I could buy from the internal shop was handed to me. I quickly learned the 1000 Yen went nowhere. These lists prisoners were given served as a shopping record and opposite each item was a little box. I coloured in the box, indicating the item was what I needed. I'd messed up my first 'shopping list' by ticking the boxes - they had to be coloured in.

I coloured in one writing pad, one pen, one bar of soap, one tube of toothpaste, one toothbrush, and four stamps. I couldn't afford shampoo, but I was able to take what others left behind; that was prison luxury.

I remembered back to the sensations of washing my hair and showering for the first time in six days. The almost inexplicable sensation of being cleansed inside and out when even my mind felt filthy, but I still hadn't brushed my teeth. The first time I brushed my teeth was on day fourteen, when I got the goods from the shopping list. Taking a bath or a shower was an activity I'd taken for granted before, something many of us do. In prison, it became a treasured joy. It was a luxury I looked forward to, twice a week if I were lucky, that there were lady officers available to supervise this ritual that I craved. I noticed that by showering only twice a week, my skin was beautifully nourished by its natural oils, so I no longer needed copious amounts of lotions, which was quite a revelation. I missed the scents of the creams, but once one's body adjusts, it becomes quite odourless unless I was taken out on regular exercise outings.

Having a notepad and pen made a huge difference to my demeanour. I stopped rocking mindlessly, began meditating, and writing relieved some of the boredom. Now that I had a notepad and pen, I began a short, grief-stricken letter to Storm. My pen hovered over the paper for a long time as I tried to work out what to say and how to say I was sorry. 'Sorry' seemed so inconsequential and meaningless, but I knew of no other English words to express how I felt. I was not permitted to write in my mother tongue, for all letters were read before being sent. I wasn't ready to explain everything; it was all still a jumbled mess in my mind as I gradually processed the fact that I'd gone from being a confident, focussed businesswoman, to emotionally anesthetised convict in a matter of weeks. It was not only unbearable to explore and put words to for myself, but to have to explain it all to Storm was unmanageable then. I first had to master my own tender emotions of guilt and shame.

When there was an available warden, I got to go to the exercise area; this was another real highlight for me. I made the most of every small move I made to patiently and gently stretch muscle, then do exercise to raise my heartbeat and oxygenate my mind, and finish with the stretches again. The exercise became my drug, clearing away the negative, depressing thoughts and replacing them with more positive ones.

By day fifteen, I knew Storm would have received the Embassy letter, notifying her of my whereabouts. My handwritten one was on its way and that's what I imagined she would have been desperately waiting to receive. Writing it had been agonising hardship. I was petrified she'd reject me, even hate me for betraying her. I only wrote one page; it was the hardest one page I'd ever written. Plus, I had to ask her to send me money. I prayed our relationship was strong enough for her to find forgiveness, and it was. She sent me money and poured out her heart to me. It was almost too hard to read, through tear-filled eyes that dropped onto the page, smearing the words she'd so carefully and thoughtfully written.

I knew exactly why my mother had done what she did. She wanted to keep a promise she'd made to me. Storm and I discussed how difficult it must have been for our darling Mother long into the night when we were together on her off weekends. I recited Mama's pledge to me before she left.

"My darling seun," she'd said. "I promise I will always keep the family together, no matter what it takes and you, my boy, will have the education you deserve."

Now she was living the burden of the ultimate sacrifice she'd made. There was no doubt in my mind; when Mom agreed to take the package to Japan, she had no idea what she was carrying, or the implications of being caught.

My father should have been the one paying for his thieving and lies, not her. After all the years she had sustained endless abuse from him, she remained a stable, grounded role model to the three of us. For her to give in to something like this was testament to what lengths she'd go to for her family. She did what she did, not to save her business for material gain but to appease her creditors, people she was ethically beholden to. Social position or mega-wealth didn't consume my mother. What she wanted was a comfortable, honestly earned income to ensure I got a university education. For me, that's admirable. But it didn't remove the anger I felt toward Vivienne and Andre for letting her go. They had some hard times when they were both made redundant, but who did they turn to? Mom. And they simply added to her financial burden, yet she rarely complained; she loved us all equally and would do anything for us.

Even before Mom left, I didn't ask her for money. I'd heard about a job delivering newspapers which I could do from my bicycle. It was in an area of town no-one wanted to take on, so I took it on. It was hard graft for two years, but it generated a small, steady income. An ex-client of Mama's, who owned a warehouse distributing consumables, cigarettes and alcohol across the province, needed a packer. I gave up the newspaper delivery work and then took on some of the IT work. It wasn't long after that I was supervising the loading of trucks in the evening and was earning more money than I could spend.

Every day after Mama's arrest, I ached, for her with a sharp cutting pain and prayed endlessly for her safety and an early release.

There was no restriction on the number of letters I could write while I was being held at Narita temporary cells. The problem was, I couldn't afford to buy the stamps required for letters to South Africa. Each letter I wrote I addressed to both Storm and Pieter to save on paper and the ink in my pen.

Storm's letter arrived with some more money for me, enabling me to write a few more letters to them, individually this time. I wasn't ready to write to Vivienne and Andre without being accusing, so I left them off my mailing list for a few more weeks.

Begging for money from my children made me feel bilious, but I was glad to have the extra pennies to spend on stamps. When letters arrived with the money in, security police removed it, changed it and added it to the small amount I had left of the 1000 Yen. Prison officials managed everything; every cent I owned and my life.

The routine in the holding cells was tedious. Green tea was the first fluid to touch my lips in the morning, and though I felt its health benefits now, the smell still turned my guts, so I'd drink it holding my breath. I seldom recognised what I was to eat, other than rice. Lunch was the same every day, and dinner was a slight variation on lunch. It took me a long time to perfect the art of shovelling sloppy rice into my mouth using chopsticks. The trick was to hold the bowl directly beneath my chin and scoop it in at speed. Historically, I was the slowest eater in the family, so this was no easy task; so much of it ended up running down my chin.

The first time I experienced the post-dinner mouth examination, done with a metal detector, I was appalled. This hideous examination was done to ensure we were not hiding anything in our mouths; it was horrific but mandatory, and thinking back, I was horror-struck by everything that happened to me during those terrifying initial forty-eight hours of capture. Every morning, after I'd swallowed the green tea, I was marched to the cupboards to lock away the futon set. If there were others in with me, we all went as a group. In the evening, it was the same procedure; then after dinner, I would lie down and cover myself with the quilt, pulling it up over my head, and try to sleep. Lights were switched off at nine-thirty pm. Even though I was often the only prisoner, the exacting routine was never deviated from.

Three weeks had passed, and I was still in the holding cells. While in this almost solitary confinement situation, I'd spend time interrogating my thoughts, most of which were full of contradictions and hard to fathom. During those dark and quiet times, I made a pact with myself; I was going to be a model prisoner to be released on early parole.

Another of my more pressing battles was that I'd endured three weeks without a cigarette. Many of my early difficulties would have been slightly more tolerable had I been able to puff on a cigarette and I craved the comfort of having one every day. Withdrawal symptoms was a war I couldn't win; the struggle for nicotine raged on, day after day. For years, a cigarette had been my constant and necessary companion. I was never a heavy smoker, but whenever I was going through hardship and emotional turmoil, I'd light a cigarette and feel instantly calmed; now I needed my daily nicotine dose more than at any other time in my life. The physical need brought bubbles of perspiration to my top lip as the craving took its hold, off and on, during the day. Eventually, I plucked up the courage to ask the exercise officer to bring me a cigarette. He made the flicker of a nod, and I lived in hope. The following day, one of the lady officers came to collect me for exercise routine. I found this odd for I was the only prisoner in, and I'd been out on exercise routine the previous day, so to have exercise routine two days in a row was unusual. She marched me to the exercise area and motioned that I should squat. While in this position, waiting for the officer who gave the exercises to arrive, my legs burned like crazy – this was a position I eventually got used to holding. There was nowhere one could sit, but it stretched the hamstrings and was a common stance in Japan. He arrived and bowed in traditional greeting to the lady officer, then he came to me and pulled a cigarette out of his pocket. A smile must have stretched my whole face as he handed the lit cigarette to me. I could have jumped up and kissed him. Instead, as one does in Japan, I put my hands together and bowed in thanks. I wasted no time in taking a long pull on it, inhaling the smoke deep into my lungs. As I hadn't smoked for some time, the nicotine made me feel blissfully dizzy as it entered my body. It was the upliftment and tonic I needed to ease stress and anxiety. My cigarette knew how I was feeling - I never had to explain my emotional state, it just knew. With each puff, a new energy I'd forgotten existed, filled me. Then I began playing joyously with the exhaled smoke, blowing circles into the air and smiling for the second time in a month, gloriously lost in a world of my own for a minute or two. I was mesmerised by the simplicity of watching the smoke rings disappear through the wire mesh that covered the exercise area and gradually vanished into the universe. This ritual became the highlight of the days I was given a cigarette. Every puff was remarkably precious as I held on to the smoke - holding it inside me like a lover would, capturing its smell and the sensations it left in my lungs. Each puff became a bizarre ceremony of blissful feelings amidst the terror of my grim future.

During the fourth week in holding cells, some of the officers dared to spoil me a little more. On the odd occasion, I had as many as three cigarettes in a day and occasionally a cup of coffee or an ice-cream cone. A visit to the library on my way back from the exercise area was another opportunity where I could hover in a relatively 'normal' environment and select a book to keep me company. On one occasion, I found a 'Fairlady' magazine from South Africa and was so excited, but when I dived into its contents, it made me more homesick so I refrained from ever looking at magazines again.

The weeks ran into months in the holding cells and I knew the officers felt sorry for me, hence the little luxuries they gave me and took huge chances giving them to me. One of them told me they'd never had one prisoner spend so much time in the holding cells before.

On the 25th of September 2002, five long months after my arrest, I was transferred to Chiba, the detention cells, where I was to await trial.

CHAPTER THIRTY-FIVE

Chiba Detention Centre was as she'd described it. I wondered, with a stab of pain, what had happened to my Filipino friend who'd provided me with the details on what I could expect in Chiba. She must have been here often to have described it in such detail. I shall not forget her kindness, but I was going to miss my cigarettes and the generosity of the officers at the holding cells. The one plus here in detention was there was a little more comfort offered and a fraction more variety to occupy one's dreary days.

There were two sections here for women prisoners. One accommodated large groups of prisoners and the smaller division, which is where I was, housed ten prisoners. As I entered, I was scrutinised again, this time by nine pairs of lifeless eyes, and a cold shiver ran down my spine as flashes of those awful movies I'd seen crossed my mind.

Things were different in detention. Prisoners who knew people on the outside or had friends and family in towns close by regularly asked them to bring in what they needed. I had no-one and no way of knowing when the next pennies would come from my children. My toothpaste, toothbrush, and other personal belongings I held so dear were not transferred with me; they had been the things that kept me sane in this hell. Now I'd have to repurchase them, and I had hardly any money left. The response to my plea to the children would only realise any funds if they could spare it. With the transfer, I wouldn't hear from them for at least another three weeks.

I watched with envy those who opened their goodie bags, lovingly supplied by their families, and it wasn't long before they generously shared so much of what was brought to them with me. Their kindness lifted me out of the swamp of emptiness that had overwhelmed me for months. This incredible generosity changed my distorted view of the Japanese as cruel and ruthless people; instead, they were kind, respectful and considerate.

As much as I wanted, it was impossible to build any meaningful friendships; the language was a barrier and communication was not encouraged. I was expected to accept their gifts as part of what prisoners do for each other.

The things I needed most, like toiletries, weren't given by the generous inmates.

In Chiba, as in the holding cells, a shopping list was provided. This one was more comprehensive but, with very little money left, I didn't have much choice. All I could afford to buy was another notebook, a red pen, one stamp for a letter to South Africa and a tube of toothpaste.

After a few weeks in detention, my financial plight became well-known amongst my fellow prisoners. It became a topic of cheerful conversation. As soon as their goodie parcels arrived, they would inspect their gifts, decide what to part with then cheerfully say aloud, 'give to alien.' And so, the pile of goodies they put to one side for me grew with each family visit. Their endless warmth and generosity always reduced me to tears and in return, they always teased me playfully.

Boredom wasn't as bad in detention, but time was a constant enemy. We had to wash our clothes, which passed a little time, but this posed a different problem for me; we had to buy our washing powder. Outsiders were not permitted to provide that, so I washed my two sets of clothing with my precious bath soap. Occasionally, a small handful was discretely passed to me by a kindly inmate while I waited for money to purchase my own.

I received two long letters from Storm during the third week in detention. Her words broke my heart. The invisible words of the heartache and emptiness she was suffering pained me even more. My absence was tearing her apart, eroding her strength little by little, and there was nothing I could do to prevent it. It took a year before I found the appropriate words to describe to her my insufferable agony and how I felt about lying to her and what it had done to me. It was the reason I hadn't answered her telephone call on that first day in Paris.

I'd not heard a word from Vivienne, Andre or Dion in those first five months. I didn't expect to hear from Andre or Dion, but I prayed I would get a letter from Vivienne. We had our differences, but I loved her and missed her as much as the other two siblings. Eventually, a letter from her arrived.

I'd had one accusing letter from my sister and one particularly sad, soul-searing letter from Pieter, telling me what Uncle Ernst had said, something neither of us will ever forget.

'My kind: Jy kan enige tyd my werk, maar dit is nie vir jou beskore nie. Jou ma wou gehad het jy moet verder gaan swot en ek sal jou ma se wense laat realiser.'

After they learned of my arrest, Uncle Ernst had held him in his arms and assured him that everything in his life would work out fine. Pieter explained in his letter how he was struggling to see how it would get better without me. He wrote: 'Mama, here is a man who is not even related to us but cares so much. He is so kind and has so much compassion. I am still speechless that he took me under his wing and has given me so much. Papa hasn't even asked after me, or how my exams are going. In his eyes, I may as well be dead.'

I sobbed rivers of bitter tears that burned as they ran down my cheeks. I read on.

'All that you have taught me, Mama, and now, with what Uncle Ernst is doing for me, will live with me forever. I hate to say this, Mom, but what you have done is another lesson for me. I still love and respect you. I know why you did it, and I know it was against your will. Storm and I know that, and we pray for you. We love you and miss you.'

I sobbed off and on for days after receiving that letter. I kept reading it until I was no longer reduced to tears by it, then the interpretation of it warmed me with his reassurance of love and only then did I find the courage to put it away.

At night, thoughts of my mother often came to me. I often felt very connected to her, so much so, it felt she was in the cell with me, guiding me, whispering to me to do the right things, that there is always a lesson to learn from one's mistakes. I thanked God she was no longer alive. She would have been bitterly disappointed, but she would not have been accusing; she knew and understood my circumstances better than most.

There was another element to my guilt; not being able to thank the wonderful man who had taken Pieter under his wing. Ernst had given him a chance to become someone and excel, and he had made Pieter's life easier.

I couldn't send him to University, but Ernst sent him to college.

All photographs and letters sent to me were guarded carefully; they were my visual lifeline to my family. The little Filipino lady had warned me they take letters away once they have been read. I hid two small pictures on me, which amazingly they never found. I had one of Pieter and one of Storm. Every night, I held them flat against my stomach and imagined their energy and love feeding into me as I lay quietly meditating my future.

An unfortunate turn of events rocked the excellent reputation I was trying so hard to build - it was all over a toothbrush. Though I may have banged on about personal hygiene and its importance to me, it would never have crossed my mind to steal from an inmate, or anyone, for that matter.

The cells were checked for discrepancies every day. Checks took place while we were out on exercise routine. On this particular day, they came across a toothbrush I was given when checking through my belongings. The problem was, the name of the prisoner who'd given it to me was on the toothbrush and she'd left, so there was no-one to verify my story was true. Rules were rules - rigid and strictly adhered to here, and to my detriment, through innocence once more, I learned another hard lesson and was severely punished.

The punishment was brutal; locked into solitary confinement, where I stayed for a long time. Presumed 'theft' was a serious black mark against me. I tried to explain the legitimacy of how I came to own the toothbrush, but the warden, who didn't have a good command of English, refused to believe my genuine story. He was convinced I was a thief. Wardens always think you are lying, and in some cases, you don't even have to open your mouth. I had to accept that reality.

In solitary confinement, there is nothing - nothing at all but four white walls. I wondered how long I could hold onto my sanity. Was this where I would lose my mind? Was it going to be within these four white walls where I would mentally snap? Terror took on another new meaning. I didn't want to wallow in self-pity, I didn't want to live the 'victim' mentality within these confines, but it grew like an infection. The road to insanity is a slow, quiet, cruel process that took me down some very rough tracks where treacherous sinkholes of manic depression tripped me up. Mealtimes were a minor distraction, and with each mouthful, I'd count how many times I could chew one mouthful until it dissolved. I'd sip on water and green tea, swirling the liquid around my mouth before swallowing, visualising and sensing its passage to my stomach. It was surreal and absurd, but I loved every sip as my mind wandered over steep, treacherous mountain paths, threatening my existence on earth, but I'd come down the other side and into the desert where I became lost and thirsty for hope. On rare occasions, very rare occasions, the solitude in the single room was a welcome indulgence; it was quiet. Hope. An optimistic state of mind, they say, based on an expectation of positive outcomes in one's life. There was not much hope vibrating through my soul. As a verb, its definitions include: "expect with confidence" and "to cherish a desire with anticipation."- How I wished those words could stick with feeling. Courage and the mentioned hopeful desires hung in my brain like the low-lying fog across the desert in the early morning; opaque and impossible to grasp. When it cleared, flashes of intense light beamed through, and I found a few positive thoughts, warmed by rays of purpose and my senses became razor sharp. But most of the time, I numbly endured the three long, lonely weeks in that cold, emotionally chilling box and remained, what I considered to be sane. I found the answers to many questions about my life and my purpose. Panicked needs lead to unclear thinking. Depression leads to all sorts of ill-conceived plans, and the reality of an ill-conceived plan was this imprisonment. All I had thought about was how to get my hands on 'fast money.' My intentions were good, but obtaining it was not.

I'd fallen into the trap, something I intuitively knew never worked. 'Fast' money, no matter where it is sourced, always has its sacrifices; never did I think it would put me in jail, though.

But another reality check looked directly at me; one I'd so often questioned in my life - money determines an outcome. Money even determines the experience of imprisonment too. We, as humans, cannot get away from the power that it holds. When we raise our spiritual awareness and give way to trusting the universe, we experience positive vibrations, I have been informed on numerous occasions. I know it to be true, but I also know that if one cannot escape the reality of one's situation, positive vibrations do not realise what is in the books. I was not in the right space to attract anything good when my business went bankrupt. I was of the notion that nothing would ever go right in my life and certainly not while Dion Du Toit was in it.

Having a few extra pennies from the children gave me the opportunity to buy a few items to make life more manageable but I also learned lots of dollars can determine the amount of time you stay in jail too! I couldn't help wondering who the deluded person was that came up with the phrase - 'money doesn't buy happiness.' It bought lots of happiness in jail and an abundance of it could buy a ticket to freedom. A lack of it, as was my predicament, meant I felt every bit of the harsh side of what life dished out behind bars in Japan and money was why I was in this hell. I witnessed what wealth can manipulate by being associated with a sweet young German lass, Heidi, who'd always had too much for free. Her family, particularly her father, dished out money when she wanted it. As a result, she grew up without values, leaving her exposed to the wrong type of people when she reached her mid-teens. Without the wisdom and guidance from parents, whose time was spent in pursuit of making more and more money, she didn't quite know how to stop wanting more herself. There is nothing wrong with wanting more, it was how she was doing it that was the concern.

She was one of the sweetest young teenage girls I'd met in many years and I was sure she had not fully comprehended the impact of her actions. She'd been caught carrying cocaine for the third time. This time, she expressed her fears that she would be spending a long time in jail and her fears brought on long fits of sobbing. Heidi told me how she'd pray at night that her rich daddy's lawyer could work his magic again. Despite this, Heidi was kind, considerate and amusing; a beautiful young girl spoiled by mega ego-driven parents. Surprisingly unpretentious, which was unusual. It was all quite contradictory; she didn't consume drugs herself but moving them, she said, 'had worked for her.' I was shocked by the vast amount of pocket money she got from her father and how little her parents seemed to care about what she did. 'When it finished, I needed more, and smuggling cocaine paid better than Daddy,' she shared with me. However, her youthful vulnerability was showing now; she was a very frightened little girl. One night, her hearing looming closer, she cried like that frightened little girl and reached out to me for comfort and maternal reassurance. Though prisoners are not permitted to touch each other, I held Heidi in my arms and let her cry until there was nothing left.

"They tell me I'm in for eight fucking years for smuggling marijuana. Cocaine is far worse." Heidi raised her eyebrows and shook her head.

"Not eight years, nein, nein. Maybe three," Heidi reassured me, "but I think I will do eight years this time. I'm scared, so very scared." And it showed. Thankfully, we were not caught comforting each other. Heidi was younger than my daughters, and that night, while we hugged and cried together, satisfying each other's needs for physical comfort, we both agreed we felt calmer for it.

I hoped this scare would stop her from doing it again, but I never mentioned my thoughts to her and after her hearing, she came back with a smile the stretched from ear to ear. Heid's father had hired the best criminal lawyer in Germany; her case was acquitted for the third time. It didn't go without warning though; if she was caught again, she would face serious consequences. And so, the many clichés, like 'with money you can get away with murder' and 'money doesn't buy you happiness,' had just played out in real-time, in front of me. Heidi wasn't directly responsible for murder, but the drug runs she was doing would have catastrophic effects on young lives that could lead to death. Innocent children were always the victims, often dying from overdoses or the consequences of overdose but Heidi didn't see that side of what she was encouraging. If we'd had more time to talk, I would have said something to her. I sat in deep thought after the outcome of her trial. I knew what I had brought in was not right but the physical consequences to one's body taking cocaine versus marijuana are worlds apart.

I was happy for Heidi she was going free and I was going to miss her. Heidi's leaving brought on the ghosts of my life, the unfairness of it, the regrets, the shame and self-loathing which wrapped itself around me like a serpent squeezing the life force from me. I had to stop feeding this anger and hatred, but it was a good companion sometimes. Real anger often prompted crystal clear thoughts for me, and the night Heidi left, I prayed for the first time in a very long time. I prayed for my little German companion, asking God to stop her doing what she was doing. If He never listened to my problems, perhaps He'd at least help her.

I asked Him to help me remove the blame game I was playing which I could shed. If Dion hadn't robbed me blind to feed his addiction for alcohol, I wouldn't be here. How was I going to forgive? If I'd listened to my instincts and not my middle child - I wouldn't be here. I had to stop thinking these thoughts; it only made it all harder to bear. In reality, the bitter truth was I was here because of...me! I could no longer place any blame; I had to take responsibility for *all* my choices. It was me who'd made a choice to give Dion endless chances, it was me who'd given in to Vivienne's pleas to help her father. I'd said I would do the delivery of said unknown package to Japan which took Andre out of the equation. I understood about choices and responsibility, or did I? The question was, how was I going to convert my bitter thoughts into forgiving ones? What I'd done was not right - I'd accepted that, but I wasn't a criminal, and that was why it hurt so badly.

I couldn't deny the envy I felt when I hugged Heidi once more before she left. I missed her cheerful demeanour in the days that followed. She was a little ray of sunshine in my gloomy future. We'd understood each other, not just in spoken language. I spoke Afrikaans, she spoke German, and we managed to understand more of what each other said than we thought. It was good to talk in my mother tongue, even if it wasn't for long. Heidi and I exchanged a few letters after her release but in her last one, she told me she'd been caught again, this time in Australia. After that, I never heard from her again.

Before she left detention, she generously gave me some of her clothing, a nightie, an expensive warm jacket I cherished, a 'T' shirt and two pairs of socks, all of which I graciously accepted. Winter was approaching, and the nights were cooling down rapidly; those extra clothes helped keep me warm. I felt the warmth of her kindness keeping my toes snug. Because her clothing, having been privately owned, was never marked like the toothbrush saga, I could keep them without retribution. The socks were the most favoured, for my feet suffered the most.

Chilblains were the bane of my life. They often kept me awake as they throbbed painfully, but Heidi's expensive thermal socks kept the bitter cold out better than any other socks. Two weeks after Heidi left, six of us had our cases heard and, for the first time since arriving in Japan, I got a taste of being handcuffed - Japanese style. If it weren't so humiliating, it would have been interesting. An intricate system of knotted ropes tied us together in a long line, leaving a complicated and equally intricate sense of worthlessness. We were bound together like slaves, reminiscent of those cruel days back in the distant past and consumed by emotions of terror and mortification and an agonising vulnerability, all entwined in rope. A ruthless pain, a cadaverous system that ensured there was no possibility of escape as we shuffled our way down to the courts, tied together in grisly bondage. I'd never felt more like an animal than I did in that moment.

Today would reveal what lay ahead for me - I had no fancy lawyer.

Visions of the courtroom were intimidating. My legs mirrored the terror I felt as they dragged along beneath me. My whole body was giving way to terror as we were unbound and taken into the courtroom.

I'd envisioned the courts to be a massive, menacing room with dark wooden benches and high louvred windows, unapproachable policeman, marching around the perimeter, clerks of the court and translators all waiting for me; I wasn't that important. Though it was a small room, it didn't make it any less intimidating. Standing in the wooden pulpit, I began to shake while I faced the judge, feeling insignificant and feeble in this foreign land, convicted of drug trafficking. Me? A 52-year-old grandmother who'd rarely done anything unlawful. My hearing didn't last long for I was the last on the list that day.

Japanese court etiquette and protocols were respected. The Judge and officials did not recess for tea twice a day, lasting up to an hour each, and then close court at four like they do in South Africa. Lunch is a quick fifteen-minute recess, and no-one moved to pack up when the typical working day ended. The proceedings continued until the list was complete and every case had been fairly heard, no matter how long it took.

The procedure was so unlike home, where the backlog of cases is carried forward to the following week, month or even year depending upon the mood.

The discipline, ordinance and general respect in Japan had a lasting impression upon me. I swore I was going to try and adopt a similar way of life when I got out.

I was asked to confirm my real name and my South African identity number - I could hardly speak.

"Are you aware of your conviction?" The judge asked.

"Yes, Sir."

After a lengthy exchange of papers and discussion in Japanese, the State Lawyer, who'd been appointed to represent me, said my hearing was postponed until December.

I was devastated. Tell a lie once; it lives with you forever and this is why I'd reinforced the importance of not fibbing with my children. They didn't need reminding though; they'd heard enough of them spill from Dion's mouth. But now they were living the real-time pain of mine, and the consequence of Dion's lies and dishonest actions.

I was told I would be notified of the date and then I was dismissed. This decision meant another three months in detention. The longer I waited, the longer my stay in Japan.

Even though I spoke the truth and tried to remain a model prisoner, I had to remind myself a prisoners' word has no value. The authorities didn't care what I thought; I was a criminal. It was a bitter pill to swallow.

CHAPTER THIRTY-SIX

Winter was settling in fast; the cells were freezing during the day and even colder at night; pneumonia was probably going to get me before the hearing. It was already the 1st of December, and I'd heard nothing of my pending court case.

I'd been in for eight months with no idea on the sentence I was going to have to serve. I had no clue what prison they'd transfer me to either. The wait was cruel, but finally, notification came through; my case was to be heard on the 5th of December.

Standing before the Judge once more, he asked the routine questions, and I answered without feeling the same level of nerves I had on the first appearance. The South African authorities had confirmed I was Elizabeth Johanna Du Toit and the identity number I'd given them was correct. The judge turned to the state lawyer and engaged in quiet discussion. I kept my eyes focused on the two of them; my jaw clenched from tension, then my neck began to spasm as I prepared myself for the verdict. I didn't move an inch as he turned back to face me and began to speak.

"Elizabeth Johanna Du Toit, I find you guilty on all counts. You are sentenced to four years' imprisonment, with an eight hundred thousand Yen fine," the judge announced. The sound of the gavel crashing against another wooden surface reverberated through my consciousness. Numbed and powerfully immobilised by an invisible force, his words kept echoing in my head.

Fewer years hadn't registered yet; it was the sting of the fine that was hard to bear.

'How was I going to pay an eight hundred thousand Yen fine?'

The rest of what the judge said filtered in and settled somewhere in the dark recesses of my mind. During this hearing came the realisation of what a mistake it had been requesting a translator. He'd screwed up my case by suggesting that four kilograms of marijuana was a severe crime and could kill many Japanese citizens. I instantly thought of Heidi and thought I should remind the judge of her case.

The injustices caught in my throat, as they had done before, and burned as I shifted irritably in the enclosed podium.

"Sir, you heard the case of……….." I was quickly shut down.

What kind of justice was this?

I wanted a re-trial and appealed immediately; miraculously, he granted it.

It was late into the evening when I was taken back to the cells. The only people left at the court by the end of the day were the driver, a lady warden I'd got to know, and me. Being the only prisoner, they didn't feel the need to cuff me, thankfully. As the van doors closed, my world came crashing down around me, and I sobbed as deeply as I had done on the first day of my arrest. It was dark in my world, and pitch-black outside, mirroring exactly how I was feeling. My heart-wrenching sobs must have tugged at the warder and, protected by the darkened interior, she took the liberty of comforting me and folded her arms around me, whispering in reasonable English.

"No worry Ma'am, prison not so bad, you see. Be smart, like you are here in detention, and very good in holding cell, you have no problem."

They were the kindest words I'd heard in months. The warmth of the warder's arms around me stilled my quaking body. A few minutes later, I began to wonder how she knew that I'd conducted myself in an exemplary fashion in the holding cells. Was she telepathic, or could she see I was not a regular type of criminal? She'd just read my mind for I'd been thinking about the man who had spoiled me in the exercise area.

The kind man was her brother, she told me.

"He say, you velly good woman." An absurd thought flashed in mind as she said it - I wished Dion could have heard this woman's sentiment.

It was late when we finally got back to Chiba, and I wearily climbed out of the bus, looked up at the night skies - glittering stars danced across the black velvet sky like they do at home - and tears came pouring down my cheeks again. Not only did the vast expanse of starlit skies tug at memories of home, I knew it would be a long time before I would gaze upon skies so beautiful again.

A solitary, lonely realisation of what lay ahead, a process of illusion and disillusionment would go on endlessly, without anyone to share it or talk it through with now Heidi had gone. A desolate emptiness and a ghastly hollowing in the pit of my stomach filled me. I sat on my futon while turbulent emotions wracked my mind in response to rocking on my haunches once more. As I rocked, my thoughts began to drift toward preparations for my appeal hearing. I nodded off occasionally, while sitting and rocking gently, and felt utterly exhausted the following day. Four years was an eternity –a lifetime in those moments; this added to the time I'd already done, but more troubling thoughts were about how to raise eight hundred thousand Yen while in jail - I couldn't ask my children to pay it.

Somewhere in between the tears, sleepless nights and the challenging thoughts on what I'd lost, the heartbreak, the loneliness, guilt and the bleakness ahead for four years, it was time to dig deeper than I ever had and find the strength to go on as a model prisoner and fight for parole.

Thankfully, Storm managed to scrape some money together for me to buy stamps, a notebook and writing paper. In my next letter to her, I asked her to send me as many facts and statistics on cannabis as she could obtain officially. I had to prove that heroin and cocaine were considerably worse than what I'd been carrying, and this time, I would represent myself. During those deplorable, agonising long days waiting for a reply from Storm, I learned through the kind efforts and quiet explanations from a handful of the lady warders, that I would earn money once I got to jail – the relief was immeasurable, and I began to sleep less fretfully. A deduction off my wages would go toward reducing the fine over the four years.

"You velly good. You will get fine job," one of the warders had said to me, which made me laugh; something I'd rarely done over the past months. I was sure there was no place on earth closer to hell than this, and there was certainly nothing funny about it, but her sweet words placated the living torment.

I couldn't begin to utter that I was *looking forward* to going to 'proper prison', but with the first court case behind me, moving to the main prison meant I could commence my sentence and start working. I'd ached to do something constructive after all this time of torturous waiting and now that we were heading towards Christmas, I was told we would get a few extra treats and the exercise area was more fun, but it only made it worse for me.

The Japanese do not celebrate Christmas, but out of respect to us 'aliens' who do, a few little 'sweet delights', and a slice of fruit cake at dinner only served to trigger emotions so intense I found it hard to swallow. Chewing and crying couldn't be synchronised – all I wanted were my children, and the birth of Christ showed me how tormenting the celebration was without them. He'd not listened to me. I was not one of His lambs. I was an outcast even though I'd faithfully prayed so hard for so long. Through all the years of abuse from Dion, I'd prayed more for his issues to be solved. I'd asked for His help to guide me to help him and protect my children - my prayers were never considered.

'Ask, and thou shalt receive,' I felt was a load of bollocks in that moment. 'I'd asked often,' I thought with acid cynicism.

Then New Year filled the void - a time the Japanese people celebrate, but the only excitement I could muster was the knowledge I was one day closer to presenting my case and, hopefully, shortening the length of time I'd be here. New Year celebrations were cheerier than Christmas and lasted three days. The food improved, which made us all more cheerful; we even got sweets. It astounded me what pleasure and comfort I derived from a handful of sweets in those bleak times. That first Christmas and New Year passed quickly; a week of pain and emptiness I shall always want to forget, then life went back to the normal drudgery.

If any changes to a prisoner's situation happened or there was to be a transfer, we were only advised the morning it was going to happen, so there was seldom anything to look forward to, and the celebrations were behind us till Easter. There was no such thing as an advanced warning here. I had wished upon those magical stars, floating around in the universe, that I'd gazed upon earlier that my name would soon be called, but the days dragged on into weeks, and I heard nothing.

Early one morning, with my nose dribbling from the cold and my fingertips numbed by the fierce, crisp air, I learned that parole would not even be a consideration for the first two years. My next hearing would be for me to try and reduce the term and the fine, but if I was here for two years, come what may, I had to adopt a more positive attitude, which I did. The reward happened a few days later - I got a cigarette and a cup of coffee; the first in weeks while in the exercise area. I was stunned. After a cup of hot coffee and a ciggy, even the icy cold wind couldn't chill me, and while I was busy with my two favourite things, I decided to take up lessons in Japanese and learn more about their culture -actions spoke louder than words in prison and they respect those that strive to be better.

I'd already noticed the warders and guards recognised I was not a 'true' criminal, and they clandestinely looked after me from time to time.

Through my past years living on and off with an addict – a selfish, alcoholic, sociopath, psychopath - it had forcefully taught me a great deal about tolerance, and if nothing else had served me throughout the relationship, that lesson was serving me now. The little 'niceties', like a cigarette and a cup of coffee provided for me occasionally by the friendly exercise warder, made the days in detention a little less wretched.

CHAPTER THIRTY-SEVEN:

Tochigi Prison

"Eee..lez..bet," the warder's voice boomed out across the cells. My name was called at last. A small smile of relief stretched my lips, followed by the name of the prison; "Tochigi Prison."

Tochigi is a prison mainly for lady 'aliens.' They called us 'aliens', for the Japanese find it impossible to pronounce "Foreigner". Having a phonetic alphabet, the word 'alien' was easier for them to pronounce. This description for us foreigners was very apt I guessed, for everything around me and my circumstances were alien; perhaps it wasn't quite as bad for some of the others. There were a lot of pretty hard women in detention.

I was transferred to a single cell again, and just as before, everything I owned was re-counted and checked then packed and stowed for the day I would finally be released. The preciseness of the Japanese people left an indelible impression on me; being a neat and orderly person myself, I respected the discipline, but the re-counting of the seventeen clean tissues I had arrived with was stretching it a bit, and I had to smile as they went into the suitcase in perfect folds, like a flawlessly ironed pillowcase.

The following day, the 6th of February 2003, after two hundred and seventy-eight grim days in holding cells and detention, I was about to begin my sentence. Another day closer to going home.

To suggest I was excited would be absurd, but the thought of being put to work and earning an income excited me; meagre amounts as they were to begin with, it was a start. Seven of us were being transferred to Tochigi that day. We were lined up, cuffed in the ghastly ropes and squashed into the transfer vehicle with the windows closed and the curtains drawn. I'd never experienced claustrophobic panic before, but I did on that journey.

It was snowing that day, and though I only got a glimpse of the exquisite beauty that surrounded us, I kept that picture in my mind and remained totally focussed on it in an effort to prevent the panic from overwhelming me. The heavy snowfall made the surroundings quite surreal; it was so quiet, and the first time I'd ever seen snow. A child-like urge to touch it and play in it was a healthy desire, I thought, so as the waves of claustrophobia came in, I'd breathe in the different visions of the sea of snow I'd caught a glimpse of, but as the journey progressed, it got more stuffy and I fought to hold onto those visions as I inhaled the toxic breath of six other prisoners.

The transfer journey took four hours, cooped up like chickens; a journey that again hammered home the grim reality of being a criminal. Thankfully, the heavy snowfalls forced us to stop every so often, and a lovely icy wind blew into the bus, which freshened the air within, while snow chains were attached to the wheels and the journey would continue. Then, as soon as we were out of the deep snow, the driver would stop and remove the chains. These 'breather' stops were a life-saver.

A letter from Storm had arrived the day I was transferred to Tochigi prison, and they handed it to me once the booking-in process was complete. With the letter was an unexpected parcel with some of their clothing and more money. How blessed I was to have such a loyal, loving daughter. I was so excited to have in my hands all the endless research she'd done on cannabis to present at my appeal hearing. Then I read her heart-wrenching explanation of why she'd sent me the selection of clothing she had. She'd asked each family member to contribute a piece of clothing that had an emotional attachment. This simple gesture was intended for me to feel the person close to me when I wore the item. Tears poured down my cheeks despite me thinking I had cried so much already I'd not be able to produce more tears.

Two lady warders sorted through the clothing, piece by piece, and as I watched, little bits of my heart broke. I was only permitted to keep certain items, but I held them all close to me and breathed in the familiar smells as I cried, visualising the face of the person who'd parted with their piece of them, just for me, before the items I wasn't allowed to keep were taken away and packed. They were the emotional food I craved, and at last, the items that I could keep would keep me warm.

Prison-issue was a dreary blue-grey dress; good quality, roomy, comfortable and practical – absolutely in line with the Japanese culture. As I signed for the issue of my prison garb, an absurd thought flashed through my mind and I could hear the sweet, innocent voice of Lena Zavaroni singing, – 'If my friends could see me now,' and I smiled, then noticed a questioning look on the warder's face - I couldn't share my thoughts; she was unlikely to know the song or see the humour of it and the moment was gone. Three pairs of panties, three bras, three thermal vests with matching long johns, two jackets, one a warm lumber jacket, the other a lighter one, cotton socks, extra slacks, and an extra blouse were issued; my wardrobe for the next 4 years. Once we'd got our issue, we had to sew our name tags onto each article of clothing and each label was thoroughly checked to ensure the sewing was perfect and sewn central to the manufacturer's label as instructed. If it was incorrectly sewn on, or untidy, the warders pulled it off, and the process was repeated. Some of the ladies had never used a needle and thread in their lives, and it took them days to complete. Once that tedious task was completed, they issued an item referred to as 'the pot.' The pot is like a thermos flask which was really useful at night when I wanted extra water. We were also given the most disgusting toothpaste powder, a toothbrush, face cloth, a futon, a woven head cushion and a bar of soap. I was delighted I didn't have to buy these necessities and could brush my teeth every day and guessed I would get used to the toothpaste. A bottom sheet, a pillowcase and two woollen blankets. This was heaven.

The furnishings were sparse but adequate; a small wooden table and chair, a trunk in which to place my clothing, even a small television sat on the lid of the chest. Mounted on the wall next to the washbasin was a wooden shelf, a tiny wall cabinet and a western-style toilet but without the seat - at least I didn't have to share the loo now. A wooden partition separated the toilet from my 'open plan' living quarters. Though I was still visible while seated, I'd become numbed to that after all this time. One and a half metres by three and a half metres was my new cell's size. I was in the new block. These cells were considered 'luxury' in size and the building was right on the edge of the prison grounds. I had a beautiful window in my cell - it obviously couldn't open, but it was over a metre in height and about sixty centimetres wide; my window to the world, a world where I intended to put my broken vision, shattered hope and lost sanity back together, piece by piece.

Being considerably taller than most ladies here and massively taller than my Japanese counterparts, I was not able to stretch out entirely on my futon; my feet got squashed up against the wooden partition, and having always had circulation problems, this exacerbated the problem in my toes. After a few weeks, they began to change colour, and it wasn't long before I had minimal sensation in any of them. At night, I'd sit rubbing them for hours to get the circulation going, giving up precious sleep. Two toes on each foot had darkened to a deep blue, and I insisted on seeing a doctor. What started as painful chilblains changed into a condition bordering frostbite, though not quite as severe. I'd asked to have the warm woolly socks Storm had sent, but they wouldn't relinquish them; I couldn't see how they could be dangerous, but apparently some had ended their lives using socks, so I resorted to wearing three pairs of my other socks at night and snuggled up in the fleece tracksuit top and the snug warm jacket Storm had sent me. Only then I did I get a decent night's sleep. I was given medication and gradually the colour returned.

There were rules to walking, talking, eating, sitting and even sleeping correctly and this was pummelled into our brains during the first two weeks. Scattered within the vast prison grounds were an assortment of essential buildings and learning their whereabouts was of paramount importance. The square block closest to my living quarters was where most of the general activities took place, and I could see it from my window; yes, my luck was changing. My cell was in an excellent position, and I wondered if this cell was selected for me because of my behaviour over the past eight months, having endured the gravity of the holding cells and detention far longer than anyone else ever had.

Whatever had caused this stroke of good fortune, my window was my saviour. Looking out every day, I became familiar with the prison grounds I could see and the view of the mountains beyond.

I'd passed the humiliating physical examination on arrival; the x-rays revealed nothing hidden, my dental check was completed without a hitch and the medication I required to keep cholesterol at manageable levels was all in place. I learned much later that I was one of very few who'd passed all this without any need to be questioned. I also had a brand-new futon, but my toes took weeks to heal and I still had a hundred and four weeks to endure without parole being considered.

My official prison number - 'Ni sen ju itchi,' - number 2011 was stored to memory.

CHAPTER THIRTY-EIGHT:

The First Year in Prison

Nothing here was how I'd imagined it would be.

I kept asking when I would be put to work and was sure we were left wondering on purpose.

I'd excitedly filled in the questionnaire on what I could do and in what fields my strengths lay. The waiting game continued for a few more days until I got the good news. I was to work in the paper bag factory. Curiosity became a sensation I'd long forgotten even existed — me, working in a paper bag factory; this was not what I was expecting.

To begin with, I felt humiliated, then common sense quickly prevailed. Any form of work was better than the endless boredom. Purpose, in any way, was what I urgently needed to stop the useless practise of counting the days, weeks, months and years I still had locked in this hell.

'The chains of the body are often wings to the spirit,' I had heard someone say in the past but couldn't recall who had said it. But more importantly, instinct and intuition were to protect me in here.

My first working day began on day ten in Tochigi Prison. I noticed some unsavoury looking women, ones I knew that keeping my distance from was a matter of survival. Some of them were in for life, some for murder, some manslaughter, child abuse and numerous cases of theft and rape. There was an assortment of horrendous crimes and plenty of short-term prisoners in for shoplifting. Plenty medium term – up to five years - were like me, in for drug and other forms of smuggling. There were approximately 900 lady prisoners at Tochigi.

The morning I started work, the group of us who'd been selected to work with the paper bags were shepherded down to a large open room where boxes of paper bags were everywhere. The instruction on how to fold them correctly began. It was the most unstimulating task I'd experienced. The job of folding paper shopping bags didn't match the answers I'd put on my questionnaire. I did some investigating; everyone starts with a menial task that plays the boredom tune to perfection. The Sensei watch and assess your attitude toward mindless tasks; Sensei's first impression was important. The book cover of who you are. It determined the type of working life you'd have in prison from then on.

Every week, boxes of paper bags got delivered to the prison. We unfolded each bag, secured thin tape along the bottom, folded it flat to seal it and stacked them. From there, they were sent on to another group who packed them back into boxes. It passed the time, and I got paid. After a few weeks, I knew I'd go mad, but I kept keep telling myself things would get better.

To break the boredom and motivate us, the Sensei's held weekly competitions. The individual who packed the most bags in a day won and earned incentives. These were not designed for fun, but to test our work ethic and to help motivate us. The more paper bags one folded, the better one's ranking became and gradually, I began to understand their carefully planned system of individual assessment. Each prisoner had to prove they were worthy of their questionnaire — a carefully designed test to judge our ability, commitment and strength of character.

I won the competition for sealing the bottom of the highest number of bags more frequently than anyone else in the group and got promoted fast.

My first reward was a more extended stay in the exercise area. But the longer I stayed out, the more I craved a cigarette. However, my working life in prison progressed well; winning all the competitions for a few weeks in a row, I did get a few cigarettes and then I was promoted to 'checker'.

Catapulted into a position of responsibility, it was now up to me to motivate my team. I worked along with the group, ensuring the bags were folded with precision, stacked accurately and we got ahead of the other teams.

Ten folded bags lay in the box one way, then ten across those in the opposite direction. They all had to lie perfectly flat before the box got sealed. Monkey see, monkey do. Despite this, I managed to inspire my team to follow my example. We won every competition; first for the neatest, first for the most substantial quantity packed in a day and so on. Our Sensei told me other prisoners were asking to join my team; this was a huge compliment and noted by the senior Sensei. The next competition we won was an extra shower a week - a significant treat for me for we only had two showers per week.

It was back-breaking work, all done on the floor. I was even called 'old alien' for I was at least fifteen years older than the rest of my group. The rewards kept coming, and as a team leader, my pay went up. My first pay was the princely sum of 32 Yen for three weeks, but it was Yen in the right direction and soon I got promoted to 'packer'. A packer was considered a responsible position and an honour to achieve so quickly, and only awarded if the Sensei found the person trustworthy because, at the end of the working day, the packer took the boxes from the packing room, and put them in the store unaccompanied by a guard and returned without trying to escape.

Both Sensei were impressed with my work ethic, and I quickly earned their respect and trust; one step closer to my goal.

During the sixth week, I got another promotion. I was to leave the paper bag factory and join the factory that manufactured dainty, pink ballet shoes - one step closer to what I' put on the questionnaire.

The Sensei also rewarded my efforts by telling me I was one of the few prisoners who'd ever got promoted so quickly. I was delighted. I hoped it would be reported to the right people and work in my favour at my appeal hearing or early parole.

I worked on my appeal every evening before the lights were switched off at nine-thirty. I had the copy of the South African police papers on cannabis from Storm and trusted this would stand me in good stead.

During this time, I'd cautiously befriended another Filipino girl who was in for murder. There was something gentle about her that suggested to me she wasn't a murderer, let alone a criminal, much like me. She had a sad warmth about her, and I could sense there was something wrong. My assumption proved to be correct.

We became close, as close as one can get to another prisoner, and she spoke English. Her story was a tragic one of being cruelly framed when an intruder had fatally stabbed her husband in their home. She found him on the floor in their sitting room; the stabbing had killed her husband and her natural reaction had been to rush to him and hold him close to her while she grieved her loss, then she called for help. She had his blood all over her and was accused of murdering him. A team of lawyers were still fighting Darna's case. She was a small, gentlewoman with a beautiful porcelain face, now etched with lines of pain and grief. Her large, antelope-like eyes spoke of the hurt and suffering she'd endured and their youthful sparkle was lost with her husband and now she'd lost her freedom too.

She was appealing her case for the second time and offered some useful tips. She suggested my written defence should be checked by one of her lawyers before my hearing. They seemed to think it was well-presented and should impress the judge, so I felt confident to hand it in. It was given to my lawyer to submit to the Judge, requesting an appeal date.

Cannabis, a 'mayaka' – (Japanese for drug) ingested or smoked, was not as dangerous as cocaine and heroin. I also compared it to alcohol and cigarettes, both available on the open market, but more hazardous than cannabis.

The mortality statistics were given by The National Institute on Drug Abuse in America, (which I thought were extremely important and included them). They proved, I thought, that 'many Japanese people would *not* die.' The statistic went like this:

American Deaths caused by addictive substances- 2001 survey

Tobacco – 400,000

Alcohol – 100,000

All legal drugs – 20,000

All illegal drugs – 15,000

Caffeine – 2,000

Aspirin – 500

Cannabis – 0

I felt this said it all.

Shortly after submitting my case, I received a small notelet in the post from Storm with this little poem written in her hand.

Diamond Droplets

'Diamond droplets in the tree, twinkle there for you and me.

Little stars in the darkest night, they are there to show us the light.'

I needed the light now, more than ever. I couldn't stop reading it, and each time I did, tears welled up in my eyes.

Oh, how I longed to stand beneath the African skies again; clear and unpolluted.

Based on the evidence, the Judge would then decide if my case was worthy of appeal. A week later, the lawyer informed me the judge had not accepted my case, saying I must have been an active part of an organised drug syndicate, considering the depth of my knowledge on cannabis - appeal denied.

Aghast, I said to the translator, "tell him I obtained the information to prove that cannabis is not going to kill many Japanese people. I was provided with the information by the drug squad section of the South African Police. I am not a hardened criminal. I am a mother who was trying to protect her children from a sociopath." I was shouting, and my lawyer scowled with disapproval. I wasn't letting go of this opportunity, and he finally agreed to explain to the judge the misinterpretation of my first trial. I waited, holding my breath, dripping with sweat and consumed by frustration. I was granted another appeal hearing the following day. I sat in a dreary little office beside the court while the lawyer and the judge decided on my fate. An hour passed, the most extended hour of my life, but the news was not good.

"The Judge says your sentence is suitable; there will be no changes and no further appeals permitted. Eight years is the regular sentence. You are only serving four. After two years you may request an appeal for parole."

"After two years?" I gasped. It was what I'd been told already but I wanted to know if they counted it from the time I was captured. "What about the eight months I sat in holding cells and detention? He'd not considered that?"

The lawyer did his best to calm me, but nothing anyone said helped.

Case closed. That was it. No little diamonds were glittering in the sky for me.

A chilling thought. I sobbed for hours; then I was sure I'd heard a voice saying, 'You will get through this; just open the doors to faith again.' I looked around me to see where the voice had come from. There was no-one near my cell. Who'd just spoken? The message sounded so clear I shook my head and stood up, looking around again. There was no-one in sight.

'Yes, I'd make it - parole was one hundred and four weeks away. I had to make it.

I'd turned one corner successfully and gained the Sensei's trust. There were ten factories within the prison grounds, and each factory had several divisions which contributed to a considerable part of the income derived for running the prison. The Sanseis clearly understood the value of placing prisoners in a factory that produced happy workers, even encouraging us to speak up if we needed to be in a different section, providing we proved ourselves first, of course. It was essential to them that each prisoner had the opportunity to reach their full potential. There was such wisdom in their methods.

Administration and office work were the best-paid positions. Though I had exceptional administration and accounting skills, I avoided this work for I needed to be creative. More importantly, I'd highlighted my sewing and upholstery skills on my questionnaire, and now I could prove it in the ballet slipper factory.

Prisoner sentence identification is indicated by wearing coloured badges above the breast pocket on the left-hand side of our shirts. Short-term prisoners and new prisoners wore a red badge, prisoners in for more than six years wore a green badge and prisoners in for life wore a white badge. The white badge-bearers filled me with an uneasy fear; I steered clear of them whenever possible. Not one of them expressed a glimmer of emotion in their dark eyes; their eyes were lifeless dark pools. Most of them were bullies and caused terrible misery amongst the short-termers; mostly done on purpose. Most of the time, they left me alone. Though some jeered at me or deliberately bumped into me and tried to fleece me, I always managed to knock them away before they got a grip of me.

The day arrived when I was to start my new assignment. Sixty-four of us left the paper bag factory.

Only the most skilled got to the ballet shoe factory. I learned later the only reason they were giving me a chance in the ballet shoe manufacturing process was that I'd proven to be trustworthy in the previous factory. The fact I had many years' experience on sewing machines was only a minor consideration at this point. I also learned this was an impressive assignment, but the best part for me was the significant rise in my monthly pay.

I must have made a good impression in my new role for, only a few days into starting, I got a brand-new pillow as a reward. This reward was for proving I could sew and hadn't lied in my questionnaire. I was ecstatic; little rewards like this pillow made some days more tolerable than others.

Any reward is considered a prestigious recognition in jail. Recognition is celebrated for all prisoners to witness but getting them as often as I did was a double-edged victory. I gained very little favour with fellow prisoners and there was a backlash of nasty jealousy. I wasn't there to gain respect from fellow prisoners but trust from the Sensei.

Stupid things become significant in jail — things one takes for granted in ordinary life. Food had never been a priority to me. I thought of it only as a necessity, but, in jail, it became an important part of my day.

There was the vile 'Azuki'- a maroon-coloured bean which was served often and prepared as a sweetish paste and always accompanied either a potato salad or a slice of tomato and two or three leafy salad greens. I never got used to the taste of it.

What I missed was my coffee serving with each of my meals. Coffee or 'black tea' was always served black and only on the 'alien meal' days, those being Tuesday and Saturday. On those days we could have milk in our tea or coffee. 'Tamanegi' – egg or Nori - a thin compacted seaweed accompanied by fermented beans, served in a Styrofoam bowl with a sachet of soya sauce and known as 'shoyu', was another meal I loathed. And a few others were positively repulsive. But, after a year in prison, the acid reflux I'd suffered with never plagued me again. However, the post-meal mouth inspection did. An utterly humiliating routine as the Sensei gaped into our mouths, one by one, checking we'd not hidden anything in the smelly depths. Then we were checked to make sure we had not concealed anything in our clothing.

'Goodie packs', a preposterously exciting privilege generally consisting of a packet of crisps, a handful of biscuits and sweets with either a sugar-loaded fruit juice or a sugar-loaded flavoured milk, were a treat. We loved them and they became the mainstay of my dreary, awful existence. But, these goodie packs became a terrible dilemma for me; I could never finish one at a sitting, and, if I took one, it was marked on the purchase sheet and deducted off my salary. I could not afford this, but in the end, denying myself became pointless and only made me crave them more.

Retail therapy was a thing of the past, ruined by rules and the scarcity of funds, so every purchase had a carefully monitored life expectancy. For example, a bar of soap and a tube of toothpaste had a life span of two months. If it didn't last, they required a reasonable explanation as to why it hadn't lasted. But no matter what reason, it was never considered reasonable. This happened to me once - soap and toothpaste always lasted two months to the day after that. Shampoo, face cream and washing powder had the same rule tag, and empty containers had to be handed in and accounted for; no empty container - no replacement. True to Japanese culture, there was always a pay-off to motivate prisoners to follow the rules.

A good work ethic earned respect. Mine was exemplary and earned me two extra showers a week, so I had to recalculate how much soap to use.

Sometime during the first month in Tochigi, the new prisoners were shown to the library for the first time. I was astounded at the massive selection of books there. There were thousands upon thousands of book titles in seventeen different languages, and each language had hundreds of different titles in assorted genres. Among so many books, I never found one written in Afrikaans. I wondered whether that was a good sign or not.

We were permitted to select five books and one magazine, which we exchanged every two weeks. Each visit, I went quickly to the English section, affording me an additional ten minutes to get a better selection of my favourite love stories. The 'happily ever after' fluffy ones became my favourite, helping overcome anxiety and depression.

The maze of five-foot-high book-cased passages was a sanctuary I loved. I felt safe in those quiet moments being nourished by such a variety of intellectual nectar, stimulating my imagination.

In one of Pieter's letters, he'd suggested I look for an author called Stephen King. 'Mom, they are brilliantly written!' So, on our next visit to the library, I took out the novel - 'IT'. Though the contents of the book didn't prompt even the remotest smile, the choice of author my precious son had selected for me did. In an obscure way, it made me happy that Pieter had no concept of what I was experiencing. The dark, sinister and scary Stephen King novel did nothing to lighten my already sombre mood, so I stuck to soppy love stories with a – 'and they lived happily ever after,' ending. Hard-wired horror and suspense I lived with daily. I didn't need it in book form too.

The days got busier; the nights remained an emotional hell. No matter how often I fought against negative thoughts, the yearning for my children was so powerful, my heart felt trapped, and tears came easily and regularly.

The worst craving was the need to feel the warmth and touch of the loving arms of my children around me.

CHAPTER THIRTY-NINE

Working in the ballet slipper factory gave me renewed hope for early release. Every morning, I'd get up and say to myself, 'Elizabeth, you will get parole. Keep being positive.' Then I'd send gratitude and love to the universe in meditation and that little ritual would begin my day.

The promotions and rewards kept coming. With every exciting move up the ladder came more significant pay rises and some great bonuses. The morning ritual I'd put together was my lighthouse during the tough, stormy times. I got knocked about when jealousy turned calm waters into raging torrents, which happened every time I got a reward.

I got caught down one of the passages in the library after my new undies reward, when a green badge prisoner grabbed me and sank her teeth into my arm, but I didn't dare yell out in the sheer agony of it. Bruising easily anyway, her teeth marks stayed on my arm for weeks, apart from it being extremely painful and unnecessary. Jealousy comes out in all ugly forms in jail, and after I'd received my new uniform, naked and vulnerable while in the shower, a white badge woman tried to rape me. Stunned, I nearly broke her arm trying to get rid of her as it got caught between my thighs. Suppressing an agonising scream, she fled quickly before being caught and stayed away from me after that. I had thought of reporting it, but that would have attracted a worse situation.

The third reward in quick succession, all of them earned within five months, was a brand-new 'Parka' type jacket. That was deemed to be one of the grandest honours and a silent warning for me to stay on high alert after receiving it, even for as long as a few weeks. Hatred, jealousy, envy; emotions like these are dominant in prison. They fill the air, they fill the cells, they fill the workplace and permeate through the exercise areas; there is no escaping them.

As far as fellow prisoners were concerned, I'd progressed from a paper bag packer to manufacturing ballet slippers too fast. The next post I was awarded meant few spoke to me. The Sensei trusted me enough to recommend the post of chief machinist. I was thrilled, for it meant a considerable hike in my pay.

In the trimming section, I checked every stitch. Yes, every stitch, then I'd trim off excess thread so when I progressed to machinist, I knew what I was in for. No trimmer was going to throw a slipper back for me to re-do.

I had a perfect source of natural light from the window I sat next to, and could look out into the distance when I became cross-eyed from the intense concentration. I was lucky enough to catch these moments to rest my tired eyes and had the good fortune of being able to utilise the natural light, though I still needed the sharp light of the machine's bulb shining down on the slipper fabric. Most of the others weren't as lucky. I knew every stitch I made was perfect. The ladies deeper in the factory struggled with their lighting, which put an enormous amount of strain on their eyes. None of this work was kind on any of our eyes and shoulders. The process of making ballet shoes worthy of the dancer that wears them is an intricate process of manufacture I'd not appreciated before.

Prior to becoming head machinist, I was put through the rigors of stitching on a square of material with pre-marked lines drawn on it. When I first sat down at the machine and was given this marked square of fabric, I considered it quite an insult to my machining ability! I laughed at my reaction when I understood the system and the level of difficulty. To get into the swing of making these delicate slippers, I was made to sew two or three stitches along the pre-marked line then stop, lift my foot off the controls, then sew a few more stitches and so it went on until my ankle screamed and my calf muscles resigned. I could hardly walk after that day. Once I'd perfected that phase, I moved on with a whole new appreciation of the importance of this training, for the seams on a ballet slipper are very short, with endless curves. It is impossible to sew fast when such precision is required. If the quality controller returned more than four slippers, a black mark was issued. I ensured black marks against me rarely happened. As good as I had been on a sewing machine, I learned foot control with considerably more skill.

The Sensei's eagle eye was as skilled as the keenest bird of prey. She recognised a good catch when she saw one and swooped on me as a prize catch. She'd spotted I had proper attention to detail, I was accurate and committed to excellence. She respected my work ethic too, and that is what shot me up the income highway.

Within our factory, there were clearly defined divisions. Each division head was a long-term, white badge prisoner who'd proved herself and lauded over her podium, watching over her assigned brood of machinists. She was also the only person a prisoner was permitted to communicate with, and the only person authorised to move around freely.

After several weeks of excruciating immobility, legs tingling or burning, I progressed from those tiresome steps, got my rewards and left that painful work behind me, becoming the leading seamstress, but it was insufferable monotony.

I continued manufacturing pink satin ballet slippers for months and began to wonder if it was what I would be doing until I left prison. I'd been in the slipper factory for roughly a year when I started making the more specialised leather ones. I had the top post. Another substantial income boost and elevation to my status, and now, at last, I was left alone, and the bullying and threats ceased.

Once the top part of the slipper is complete, binding is sewn around the top edge of the shoe. This is where the cord slides through and must run freely inside the binding to allow the dancer to tighten the slipper to fit the foot perfectly. My machine had a specialised binding attachment and the concentration required was more intense – it was good for me, keeping my mind focussed. I wasn't sure how many more promotions were open to me in this factory, but the one position I wanted was to head one of the divisions. Once I got there, I could move around and talk to some of the lady machinists.

Sitting at my cell window one evening, revelling in my last promotion and staring out longingly at the mountains, I was interrupted by the delivery of a letter from Storm. Inside was a photograph of my second grandson. For long minutes I starred at the picture of my grandson, sadness eating away at my insides while another deep sense of guilt persecuted me. Delighted though I was to receive the photograph, and knowing it was sent with all the best intentions, it left me weakened by a renewed self-loathing; I should be with my children, not here, staring out a prison cell window in Japan.

Unfolding my legs, straightening my back and closing my eyes, I heard the voice again. A powerful light flashed bright and beautiful; then it was gone.

At the end of a busy day, the Sensei signalling to switch off all machines; then I saw that light again beam across the skies. These I understood to be the signatures of reassurance that I was not alone. That night, I crawled onto my futon and thanked God for coming to my rescue; even the stigma of being a criminal became more comfortable to bear.

A brand-new futon with brand-new bedding came with an abundance of brand-new problems I'd thought were over. But this time, I handled the nasty bullying with God's guidance. Even sleep was more peaceful; terrifying nightmares didn't plague my nights quite as often. At last, I began to feel I was on the fringes of accepting this journey and the lessons. Standing alone in this threatening arena, watched by those with folded arms and lots to say, I'd been torn and whipped about by the storms of life in this arena, my body maimed, and my garments of clothing torn, but with honour, I'd leave.

I'd just finished my umpteenth pair of slippers when I was called to the head Sensei's office. Being summoned to the head Sensei's office generally meant trouble.

He was one of the few male staff in the jail. Stress levels peaked; I couldn't think of anything I'd done wrong. It is the primary response in jail, and sure enough, his opening question wasn't encouraging.

"Why are you not putting more of your earnings toward paying off the fine?" he asked, like this alone was a crime. I stood there, not knowing how to answer. I had no control over the deductions.

"E... liz...bet, you must pay 1000 Yen per week now, " he insisted.

I would be left with very little to buy the few things that made my life bearable, and I expressed my concerns. Stamps, pens and notepads were my number one priority; I could go without the rest if I had to.

He nodded and dismissed me.

Hope, my powerful weapon against depression, had been dashed. To my surprise, at the end of the month, my income, even after the new deduction, brought hope racing home. He'd doubled my earnings; my fine was reducing significantly.

I realised then, as I had previously in my life, even when things are dark and grim, when I'd tried and tried, over and over again and hadn't allowed others to discourage or insult me, even those who enjoyed humiliating me after Dion's disgusting escapades, I could hold my head high; even now I could be proud of me. I was brave for an innocent farm girl who'd grown up in the humblest of environments. The Sensei recognised these traits and dished out the honour I deserved.

While taking a moment to look out the factory window before switching on my machine, I noticed a spider hard at work in the most distinct web I'd ever seen. The spider's hard labours captured my attention to such an extent that I didn't want to look away and get back to work. I had been so absorbed by the miniature battles going on within the web, I never realised the Sensei was watching me as carefully as I was watching the spider. She interrupted my spider moments by saying in broken English that she was impressed with my work and would ask Senior Sensei if she could teach me to be the overall supervisor of all the divisions. My mouth dropped open; I could have hugged her but didn't dare, of course. This was huge; perhaps it had been worth spider-watching with such intensity.

This was an astounding promotion resulting in me being one of the highest-paid, short-term prisoners they'd ever had at Tochigi. I was proud of my achievements under such trying circumstances.

God was answering my prayers at last.

The boredom and immobility I'd endured for months were over. At last, I could move around and put my spoken Japanese skills to good practice.

Issuing new machine needles was one of my new tasks, though it didn't happen often. Breaking a needle was seriously frowned upon because a broken machine needle could do severe damage or even kill someone if thrust deep into an unsuspecting jugular. And, one thing I knew for sure, I didn't want to meet my end as a jealous inmate plunged a broken needle into my neck. So, when a needle did get broken, every single piece of it had to be handed in before I would issue a new one.

I introduced a reward scheme to stop needle breakage, for there were some who broken them on purpose. Those engaged in the practice soon stopped it. Apart from issuing them, I changed them, altered tensions, taught newcomers and operated a machine if one became empty.

The days were more varied at last and sometimes I was even asked to fix a machine if the Sensei couldn't or was having difficulties; the only benefit of owning a sewing shop years back.

Despite the job variety, emotional emptiness remained a close companion. But what always amazed me, was how adaptable the human soul is, once acceptance is fully committed. And it's amazing how hardened one becomes, trying as I did, not to become cynical, a disposition I always disliked.

I found learning to speak Japanese difficult but inspiring. Receiving the warmth expressed in letters from my children and family kept me sane, and I learned a new meaning for the words time and hope.

And now, here I was, in the top post I'd prayed for. I couldn't help wondering if I got parole, would the balance of the fine be written off? Was that possible? Did that sort of thing happen?

Back to Japanese lessons; to brush up was essential now. My poor tutor, how patient she was. I found Japanese very difficult to learn to speak, it is an agglutinative, mora-time language I often found impossible to get my tongue around. Its history dated back to the 8th Century. Simple phonotactics with a pure vowel system, spoken in subject-object-verb; a language I never truly grasped, but these extra lessons helped as the head the ballet slipper division.

'Keemusho kara no shakuhoo' – released from prison; 'this is what I will sing when I get parole,' I thought.

'Irasshaimasc, doozo o-hairi kudasai'- 'Welcome, please come in.' Now that was a tongue twister and it took lots of practice to get that right.

Once I was confident enough to ask, I approached the head Sensei, asking if it would be permitted to begin our days in the factory with singing the Japanese National Anthem, 'Kimigayo.' He was delighted and soon the other factories followed suit. It was a great motivational, patriotic way to start the day. There is a verse in the song that reflects the culture and expressed respect. The basic meaning of the anthem is; 'May the reign of the Emperor continue for a thousand, nay, eight thousand generations and for the eternity that it takes for small pebbles to grow into great rocks and become covered with moss.'

The words resonated with me.

Many, many days throughout my imprisonment, I'd have what I called 'my mind wanderings.' These wanderings took me back into the veld, into the wild, wide-open spaces where I grew up. How one appreciates those unspoiled spaces when they are gone. Inhaling deeply, I pretended I could smell the dust or the freshly fallen raindrops on thirsty dry earth. The deeper my thoughts became, the freer I felt, and my mind tricked me into believing I actually could smell those wondrous smells of my African childhood. It was when immersed in these blissful thoughts that I received the first letter from 'Gogga'. To begin with, I didn't want to read it. His timing was impeccable. It took me days to open the envelope and read it. He was writing to tell me he hadn't had a drink for weeks and was very proud of himself. 'I feel clean, clear and calm - I wish you were here with me.' I didn't have the same sentiment, but the contents, when he wasn't talking about himself, had some surprising tender touches; he even admitted having sensations of guilt, something I didn't think he was capable of.

He seldom asked how I was coping with prison life, but in his next letter, a glimmer of reflection was expressed. The worst part about all the letters I received was that I knew all these deeply personal things had been read by a third person - the censor - and I cringed. I read on.

'You know, I've always thought that you viewed me as a nothing, a failure — someone who never learns from their mistakes. But now, I finally see how you tried your best. It was me who saw the wrong side of you. I promise to 'make a plan' to pay for your ticket home. Love you always, Dion.'

I read that letter repeatedly and cried endless tears each time; I hated the bastard; or did I? I couldn't fathom my reaction.

CHAPTER FORTY

Once a year, the Sakura Festival is held, creating a wave of excitement within prison that spreads like an infection. The Sakura is the national flower, translated it means cherry blossom. The Festival is internationally renowned and enjoyed by many visitors to Japan, even those of us visiting behind bars.

On the morning of the opening day, we were marched to the sports grounds to participate in what I know as Boere (farm) sports. It was a refreshing change; a day of rope-pulling, volleyball, skipping and rounders competitions, plus other games they play in Japan I'd not played before.

The factories were divided into groups and I opted for the skipping competition. It brought back memories of boarding school days and brought relief from the drudgery of everyday life, and we won it.

Since the festival, and on an occasional Saturday, they introduced inter-factory games, and pop music festivals. It seemed absurd that the first song I heard at a 'pop' festival was a Japanese rendition of 'New York, New York,' and it left me desperately homesick.

Since the encounter with God, while sitting at my cell window, the pull to attend church became quite intense. I felt the need to be a part of His flock again. The options were Catholicism or Buddhism. I knew nothing of Buddhism and was somewhat hesitant about Catholicism. I took the Catholic opportunity and joined their prayer meetings and services; they were of the Christian faith, which I understood, and the meetings were conducted in English.

The opening blessing had a powerful effect on me. We stood in front of our chairs, ready to welcome the priest, when suddenly a voice echoed through the building, sending shivers down my spine. It was the priest singing the sensational hymn, 'Amazing Grace,' as he walked into the congregation. Moved by the timbre and magnificence of his voice, tears rolled down my cheeks on their own accord, lifting out the darkness I'd stored for twenty long months.

That evening, I sat cross-legged on my pillow at my window, which, in my mind now mimicked an altar, and in a jerky whisper, sang my favourite hymn; 'Jerusalem,' and closed my eyes. Later that night, while I lay meditating, contemplating and philosophising, I found a connection to my inner soul and faced buried truths I'd never wanted to face and questioned some of my cultural beliefs and whether they all served me. I'd worked on a multitude of thoughts, but deeper stuff seemed to be happening now, feelings I'd seldom allowed myself to acknowledge. Picking up one of the books I'd sourced in the library, a little poem fell out of the book and I read it.

The poem touched me, teaching me a little more about me, and added immense warmth to my chilled soul, blending beautifully with the thawing the minister had begun.

> Life's threads all form a pattern,
> Some silver, some gold.
> And there are new and finer threads
> To mingle with the old.
> Some tiny threads are broken
> A stitch or two is skipped,
> But when the work is finished
> The pattern isn't ripped,
> It forms a perfect blending
> Of all of life's great dreams

> With love we form the border
> With sorrow, sew the seams
> So, fold the pattern to your heart
> Sweet memories are the dearest part.

From then on, the moment a negative thought came to mind, I'd think of the poem and soon I could recite it word for word. Those words were the thread of gold that helped keep me motivated in the days, weeks, months and years ahead. I pasted the little piece into my journal and considered it another lesson that would serve me for the rest of my life.

All the hurt, my pain, my shame and regrets, resentment, bitterness and hate had been like open wounds festering for so long. In tiny increments of self-love, others' love, kindness and remarkable thoughtfulness, from sources I'd never anticipated, the uncomfortable sensations within were being put back together, piece by piece. But, no matter how my thoughts had changed, the first Christmas in Tochigi Prison was the greatest torture in this adversity. A tsunami of the most horrendous compilation of emotions, magnified by desperate loneliness and a mournful need to be with my children, smothered me. An agony so indescribably devastating it set me back the months of hard work I'd done on myself.

It began on the 19th of December 2003, at the Christmas Mass.

In my view of the mountains on that morning, they were sprinkled with a splattering of light snow, a vision like a picture postcard. The air was crisp, though the sun was shining, and the wind whipped across my cheeks as we marched from the dining hall to the hall where Christmas Mass was being held. On the way across, I noticed a pigeon sitting in the snow, its feathers all puffed up and for a fleeting moment, I wondered if its feet were as cold as mine.

This was my first experience of a Catholic Christmas Mass. The first Christmas in detention I'd blanked from my mind; I scarcely remember it, other than the tears.

When Father entered the hall, he was carrying with him a porcelain baby boy doll dressed in swaddling clothes and today, it represented baby Jesus. At the end of the service, Father passed 'baby Jesus' around, asking each of us to hold baby Jesus in our arms, to look deeply into his eyes and give thanks for our lives.

I had the most poignant connection to the holy spirit I'd ever experienced. I cradled the child in my arms, who, for a moment, felt so authentic and tearfully whispered my gratitude for sparing my life, a life I had so often wanted to end. Baby Jesus's face, hands and feet were porcelain, but the body was soft; it felt so real, as real as the emotion that was pouring out of me. I saw life in those glass eyes as the lids flickered open and closed while the doll-child moved in my arms. I knew, in that instant, God was beside me, He understood the depth of my pain and guilt, and it was time to forgive myself. During the divine celebration of an extraordinary life, and, before I passed baby Jesus on to my neighbour, I rejoiced at the birth of the new me. It was time to graciously and fully accept the difficulties and harshness of prison life.

It was one of the most meaningful Christmas Services I'd ever experienced.

On the 23rd of December, we celebrated the Emperor of Japan's birthday, quite different celebrations from the 19th. The variation in food during the festivities had more meaning to us 'alien' inmates than the Emperor's birthday, as there were all sorts of delicacies like icing sugar-coated doughnuts and other cakes we rarely saw.

On Christmas morning, the church distributed a printed Christmas prayer and a heart-warming thought-provoking letter to carry us faithfully into the New Year; there was no service.

THE PRAYER

> Joy is to be shared. Let us pray to Jesus our Lord that
> the Good News of his coming may warm the hearts of all,

and let us pray that;
Today may be a feast of joy for all our families and
For all to whom we bring a bit of happiness today
That today maybe a feast of joy for all children
Far or near,
To those who are happy and those who hunger and suffer
That today is perhaps a feast of faith for those who know the Lord
And for those who do not yet know him
That today may become again a feast of
Peace for those divided by quarrels
For countries divided by war
That today may be a feast of joy for all our
Christian communities and that we may share
That joy as we go together in the Lord's way of peace.
Let us pray to the Lord
Lord Jesus, you are one of us. Help us to
Become more like you, that we may become your joy,
as you are ours,
Now and forever
Amen

The prayer held a more profound meaning now. As I read, I cried softly and often that day. I cried for my children, I cried for Dion, and I prayed for them all. My sobs were no longer gut-wrenching blasts of intolerable physical pain and unimaginable suffering, but gentle sobs of personal forgiveness and messages of unconditional love.

I asked the Lord to show Dion the road to recovery. The children's letters told me he was still drinking heavily, though he'd have weeks where he wouldn't drink, but those were short-lived. He'd been job-hopping as usual, either resigning or getting himself fired. My fantastic, once-prosperous business that had collapsed because of him, still stung but I was working on forgiveness. In one of Storm's letters, she'd mentioned having banned Dion from entering her home. Now, under normal circumstances, it would have infuriated me that his behaviour was so unacceptable that even his own daughter wouldn't allow him into her house. Instead of feeling this intense anger and disappointment to the same levels, I found comfort in offering up a little prayer for them both.

That night, after consuming a rather unusual, but special Christmas dinner, I went to bed holding baby Jesus in my mind; it was a treasured peaceful night.

The following day was the last working day of the year in Japan. We gave the factory a spring clean, closed at 3 o'clock, and as I locked the factory door, I was handed another letter from Storm. The timing could not have been more perfect. Though this first Christmas in Tochigi had been an emotional mix of emptiness and enlightenment, reading her letter was still extremely hard, sending shooting pains through me as I read.

Throughout the Christmas week and into New Year we received a variety of interesting goodie packs we could take into our cells, which was comforting, but they had to be finished by the 31st. On the eve of the 27th of December, looking out my window was like looking at a real-life fairy tale; everywhere was white with snow. The tree's sparkled in their white coats, the roofs of the prison were blanketed in snow; it was magnificent. A white Christmas is not something we Africans experience. I knew this New Year would be a better year for me.

Weirdly, on the morning of the fourth day into 2004, my waking thoughts were of 'Gogga.' I opened my eyes and found myself praying for him. And later that day I received a letter from him, and like Pieter's letters, he too asked if I remembered various songs we had loved so much. The one he mentioned in this letter was - 'You Can Make Me Whole Again.' This reduced me to tears. It wasn't Dion making me whole again, though I heard his exquisite voice singing it to me. I wished with all my heart that the man I had married all those years ago hadn't changed into the ogre that beset our marriage and made our lives a living hell. Perhaps my prayers of forgiveness were being transmitted, for this letter contained unusual emotional dialogue and was hard to read. I wondered if he finally meant what he was expressing.

'Would I ever be ready for him to serenade me again?' Even with God's help, I doubted it. Even with God's help, I was sure I'd not be able to forgive him fully for all he'd put me through. I'd endured twenty-five years listening to empty apologies and endless lies; now it was time for me, even if it was in this God-forsaken place. Because I'd never forget all the pain he'd inflicted upon me, and our children, I knew it would take more than just one deeply moving Christmas Mass in Japan to forgive him. His letter ended by saying, 'Be strong, my love, your ever-loving husband. I love you.'

If he'd said that only weeks before the Christmas Mass, I would have angrily torn the letter into tiny little bits. Though I still had a long way to go on this journey of forgiveness, I was considerably calmer in my response to those words.

That afternoon, we watched a movie called 'Pay it Forward' with Haley Joel Osmond. It was excellent. The theme song was, 'Call on Angels' - I wondered if that was another message.

The following week, while in the library, I went in search of spiritual and religious books to add to my uplifting love stories that gave me hope and inspiration that love could be found, even if it was only fantasy.

CHAPTER FORTY-ONE

The Christmas celebrations had shifted my old thought processes into something new and I realised how hard I had always been on myself. My mother, bless her, had done an excellent job of entrenching a powerful belief system in me that I had to remain strong and in control of absolutely everything I did. I had lived with the illusion that I had been strong and in control. It was only now, after all I had endured and still had to endure, that I could see how detrimental that belief was. The only thing I was in control of now were my thoughts, and with them, I was going to carve out a better future for me. I accepted, with warm gratitude, that there was nothing wrong with the framework of Mother's teachings. Her intentions were pure; her admirable inner strength had served her when Papa passed away, but they'd left an ingrained fear of failure within me. This was the fear I was struggling to crawl my way out of now, even with God's assistance, though I felt more confident my journey to redemption would be more manageable now.

I smiled as I thought back on my initial horrified thought of being forced to attend a *Catholic Mass* on Christmas Day, not being of the Catholic faith. It completely went against all my beliefs and I realised then how inflexible we can become.

During bible study or in a service, when Father read from the Bible, he explained *his* perspective, then asked us all to give the wise words some thought from *our* perspective. It was a perfect, unobtrusive way of allowing the interpretation to become our own. He never forced us to pray or beg the Lord for atonement of our terrible deeds and sins. Instead, he filled us with hope and an intricate understanding of being simply human.

Slowly, like the passage of a tortoise, I began to see life through the angelic eyes of the hare.

I was able to reach out to Vivienne, now that I understood her struggles from a different perspective and her letters, and mine to her, took on new meaning.

'Love the unlovable,' he taught us in Bible study. It was a concept I struggled with to begin with, despite having welcomed God's guidance into my life again. Jail was indeed a lonely, solitary life, but it was easier now.

> The little choices we must make
> Will chart the course of life we take
> We either choose the path of light
> Or we wonder in the darkest night

The author was unknown, but I found it in the library and copied it into letters to my children with the hope they'd make better choices than I had.

Storm's letters and poems kept me motivated when I hit emotional low spots - she wrote almost weekly - or I'd ask to speak with Father Bradly.

"Elizabeth, my dear, you need to remember a famous quote.... I'm sorry, it escapes me who said it, but it goes something like this.... 'people are not disturbed by the things that happen, but by their opinion of the things that happen."

I thought long and hard on the wisdom of those words, for they had deeply resonated with me and I have never forgotten them.

CHAPTER FORTY-TWO

I watched, from my window, the dazzling sunsets. Their colours changed the fluffy white clouds to puffs of orange, gold and yellow, each with a perfect silver lining until the last rays of light were gone. Songs I'd forgotten would fill my mind as I watched the sun slowly fade and I'd sing them quietly until it was dark. Once the last rays were gone, I'd turn my attention to the photographs Storm and the family sent. The most recent was of Storm standing with her father; still so handsome it caught my attention, surprised by the desires the image of him provoked, desires I didn't want to deal with in prison; sensations I never thought I'd feel again. There was never a moment's doubt; I still loved the Dion I'd married first.

In the morning, I'd see another glorious day bloom, showing a completely different palette of colours that washed across the skies and helped brighten my day.

April 2004. The second-year anniversary of my arrest. Sublime, but it was a great celebration for me. I was halfway there if I had to complete the full sentence.

I walked into the factory with Sensei and switched on the radio and, 'Have you ever seen the rain,' was playing. I loved that song. It was a perfect song to listen to as I secretly hoped the possibilities of a parole hearing were approaching.

I'd given up daily exercises for the past two weeks. My entire body hurt from the machining; I needed to rest. I'd asked to go to the dispensary to get pain killers, but they said I wasn't sick. I needed some powerful analgesics, as every joint in my body ached painfully. Because I wasn't considered sick, I requested to see the doctor to have my cholesterol checked instead. It was dangerously high; he cautioned I could have had a heart attack. After those results, he advised it was essential for me to have checks done every three months.

During this horrid low, burdened by awful joint and back pain, my assistant, a vicious, long-term prisoner whom I disliked immensely, chose this time to come on to me. Like a lioness watching and stalking a sick animal, she cornered me. She was strong and rubbed herself hard against my body, telling me I was very pretty, which thoroughly repulsed me. I managed to push her away with more force than I'd anticipated and knocked her to the floor. I was terrified there were going to be terrible repercussions, delaying my parole application, or worse still, losing my responsible position. Thankfully, not a word was spoken of the incident, though she told me later she was hoping to get me into trouble. Bitch! She left me alone and a few days after my medication was changed and I was feeling stronger, I got notification that I would only be permitted to apply for a parole hearing in July 2005 - fourteen months away. I sank back into a dark emotional pit, more raw and devastating than before. I wondered if knocking the assistant head to the floor had anything to do with this.

Seven weeks later, Japan was shaken by two earthquakes. I was sitting in my usual position, looking out my window at the mountains, trying to re-establish some positivity back into my life, when a deep rumbling filled the air, followed by a frightening shaking of the earth. The whole building shuddered and I thought it was about to crash to the ground - for a fleeting moment, I wished it would. A few minutes later it was over, but the following day, during the morning, we got hit by a stronger tremor. The Senior Sensei sent an urgent instruction that echoed through the factories – 'switch off machines and sit on the floor,' and we all slid off our chairs and put our heads between our knees as the building shook.

Sitting cross-legged next to Senior Sensei, I got the chance to question why my parole hearing had been shifted, forcing me to wait over another year. He informed me there was nothing he could do to bring it closer but assured me he'd submitted many 'good behaviour' notices.

The earth tremors settled, but my internal ones stayed with me all day. I found it impossible to concentrate and cried off and on throughout the day - I had tried so hard; this news was so demoralising.

That day, during afternoon exercise routine, Sensei brought me a cigarette; I hadn't had a cigarette for months; even that didn't help.

I stopped looking out my window with sparkling eyes. I stopped praying. I even stopped going to bible study and performed all the daily routines robotically. I felt no emotion; it had rumbled into the earth with the quake, where it was to be stored until my release. I sank back into nothingness, my soul needing to hibernate for the winter; I was dead, but my body worked and worked and worked on autopilot. This was cruel; this was merciless, and for the next three long months, I lived in this pit of ever-increasing depression until an accident in my section stirred me from the dangerous spiral I found myself in.

Under my watch, in front of my eyes, I witnessed, with traumatising horror, an in-mate emotionally snap. I was shattered, but what struck me a blow within me - I wasn't far away from mentally snapping too. The once balanced and powerful internal self-control my mother installed was gone. I was teetering on madness. I could feel its talons gripping harder and the shock of witnessing the most gruesome dance of self-destruction any human could witness stopped me in my tracks and woke me from a madness slumber. A numbed state where I didn't care anymore.

The girl was Polynesian, petite and shy, and seldom spoke to anyone. She was in for drug offences. I had observed her carefully – well, I thought I had. I remember wondering why she was so reserved. She was a good seamstress and very meticulous. Externally, she appeared to be focussed, but her demons got the better of her when she made a trivial mistake on the pair of ballet shoes she was working on. It began with her rocking on her seat, then as human tolerance became more and more stretched by her internalised emotional trauma, weird sounds hissed out her mouth with strands of saliva, then she erupted with agonising screams as if she were being torn apart by some invisible force from the inside out, and she threw herself on the floor, writhing and jerking in spasmodic asthmatic-like gyrations, banging her head against the floor as if she were beating a rag doll to death. Blood burst in spurts from her head while she repeated the thrashings, then she grabbed the ballet shoes she'd tossed on the floor and hurled them across the room. My immediate reaction was to rush to her and stop her from doing herself more damage, but I knew I could not do it alone. Her mind had gone; her body was performing a grotesque suicide for all of us to witness. By the time Senior Sensei entered the factory, it was too late. She completed her macabre dance of death so quickly and with such power. She stood up, smashing her head into the top of my sewing machine. The threader guides embedded into her skull and the needle arm ripped through the flesh of her face, tearing it away from its moorings. Then she sank my cutting scissors deep into her chest with a departing deathly groan as she fell forward over my machine, her body twitching and spasming before it hit the floor with a horrifying thud, shuddered violently and she heaved out her last breath and was still. We all stood watching, in rigid horror, as the emergency siren rang out, chilling even the most hardened inmates.

'I could have been next,' I thought grimly, as we silently watched her limp, torn body being lifted onto a stretcher, covered with a sheet and removed from the factory.

The mood was grim, but as I was the one in charge, I chose two others I could trust to help clean up the morbid mess. Sensei's voice exploded in my head and brought me back into the room. He'd shouted at me twice before I acknowledged his instruction, so intensely disturbed was I. Sensei helped organise cloths, bowls of water and disinfectant. It took immense effort to stop myself from vomiting as we removed pieces of facial flesh, tangled up with hair and congealed blood off the cotton holder and needle tensioner of my machine. One of the helpers could take no more of it and fainted. This was a gory reminder of what can happen when the human mind can take no more isolation and punishment.

Once we'd got the area cleaned and my machine was freed of human flesh, blood and hair, we were marched out of the factory and down to the exercise area where we could mingle, rest, communicate and reboot our minds. Two off-duty Sensei came to talk to us, and the Catholic Father visited us, offering words of wisdom to soothe our battered thoughts from the horror we had all witnessed. Her suicide made me doubly vigilant from that day forward, and I always kept my cutting scissors in my uniform pocket from then on.

What helped my mindset was, on the 16th of July 2005, I was informed my first application for parole had been submitted, which gave me hope. I was so excited I wrote a letter to Storm letting her know I would be home soon, then I had to let them in on the devastating news I wasn't coming home; parole had been denied without explanation.

I applied again, but again it was denied. This time I insisted on a full explanation as to why I was being denied parole, when I had done everything in my power to prove I wasn't a criminal in the real sense of the word, and would never consider doing anything illegal again in my life, no matter the circumstances, for this was a mistake too enormous ever to contemplate making again.

The only answer I got; 'It is still too early.' I was furious.

"Too early for what? Too early for whom?" I screamed at the senior Sensei. So practised were they at not answering prisoners' demands and cries for help, he stared past me in uncomfortable silence.

On Sunday the 18th of December, three prisoners were released on parole – that was more punishing news for me. A fellow prisoner understood my anger, and while in the exercise area, she came to me, pointing with her index finger to her head, she said, "Stupido, you."

"What you mean?" I asked, gesturing with my arms.

"You too good to go, make too many slippers, too honest – Sensei needs you." The penny dropped, but I was still spitting mad. The three released were Green badges.

What to do? I wouldn't drop my work standards. I felt sure there was more to it. I'd learned many years back that no-one is indispensable, but now I found I'd worked myself into a position of being vital in this environment for a time period. There was precious little I could do to change it. The factory closed early that day - a movie was being shown for the afternoon, turning my burning anger right back into deep sorrow.

The movie was of the Life of John Lennon, 1940 – 1980, and the theme song was "Stand by Me".

I wept through the whole movie struggling with crushing conflicting thoughts. Gogga used to sing that to me, on the infrequent occasions he ever felt guilty.

'When the night is dark, and the moon is the only light I see……' I remembered his smile. 'Darling, darling stand by me…'

Oh, how I had. I'd stood by him through thick and thin. I'd tried so hard for him and look what it got me – four years in jail. Now it appeared I'd tried too hard for parole, sealing my fate. I wondered if I'd ever get out early and the awful, intolerable human emotions, resentment and bitterness, were back. How would I ever get over it? How could I ever forgive him? The ongoing battle between negative and positive emotions fought each other for lead position in my head and my heart, while fear and the encroaching cold weather kept me alert. Winter was back with a vengeance this year, chilling my mind, my body and my soul, all of which hovered around freezing point, battered by cold winds from Siberia.

Christmas day, 2005 came and went, and 'Oujaar' celebrations were about to begin. This one was just like the last, except for a letter from Pieter who'd enclosed a little poster for an indoor cricket match he'd organised as a fundraiser toward my flight home – what a heart-warming gesture and Christmas present. God had given me amazing children. It was time to start working on those positive affirmations again and go back to communicating with God.

"Good-bye, 2005." Time was passing. The winds had dropped, and it was almost peaceful but for my thoughts. Sometime during 2006, I would be home with my family. I did not stay awake for midnight that year; instead, I drifted off to sleep, my night filled with fitful dreams and visions of me being reunited with my family once more.

At 9.30 am on the 3rd of January 2006, I was holding in my hands, with disbelief, another request for an interview for parole. I'd just about completed my sentence; their timing was ruthless and inexplicable.

"Third time lucky," I prayed. The difference in the questionnaires gave me hope. There were three strange questions this time, ones I'd not had before.

What things have you thought about during these past four months?

Describe what you feel and think about your crime.

In order not to commit a crime again, what kind of life are you going to have in the future?

I was worried my answers in English may be detrimental to the outcome. 'Lost in translation' had happened to me before. Now I had to depend upon my new-found faith and belief that God would guide my answers.

Thoughts over the last four months? The previous four years, I could honestly say, they had been plagued by shame and guilt. I was desperate to get home to redeem myself with my family. I was returning home a criminal – an international criminal. It was an impossible realisation. A colossal mistake of trust and misjudgement that any sane, functioning, loving mother would have made was my justification. God knew I'd never had any intention of doing anyone harm. I'd allowed my ex-husband to destroy my success and force me into a disgusting muddle of lies, deceit and despicable behaviour, which had finally led me here. This was his final gift to me as I tried to get away in case I murdered him, for that is what I was being driven to do.

The last four months? I'd lived with regret, grief, heartache and despair. I'd wallowed in self-pity – what more did they want me to say? How many times did they want me to agree I'd made the biggest mistake of my life?

How do I feel about my crime?

Demeaned, humiliated, shamed -they knew I loathed what I'd done, but I had accepted the responsibility of my actions. I believed I had proved that my morals and ethics were sound and unquestionable. Why did I have to regurgitate the disgrace again? The wound in my heart would always fester.

I had a few days before I had to hand in my answer sheet and decided to allow the process to happen on its own. A new set of suitable answers would slip out from somewhere. The answers came to me while watching the movie Titanic, hidden in the hauntingly beautiful musical lyrics.

Thursday, the 12th of January, 2006 - The day they were to call me for the interview where I would be asked to read the answers I'd carefully scribed and await the decision of one man.

I always hated this 'waiting to be called'; it made my hands damp and clammy, and a cold sweat of apprehension covered my body. I'd put heart and soul into the previous interviews, and all I'd been served was more bad news. This time, the Titanic wasn't going to sink. This time, love and divine guidance would steer me around the icy cold hard places I'd been kept in for four years, and I'd come out in the sunshine, victorious.

That day also marked the day I had completed three-quarters of my sentence; the worst was already over.

Finally, I was called. I stood up; I read out my answers, my voice filled with honest sincerity, then I sat down again. I kept my eyes cast toward the floor, and my hands clasped together and gripped between my thighs. The tension was spreading across my shoulders, and a dull ache had snuck into my temples as I waited.

"Elizabeth, did you hear..........?" the Parole Officer asked again.

"Hear what?" I asked, amazed I'd even been spoken to.

"Internal parole is approved." I heaved in sadness at his familiar words.

"Internal parole was approved last time, Sensei, and I'm still here." I curtsied and left the room with a heavy heart. Nothing I did or said worked with these people, but I noticed the Parole Officer shake his head and he said something in Japanese I didn't understand. A month passed, and I still had no idea of when I would be called and notified of the decision taken by the External Parole Officer. It was Pieter's birthday soon, and I desperately wanted to be home for that.

Monday the 20th of February - still no news. I was missing Pieter's birthday; another year celebrated without me. I was not just counting the days, the weeks, and months, but the hours, the minutes, and the seconds now, even though I knew it was a pointless exercise - it just made it all go slower, but I couldn't help myself.

The only real positive thought; I would never have another Christmas or New Year in jail.

CHAPTER FORTY-THREE

I woke in a better mood than I had in months. Perhaps this was the day - the 22nd of February 2006; dare I hope? I greeted my section as always, suppressing a smile I wanted to wear for no apparent reason.

"Ohayogozaimasu," (good morning) I said, using a monotone voice and they responded the same way. None of them were waiting on parole advice, it was only me this time.

The drone of the machine motors whined as they started up, marking the beginning of another day of precision work, after we'd sung the National Anthem. The monotonous humming continued throughout the day and became so lodged in my brain that it took hours for the sound to leave my consciousness at the end of the day. But more beautiful ballet shoes would be completed today and shipped around the world and, despite the daily repetition, I was proud of what my girls produced. The phone had rung in the factory a few times and each time I jumped at the sound, and a few ladies who noticed, smiled at me. They knew I was waiting for that parole call. Everyone was working perfectly this morning. Checks complete, I settled back on my machine and started it up. My gut twisted with anticipation; I found it hard to concentrate, let alone sew. I switched off the machine and walked up and down the rows of my machinists, checking each one and asking if anyone needed help, but it was more to quell my anxiety. Just before the lunch bell rang out, so did the phone. This time it was for me.

Tears of relief streamed down my face, and my hands automatically closed in thanks as I raised my eyes to the imaginary skies above the roof and thanked God for His loving guidance. My group of seamstresses all rejoiced and clapped for me. I bowed in grateful thanks to them and quietly asked for Him to bless those I was leaving behind. Then they all stood and bowed, silently returning the respect, then sat down and went on with their work. It was an incredibly touching response. I knew then I'd done an excellent job and that mattered to me more than anything.

Sensei gave permission for me to thank each one individually for their dedicated work and for taking care of me. I really wanted to give each one a hug, but that was not permitted.

I stood at my podium and waved to them all for the last time.

"Sayonara - Goodbye, we will never meet again, but I will never forget you either. God Bless you all," I said in Japanese.

The External Parole Board had only deducted six months off my sentence. It was hardly parole, considering I'd spent a total of nine months in detention and the holding cells, but it was better than nothing.

I was going home. I had to say it aloud for it to penetrate. 'I am going home!' I shrieked happily, as I was escorted back to my cell; cell number 248. Will I ever forget it? Like a coil unravelling, I could barely contain myself.

To utilise the burst of energy that had filled me, I got to work, spring-cleaning every inch of my cell. This amount of happiness coursing through my veins was a brand-new sensation; I had to do something useful with it.

I scribbled a short note to Storm and handed it in for posting. This time I was definitely coming home; no false alarm. Busying myself with getting my cell clean and tidy, I thought about our meeting at the airport; it was going to be hard on us both; poignant but complex. I let her know I wanted no-one else to meet me but her and wanted no-one else to know I was coming home — a date I couldn't give her yet.

Everything moved fast now. The following day, I was moved from my spotless cell to a single waiting cell. To all intense and purposes, I was free, but when you are a criminal, you're never free, and I was still within the prison walls.

I couldn't help but feel free. How else was I supposed to feel? I had a private shower cubicle, and I could shower every day; that was exhilarating, that was freedom, the ultimate heaven and worth celebrating, and I had my hair cut and styled, and for the first time in 5 years, I felt alive.

Then the warders and I carefully checked the inventory against every single item I'd ever possessed from the moment I'd arrived in Japan. There, among the clothing and other articles, were the 17 tissues I'd had when I was captured. I looked on in awe; then I couldn't help myself and burst out laughing. The gentle lady warder looked at me with a confused expression, and I suddenly realised how disrespectful that was and apologised to her. Freedom had gone to my head, and I'd forgotten my manners in that moment of elation.

Seventeen tissues – all still there, neatly folded and accounted for in precise Japanese style; absurd, but anyway. My old toothbrushes, toothpaste, even the half bottle of shampoo! The warder's petite round face lit up, satisfied it was all still there, then finally she laughed, two little dark eyes became slits in a round creamy-coloured face, and I laughed with her. The suitcase filled very quickly, so she kindly arranged another bag for me, and we filled that too. I'd be overweight. I left some of the unnecessary things behind and shoved the tissues into my handbag; I'd be needing those.

I waited in my new cell for a week and imagined myself walking out the prison gates, head held high, breathing freedom deep into my lungs. I pictured myself climbing into the cab; there'd be no need for curtains this time, no need for rope handcuffing, I wasn't a criminal anymore, I'd paid my dues. I was looking forward to seeing a small part of the countryside for the first time, other than the view from my cell window.

The vision I'd had, and reality were starkly different. It really wasn't how it is shown in the movies, and I had to keep reminding myself of this.

I went out the same way I came in - cuffed and bound with horrid rough sisal ropes and transported in a curtained vehicle. I never did get to see any of the country. What I did learn on my way to the vehicle was they could not have released me any earlier, for it was only a week ago that my fine was fully paid up; my dreams of parole after two years had been in vain.

It was clammy and humid inside the vehicle; a fleeting moment of excitement was quickly overtaken by nausea. When we stopped a few hours later, I was off-loaded and marched to the basement of a tall building that was marked - Immigration Cells. The cuffs were removed, and I was locked in my cell; the last cell in the line of cold concrete boxes. I could only assume this mysterious building was part of the airport, but it was very different from the holding cells coming in. All I wanted was to get the hell out of this dingy catacomb that was icy cold from air conditioning blasting freezing air that whipped around the cold bare concrete walls in this basement prison.

Freedom doesn't come without enormous cost, just as my fellow countryman, Nelson Mandela once told. And 'freedom' is an all-embracing word that has many meanings, as I discovered. Just a few short weeks away and I'd be free from the burden of imprisonment, but what lay ahead emotionally was making me feel rather anxious. I prayed the work I'd done on myself was strong enough to withstand the coming emotional onslaught. It was going to be huge; I knew that. My darling brother, though I'd not mentioned him while I was in prison because my children were the mainstay of my sanity, was, in fact, a powerful voice within my head and in my journal ramblings. He was my rock, whether we communicated or not.

I sat entombed in the basement of an unknown building; a chilly reminder I was still regarded as a criminal in every sense of the word. I learned from the others this was where all foreign criminals were brought when they'd reached the end of their term and were either waiting for travel documents, airline tickets, or family to collect them. For me, it was like being in a long dark tunnel without a light. I had no idea how long I'd be here, how quickly travel documents could be attained by Storm, when I'd be given my airline ticket or what would happen next. All I knew was I was almost 'free.'

A line of stark white washing machines stood in a row against the wall opposite to the cells. Their doors lay open like gaping mouths, ready for dirty clothes to be fed in, cleansing away the stench of captivity for the last time. The showers were good; civilised cubicles where my breasts were no longer exposed to forty prying eyes, thankfully; these cells were multi-sex, another thing that unnerved me somewhat.

Scattered around were a few gaming machines, dispensing machines and a couple of table-tennis tables. There was the normal assortment of candy dispensing machines, cool drink and crisp dispensers seen in shopping centres, goodies I'd not laid eyes on for four long years

At 9 pm, the guards came around and locked our cells, then opened us up again at 6 am.

Two public telephone booths stood, bold and blue, near the washing machines, beckoning us to connect once more with the outside world. It was the most sought-after spot in this cold, characterless basement, and we stood in queues to make that one important call.

My gut churned as I stood in the line, wondering how I'd deal with hearing Storm's voice again. I had to hold myself together. The call I'd dreamed of making, the announcement of my freedom at last. A call I'd so dearly hoped to have made much sooner. Standing in the queue suddenly made 'freedom' a more significant reality and quelled the horrors of my nightmares, but initiated a whole lot of others I'd have to face.

A call to South Africa was expensive; money was tight and there was a seven-hour time difference. When I finally reached the head of the queue, I mentally calculated it was about 2 a.m. in South Africa and Storm would be fast asleep, but this news required me to wake her. I stood nervously, fiddling with my fingers and hair and shifting my weight from one foot to the other, wondering if it was fair to wake her; should I call her now or wait? But I'd waited too many long years for this moment, so the decision was made - it was worth taking the chance.

Storm had just completed a twenty-four-hour Police shift. The National Elections in South Africa were in full swing, and she'd just come off duty and was about to fall into an exhausted sleep when she answered my call, wearily and unenthusiastically, thinking it was another call out. The telephone reception was dreadful, so I kept shouting down the line, saying, "Hello, Hello, Hello." In a final attempt to make her aware it was me, I shouted her nickname as loudly as I could and heard muttering in the queue behind me.

"Meid, Meid, it's me, I am free, I need to get home."

"Ma...maaa," I heard her say, her voice breaking up, husky with emotion but obvious, even with the bad connection. The crackling made conversation difficult, so we arranged a time to call the following day, and I placed the earpiece back on its holder. Turning away, not quite knowing what to do with myself, I walked slowly away from the queue of others waiting to do the same thing I'd just done and sat in my cell sobbing tears of relief, confusion and bewilderment. Everything I was dealing with at that moment and everything I had dealt with over the years came crashing down on me — a mingling of outrageous happiness and bitter regret all churning in the cauldron of the love I was feeling for my daughter. Nothing I'd thought of or primed myself for had prepared me adequately for this.

Tomorrow we would talk again and arrange my exit from Japan.

Freedom, yes, the one from jail, was indeed just around the corner. Emotional freedom would follow later.

CHAPTER FORTY-FOUR

So, my life's' journey had been one filled with difficulty and insurmountable tests of courage, tenacity and wit. What other nasty surprises lay ahead?

This final test of endurance was colossal enough; then I learned I had to endure another month of hell in these freezing cells, waiting for my ticket to arrive.

My telephone call had led to a few hectic weeks for Storm dealing with inefficient bureaucracy while I impatiently waited, and of course, time went really slowly.

Before I could fly home, a temporary South African Identity Document had to be issued. Inevitably delayed by the jumble of autocratic red tape and the application of things being done in African time within the Internal Affairs department, it took an unusually quick three weeks. Only once Storm had my official ID document could she book my ticket home. Then as timely as the other setbacks, planes only departed from Tokyo to Johannesburg on Tuesdays and Sundays. Storm had booked my flight for a Tuesday departure, but unbeknown to her, that particular Tuesday was a public holiday in Japan. Only a skeleton staff was on duty which meant another excruciatingly long week's wait. Apart from being the longest month imprisoned, the last week was one of the longest weeks of my life.

Once the flight was confirmed, I learned I was not where I thought I was. I was not living in the guts of the airport buildings at all; I had another four-hour journey to get to Narita airport in a curtained minibus and was still considered bad enough for them to handcuff me, only this time in the conventional handcuffs. As we were permitted to talk to the warders, I wanted to know why I needed to be handcuffed and why we couldn't look out the windows and view the passing countryside, if, for all intense and purposes, I was no longer a prisoner. Her answer shocked me. Perhaps I shouldn't have asked.

"You do not have a visa to be in Japan as a South African resident," she answered. "You are an illegal visitor."

I finally made that longed-for exit from Japan on the 28th of March 2006.

The stigma of being a prisoner stays firmly glued; no matter how one views oneself, it is not how everyone else sees you. There was still more disgrace to live through.

At the airport, foreign ex-prisoners were dealt with in the basement of the building and shoved into vile-smelling cells, nothing like the clean holding cells when I came in. I'd learned to deal with just about every form of humiliation, but this final blow was the hardest, for I'd psyched myself up for this passage to freedom as being so much easier.

I was collected a few hours later, handcuffed again and led to the plane via airport passages not used by regular commuters, and formally handed over to a hostess who led me down the aisle to a seat at the very end of the plane. I was the first onto the aircraft.

'Normal travellers couldn't have their space violated by a criminal like me,' I thought with bitter cynicism.

I was seated in a special seat hidden behind the galley that housed the last block of passenger ablutions. I was not permitted to carry hand luggage of any sort - just in case I blew up the aircraft! Anyone would have thought I was some mass murderer. I could understand this type of treatment for serious criminals, but I wasn't one of those and had spent nearly four years proving it. I was a normal South African grandmother who'd made an error of judgement and was dying to get home. I'd paid dearly for my mistake and wanted this whole ordeal over without adding more degradation. My hand luggage was taken and stowed elsewhere; it would all be handed back to me upon landing in Singapore where we would be changing planes.

Upon landing, I was escorted directly to the other plane ahead of all the other passengers and taken straight to the back of the plane again and ordered to fasten my seat belt. Stripped of all dignity now, I cried rivers of tears. Being so close to 'home', I felt my mind give way. My subconscious thought must have been, 'Oh well, I don't have to fight for survival and recognition anymore,' and tears of shame, tears of happiness at knowing I was on the last leg, tears of processing the meaning of freedom, tears of haunting hardships; I cried tears for every human emotion with intensity.

After take-off and once the plane had levelled off, I was served the meal first; surprisingly. Probably because I was in the galley where the food was stowed. After four years of prison food, aeroplane food tasted tantalisingly good. The only plus of being stuck at the very back of the plane was that I had two seats to sleep across, and after my long sobbing session and a good meal, I fell into a deep, emotionally exhausted sleep and was woken by the stewardess asking me politely to fasten my seat belt for landing.

"Am I home?" I asked her, rubbing my eyes, amazed.

"Yes Ma'am, we will be landing in 20 minutes."

I quickly went to the toilet, splashed cold water on my face, brushed my teeth and ran my fingers through my hair. I could feel the excitement rising as the plane was dropping in altitude, rapidly descending toward the earth I loved so dearly, and moments after taking my seat, we touched down on African soil. Choked with emotion, I had to keep swallowing as the lump in my throat threatened.

The plane taxied into its allocated parking spot, and I heard everyone unclip their safety belts in unison; I was instructed to remain seated - I would be collected by Airport Security Personnel.

When I eventually exited the plane via the door furthest from the front of the aircraft, I could smell the ground, the earthy smell of Africa and it took all my strength to remain poised as I stepped onto the luggage carrier platform which criminals share with the cargo. Nothing was normal, and every process took ten times longer. I began to panic for I knew Storm would be waiting for me at the standard international arrivals area - as one does.

I didn't know what to do, then I was taken into a hall and told to sit; someone would come for me.

Eight o'clock came and went. I was frantic, agonising over the thought that Storm may assume I'd missed my flight and possibly leave the airport – but that was an absurd thought; amazing how bizarre one's thoughts can be when panicked and common sense flies out. I illegally left my seat and went to find someone who would get a message to Storm to tell her to wait; there were more formalities I had to complete. I found no-one who could be bothered to help and was met with a barrage of 'No' answers; then I found someone who enlightened me.

"Excuse me, Sir, but why is this taking so long? I need to let my daughter know she must wait for me," I urged.

"They are checking your luggage," the official answered and I felt like saying, 'Looking for bombs, are they?' I refrained from being sarcastic.

"What, again?" I asked with an irritable shake of my head.

"Yes, Ma'am, again," he snapped.

Two hours later, on the 29th of March 2006, after flying for nineteen hours and waiting for many others, I was technically a free woman. A kind porter loaded my luggage onto an airport trolley, and for the first time in four years, I was free of handcuffs or rope bonds, dressed in civilian clothing, and pushing my luggage trolley, free to go where I pleased without a security escort. It was liberating, but oddly frightening too.

I walked through a different set of immigration and customs gates and there, standing forlorn and alone under the glaring artificial airport lights, stood my precious daughter. I was horrified how thin and gaunt she looked. Her once beautiful glowing skin was now sallow and grey with the etchings of sadness, worry and fear that had woven a delicate web around her friendly warm brown eyes, that even at a distance, I could see were sunken back in her head. Guilt, oh the guilt, along with a collage of other emotions at war with each other dampened the happiness at seeing her and being on home soil.

Then she saw me, and a sob caught in my throat as we ran into each other's arms, sobbing, holding each other tightly, savouring the smell and feel of each other, storing it to memory, never to be forgotten. I pulled back from her first to release the grief-filled space between us, giving space for happiness to pour in and tearfully asked, "Why are you so thin, Meid? All I saw was a big nose." I giggled through my tears, holding her close again and breathing in the smell of her soft brown hair that was lightly apple-fragranced.

For a moment, she couldn't answer and cried harder. Finally, unlocking ourselves from each other, looking questioningly into my eyes like she used to as a small girl when something had gone wrong, she said, "Mama, you are so thin and fragile too, look at you."

The years without me and the stigma attached had been a far greater strain on her than I had understood. My last vision of her was when I'd left; carefree and happy; now she was ravaged by shame, loss and heartbreak. Could I ever find that quest for internal freedom without guilt?

For the next half-hour, we couldn't stop touching, hugging, giggling, crying - drunk with a surreal relief. Emotionally disorientated, Storm struggled to find where she'd put my passport, lost somewhere in her handbag while we stood in the queue at Bureau de Change, but it came to light, and we giggled again. After doing the exchange, still giddy with the joy of being reunited, we couldn't find where she'd parked in the covered parking. This time we looked at each other and erupted in laughter; it was a joyous disorientation and eventually we were on the road home.

There was so much to say, but where does one begin when there are raw truths to deal with? The drive home was a concoction of awkward moments that swung from tears to laughter, back to sadness and excruciating pain that tore at my conscience as I released a few of the raw truths. I knew I had to give myself time.

"How is my darling boy?"

"He's coped, Mama, we all have. You taught us how to cope, but our grief and yearning for you has been hard on us." Storm answered truthfully as tears rolled down my cheeks again.

"Mama, we all forgave you long ago; it was not your fault," Storm said quietly with depth and tenderness, provoking continued tearful sobbing.

"Papa should have been jailed, not you," she added bitterly. Forgiveness didn't resonate in her voice. The mention of Dion's name brought about other questions I had to know.

"He doesn't know I'm home, does he? I do not want to see him." It would take me a few weeks to settle back into 'normal' life and Dion was not going to disrupt that if I could help it.

"No Mama, he doesn't, and for now, you don't have to see him, but you will at some stage." I simply nodded.

Our journey home passed with only glances at the passing countryside. I'd missed so much of it, but our constant chatter was more essential, and soon we were pulling into the driveway of Storm's new house where my precious grandchildren waited.

Little Rick, born while I was in jail, was now seventeen months old. Rika, who'd been seven months old when I was jailed, was now five. All those years of her childhood I'd missed. She came tearing out the house to greet us. I jumped out the car wrapping this precious child in my arms, her little body close to mine, and knew in that moment no other hug compares to the unquestioned purity of one from a child.

As I walked into their new home, arm in arm with Storm and holding Rika's hand, a familiar tune was playing, I assumed on the radio and one I'd not heard for years, and didn't associate it with my homecoming; then it hit me - it wasn't the radio.

'Tie a Yellow Ribbon Round the Old Oak Tree, was playing, welcoming home the prisoner who'd returned to her family. Standing on the coffee table in their lounge was a love palm, bound with yellow ribbons and a big chocolate cake sat next to it. The sights and sounds so touching, its meaning so real, with little Rika looking up at me with expectant eyes, I knew in an instant I was forgiven and loved unconditionally.

Could a mother dream of anything more?

I stood and unashamedly sobbed while Rika looked down at the floor, not sure what to do with the sobbing Grandmother she didn't know well. She squeezed my hand, just as her mother had done when she was a child then looked up at me again and I smiled awkwardly. Little Rick slept soundly in his cot as if the music had extended his peaceful slumber. We'd meet later. Time was no longer a pressing issue that had dominated every second of the last four years.

CHAPTER FORTY-FIVE

The delicate and delicious smells that wafted from Storm's kitchen made my mouth fill with saliva. I felt like a Labrador desperate to get hold of food, any food. Storm had insisted I was not allowed in the kitchen; she wanted to spoil me with the kind of meal I'd often said in my letters to her that I'd missed the most.

Eating with a knife and fork was an absurdly alien experience. I hesitated a moment, letting my hands rest on the cutlery, thinking back to the holding cells and how I'd sobbed with frustration at the difficulty of eating with chopsticks; how I'd longed to hold a knife and fork then, slicing through a juicy piece of South African beef. I felt their eyes on me, and I looked up at Storm and Robert watching me with amusement sparkling in their eyes, as I sliced through the roast beef and put it my mouth; nothing had ever tasted so good. I swallowed quickly to appease the callings in my stomach, then slicing another piece of meat and a slither of roast potato, I lifted the loaded fork to my mouth, relishing the tastes of old, savouring long-forgotten flavours and cherishing the moments of being home with family once more. From one taste sensation to another, Storm had provided it all. The second course of 'Koeksisters' was nectar to my numbed taste buds, creating a delightful chaos of rejection in my tummy.

Storm had taken a week off work to celebrate my homecoming. After dinner, exhausted, but refusing to part from each other, we curled up on the sofa together and kept up the constant chatter like two hungry hyenas at a kill.

Robert discreetly disappeared, leaving us the intimate space we needed as mother and daughter to tear away at the pain we'd endured for so long.

"I prayed so hard for you, Ma. While you were in the holding cells, I prayed for your release; prayed that they'd discover there had been a mistake, the same when they moved you to detention; but you never came back. I remember you telling me you had lost your faith in God, and I did too, for a time, when anger couldn't find the answers to my questions. Work was a continuous nightmare; everyone knew you'd been caught smuggling drugs, so working in the Drug Squad was precarious for I was under constant surveillance. For a few months, I even hated you, Ma, then all I could think of was you rotting in a jail thousands of miles from home, and I was helpless to protect you. So, I redirected my focus and cultivated a more positive approach, but it took longer for me to forgive Vivienne and I hated Andre. I banned Papa from coming to my house. I hated the world then too. Only Boetie and Robert could enter my shattered world. Boetie was so strong; sometimes, it was just a veneer to hide his pain, but I was so proud of the way he sorted out his own life without Papa's help." I sat listening intently to what Storm had to say. There was so much she couldn't say in her letters to me and I knew in the next week she would have the time to clear away the ghosts and we could begin our healing journey together.

"Oh, my angel, remember if God had answered my prayers and sent me back when you asked him to, I would have come home and committed murder, and that would have been worse. I hated Papa; I hated him with such venom; it poisoned my mind; there was no clarity then. If I'd been chucked in jail here, we wouldn't be sitting together talking as we are." I hesitated while I tried to find the appropriate words to what I wanted to say next.

"There are no gentle ways of putting this, but I would have strung myself up or slit my wrists had I been jailed here; I'd even considered it a few times in Japan."

Storm nodded; she knew what life in a South African jail looked like. It was time for bed; I yawned, too much emotion and a belly full of forgotten taste sensations, it was time to sleep.

"Just one more question, Ma," Storm smiled with a pleading look in her eyes.

"Okay, then we must get to bed." I yawned again feeling more relaxed than I had in years, but I was emotionally exhausted too.

"Why didn't you answer my phone call the day after you left?" It was the one question I'd been waiting all these years for her to ask.

"I couldn't, Meid; I just couldn't. You know how sickened I was with guilt. You know how I detest blatant lying, plus I was scared to death, only more lies would have tumbled from my mouth, and I couldn't bear the thought of that. Why do you ask?" I leant forward and pinched her cheek affectionately and then she dropped her bombshell.

"The day after you left, I received a call during my lunch break, and if you had only answered my call when you were in Paris, I would've told you that I'd just won two hundred and forty-six thousand Rand in a competition I'd forgotten I'd even entered and you need never have gone to jail. I could never bring myself to tell you until now."

THE END

EPILOGUE

Despite the devastating news of the phone call, I slept well.

'How?' you may ask. 'It is what it is,' is my philosophy now.

I'd grown in jail; I'd shamed myself, blamed myself, loathed myself and now the rarity of living, happily fragile and accepting of that human fragility, allowed me to sleep well that night without yearning for what could have been.

The following morning, I called Pieter, who was thrilled to hear my voice and excited I was finally home. Another emotional conversation happened, of course, but rather than shying away from hard truths, I looked forward to understanding his deepest feelings and how, together, we could all heal the wounds of the trauma and learn from it.

Twenty-four hours later, the editor of the local newspaper called Storm, asking if I would permit an interview, which I reluctantly agreed to, even though I felt mildly annoyed by the intrusion and wondered how the news of my homecoming had already leaked out into the community. Someone must have seen Storm and me in her car on the way home. What the heck, I had to stand tall; I didn't need to make apologies to anyone except my family; the public just wanted some juicy news. Humans thrive on others heartache and hardships.

It took another twenty-four hours before I called Viv and Andre. This was a harder one to cope with, for no matter what one tells one's self, it had taken time to process their part in all this and it still stung a little. Forgiveness and love always step in for me, but finding the right vocabulary to articulate my feelings over the phone in that moment, and face the injustice of their actions appropriately, was hard. There had been many letters back and forth from Viv over the years, but actually speaking to her seemed to conjure up what I'd not dealt with correctly. I'd learned in prison that whatever happened in my life, I had choices and I had to take responsibility for them, which I had, which translated another way means the ability to respond, and that was the key in this instance. I could embrace what had happened and lay no blame, move on and nurture our relationship, or I could kill it. I chose to embrace it.

The following week, Dion rang. He'd seen the newspaper article and wanted to know why none of the children had told him I was home. After all these years, it was still all about him, and though I felt momentarily annoyed, I also felt sorry for him too. His entire life was a plea for attention; it was so entrenched.

My inner peace was complete though; I was reunited with all my family, and to my amazement, I also received an incredible number of unexpected 'welcome home' calls from the community, touching me deeply- with so many of them, there was no finger-pointing and gossip, but admiration and awe of what I'd gone through.

I spent hours discussing with myself, and Storm, what I was going to do, where I was going to live, how I would earn an income. Who in this town would give me a job knowing I was a convict? Should I remain in Bethlehem? The only thing I was sure of; I didn't want to be far from Storm.

A month later, I found an insignificant little job that helped raise my self-confidence when dealing with and facing the public. I sold milk and cream for a farmer in a dairy shop.

Facing the challenges of reintegrating into 'normal' life was very difficult. I knew it would be, I'd accepted that, but with the overwhelming love and support from my family and more friends than I realised I had, it eased the transition from being a cocooned pupa into a beautiful butterfly and I began to spread my wings and fly a little further on.

Of all the many lessons I'd learnt from my experience in Japan, and how I got there, the most rewarding was being able to feel the meaning of unconditional, pure love and forgiveness and from that follows a deep understanding of setting personal boundaries without feeling guilty for doing it and that was why I was able to allow Dion back into my life until he ended it himself.

It was then it struck me that life really does revolve the same way our wondrous planet does - round and round in big, astounding circles and so often there is simply no explanation for the way it turns out.

Lightning Source UK Ltd.
Milton Keynes UK
UKHW020954270420
362382UK00008B/64

9 781916 309685